A QUEEN'S /

by Sam Burnell

•

First published in eBook and paperback
2019

•

© Sam Burnell 2019

•

Please note, this book is written in British English, so some spellings will vary from US English.

For Rio and Mooster

Character List

Fitzwarren Household

William Fitzwarren – father of Richard and
Robert
Eleanor Fitzwarren – his wife
Robert Fitzwarren – Richard's brother
Jack Fitzwarren – William's son
Richard Fitzwarren – William's son
Harry – Richard's cousin
Edwin – Servant of William
Jon – Servant of William
Ronan- - Robert's Steward
Master Juris – William's physician

Lawyers

Master Clement – Robert Fitzwarren's
Lawyer
Master Luterell – William Fitzwarren's
Lawyer
Marcus Drover – Clement's servant

The English Court

Edward Courtenay – Plantagenet
descendant with tenuous claim to the
throne
William Cecil – Secretary of State
Somer – Crown Servant
Christopher Morley – Cecil's man

Other Characters

Catherine de Bernay – Elizabeth's servant
Myles Devereux – London Merchant
Matthew – Servant of Devereux
Master Kettering – Governor of Marshalsea

The Tower

Master Hunt – Prisoner governor
Jeriah – a gaoler
Simon – a gaoler
Master Harper – a gaoler

Christian Carter's Household

Christian Carter
Harry – Christian's illegitimate son
Coleman – Christian's servant
Tilly – household servant
Anne – Christian's wife

PROLOGUE

†

The health of the monarch can never be a private issue. Philip had returned for a scant few months in March 1557 and left again in early July of the same year, and the Queen again favoured the idea that she was pregnant. There were few, however, who shared the notion.

Towards the end of the year her expenditure on her wardrobe even outstripped the excesses of her father, for additional cost was required as the dresses and gowns held in the royal wardrobe would no longer fit around Mary's swelling abdomen. Her courses had stopped, but detailed enquiry of her ladies in waiting by Cecil's officers and consultation with the Queen's physicians did not lead to the conclusion that she was carrying a child. And Mary at forty-one was now deemed to be past the years of child bearing.

By January 1558 there were real concerns for her health, and during March

Mary took to her bed with a fever. London had been blighted by an epidemic that was sweeping the population away at the rate that the plague had. The situation for the citizens of the capital was worsened by the fact that while the plague would carry its victims to the hereafter swiftly in a few days, this latest sickness left the afflicted with a fever that could last for weeks and even months before it finally ended the suffering of its victims. The citizenry of London were weighed down now by the burden of their dying rather than just their dead. Hospitals were full; those who could leave the capital had, and churches were now housing rows upon rows of sick and dying Londoners. The carts carrying the deceased to the communal pits trundled endlessly through the streets.

It had been Morley's task to corner a very reluctant Master Hardy, one of the Queen's physicians. Morley's first attempts to lay some searching questions before him regarding the Queen's health had been rebuffed. However, when the doctor had received a summons to an interview in Cecil's offices, it was an invitation he could not decline and his bravado was somewhat lessened by the austere surroundings and the close proximity of Cecil's offices to The Tower.

Hardy, when pressed, confirmed that the lady had contracted the sickness that had taken so many of her subjects. However, her condition had improved and he had no fear for her immediate health. The Queen was, however, suffering from melancholy spirits attributed to the loss of her husband and the current blight that was affecting England. Morley was able to take to Cecil news that although ill, Mary's condition was not viewed as perilously so.

CHAPTER ONE

†

Finally, they were as far north as they could go. Jack felt as if he had been physically hurled through Europe, and now he had fetched up against a solid barrier that even the Knights of St John could not break down.

The weather.

Prowling along the shoreline, glaring at the white crested waves and the wind-whipped clouds, frustrated and angry, he readily vocalised his feelings. Emilio did not seem bothered and Richard also remained calm in the face of this halt to their progress. That Andrew Kineer could now be ahead of them and on the opposite side of this narrow, boiling waste of water did not seem to be as infuriating to his companions as it was to Jack.

"Can we go back?"

Jack wasn't alone: one of Emilio's men walked with him along the harbour wall interrupting his thoughts. Wherever they went on this journey they did not go alone, and Jack had, by now, got used to it.

Emilio remained with them, but their escort changed constantly: the men indifferent, under orders simply to ensure that Jack and Richard arrived at their destination.

When he finally returned he was truly soaked and both men headed towards the kitchens where the largest fires would be burning. The house was attached to a large warehouse and a high-walled enclosed yard which protected the business of the wine merchant who operated there. Although Jack was not sure, it seemed that the operation belonged to the Knights, which did not surprise him. Edward Hillcrest had introduced himself as the controller, and though he was not wearing the garb of the Knights, he was soberly dressed and he had documents for Emilio. Jack guessed that if he was not a member of the Order then he was somehow closely associated with it.

Hillcrest was organising the last leg of their journey. Currently rocking against the harbour wall was a ship filled with barrels; her destination, when the wind dropped, would be London. Despite his orders that these men were to be transported with all speed, he was not going to risk the ship. Even when the waves lessened and the skies lost the storm clouds two days later he still refused to allow the ship to sail. She was a Fluyt, a flat-bottomed merchantman, much like the *Dutch Flower* they had travelled on over a year ago, and she needed kind seas to ensure her safe passage. Already other boats had left the harbour, and others were readying to do so.

It seemed Richard was more impatient than he appeared, he had already found a ship in the harbour preparing to sail. The *Lily of Ireland's* destination was Dublin but for a price she would drop them and a small boat close to the English coast.

Emilio was persuaded only because he had received a communication that had confirmed that it was more than likely Kineer had remained onboard a ship and had taken a seaward passage to England. That being the case, the longer they remained trapped by the ill weather the more headway Kineer could be making. If his passage had taken him to a port on the west of the country he could, in theory, have avoided the angry waters of the channel.

Emilio had attempted to argue that Kineer could be confined to a harbour just as they were, but without evidence it was difficult to maintain and eventually he conceded to Richard's plan. They would take the direct passage to England, and the men he had with him would follow on

Hillcrest's merchantman and meet them in London.

Consequently Jack found himself victim to the worst sea crossing of his life. He hated boats; his fear of them had worsened after the *Santa Fe* had turned on her side in Grand Habour in Malta, nearly taking them all to the bottom with her. Richard had laughed at him, but Emilio at least seemed to share his concern, and although the sea did not make him as sick as it did Jack, it was obvious that the passage inside the stinking, archaic ship bound for Ireland was not one he was enjoying.

†

Jack's courage was tested to the full when he had climbed down from the ship into the small rocking boat with Emilio and Richard. Heart beating fast in his chest, he could feel the panic rise as the boat rocked alarmingly beneath him. Richard fastened a hard grip on his elbow and pulled him down onto the bench before he had time to lose his balance.

"There's an oar there. Come on, we need to get away from the side of the ship or we'll be smashed against her," Richard yelled against the wind.

Jack's hands shook, but he found the loose oar, and, in the near darkness located the rowlock to drop it into. The two men he was with were shouting to be heard.

A sudden jolting impact jarred them all and Jack nearly lost his hold on the oar, the skiff was too near the ship and had bounced from her wooden sides.

"Row! Jack match me. Now!" Richard commanded.

All Jack could see was his brother's white knuckles wrapped around the shaft of the oar as he pitched it forward before beginning the stroke to haul them away from the ship.

Jack's first stroke failed. When he hauled the oar back it skidded through the wave tops, the angle wrong. The second was deeper and he felt the boat straighten and move forward with the force of the stroke.

"And again!" Emilio shouted from behind them.

Jack gritted his teeth and drove the oar through the water with as much strength as he had.

"Back now, together. You English rats are supposed to be born sailors so what's wrong with you two?" Emilio called out through the wind and spray.

Jack knew Emilio's tirade of caustic comments were meant to divert his attention from the journey towards the shore, and he was thankful. Swallowing hard, his muscles complaining, he pulled again hard on the ash shaft of the oar, concentrating on nothing other than the wood in his hands. Making each stroke as powerful as he could, lifting the oar from the water at the end of her travel and reversing the process, Jack closed his eyes tightly against the salty spray and hauled the oar back again with as much power as he possessed.

"Look, we've passed the headland," Emilio called. Jack didn't look but he was suddenly aware that the boat was rocking less erratically and the spray that the wind had lashed over the side into Jack's face had stopped.

"I can see the shore, come on we've not far to go." Emilio, sitting facing them, was looking over their heads towards the land.

"How far?" Jack managed as he leaned forward to return the oar to the sea for another stroke.

"Too far for you to swim." It was Richard who replied. "So keep damn well rowing."

"If your ship had sailed then I'd be in London by now!" Jack growled, his eyes stinging from the salt water.

"Even the Knights of St John cannot control the weather," Emilio replied scathingly.

"Oh, and I thought that would be easy, doesn't your father know the Pope?" Jack shot back, his mood still black.

"My father is the Pope's uncle, which makes him my second..." Emilio began to correct Jack.

"I am sure at some point that could be useful, but not today," Richard shouted. "Now bloody well row!"

If there was a reply from Jack it was one Emilio could not make out. Jack, cursing, dug the oar his hands were wrapped around hard into the water, still matching his brother's pace. Emilio steered the small boat toward the darkened shoreline, visible only as a dim white line where the waves broke on the sand and gravel.

As the prow of the skiff crested a shore-breaking wave, it lifted high in the air, then dropped suddenly.

Jack stopped dead mid-stroke.

"Pull you useless galetoi, or she'll turn over," Emilio shouted.

The skiff had begun to turn sideways to the surf and the current beneath pushed her towards the shore at an alarming angle, one wave after another buffeting her viciously.

Jack waited until Richard had lifted his oar and was about to dip it back into the water before he matched him again. The prow swung towards the shore again, and in two more strokes she was pointing in the right direction. Another wave behind them pushed them forward and all three men felt the hull bite into the sand and rocks of the beach. The oar in Jack's hands bit into the sand and the next wave coming in behind them spun the small boat around the pinioned oar.

"Out, get out, we're on the beach." It was Richard's voice, he was already jumping over the side of the boat. "Jack, come on before she gets pulled back out."

Emilio was already beside Richard, waist deep in the tugging water.

"Come on!" Richard shouted, his hands on the sides of the boat as the tide dragged her back towards the channel.

Jack realised he had no choice but to obey since Richard was now chest deep in icy water as he clung to the retreating boat. Scrambling over the side Jack dropped into the water and felt his breath sucked from his body by the shock of the cold.

How they made it to the shore he couldn't remember, instinctively he followed the push of the waves and soon his soaked body, streaming with sea water, emerged onto the gravel beach. The pack on his back was soaked and heavy and when the water ran backwards as the waves retreated he lost his balance and fell onto his knees, the next wave covering him and pushing him into the stones and sand. Jack crawled on his hands and knees far enough up the gentle incline of the beach to be out of reach of the waves.

There was the noise of a man coughing in the dark next to him, and then Emilio gasped, "What a welcome to England!"

Nothing that morning was to be easy. They had landed on a sheltered beach, but entry to England was still barred to them by high, crumbling cliffs. Pre-dawn light seeping over the distant horizon guided them in the wrong direction along the shore, and after an hour they found their escape blocked by rocky promontories that projected into the sea. Cold and soaked still, they retraced their steps.

Jack was sure they had already passed their landing point and was annoyed to find the boat they had rowed upturned and partially buried in the sand. A hasty search failed to locate the oars so there was little point in salvaging it and they pressed on. Now it was fully daylight all of their eyes were fastened on a gentler slope running towards the sea, and what looked like a path running up it and away from the beach.

The weather, it appeared, had not finished with them to Jack's annoyance, and before they started their ascent from the beach the rain began. It made little difference to their saturated state, and as Richard pointed out at least they did not all now look as if they had swum ashore.

By the time they had reached the relative sanctuary of the Inn in the village of Woodton, Jack's feet were blistered and bleeding. Dropping on to the first available bench he cursed and gave voice to his thoughts, leaving his brother and Emilio to deal with the innkeeper and the necessity of procuring a room and food.

Within a very short space of time Emilio's money and Richard's calm insistence had secured them a room and the services of one of the inn staff to dry their clothes and provide them with food. Richard had explained they were travellers to London who had been caught in the recent storm and had lost their way, all plausible enough, and the innkeeper was only too happy to profit from his newest arrivals' misfortunes.

The inn was attached to the village bake house and the bricks of the ovens were soon covered with drenched clothing and sodden boots.

"That shirt is still wet. Come on, off with it." Emilio was already stripped to his breech hose and had dumped his shirt into the waiting servant's arms when the man had returned to their room for a second time to collect more wet clothing.

Jack pulled the clinging wet linen over his head and added it to those already draped over the man's arms. Swiping a blanket from the bed in the room he peeled away wet hose and wrapped the rough material around himself.

"Shy as a bride," Emilio said, laughing as he dropped down naked to sit in front of the lit fire.

"No, I just don't like being cold," Jack replied. Wrenching another blanket from the bed he dumped it on Emilio's head, pitching a third to land on the floor before his brother, who was struggling to undo ties with leaden fingers.

They had barely finished the food that had been delivered to the room when the first pile of dried clothing arrived. Linen shirts smelling of yeast and fresh bread came back first, warm and with flour dust in their creases. Woollen hose took longer; sea water had penetrated the fibres and the smell was acrid even though they were now dried. Then the footwear came back. Jack's boots had dried too quickly so the leather along the back seams had cracked, the creases around the ankles no longer soft and pliable but now rigid and unyielding. His feet, sore and blistered already, complained as soon as they were forced back inside the tight hard leather.

Jack pulled hard at the top of his boots, trying to stretch out the creases that he could feel biting into him. "Look what they've done to them!"

Emilio, whose footwear had survived the drying experience, leaned close to him and laying a hand on his arm said, "There is little they could have done you have not already tried yourself. Jack, they would make a cobbler give up in despair."

Richard, palms flat towards the fire, asked over his shoulder. "Are those the ones you got from Robert?"

"So what if they are?" Jack was still trying to stretch the leather.

"They are not his boots?" Emilio cast the question towards Richard.

"No, he stole them," Richard supplied, grinning.

Emilio picked up Jack's leather jerkin that lay on the floor next to him and, eyeing Jack seriously, he asked, "Please do not tell me you also stole this?"

Jack, his expression murderous, snatched the jerkin from Emilio's hand. "There has not been a lot of opportunity to acquire anything else, has there?" The accusation he sent in his brother's direction.

Emilio, his voice serious, said, "I thought it was just your spiritual needs I was faced with, however it seems I am to be your provisioner as well."

"Leave him be." It was Richard who spoke, and he slid a tray with cheese and fresh bread towards his brother. "Jack is never in a good humour unless his stomach is full, surely you've realised that by now."

Jack chose to ignore both of them, but not the tray, and began to break off lumps of bread with his fingers and push them into his mouth.

"Well," Richard voiced, speaking to neither of them in particular, "the innkeeper has horses we can buy, and if Emilio is willing, then that would be the fastest way for us to get to London. I don't think Jack's boots are up to the journey on foot."

Emilio nodded in agreement. "And do you know where we are?"

"Ah, now this is not good news. If the ship had crossed the channel as her captain said she would, we should have landed closer to London, but the wind has taken us further down the coast and we are at Woodton."

Jack, whose general grasp of geography was not great, looked confused. "And what does that mean?"

"It means we are about three days ride from London, maybe four," Richard answered evenly.

"Three days!" Jack blurted.

"Maybe four," Richard corrected.

"You said the captain would take us to the coast south of London!" Jack said accusingly.

"That hasn't happened, we need to deal with the consequences. It is a little late to debate the fact that the delivery was not quite what we had in mind," Richard said tersely.

"He is right," Emilio said, siding with Richard, "I have enough to buy us horses, and the sooner we set out for London the better."

"Buying three horses and tack is going to cost you quite a lot of coin," Jack pointed out.

Emilio leant over and cuffed Jack round the ear. "Well you had better come with me and make sure the deal I make is a good one."

"You!" Jack blurted. "You can't go and barter for the horses."

"Why not?" Emilio, dressed now, was on his feet.

"We're in England!" Jack pointed out, as if that was answer enough.

Emilio looked at him squarely, his brow furrowed in confusion. "I know that, idiot. So why not?"

"You're Italian?" Jack ventured.

"This is becoming tedious." Emilio had set his feet towards the door already, then turning to Richard he said, "The innkeeper you say."

Richard nodded. "Yes, his brother has mounts for sale."

Jack, ramming his arms through the sleeves of the leather jerkin Emilio had discarded on the floor, scrambled to his feet. "You can't let Emilio go," Jack said to his brother.

Richard grinned. "I'm not. If food is your first weakness, then buying horses is your second."

"And I suppose predictability would be my third," Jack shot back as headed towards the door.

"No, no Jack it's not. Go, make sure he spends his silver well, then the sooner we can set out to London," Richard replied, his tone conciliatory.

Emilio knew his horses well enough, but when faced with such a dismal selection as the innkeeper's brother had for sale, he despaired. Flinging his arms wide he declared that he had never eaten anything so poor, never mind ridden anything that lowly on the equine scale.

†

Richard pulled his cloak closer around him and waited while Jack concluded his negotiations for the horses. The innkeeper stood at his side, leant towards him and said, "Your lad knows how to drive a bargain."

"I wish he would do it a little quicker, before we all freeze to death." They were standing under the eaves of the inn and Richard stepped sideways to avoid a shower of water that had changed course and begun to drip on his right shoulder.

The innkeeper turned his eyes skyward. "Bloody rain, we've had four months of it. There's not a field between here and Dalton that's not under water."

"It's been a bad winter then?" Richard asked.

"Bad! Christ where've you been?" the Innkeeper looked at him sideways.

Richard regarded him with a cold stare. "A few places."

"Well, it's not stopped raining since St Edwell's day. There's no fodder for the livestock, and no fields to keep 'em in. Farmers are having to keep them penned in barns, leave them in the fields and they'll drown. My other brother, Aldren, has a farm down past Dalton and they've had to slaughter all his animals. There's nothing left to feed them on, so they either starve or you salt and cure them and get what you can."

Richard's eyes wandered back to where his brother was shaking his head as another horse was led out for his inspection. It was dismissed immediately as unsuitable, and the stable hand was sent to fetch another. Richard swore silently. So far Jack had one horse picked out and still needed another two.

"And word from London is even worse," the innkeeper continued.

"Is it?"

"Aye, wheat prices have nearly tripled after the crops were flattened and rotted in the fields at the end of last year. Stocks are being brought in from Holland, so I've heard, and that's putting the price of everything up, bread, beer, you name it."

"And horses probably!" interjected Richard, his tone acid as he watched Jack flatly refuse to pay the asking price for the new horse that was being led around the yard for his inspection.

"Well of course," his companion commented, taking Richard's words at face value. "Feed prices are up, with no grazing the price of horses is on the rise as well, and your lad is picking out some good un's there."

"I'm hoping he'll make a final choice before we all dissolve," Richard said sarcastically.

The man grinned. "Where are you headed anyway?"

"London," Richard supplied, his eyes fixed on his brother who looked like he might have finally found the last beast he needed to complete his purchase.

"Good Lord! That's a place to avoid, they've got the sweating sickness running though the city worse than plague. We've a few local lads who normally go and work on the docks, but not this year, they've stayed at home. Dropping like flies they are."

"And to think I was looking forward to returning," Richard replied dryly.

The innkeeper laughed and slapped him hard on the back. "Cheer up lad, it wouldn't be England if it wasn't pissing it down."

Jack had finally selected the three horses he wanted to buy, now he just had to nail down the price. Richard groaned inwardly as the process of a hearty negotiation started. The price agreed to after half an hour, Jack led his new acquisitions towards Richard. The innkeeper absented himself once the deal was finalised—no doubt to go and claim his cut for providing his brother-in-law with the customers.

"You want me to ride a cart horse?" Emilio, who had just arrived, declared, looking wide-eyed at the beast he had been handed.

"Solid, tireless, and with a gait that won't shake your bones to pieces over the next three days," Jack replied, smoothing his hand along the neck of the horse he had passed to Emilio.

Emilio's eyes were alive with delight and a moment later he was in the saddle pulling the reins tight in his hand. "So, now I shall find out what it is like to ride an English gelding."

CHAPTER TWO

†

The shutters on the windows were closed fast against the uncertain light of the evening, the illumination in the room coming instead from a reliable warm glow provided by candles and lamps.

Somer was dining with Cecil.

Somer had declined Cecil's invitation to meet with him in his dreary offices. Knowing Cecil well enough to realise that he preferred to control everything, the location and situation of a meeting would be something he would readily turn to his advantage. Pleading his advancing years, which was true enough, Somer had instead requested that Cecil join him at his London house for dinner.

Age, so far, had only robbed Cecil of the accuracy of his eyesight, whereas Somer felt the advancing years spreading through him like vines, twisting through his body, squeezing joints painfully, tightening around him, making him stoop and slowing his movements. At least, he mused, tonight his infirmity had been to his advantage. Rather than having to wade through the rotting mass of London, Cecil had been forced to come to him. Somer was fairly sure Cecil was cursing the sumptuary laws. They dictated how many courses a man could serve at his table as defined by his status. And Somer, entitled to serve six, was ensuring his table reflected his rank. So far they had been served roasted quail, a game pie which was currently the cause of Somer's indigestion, a pheasant tart with a rosemary jelly, steamed salmon in an aromatic wine sauce, a delicate custard laced with nutmeg and cinnamon, and before them now lay the final course. Crisp delicate layers of pastry, crusted with sugar and hiding a filling of hot, sweet spiced apple. The dessert was expensive, a testament not only to the skill of his kitchen staff but also to his wealth.

Somer had little doubt that Cecil had not wanted to attend, but neither could he readily refuse. The meal, the pleasantries, and the light and pointless conversation had persisted now between the two men for nearly two hours. Somer was trying to keep an amused expression from his face, knowing that Cecil was suffering inwardly. Here was a man who liked to come to the point immediately, gather what information he needed quickly, assess it, plan a response and then execute it. To have to discuss the epidemic that was gripping London *and* the economic crisis *and* rising prices *and* the weather *and* its tragic effects on Somer's wife's flower garden was truly making Cecil suffer.

Cecil, in his thirties, with a body that was as busy as his mind, sat and tapped his fingers on the table with one hand and turned over a knife repeatedly with his other. His eyes flicked constantly between Somer's still-full plate and his host's face, Cecil impatient for the meal to conclude, the servants to clear the table, and the business of the evening to commence.

Finally, Somer relented. As host, social decorum decreed that he control the path the conversation was to take, but finally he asked a question that allowed Cecil to guide it in the direction his guest wished.

"So tell me, how is life at Court?" Somer asked with a wicked glint in his eye; he could almost see Cecil relax and then focus as the door had finally been opened and he was allowed to raise the matter that had been the unspoken subject of the meeting.

"There are many, John, who want the issue of the succession finalised. It is becoming a focus that many on the Privy Council are overly worried about." Cecil, a deep frown lifting from his brow, came straight to the point, finally releasing the knife he had been toying with, his hands folded on the table before him.

"We are alone. You can speak honestly of your concerns," Somer replied, his tone genuine and honest, settling back in his chair, holding his wine carefully before him in two hands.

"There are few options, as you know, however one needs to be selected. Once a settlement is made then the focus of the council can change to other, more relevant things," Cecil explained, his dark eyes fixed upon Somer across the table.

"The choice is, I assume, between Philip and Elizabeth," Somer stated unnecessarily, his lips pressing hard together.

"Chiefly yes. There are other names, but in all reality there are just these two," Cecil answered, his tone grave, nodding in confirmation.

"It remains an issue that Her Majesty needs to address, I agree," Somer's voice, as always, remained polite and level, his expression cordial, denying the casual observer any clue as to his real thoughts.

"I believe even her Majesty realises she cannot forward Philip as her heir, vesting England in Spain's hands is not an option that any on the Privy Council will endorse. If she does, then we are likely to see some troubled times ahead." Cecil picked up the knife and began tapping the blade on the table to underline his point, a telling sign of his continued impatience.

"Civil war?" Somer said with mock disbelief, his eyebrows raised.

"Worse. It would divide the country, yes, but it would also be a claim that Spain would not be easily dissuaded from pursuing," Cecil replied, his disparaging tone telling Somer that he found little amusement in the situation. "Can you see them leaving us be?"

"It is an unpleasant prospect, I agree. Do you have a more equable solution?" Somer asked quietly, forcing his voice to adopt a serious note again.

Cecil inclined his head before continuing, his right hand tugging absently at his earlobe. "It is a matter of vesting the succession in Elizabeth in a way that satisfies all factions on the council and, of course, Her Majesty."

Somer's eyebrows shot up for a second time, and sarcasm tinged his reply. "Good luck with that! You can negotiate until Doomsday and you'll never get them to meet eye to eye."

It was a fairly simple division. Elizabeth had supporters, especially amongst those of the Privy Council who saw her as a champion for the Protestant cause. They would back her in her own right if Mary named her as a successor. Then there was another Catholic faction, who distrusted

Elizabeth, and sought to control her. If she married Edward Courtenay, devoutly Catholic and until recently Mary's favourite cousin, then this was an Elizabeth they could support. One who could be controlled by her husband, a man they in turn could control.

"I know. Both factions need to feel they are on the winning side, and Her Majesty also rejects her sister as her successor." Cecil's tone told Somer he was far from admitting defeat on this issue. He had abandoned the knife and his right hand had found a fold in the table cloth that he was worrying between thumb and finger.

"So you've three separate masters whose arguments you need to champion. I can't see you reconciling them," Somer said honestly, setting his glass down carefully on the table.

"There is a way. A path through this that I can see that will secure the succession and keep every party united," Cecil supplied, the muscles around his mouth tightening, and added, "however, I need help."

Somer knew that confession had just cost Cecil dearly, but he kept a smile of triumph from his face, instead furrowing his brow in a look of concern he asked, "Of course, if I can help, I would be glad to."

Cecil's hand returned absently to his ear, and with reluctance he said, "It will need to be carefully managed, but I believe it is possible."

Somer settled back in his chair, sipped his wine, and enjoyed Cecil's discomfort. The man hated having to ask for anything. Somer pursed his lips and said, "Pray, tell me then, how you aim to get Her Majesty and the two opposing factions of the Privy Council in accord."

Cecil adopted a business-like tone, and leaning forward he selected Somer's salt cellar. "This is Elizabeth's supporters. They are in a fairly perilous position." He placed the salt down firmly in a clear space on the table. "They cannot openly flout the faith as a reason for their support of Elizabeth, however I have, I believe, ascertained most who fall into this faction, and separated them from..." Cecil picked up an equally ornate sugar bowl and placed it next to the salt cellar "...those who will outwardly support Elizabeth but only if the Catholic faith is preserved. They will only back Elizabeth if she marries Courtenay."

"So you have a plan to reconcile them?" Somer asked, letting a note of incredulity edge his voice, his eyes running over his rearranged tableware.

"I will never reconcile them. Although I believe I can make both sides believe that they are going to succeed," Cecil said, picking up the salt cellar and holding it in the air between them. "If her Protestant supporters believe that there will never be a wedding to Courtenay then they will support Elizabeth as Mary's successor." Cecil placed the salt down with a decisive thunk on the table and raised the sugar bowl, "And if the opposing faction believes the wedding will take place then they too will support Elizabeth."

Somer held up his hand. "I am sure you are going to explain this to me, but don't forget Courtenay's own ambition to claim the throne caused Mary herself to banish him from England."

"True, the fool didn't really leave her with much choice, however he was once a favourite and banishment is not The Tower is it?" Cecil replied, his hands empty now, had found again the rucked edge of the table cloth.

"Accepted. Go on."

"So, Elizabeth needs to outwardly favour the match which will secure her the adherence of Courtenay's supporters, and then her other supporters simply need to be convinced she is doing this merely to secure the support she needs but would never go through with the wedding," Cecil concluded, his hand moving the sugar bowl away from the salt cellar.

Somer digested the simplicity of this argument for a moment, sipping his wine, before he responded. "I am sure you are able to execute the mechanics of this. However, there is a third point on your triangle. Her Majesty, and she is opposed to Elizabeth as her successor."

Cecil nodded. "She favours Philip, I know. Though I believe this is where you can help."

"Me!" Now Somer was surprised. He held little to no sway over Mary.

"Yes." Cecil's small dark eyes bored into him, watching him carefully, ready to gauge his reaction to a suggestion he was about to make. "Years ago you showed me a paper with the sole intention of having Elizabeth released from The Tower. I agreed, if I remember, the chaos that it could have made had it been released was not in the interests of Her Majesty or England."

Somer watched him equally carefully, his fingers tightening involuntarily on the wine glass. "Go on."

"That paper could be used to persuade Mary that Elizabeth is the rightful heir," Cecil stated simply.

The meeting was concluded soon after, and Somer was left alone with his thoughts. He returned to his study, removed from a box in his desk the paper Richard had given him, and smoothed it flat. Marked with age, creased and somewhat stained with the faded dried blood of the messenger who had delivered it, this was a deposition that he knew could never be made public. Signed by one of Katherine of Aragon's ladies-in-waiting, it confirmed that Katherine had suffered an early miscarriage. The unfortunate event, however, had not occurred whilst she had been wed to Henry, it was dated to the time when she had been married to Henry's brother, Arthur. Henry had married his dead brother's wife, claiming that Arthur had never consummated the marriage. What Somer held in his hands showed that he certainly had , and Henry's marriage to Katherine should never have taken place. Quite simply it made Mary Tudor illegitimate. Cecil's hope was that this truth would force Mary to name her sister as her rightful successor.

✝

Richard found the journey to London was uneventful and straightforward, albeit slow. The innkeeper had not lied. Rain had indeed tormented England for months. The roads were mired; the fields under water, and the rivers and streams had burst their banks. His brother, back on home ground, seemed to breathe easier.

Jack liked the food, and delighted in the fact that Emilio didn't, even more. It had been a long time since English had been a language Richard heard all around him, and one he used daily, and the feeling of being home was one he had not expected, especially as he did not have anywhere he could really call home.

It was their second night in England and they were forced to stop early, he had wanted to press on further towards London, but Richard had to relent when he found out that it would be about twenty miles along the road before they found somewhere else to spend a dry night. Leaving Jack and Emilio to stable to horses, he went to secure their accommodation.

The rented room was probably the best the inn had to offer. A peat fire was burning in the hearth, low wooden beds were set against the walls and the closed shutters were keeping the worst of the rain out.

For a few moments Richard found himself alone.

The mask of calm proficiency fell from his face. Stupidly he had allowed himself to look too far down the road ahead. Groaning, pressing his fingers into his eyes, he tried to stop the thoughts running unchecked through his mind. It was a harsh admission to acknowledge that he could no longer deal with much more than the immediate future, the task at hand. He could not fit together the pieces of the puzzle that were to be their future. Like some broken vase he was clutching at the larger recognisable shards and the rest, scattered and smashed, he could no longer order.

He had to get to Christian first.

Fulfil this bargain, free the rest of the group, and what happened to him after that he no longer cared. His back to the cold damp wall, Richard slid down it until he was sitting on the floor, knees drawn up, elbows upon them, his face covered by his hands. But closing his eyes would no longer shut the world out like it once had.

When he heard the tread of steps on the stairs outside the room he knew they were too heavy to be Emilio's. A moment later the door opened and Richard, raising his head from his hands, schooled his face too late as Jack opened the door.

"What's the matter?" Jack asked immediately, dropping his pack onto the bed he wished to claim.

Richard met his brother's enquiring gaze. "I need to get to Christian before Kineer does, everything seems to be trying to stop me, that's all."

"We will succeed." Jack seemed relieved, squeezing his brother's shoulder briefly before dropping to sit on the edge of one of the low beds.

"I have to believe that," Richard's reply was distant and automatic.

Jack, it seemed, had thankfully decided to change the subject. "When we have done this, when we have ensured the weapons are headed to the Order, what then?"

It was the first time either of them had mentioned the future, or spoken about a time after the immediacy of the task they were facing.

Richard regarded Jack with a serious and troubled gaze. "I don't know. Sengle told me he would release the men and Lizbet, but will he?"

Jack smiled. "Well one thing we know for sure, they'll not want to keep Lizbet. Christ! Can you imagine her in a convent?"

"At least she is safe," Richard was in no mood to share his brother's amusement, dropping his gaze back to his hands.

Jack, chastened by his brother's tone, replied soberly, "I worry about her as well. But with Emilio's diligent planning, how can we fail?"

Richard looked up at that, regarding Jack closely, and asked, "Do you know who Emilio is?"

Jack looked at him in confusion, but his instant answer was, "An insufferable

Italian who thinks he's right about everything."

"That's not what I meant," Richard replied, "And you know it."

"He's a Knight of the Order." Jack added.

"And?"

"And what?" Jack sounded confused, "He's a soldier and an admirable commander."

Richard shook his head. "I didn't say what. I said who?"

"You are speaking in riddles. Tell me what you mean, I'm not in the mood for your games," Jack spoke bluntly, as he tried to pry a wet boot from his left foot.

"His uncle is Charles V, the Holy Roman Emperor, his brothers are among Philip of Spain's generals and his sisters are married to some of the most powerful families in Europe," Richard explained patiently.

"So?" Jack shrugged, dropping the boot on the floor and starting to work on removing the second.

"Should his status not be important to you?" Richard persisted.

Jack, looking utterly confused, was still battling with his right boot. "I know, but what difference is that to me?

"He is the most powerful and most highly connected man you have ever met and you don't take advantage of that?" Richard sounded incredulous.

Jack had managed to free his boot from the suck of the water that soaked the inside and dropped it next to its companion, observing his cold wet feet gloomily. "I have, he doesn't seem to mind sharing his skills with me."

"Jack, I'm not talking about his skills," Richard replied, then, "here, throw your boots over. I'll set them next to mine near the fire to dry out."

"What then?" Jack sounded confused as he kicked his boots towards his brother.

"Leave him be." It was Emilio's voice from the doorway, then he used the name that he knew annoyed Jack the most, "I like Jacque just the way he is, stop trying to corrupt him."

Both men looked up from where they sat, to find Emilio leaning against the door frame.

"How long have you been there?" Jack asked, squeezing water from the wool encasing his frozen feet.

Emilio pushed himself away from the wood. "Too long, I have no doubt." Then placing a hand on Jack's shoulder and leaning over him said, "If an 'admirable commander' is the only compliment I can gain from you then I shall value it. A compliment given with honesty is one to be treasured."

Jack flushed and then scowled at Richard. Richard found himself grinning back. Jack was, he had to admit, good company.

✝

Their stay at the inn had coincided with a village fayre, which event was taking place despite the weather and, for Jack at least, was providing a much needed distraction. Jack found Emilio where the noise was loudest. Perched on a wall watching a wrestling match. The Italian had one knee drawn up, his chin resting upon it and there was a look of mild interest on his face. Jack pushed his way through the packed crowd, climbed up the wall and sat down next to him

"I would not have thought this a sport you would enjoy." Jack spoke to Emilio, but his eyes were on the current two contestants inside the ring of cheering men. Locked in combat, arms around greased bodies, they heaved and pitched against each other trying to effect a throw.

"And why is that?" Emilio replied, his eyes not leaving the combatants.

Jack looked between the fight and the Italian. "It is brutal, vicious, and although they are both near enough naked, I can't see either of them being to your taste."

Emilio ignored him and pointed a ringed finger towards the taller of the two wrestlers. "He looks like the natural winner, taller, bigger, stronger by far than his opponent, and to make sure as much money changes hands as possible the other is letting it look as if he is losing ground."

"He is losing ground," Jack replied, his eyes on the shorter man, whose face was contorted into an agony that told of the physical battle he was currently undergoing.

"No, Jack," Emilio corrected, "he looks like he is. Watch."

"I am watching. He'll be on the floor in a moment."

"You are not watching. The bigger man has a hold around his neck. He can't close it and suffocate his opponent because of where he has his arm," Emilio explained patiently.

"That's just luck," Jack replied, although he had to admit that what Emilio said was correct. No matter how hard the bigger man would try to close the hold against the other's windpipe he couldn't, because of the locked arm the other had against his chest.

"It's not luck, he's used several other techniques as well which he didn't learn by accident," Emilio observed.

Jack watched carefully. The fight certainly looked as if it was going in the bigger man's favour. The two struggling men rotated together through a half turn, and the smaller man dropped his head towards his chest. The tout flung his arms wide, declaring he'd take no more bets. There was a cacophony of complaint from disappointed gamblers, and in that moment when most of the spectator's attention was on the tout and not the wrestlers, the smaller man broke the hold of the larger and with a speed that surprised Jack, had his opponent pitched and rolling on the ground a moment later.

There was a united groan of complaint for the onlookers.

"I told you," Emilio replied. "The smaller wrestler and the tout are working together."

It wouldn't be the first rigged match he'd seen, but Jack was still not convinced by Emilio's argument. "I thought the only thing you wrestled with on Malta were your consciences?" Jack said dryly.

"Please Jack. It's a sport of kings. My father believed he was King Chronicus and that having his sons crushed and bruised by a series of trainers would liken myself and my brother to Plexippus and Enetus," Emilio said, then tapping Jack's arm with his own, he said, "Look here we go again, same man back in for a second bout."

"Against the blacksmith by the looks of it," Jack mused, looking at the new challenger.

"It will make no difference. The defending champion is fighting on skill and not on his strength," Emilio replied.

"That man is twice his size, he will pull him apart," Jack's voice was incredulous.

"Shall we have a private wager?" Emilio said, tipping his head towards Jack's.

"You know I don't have any coin." Jack did not like being reminded of his penniless state.

"Oh, you don't need silver for this wager," Emilio said smiling.

Jack cast his cold blue eyes over the Italian's face. "Go on then. What do you want me to bet?"

"If he loses, and is torn apart, then you can have this." Emilio had taken one of the rings from his hand and held it up for Jack to view. It was indeed a valuable prize.

"And if he wins?" Jack said, his eyes on the ring.

"Then I get to put you on your back in the dirt down there," Emilio said, his face deadly serious.

"You!" Jack blurted. "You think you can beat me?"

"I know I can. And if I lose then you can still have this," Emilio held the ring up for Jack to see for a moment longer before he dropped it back onto his finger.

"So, if he wins," Jack pointed at the bigger of the two wrestlers, "I get that ring, and if he loses and I beat you then I still get the ring?"

Emilio inclined his head in acceptance of the proposal.

Jack grinned. "You have given me not one, but two chances of success and I shall take them both."

Emilio raised his eyebrows and returned his attention to the match that was about to take place below them. The bout was a short one, and Jack was more than a little annoyed with the outcome when the blacksmith had his feet parted from the ground and landed on his back with a force that propelled the air from his lungs. As Emilio had predicted, the champion retired at that point having earned himself a large enough purse for the evening, and two of the spectators stripped to their hose and entered the ring circling each other.

Emilio clapped Jack on the back. "Come on then."

The Italian stood on the narrow wall, his hand on Jack's head for balance, neatly stepped past him and made a quick descent to the ground below. Richard was on the edge of the ring of spectators. Emilio divested himself of his rings, including the one he had offered to Jack, and dropped his doublet and shirt into Richard's waiting arms.

"Do I get him back in one piece?" Richard said quietly, as he deposited Emilio's clothes on an empty trestle.

Emilio, his back to Jack, grinned. "Of course!"

"I heard that! You are serious then?" Jack shook his head, not constrained by either jewels or artful clothing he had dropped the leather jerkin he wore onto the ground next to the wall and shrugging his linen shirt over his head dropped it on top.

Emilio pushed his way to the front of the ring, with the confidence of a man who was convinced the event had been arranged solely for him. Jack, his arms folded, and wearing a look of mild disapproval, stood next to him.

When the last challenger had been pitched into the dirt for a second time and crawled from the ring, Emilio entered and Jack stepped in behind him. The bout was a traditional best of three, and the men were supposed to wait while those watching placed their bets. Emilio, however, was not going to afford the spectators this opportunity. Moving towards Jack he flung his arms around him and forced Jack to match his stance. Jack, both arms behind Emilio's back, locked his hands together and tightened his hold on the smaller man. Jack was never sure how it happened, he felt the pain in the back of his left calf, his balance wavered, and then his left shoulder was digging into the ground at Emilio's feet.

Rolling onto his back, a look of open surprise on his face, he stared up into Emilio's impassive face.

"Again? Or do you concede?" Emilio stated, his arms folded.

"What? No," Jack rolled onto his front and sprang back to his feet to face Emilio.

It was with a lot more care that Jack closed in on Emilio a second time. He had been the victim of a trick, of that he was sure, and it wasn't going to happen again. His hold this time was firmer and his feet, squarely planted against the ground, were a little further away from Emilio's. Their muscles tight against each other, they waited for the shout to start. Jack had every intention of landing Emilio face down in the dirt, the hold he tightened around Emilio's back was brutal, and he could feel Emilio's muscles hard under his own.

Using his weight he tried to twist to his right and pull Emilio's body down, the lighter man instantly loosened his hold and reapplied it, with both of his hands now locked around Jack's neck. The effect was instantaneous. Jack found his own strength turned against him, the resistance he had been straining against was gone and again he found himself lurching off balance. This time he was planted face down by a well aimed kick to the back of his knee that folded his legs beneath him.

Cheers for the victor rang in Jack's ears as he pushed himself back up on his elbows. An open hand appeared in front of his face and Jack, realising he had just been taught a lesson, ruefully grinned and allowed Emilio to pull him back up.

"A victory without a prize is a poor one," Jack said, brushing dirt from his chest.

"Oh, don't worry I have a prize I shall treasure," Emilio said, smiling broadly.

"You are as bad as my brother, but you have a few tricks I would like to learn," Jack said graciously. Jack ran his eyes over the half naked man before him as if he was assessing a horse. Emilio's dark skin lay tight over lean muscle, the arms and shoulders were those of a swordsman, and over his body were a number of faded scars, the freshest of these that had not had time to fade was a white line running across his ribs under his right arm.

Emilio didn't seem annoyed by Jack's critical gaze, and when Jack's eyes came to rest on the most recent scar Emilio smiled broadly. "Can't you remember giving that to me?"

Jack's brow furrowed, and he said defensively, "Me? I've not laid a hand on you."

"You cut away the cuirass, remember?" Emilio replied.

"I'd not realised," Jack said. The cut must have been a deep one to have left such a ridged line across the man's ribs. He'd also not expected to see so many other marks on the Italian's body, under his perfectly white linen Jack had always assumed that the Knight's lithe and muscled body had been one favoured by fortune and status and would be unmarked and unscarred.

"You seem surprised. You are not the only whose body has tales to tell," Emilio replied. He retrieved his linen shirt and dropped it back over his head, the ties undone. It dropped lopsided over one shoulder but Emilio seemed not to have noticed. Shrugging into his doublet and looking now particularly slovenly compared to his usual standards he tucked an arm under Jack's and steered him away from the men still watching the wrestling. "I think you owe the victor a drink at least."

Jack allowed himself to be led towards a vacant table where he took a bench opposite Emilio, summoning for ale which was swiftly delivered.

Emilio swilled the ale around the earthenware cup in his hand before tentatively sipping at it, his nose wrinkled. "How do you drink this? It's so sour."

Jack drained his cup and reached for the jug to refill it. "Easily. Sometimes having low standards does mean you're not easily disappointed."

Emilio laughed. "Jack, only you could appraise yourself as having low standards."

"I have low standards when it comes to food and ale. As long as it's edible it will do. You've never been hungry, so you wouldn't understand," Jack shot back.

"Accepted. And your high standards? Are those some I've not noticed?" Emilio asked mischievously.

"Very funny," Jack said sarcastically, then snatching Emilio's abandoned cup from the table he said, "Give me that here, if you're not having it I will."

CHAPTER THREE

✝

Marcus Drover, Lawyer Clement's assistant, returning from an errand for his master, recognised the mounted man approaching. It was one of Clement's clients, and quickening his pace Marcus bounded down the path, up the two wooden steps and darted through the door to warn his master.

"It's Fitzwarren," Marcus blurted the warning through the partly opened door to Clement's office.

A look of instant panic contorted the lawyer's face. Standing quickly, his eyes darted around for an escape. "Tell him I'm out." There was a door from his office leading to the yard at the back and Clement quickly headed towards it.

Marcus looked around helplessly as he watched his master disappear and heard the noise of the firm's richest client slamming open the front door.

"Clement!" Robert Fitzwarren bellowed, his feet treading the boards leading to Clement's empty office.

Marcus took one hesitant step towards him and then, obviously thinking better of this act, took two in reverse. "He's not in, Sir."

Robert looked beyond Marcus towards the partly opened door leading to Clement's office and, ignoring the servant, pushed his way into the room.

Clement was no longer there.

Robert, growling under his breath, cast his eyes around the lawyer's chaotic room. He saw the unstopped ink pot and next to it the pen. Navigating through the wasteland of papers stacked on the floor, sending files tumbling in his wake, he rounded the desk. Pressing the flat of his hand to the leather of the chair seat, his eyes met those of Marcus who was hovering nervously in the doorway. "Where is he?" Robert shouted. Marcus didn't answer but glanced towards the door in the corner of the office. A moment later it was dragged open and Robert glared at Clement who yelped involuntarily when he saw him, caught before he had managed to pull open the yard gate and make good his escape.

"Get in here now! Or I will give you a reason to hide, Master Lawyer," Robert commanded, stepping back into the room and dropping heavily into Clement's chair.

Clement, his hands bunching his dusty, stained lawyer's robe, entered the room, skirting the edge and brought himself to sit nervously in the client seat opposite Robert.

"This is all your bloody fault, and *you* are going to set it to rights," Robert growled.

"I don't understand, Sir." Clement's voice, high-pitched and nervous, shook as he replied.

Robert's fist slammed down onto the desk. The ink pot tipped and the contents spilt out over the papers Clement had been working on before Robert had arrived. The lawyer, his eyes widening as he saw the ruined papers, let out an involuntary wail of despair. Robert angrily balled the dripping papers in his hand. Parchment cracked, ink dripped, and the lawyer's red seals crumbled in his fist.

"Do you care more about this than my affairs?" Robert thrust the spoilt papers towards Clement across the desk, the ink making tracks down his forearms, staining his doublet.

Clement, shaking, didn't answer.

"Do you?" Robert flung the saturated mess towards Clement. The lawyer flung his hands up to his face as the parchment slapped across his cheek.

"You do right to cower. That bastard was supposed to die in Marshalsea, remember?" Robert growled.

"Kettering didn't..." Clement's voice squeaked.

"I don't care what Kettering did or didn't do, it's your fault. My father, imbecile that he now is, has signed over my inheritance to that sack of shit, and you, Master Clement, are going to reverse that," Robert said, leaning threateningly across the table.

Clement's eyes widened. "Your father?"

"Yes, his lawyer Luttrel has rejected the sale of the manor, declaring that I have no title, and my bloody father has confirmed that he has signed over everything to his bastard son." Fury burned like wild fire in Robert's eyes.

"But, if he's a bastard then he can't inherit," Clement replied swiftly.

"Apparently he can after my father's lawyer, Luttrell, concocted some scheme," Robert growled.

"Luttrell? I know him, I thought he'd retired. I was surprised to see his name on the documents we received concerning that land transaction," Clement said, relieved that the conversation was moving away from himself and on to a safer topic.

"Find out what Luttrell has done, and find out what you need to do to undo it.

Do you hear me?" Robert boomed across the desk.

Clement nodded so rapidly his black lawyer's cap became detached from his balding head and slid over his eyes.

"How can this happen?" Robert complained again. "He's a bastard, the law is clear on inheritance."

"I will try to find out as much as I can," Clement said, swallowing nervously. *Why couldn't the lot of them just get into a room and kill each other,* Clement lamented silently.

"Don't *try,* you idiot. I want better than that. Find out what is happening and send me a message before the week is out with what you are going to do to correct this. *Do you hear me?"*

Clement was still shaking when he heard the front door slam marking the exit of his furious client. How had he ended up in the middle of this? It wasn't fair. Clement knew only too well from his dealings with Richard Fitzwarren that Jack was the rightful heir, and he'd even produced a document for Jack to give his father William to sign. He had to suppose that it was as a result of this that Lutrell was now refuting Robert's right as heir.

If Robert found out about this, Clement had no doubt at all what he would do. The simple fact was that he had to work out which of the Fitzwarrens he feared the most. Richard was likely to let the leash slip on his brother, a man that Clement had contrived to place in Marshalsea. It had only been Richard's restraining hand that had stopped the man from putting a knife to him when they had confronted him in his office.

Since then he had heard nothing from them. Maybe they were dead? More than likely they were out of the country. That meeting had been nearly two years ago and the lapse of time was deadening the edge of his fear. The Fitzwarren he feared most was the one now closest to him, the more immediate threat - Robert.

The de Bernay case was still ongoing. Robert should have been grateful; it had been through Clement's diligent enquiry that he had found that the wealth of Assingham lay not in the manor but in the vast woodlands that de Bernay had bought and appended to his property. Clement tapped his fingers on the arm of his chair thoughtfully. Some success on that front might appease Robert, perhaps direct his mind elsewhere...

Clement discarded that false hope quickly. William Fitzwarren had been one of the old King's trusted elite, and Clement had no doubt he would have stuffed his coffers to the brim with the land and property deals Henry had brokered after raping the church of her assets. Acquiring for Robert a small manor in Bedfordshire and some tracts of land was not going to make up for his lost inheritance.

Clement could, when faced with a legal problem, be particularly inventive, especially when that problem involved his own well-being. Immobile, still seated in his client chair, his eyes stared across his office unfocused. His mind though was racing, running down one legal path and then another until he could find a process that might work. After an hour, when his arse was completely numb, he had the beginnings of an idea.

"I could…"

Clement smiled to himself. William Fitzwarren might have been able to change his inheritance, however a man who was convicted of treason could not inherit. Richard Fitzwarren was wanted for treason: as yet there had not been a trial, but the writ existed. Jack was wanted for murder, but if Clement could tie him close enough to his brother then a charge of treason could also be leveled at him. The charge in itself would not bar his inheritance but if there was a conviction, that would. Not the easiest route to pursue, but it was possible that the conviction could be obtained *in absentia*. A very plausible argument could be made to the effect that neither Richard nor Jack would ever return to England.

Clement pulled his cap from his head and scratched, then raked his fingers through his thin grey hair. William Fitzwarren's property would be vast, and it was not only his property that was at stake but his titles as well. Everything that he had vested in Jack would be forfeit to the crown if he was convicted of treason, and Clement could see no reason why he could not raise some interest in this case given the stakes involved. Once the crown became aware of the potential worth of Jack Fitzwarren it would not be too difficult to make him complicit in his brother's crime.

It was all a matter of timing.

William Fitzwarren was unlikely to continue to want to vest his estates in Jack knowing that everything would then be forfeit to the crown should a conviction be secured and was more than likely to reinstate Robert as his rightful heir. The very nature of the crime and the high stakes it attracted meant that it was rarely successfully contested.

Treason!

Clement let his mind wander to back to the execution of William Thomas, who had been one of Wyatt's conspirators. Wyatt's rank might have bought him a swift end on the block before his body was hacked into pieces, but William Thomas had suffered the full traitor's demise. He was a clerk of the Privy Council, and Clement had been present at his execution. Gossip had said Thomas had tried to kill himself to avoid a traitor's end, and the man who was hauled behind a horse tied to a hurdle had looked like he had suffered. Whether it was at his own hands or those of his inquisitors was unclear. What had been patently clear though, when he was released from the hurdle and his rope bonds cut, was that he could no longer stand and had to be carried to the waiting rope. Noosed he had swung in mid-air, piss running down his legs. The rope had been quickly lowered and Thomas' choking had ended. It was not the executioner's desire to deny the crowd the full exhibition of a traitor's end.

Clement could only hope that Jack Fitzwarren and his malicious brother would swing from a rope as Thomas had done. Their bodies humiliated and broken, and then forced to watch as they had their cocks cut from them and burned. The lawyer's lips curled in an evil snarl. That would be an entertainment he would not miss.

This would be no ordinary case. The property issue alone and the implication of a noble's heir would make this a matter that would be ideally suited to the Star Chamber, a court comprised of privy councillors and senior judges whose proceedings were held entirely in private. It might have been set up originally with the intention of ensuring the fair judgement of the notable classes, however it was now a secret court mechanism that ensured political and monarchical will triumphed. Clement was sure that the desire in this case would be to line Mary's depleted coffers with the Fitzwarren wealth.

After clearing his desk of the jumble of files Robert had left scattered there and righting the ink pot, Clement seated himself and began his first draft of a letter he would eventually send to one of the privy councillors of the Star Chamber, William Cecil.

If Clement was careful, he reckoned he might even profit from this himself.

✝

Morley knocked on the door to Cecil's office. Moments later it was opened by one of his assistants and he navigated through the cramped space towards Cecil's desk. His master looked up as he lowered himself into the seat opposite.

"I am beginning to wonder if we are being played for fools," Cecil stated as he glared over his spectacles at Morley.

"How so?" Morley replied in his usual light tone.

"Robert Fitzwarren's lawyer is now sending me tales of treason." Cecil cast down the pen he was holding and selected a folded sheet from the pile on his left, casting it towards Morley.

"He's found Richard Fitzwarren?" Morley said, his interested immediately piqued. He leaned forward and took the sheet, opening the letter fully.

"Unfortunately not. He is pressing for his brother, Jack, to be included as complicit in Richard's crimes," Cecil said as Morley read the neatly penned letter.

"So he's of little use then. Why's he doing this?" Morley asked, still reading.

"I don't know," Cecil replied honestly. "Robert Fitzwarren has still got that case in Chancery running to gain control over the de Bernay girl."

"It would help if he actually had the girl," Morley pointed out.

"They are blissfully unaware that the de Bernay secret is not one they have successfully kept. Indeed, the case is due to be heard again in a couple of weeks. How Robert Fitzwarren intends to weave his way through this legal tangle will be interesting to watch," Cecil mused, "If I was not such a busy man I would be tempted to attend just to watch the courtroom entertainment."

"Richard and his bastard brother are not likely to be in England. I've found no trace of them and with charges for treason and murder attached to their names it's not likely they would remain here. From what I know of them it is also unlikely that they would disappear beneath the surface for very long," Morley replied, "Richard in particular has a penchant for being where he should not."

"I agree. Robert has, he says, information on why Jack Fitzwarren should be charged as well for treason. Find out what's going on, Morley," Cecil commanded, a finger settling his spectacles back on his nose.

"I will talk to him," Morley replied.

"And his lawyer," Cecil reminded him. "They've some scheme afoot and I want to know what it is."

†

Robert Fitzwarren was an easy man to dislike.

Morley knew from his previous dealings with Robert that their coming meeting would not be a pleasant one. Robert was arrogant, bad-tempered and habitually hostile to anyone not of an equivalent rank, and he had made his opinion of Morley quite clear. Last time they had spoken had been when Morley was on the trail of Richard. Robert had been appalled to hear that his brother was not dead. There had, it seemed, been an incident at Burton and it was believed Richard had perished trying to escape, crushed to death by a mill wheel. Robert was less than happy to find out that he had in someway been duped, and that Richard had subsequently been seen in London. Robert's spirits did rise though when Morley had told him that he was wanted for charges of both treason and murder, and that servants of the Crown were actively seeking him.

Arriving at William Fitzwarren's London house, Morley let his eyes roam over the opulent facade. Diamond-paned windows freckled the wide expanse of the front, and to the right was an arch gate with an oak door, studded and bearing the Fitzwarren crest prominently displayed in the middle. William Fitzwarren might be crumbling in his dotage, but his house certainly wasn't.

Ronan, Lord Fitzwarren's steward, showed Morley into a room in the spacious town house where he found the man he had called on sitting in a chair by the fire, one leg slung over the arm. Robert glared at him as Morley stepped into the room and Ronan silently closed the door behind him.

"Is this the best I get?" Robert demanded,

"Sir, I am sorry I do not understand your meaning," Morley replied, although he did understand perfectly what Robert's issue was. Christopher Morley, backed by Cecil and the weight of his office, was rarely, if ever, intimidated.

"A lackey. I report treason, by God, and I get you?" Robert spat back.

"I can assure you, talking to me is the same as if you were talking to my master," Morley said, attempting to sound as conciliatory as possible without crossing the boundary into patronising.

"What I have to say is too important to be imparted to the likes of you. Tell that to your master," Robert said slowly, as if speaking to an imbecile, and when he had finished he nodded his head in the direction of the door his visitor had so recently entered. "Out, go on."

"As you wish," Morley said evenly. He had expected little else from the man. Now he would report back to Cecil and return with a military backing that would underline his master's request, or Cecil might choose to summon Robert to his offices. Either way, he was sure, Robert would regret not taking the opportunity he had just been afforded.

Morley closed the door and stood once again in the corridor. The steward was still there, ready to lead him from the house, when a thought occurred to Morley.

"Please let Lord Fitzwarren know I am here," Morley's words halted the steward who turned to look at him, indecision plain on his face.

"Lord Fitzwarren, please let him know I am here," Morley repeated his request, his eyes connecting with the servant's.

"He'll be asleep, I'll tell Master Fitzwarren you want to see him." Ronan clearly did not want to be responsible for this meeting and took a step back towards the room Morley had just exited.

"No." Morley caught his arm, "Lord Fitzwarren, not Master Fitzwarren."

The Steward made no move to reply.

"Oh very well, I know which door it is, I shall take myself there." Morley released Ronan and a moment later he had knocked quickly on a thick oak door. Turning to the steward he smiled. "Ah, he has bid me enter."

Neither Morley nor Ronan had heard a command to enter the room, and the look on Ronan's face was one of pure horror as

Morley opened and then stepped through the door.

The room was dimly lit. Oil lamps burnt in two of the wall sconces, the shutters were closed blocking the light from the street and the room was overly warm and carried with it the foul odour of sickness. The smell of sweat, urine, and faeces was mixed with the aroma of apothecary's herbs and something else as well which Morley's nose couldn't quite translate.

The bed was empty, the covers heaped and in disarray. Morley had been here before and his gaze shifted to the chair where William spent his days, though that too was empty.

"I'm over here," a voice said from the darkened corner of the room.

Morley turned towards the speaker. "My Lord, I apologise for the intrusion. William Cecil ..."

Morley trailed off as his eyes adjusted to the gloom and he began to pick out the image of William in the darkness. Before he could speak or take a step forwards the door behind him was wrenched open and light, along with Robert, spilled into the room.

"Out! How dare you intrude on my father's peace!" Robert was in the room, his hand clawing into Morley's arm, hauling him from the room.

If Morley believed he possessed an immunity as a servant of the Crown, it was a view that was not shared by Robert Fitzwarren. Ronan, directed by Robert's shouted commands, propelled him down the short passage, yanked open the door and ejected him into the street. Morley, unprepared for the sudden assault, in shock from what he had witnessed in the room, stumbled and tripped over the threshold landing on his knees outside the front of the house.

He needed to report this to Cecil, and quickly.

†

Morley, normally a patient man who let time pass at its own pace, stalked in agitation outside Cecil's office. He'd already been told that his master was in a meeting and would likely not be available for hours, but nevertheless he had waited, needing to speak to Cecil at the earliest opportunity. He knew he would be returning to the Fitzwarren household, but this order needed to come from his master.

It was not until dusk was settling over London that Morley returned to William Fitzwarren's house. Morley knew it would be too late. It had probably been too late five minutes after Robert's steward threw him into the street. But still it had to be done, they would be expecting him and Morley had no intention of letting Robert down.

Morley's gloved hand held a legal writ. William Fitzwarren remained a peer of the realm, and he was summoned to Court.

Morley was informed by a very pale and hesitant Ronan that Lord Fitzwarren and his son had gone to their estate in Suffolk for the good of his Lordship's health.

The men who stood at his back ensured Morley quickly gained access to the house, and while the servants cowered in the kitchen the house was efficiently searched.

Morley opened the door for a second time that day and stepped inside William Fitzwarren's room. It was much as he had seen it earlier that day, the smell wrinkling his nostrils. Advancing to the end of the room he lifted the iron clasps that held the wooden shutters closed and pulled them open on their leather hinges. Turning back he regarded the destruction of this once tidy and well ordered room.

One wall was dominated by a full length painting of a woman. Her eyes, blue and bright and inquisitive, locked with his own.

"I wish, fair lady, that you could tell me what has happened here," Morley spoke quietly to the portrait.

Williams's chair was tipped over, the table at the side of it was broken, the chain attached to the bell cord ripped away and left trailing across the floor. The bed hangings had been ripped down and all the apothecary's stoppered bottles were spread over the wooden floor, some smashed, some leaking their unctuous contents.

Morley turned his eyes finally to the stool closet where he had seen William Fitzwarren earlier that day. It was empty now. Pulling a square of linen from his doublet, Morley covered his mouth and nose and advanced towards it. As he did so, his boot connected with one of the small, green glass bottles and sent it rolling forwards, its drumming passage on the floor coming to a halt when it hit the closet. The air immediately filled with hundreds of thick black-bodied flies that had been feasting on the shit inside it.

Morley gagged.

A moment later he was in the corridor, his back to the door, releasing a lungful of air and taking in an untainted one. One of the soldiers he had arrived with, a concerned look on his face, stepped towards him.

"Get me the bloody steward," Morley gasped as he tried to stop his stomach from rebelling.

CHAPTER FOUR

✝

It happened sometimes, not often, and he couldn't blame it on the opium either. In London, in the church of St Ethelreda he'd felt his strength flowing from him, his legs becoming leaden and uncertain, and once in Italy it had been the same. On more than one occasion he had wondered if the life were being pulled from him by a justifiably angry God.

This time there was no church.

This time it was different.

This time he was not even standing.

From somewhere inside him he heard a desperate cry for help. Maybe not heard it as much as felt it, or sensed it. The effect though was much the same and he could feel the strength seep from his limbs, his breathing became quick and shallow and his hands holding the reins were white and shaking. Richard knew if he had been standing he would have collapsed, and if he got down from the horse now his legs would not support him and he'd end in a heap on the floor. Despite his best efforts he must have swayed in the saddle, for a moment later an iron grip fastened around his upper arm.

"What's the matter?" Jack asked urgently in his ear.

"I don't know." It was, at least, an honest admission.

"There's a village ahead, we can find shelter from the rain there. Can you make it that far?" Jack spoke from behind a hood, the edge of which was jewelled with raindrops.

Richard nodded his reply. The road was washed out. What had once been a hard-packed road wide enough for a cart and a horse to pass was now a river bed. Down the centre ran a stream that had torn deep gouges through the surface, washing away the mud and leaving it strewn with a beach of loose stones. The pebbles rolled under the horse's hooves as they made their way down the final hill to the village, and the riders needed to plan where the hoofed feet of their mounts would go.

Richard's cob tripped, recovered, and banged into Jack's.

Richard was in the middle of the road, riding amongst the loosest stones and stepping in the deep cut forged by the water. Not a place to find sure footing for his mount. Jack pressing his heels into the hairy flanks and forced his beast across the road, pushing his brother's away from the ravine.

"Have a care!" Richard heard Jack's voice growl, but he was thankful when he felt the tug as Jack pulled the reins from his slack hands. Five minutes later he was standing next to the soaked horse, a supporting hand still holding the pommel. Behind him he heard a hurried conversation and the distaste in Emilio's voice as he replied.

Richard allowed Jack to propel him into the inn, the common room was empty, Jack pushing him towards a table near the back. He heard his brother call for ale, recognised the noise of him hauling the sodden cloak from his shoulders, and opened his eyes when he felt the bench he sat on groan with the new weight settling next to him.

"Tell me what's wrong," Jack asked, sounding concerned. "You've turned the colour of a bloody shroud."

"Have I?"

"Tell me what's wrong before Emilio arrives," Jack asked quickly.
"I don't know. It happens sometimes," Richard replied, raising a cup to his lips with a hand that still shook.

Jack regarded him with a hard look.

"It's not ..." Richard spoke with difficulty.

"Thank God for that. What is it then?"

Richard put his cup down and Jack filled it for a second time. His heart was no longer beating as hard in his chest and the tightness in his throat had lessened. Jack's blond head leant close to his. "Tell me, don't be a fool, I'll not judge you."

Richard nearly dropped the cup from his hand.

Like tumblers turning in a lock, everything suddenly fitted into place. With a clarity that had evaded him for a long time Richard suddenly saw the past, present and future synchronise and fuse together and he realised what his tired mind had been trying to tell him. He was looking along a long corridor and suddenly every door along its length had been slammed open.

Richard, groaning, dropped his head into his hands. "What's the month?"

"March," Jack answered, the look on his face one of utter confusion.

"Date?" Richard asked through his hands.

"I don't know, half way through I expect," Jack supplied quickly. "Tell me? Why is that important?"

Richard didn't answer.

"Tell me for God's sake!" There was genuine alarm in Jack's voice now as well as rising anger.

Richard's face remained covered with his hands.

"I am going to count to five, and then I am going to lose my temper!" Jack announced. "One..."

"Jack..."

"Two..."

"Please, Jack, just leave it be."

"Three..."

"Stop it Jack."

"Four..."

"Not now..."

"Five..."

Richard found his hands ripped from his face, Jack's fists fastened themselves into the material of his doublet and he was dragged forward across the table. Richard twisted, forcing Jack to lose one of his holds, but it was quickly applied to the back of his neck and he was hauled forward to land face down on the table.

"Now bloody tell me," Jack growled in his ear.

"For God's sake, Jack!" Richard spluttered against the table.

Jack twisted Richard's right arm across his back. "Now tell me or I break it."

"Bloody well break it then!" Richard snarled back, his body tight against Jack's hold but unable to pull himself free.

A cold draught swept across them as a door opened and Emilio said, "As amusing as it might be, if you break his arm, it is going to delay us."

"Get out! Leave us alone," Jack's voice was a command.

The Italian rolled his eyes, muttered under his breath in Italian, and left, slamming the door behind him.

Jack dropped more of his weight onto Richard's captive arm.

Richard cried out. Then through clenched teeth he said, "He's right. Break my arm and the journey will take longer."

"So be it!" Jack leant on it even harder.

"Alright, you stubborn bastard!" Richard gasped, realising the will of his brother was no less than his own. If he kept the truth to himself it was going to cost a broken arm, and he couldn't afford that.

The pressure on Richard's arm continued for a moment longer before Jack slackened his hold, though he did not release him.

"Well?" Jack demanded.

"I can't let this bargain fail," Richard said, his face still pressed against the table.

"Not good enough. There's more," Jack said and began to tighten his hold on Richard again.

"There is more at stake in Malta than just the men and Lizbet. Now let me go, Jack!"

"What else, what's at stake?" When Richard didn't reply Jack shook him violently, Richard gasping against the pain. "Tell me!"

"There's a child." Richard's eyes were closed as he said the words.

Jack's grip slackened instantly and Richard pushed himself away from the table, one arm massaging the ligament and joint in the one Jack had threatened to break.

"Lizbet's child. It will have been born by now," Richard said when Jack continued to stare at him blankly.

"Lizbet's?" Jack echoed as he dropped onto the bench. "Are you sure?"

"Yes, I am sure, and Sengle confirmed it before we left. The bargain I struck was for the men, for Lizbet, and for your child."

"Mine!" Jack blurted, blue eyes wide with shock meeting Richard's. "I don't bloody well think so."

It was not the reaction Richard had expected. "Are you sure?"

Jack was performing some mental arithmetic involving his fingers. "Unless she's the gestation period of a horse, it's not mine. Can't be."

Richard sat back heavily, resting against the wall behind him, his face pale.

"Why? What have you promised them?" Jack sounded wary now.

Richard dropped his head into hands. "Are you sure?"

"Yes I'm bloody sure. Maybe it's yours?" Jack replied unhelpfully.

"It's not mine!" Richard replied, his voice sounding weary now.

"How come you are allowed to vehemently deny the truth of it but not me? I am as sure as you are. What deal have you made? Tell me damn you!" Jack's words revived Richard's attention.

"I thought it was yours," was the only reply Richard could make, he had for so long believed that the child was his brother's.

"Why didn't you ask? Why didn't you tell me before now? For Christ's sake! Does Emilio know?" Jack asked.

"I don't know," Richard spoke through his hands again.

"What have you done? Richard?" Jack's voice was insistent.

Richard remained silent.

"This is a battle you will not win, brother."

Richard drew a long steadying breath. "I promised myself."

"What do you mean?"

"Sengle will release them, all of them, if I stay," Richard replied.

"Christ!" Was all Jack could manage. "You did that for me? You bloody fool!"

Jack sat in silence and stared at his brother.

"I'd have done it anyway. Neither of us would be sitting here if it wasn't for Lizbet," Richard replied honestly, and both of them knew the truth of that.

"I thought we were finished with that damned rock," Jack swiped a cup from the table and drained it in one go. "Now I know why Edward was so convinced I would accept his invitation."

"Edward Fitzwarren?" Richard said, resting his enquiring eyes on Jack's face.

"Yes. Before we left Malta I spoke to him," Jack said.

"I know. You never did tell me what he wanted. Mutual confessions?" Richard invited.

"It seems so. He'd found out I was William's heir and so could command a heavy inheritance that might be directed to the Order's coffers. That was what he wanted. I wasn't especially interested in the offer, but he was convinced I might change my mind. Now I know why." It was Jack's turn to groan now.

"He wanted you to join the Order?" Richard repeated.

Jack nodded. "I didn't give it much thought, but now."

"Jack, you don't need to, not for me," Richard replied.

"Terrible apart and even worse together – isn't that our family motto?" Jack replied laughing, "maybe we are just what the Order needs."

If there was a weight on Richard's shoulders, Jack's words had gone some way to lifting it.

"I had nothing much else planned. As long as Scranton doesn't stay on that bloody rock I won't mind," Jack said grinning.

Richard found himself grinning. "Imagine how pleased Emilio will be?"

Jack reached across the table and cuffed his brother around the side of the head. "Careful, or I'll leave you to rot on that island on your own."

"It does raise a question though, doesn't it?" Richard said, changing the subject, his voice serious once more.

If it did Jack seemed temporarily at a loss as to what it was. "What?"

"Whose child is it?" Richard placed the words carefully. "There aren't that many candidates."

"Does it matter?" Jack replied.

"No, I suppose not." Richard picked up the cup and twisted it in his hands thoughtfully. He had been so convinced the child was Jack's he'd not considered the other possibilities. And, if he was honest, he didn't want to. At the back of his mind a dark thought was beckoning to him, consciously he slammed a door in its face. He'd consider it later – much later.

†

"I did wonder if I would be seeing you again today," Emilio remarked as Richard emerged from the dark smoky confines of the inn.

Richard cast a disparaging look in the Italian's direction. "As you can see I am hearty and whole."

"Regrettably so," Emilio replied, dryly, clearly disappointed.

"And I was going to apologise to you," Richard said, shaking his head.

Emilio's eyebrows raised. "Really!"

"No, not really," Richard said and swung back into the saddle, setting his horse towards the muddy track that was the road to London.

It was his brother, though, who set the pace that afternoon, and it was a fast one. After an hour Emilio pulled his horse level with Jack's. His voice when he spoke was friendly. "Jack, we should slow, the horses can't keep this pace."

Jack threw him a vicious look. "I'll stop when I want, not when you want me to." Shortening the reins he set the horse to canter ahead leaving Emilio watching after him.

"Jack's not a patient soul," Richard said from where he rode behind Emilio.

"You are right, and it's you who has tried his patience," Emilio said, dark eyes blazing with frustration.

"He'll relent. He always does," Richard replied, a malicious smile on his face.

They completed the afternoon's journey in relative silence. Richard knew his brother was deep in thought over what he had just learned – only one of them was feeling any better as regarded those revelations. Jack's temper was short and he had snapped at Emilio, who then rode on stiff-backed and ignoring Jack, while Richard, his mind deep in thought, ignored them both. The weather kept progress slow and they only made another eight miles before they were forced to stop for the night.

Richard was more tired than he realised, his body letting him know as soon as he lay down on the straw mattress. If it was lumpy, if it was coarse, if it was bare and showed it's stuffing in places, he didn't notice. Even though the wool blanket was thin and his boots made a poor pillow he was beyond caring.

Pulling the rough material over him, his knees drawn up, he was asleep in moments.

When he awoke the comfort of sleep was gone immediately, replaced by the unpleasant cold that had sneaked beneath the thin blanket during the night, chilling his body. Richard rolled over, stretching stiff joints as he did, breath clouding above him. His feet, bare, extended out into the cold air of the morning, and he rapidly pulled them back beneath the cover of coarse wool. Richard knew he'd not warm up laid where he was, so he pulled his boots back on and with the blanket wrapped over his shoulders and cowled over his head, he left the room. Stepping over the other two still-sleeping men he went in search of warmth. Jack, always a light sleeper, opened an eye, noted his departure momentarily, before returning to his snoring slumber.

The hour was still early, but he could hear the sound of the workers in the bake house. The ovens would be lit, and his nose told him there would be warm bread. The baker's life was not an easy one, their day started in darkness, apart from those blessed few summer months when the nights never truly settled on the country, and their work was complete before dawn started the day for those about to toil in the workshops and fields.

Richard bought what he wanted, a cocket loaf, and stuffing chunks of warm bread in his mouth he traded banter with the man and two women in the bake house. He had his back to the warmth of the brick ovens, and soon the cowl had dropped around his neck as the heat worked its way into his stiffened muscles.

"Do you want another?" one of the women asked after she'd finished cleaning the wooden trough in which they prepared the bread dough, the bone scraper in her hands hanging with strands of sticky flour dough.

"Give me three, no..." An ache in his shoulder suddenly reminded him of Jack's anger the day before and an evil smile crossed his face. "Give me one cocket and two horse bread."

She smiled, dropping the scraper and shuffled through the round crusted cooling loaves on the wooden boards. "There you go, lad. I bet you ate your mother out of house and home."

Richard fished for and found the coin he needed and pressed it into her hands; with a word of thanks he accepted the warm loaves.

"I can remember when I was a lass we'd get five of these for a penny," she said, pointing at the cocket Richard was breaking open. "And now it's three!"

"With wheat prices the way they are, they need to go up again, but how do you do it?" It was the baker, his hands wrapped in his floury apron that came to stand next to his wife. "This weather is not likely to give us a good harvest this year either."

"And a hungry England is an unhappy one," Richard said under his breath.

Returning to the room shortly after, he found his brother and Emilio were up, the horses tacked up and ready.

"Here, I got this for you," Richard threw the bread towards Jack and then passed another brown loaf to Emilio.

Jack, who would eat just about anything, cast him a look of thanks. Then breaking open the bread his shoulders dropped slightly as he realised what it was. The dark brown heavy bread was made from pea and bean flour mixed in with whatever else the bakers could find. It was the fayre of the poor. "Was this all they had?"

"Sorry, everything else had been sold. That was all they had left," Richard replied, his back to Jack who could not see the smile on his face.

"I bet it was," Jack replied, more than a hint of sarcasm in his voice.

✝

When they stopped in the late afternoon the skies had decided to clear themselves of grey, and for a few hours the sun shone on England. It did little to dry the fields, but it did a lot to lift Jack's spirits. He knew he owed Emilio an apology, as he had undeservedly been on the receiving end of Jack's temper after his brother's revelation and about the deal he had been forced to accept.

Jack had thought about little else all day but returning to Malta. At first he'd been furious, knowing they had both been manipulated into accepting a decision that neither wanted. As they day wore on, however, he was forced to accept that there were very few other options available to him.

They might be back in England now, but he was still wanted here for murder, and his brother for the added charge of treason. They could have no kind of public life without the risk of being hunted down for their crimes – and Jack had no wish to ever return to gaol. They could cross the Channel back to France where they'd found paid mercenary work before, and he had no doubt they could again – but Jack didn't want to do that alone. If Richard was returning to Malta, then so was he.

When Emilio found him Jack was laid flat on his back, on top of his cloak, sheltered from the breeze in the lee of an elm tree. His liquid blue eyes, open, mirrored the sky as he watched the bird above him hover motionless. Jack heard the sound of foot steps and turned his head to observe the approaching man. He let his eyes travel over the Knight. Emilio had joined them on this journey, without complaint, and after four days now mired with the mud of England he looked no better than Jack did. White linen was creased and brown, long sleeves had been rolled back up away from his wrists to stop the material from getting soaked, and his hair, once neat, had been reordered by the damp weather, curling at his neck and across his brow. Boots, delicately stitched and made from the finest calf skin were saturated, the leather swollen and leaking. Emilio though, didn't seem to mind. Jack moved over on his cloak to make space for the other man who dropped down next to him.

"I am sorry, my brother soured my temper, there was no need for me to make you suffer for it though," Jack said, wearing an apologetic smile.

"He is not an easy man to like," Emilio replied.

Jack knew the Knight held his brother in no high esteem, he had seen Richard on their journey to Malta when he had been a victim of opium, his senses lost to him, and it was a weakness Emilio was ever unlikely to overlook. Jack's eyes travelled back up and he found again the bird he had been watching.

"A goshawk, I think," Emilio said, changing the subject, his hand raised to shield his eyes from the sun, the tone of his voice telling Jack he was forgiven.

"It is," Jack said in agreement, grateful that they were once again on easier terms.

"I miss it. I had to leave my hawks in Italy and of everything I gave up, that I grieve for the most," Emilio said, a hand still shading his face from the sun as he turned his head towards Jack.

"I do as well," Jack replied, wistfully meeting the Italian's gaze.

"You had hawks?" Emilio sounded surprised.

"No, I trained and looked after Harry's, he was my cousin and I was his servant. He hardly ever flew them; he used them only for show. I trained them for him. It was the same with his bloody horses as well, he had tournament mounts but they were never used."

"So that's where you get your skill from," Emilio replied, returning his gaze to the hawk above them. As both men watched, the bird folded its wings and dropped silently like an arrow, disappearing into the long grass of the meadow.

"William Fitzwarren and his brother were close to the centre of the Court and in Henry's time both of them took part in tournaments. William was pretty good from what I've heard. Harry's father had horses that princes would be envious of, and even when he stopped riding them the stables were kept stocked with the best horses for Harry, but he didn't use them."

"A waste," Emilio said, "my brother, Angelo, he is the same."

"I remember once... Months of work went into the preparations for a tournament, and that shit, Harry, was too scared. He took part in the melee, I rode as his second. He made a laughing-stock out of me amongst the other lads, the bloody idiot rode behind me, not in front and I took a beating for him, and one I've not forgotten," Jack's voice clouded with anger as he remembered it.

In the melee the knight rode fully armoured, the aim being to place blows against the other armoured knights in the ring. Each armed man was attended by a squire, his second, and their job was to protect their knight, to keep their attackers at a distance. The knight owed a duty to his outrider, to protect him as well, they rode unarmed and unarmoured. Harry had abandoned him and Jack had taken the full force of the attack. The rounds were short, but he could still vividly remember the pain from the blows, his ribs and his back had been a mottled purple after the event, but that had been nothing in comparison to the shame he had to bear for being tethered to a worthless master.

"I didn't know you'd ridden in the melee," Emilio said, sounding surprised. "If you are any good you can be my second, should the opportunity arise."

"Any good!" Jack spluttered, turning his head to lay his blue eyes on Emilio. "Are you trying to say you doubt my skill?"

"I've seen your wrestling skills and they leave a lot to be desired. Perhaps your tournament training still needs a polish as well," Emilio replied, grinning mischievously.

"You really know how to spoil a man's day, don't you?" Jack muttered, although his tone told the other that he was not annoyed.

"Perhaps a test of skill then, just between us, will settle this argument?" Emilio offered playfully.

"Another wager?" Jack's voice was laden with sarcasm. He'd not forgotten being dumped on his back at Emilio's feet during the fight.

"Why not? A contest of horsemanship, between us?" Emilio said, sounding delighted by the prospect.

"What's the wager this time?" Jack propped himself up on one elbow and regarded Emilio with intense blue eyes.

"Same as last time," Emilio replied a little too quickly.

"You are that confident of winning?" Jack questioned, his eyes narrowing. "Anyway, before we decide on the stakes we need to decide on the challenge."

"At the moment we lack horses for any challenge," Emilio said.

"No we don't." Jack pointed to the three piebald horses loosely tethered and cropping grass in the shade of a tree not far from them.

"Those are not horses!" exclaimed Emilio, propping himself up on his elbows.

"Yes they are, and it's a poor horseman who believes he cannot succeed because of his mount," Jack shot back, blue eyes twinkling.

Emilio regarded the horses for a moment before nodding slowly. "Alright then, we have our steeds. So what will the challenge be?"

Jack's eyes ran over the countryside around them before he declared, "A race."

Emilio sat up next to him, his face alight with a smile. Raising an arm he pointed. "From where they are now up to the top of that hill, then 'round that chestnut tree, over the wall and across the stream on the other side, along the bank, over that other wall there, through that field and back to the tree."

Jack looked over the proposed route, there was plenty of scope for cutting a few corners, and the advantage would be to the man who had the head start, getting beyond him after that would be hard.

"Are we agreed?" Emilio asked.

Jack scanned the terrain and made two deviations of his own that Emilio agreed to, and then he added a final word to the challenge. "Bareback."

Emilio nodded in agreement, and then said, "The stakes?"

Jack fished under his shirt and produced the jewelled cross he always wore out of sight. Emilio's hand caught hold of the chain and neatly flipped it over his head. The cross, warm still from Jack's skin, he held in his hand whilst he threaded a ring he had pulled from his own hand through the chain. "A good prize for the victor."

"I don't know if I dare ask?" Richard, walking over to join them, seemed to have overheard the last of their conversation. "Getting married are we?"

"A wager, and you can hold the stakes," Emilio said, ignoring Richard's comment.

He held out the chain for him to take. "And announce the start."

Richard dropped down to sit, cross-legged, on Jack's cloak. "So when does it start?"

"When we reach the horses," Jack replied.

"I think it should start and finish here. One, two, three, go." Richard announced.

"What!" Jack blurted, Emilio had already set his feet towards the tethered horses. "You can't do that!"

"I just did. So run!" Richard shouted at Jack, settling back onto his elbows to watch.

Cursing, Jack turned and headed after Emilio.

By the time he arrived Emilio was already pulling the saddle from his horse. The girth strap released, he pushed it to fall from the opposite side of the cob and a moment later he was on the horse's back pulling the reins taut. Jack, realising he was behind, mounted and then jettisoned the saddle from beneath him, the tactic bought him valuable moments and his horse's nose as they left the trees was directly behind the streaming tail of Emilio's.

The first leg of the race took them uphill, from the trees and over a low wall at the top of the gentle slope. After this there was a turn to the left. The track took them along the side of the wall and it was bordered on the other by a thick hedge of hawthorn. Whoever cleared the wall first would hold the lead along the track, and Jack knew that it wasn't going to be him. Emilio pulled his horse tight and close to the bend in the wall so there was no chance of Jack overtaking him and as soon as his horse landed on the other side all Jack could do was follow as the track was too narrow for him to pass.

The track turned an abrupt left and ran down the side of the field, then the route the riders had chosen took them straight on, over the wall and into the next field and across to a small copse of trees that Jack had added in as a detour.

There were three large elm trees interspersed with maple and shorter holly bushes. Running through the copse was a deer track, the bark from the elm trees scored and torn from the horns of the rutting stags. This was the obvious route, it was longer, but to take another was to risk being unseated by a low hanging branch.

Emilio turned his horse as soon as he could, ducking beneath the low branches of the elm and heading back uphill to turn and take the deer track back through the middle of the copse. Jack had to round the elms, but forced his horse to take a tight turn after the last one, cutting a course through the briar to the deer track. Low over the horse's neck he brought the cob on to the path at the same moment Emilio's headed down the track. Both horses were pressed side by side, Jack could feel Emilio's leg as it clung around the horse's side banging against his own. Neck and neck, they left the copse of trees.

The next obstacle was another wall, low and with space for them both to jump it side by side. Emilio would have the advantage as the turn after the jump was to the left and he was placed on the inside. Both riders set their horses to jump the wall. Jack though, pulled his back, slowed the cob to a steady canter and cleared the low wall. Emilio's horse cantering on took four more strides before he pulled her to the left, and he found Jack had made the turn first and was half a horse's length ahead of Emilio.

Jack's horse cleared the stream with ease, but a cobble, loose under the gelding's hoof, made him stumble and by the time he had regained his stride Emilio was level and both horses together crested the gentle rise leading back towards the starting point. Both men urged their mounts on down the meadow, and both sturdy horses obeyed and galloped together, manes and tails streaming back to where Richard waited.

"Either both of you were trying too hard, or not at all," Richard observed dryly when the sweating horses drew to a halt before him.

There was a hurt expression on Emilio's face. "Not trying! It was a fair race and I shall have to think of another test!" Then to Jack, "Shall we let him keep the wager?"

Jack, breathing as hard as Emilio was, nodded. Richard pocketed the chain and ring. "If it is not too much trouble, it would be good if we could get back on the road."

✝

Their next stop was in the town of Dorchester, which offered a choice of accommodation, and they selected the largest of the four inns, the Star and Moon. The tavern offered ample stabling and the services of a groom for their horses, and Jack was more than happy for Emilio to spend his money having them cared for. Wet and cold, all of them were eager to find a warm corner of the Star to settle in for the evening. The building was offering a level of accommodation that they had not experienced since they had landed on the beach nearly a week ago. Ducking through the inn doorway they walked along a short corridor and were met by the delicious aroma of pork cooking over a fire.

Jack elbowed Richard. "That's roasting meat!"

"I have a nose of my own," Richard replied sarcastically.

"Just make sure I get some, that's all," Jack said, striding ahead into the dark room littered with tables and benches. Emilio, unfortunately, was the only one of them who had any money. Jack had none, and Richard had little left after his recent spend on bread. They were both, at the moment, poorer than they had ever been.

There was a fire burning at the back of the room, an ample supply of fuel stacked next to it, and to the right was a table benefiting from the best of the heat it had to offer. Jack dropped his cloak onto a bench and claimed the table. The rest of the room was presently empty, outside it was still light, and the labours of the day were not finished yet. Men would drift in as the dusk drew in the night.

Emilio did not stint with his order from the inn kitchens and Jack was pleased to find that there was more than the three of them could eat. Meaning, simply, there was some left over for him to wrap in a cloth for the following day. Emilio and

Richard watched as he stowed away the remains of the meat that had been left.

"And were you were going to ask us if we wanted some?" Richard said, his eyebrows raised.

Jack just shrugged. "You could have taken some. I wasn't stopping you."

The inn had begun to fill, the background noise now was the low murmur of voices punctuated by the occasional bark of laughter.

Emilio tipped the ale jug towards him, observed the remaining slops, and fixed an accusing eye on Jack. "You've finished that as well?"

"Well, you know what they say, don't you?" Jack said grinning.

"No. What do they say?" Emilio said, setting the jug back down.

"There's the fast and then there's the hungry, or in your case thirsty. You'd best order another," Jack advised.

Emilio muttered under his breath before raising an arm and attempting to summon one of the serving women who pressed between the filled tables delivering food and ale. A woman who had served them food earlier acknowledged him with a wave of her hand and went to collect an ale jug. She made it halfway back across the room towards them when she was waylaid and deprived of the ale. She complained, cuffed one of the men around the back of the head, and returned to get another. This time she took another route but her progress was again halted and the jug prised from her hand. The men had pulled together three of the tables and it spanned nearly the width of the inn, forming a barricade between the ale and Richard, Jack and Emilio.

"Stop it, Al, you'll just get me in trouble," she complained, and there was a ripple of laughter that rolled along the table.

The third time she returned she was reinforced by the landlord.

"Come on, lads, let her through," the landlord's words were met with ribald remarks and mock indignation. But the blockade on the ale had been removed and a moment later the jug arrived.

"Sorry about that, lads," her words, and her smile, were directed at Jack. "This is usually Al's table. That's why he's making a nuisance of himself."

Jack smiled, took the jug from her, and pulling her close for a moment, whispered something in her ear that made her giggle.

Emilio rolled his eyes and Richard just shook his head.

Jack, meeting their disapproving stares as the girl retreated, began to pour out ale, saying, "I'm just keeping her on our side. Do you want to do without anything to drink for the rest of the evening?"

Richard turned to Emilio. "Jack is always noted for his selfless acts for the greater good!"

"Shut up," Jack said good-naturedly. "You're only annoyed because she didn't give you a second look."

The ale jug emptied and Emilio called for another across the crowded room.

Jack, his back to the long table where Al was seated, heard the comments clearly enough, as he was intended to.

"What has he just said?" Emilio had heard as well, but Al's quick derogatory English had escaped his understanding.

"He's accusing you of being French," Jack provided smiling, enjoying Emilio's reaction.

"French!" Emilio exclaimed his eyes widening, his tone indignant. "Tell them that's not so."

"No," Jack replied. "There are nine of them, and three of us. So tonight, just be French. To be fair, you do look a bit French."

Emilio banged a fist down on the table and cursed. "I'm not French!"

"This is not our town, so just ignore them," Jack advised.

Al and his cronies loud laughter filled the room. The entertainment was clearly Emilio.

"I'm not going to sit here and listen to that," Emilio growled, "I'm not French!"

"Christ! I know you are not. Richard knows you are not. Does it bloody matter if nine hog washers from the back of beyond think you are?" Jack said, annoyed now more with Emilio than Al and his companions.

"Yes! It's a slur," Emilio countered.

"For God's sake! I'm going to go and side with them in a moment," Jack said, "does it really matter?"

"Oh, I think it does to Emilio," added Richard unhelpfully.

"Don't you start!" Jack said, knowing full well Richard would enjoy goading Emilio.

"I'm Italian! Sono Italiano!" Emilio stated loudly, his voice pitched to be heard across the inn.

"No," Jack's hand gripped Emilio's shoulder and pressed him back into his seat.

Al and his group had witnessed the argument between Jack and Emilio and now catcalls and jeers were being sent in their direction.

"That's it!!" Jack flung his arms wide. "Finally I get some good food, get my arse warmed by a decent fire, and can you let me enjoy it?"

Richard was laughing silently.

"No! You damn well can't, can you?" Jack said accusingly, then turning in his seat he bellowed loudly in Al's direction.

"Bloody shut up – *he's Italian!*" Then to Emilio and Richard, "Happy now?"

Richard was already pushing himself from the table. "Jack, watch your back!"

Before Jack could rise a meaty arm wrapped itself around his neck. Jack, rising and twisting, catapulted the man over to land on his back on the table, scattering cups and the hard won ale jug to the floor.

There was a press of assailants after that. Jack, closest to Al's table, took the brunt of it until Emilio clambered onto one of the tables and began to level well aimed kicks at the heads of those attempting to pull Jack to the floor. Richard, armed with the earthenware jug in one hand and a wooden stool in the other, had already delivered a broken nose to Al, who staggered back into his companions' arms, blood pouring through his fingers.

A short man, barrel chested and with a matted beard, lunged across the table, catching hold of Emilio's leg. His strategy for attack exhausted he clung on, wrapping himself around Emilio's boot to hamper his movement.

The ale jug broke on the back of the bearded man's head. Semi-conscious but refusing to relinquish his hold he slithered to the floor dragging Emilio in his wake. The table pitched violently. Emilio, still weighted by the man's grasp, was flung forward. He struck Jack in the back, and together they took two more of their assailants to the floor with them.

Then the dynamic changed.

The innkeeper, a cudgel in one hand and his other balled in a fist, waded in amongst the brawl and began to indiscriminately deliver blows amongst the fighting patrons along with cursed admonishments.

If there were any victors it was hard to tell. The innkeeper's fury had been instantly reduced by Richard's quick promise of recompense. That put their group on an instant higher standing than Al's, and they were restored to their fireside table while Al found himself, along with his companions, banished from the Star for the remainder of the evening.

Jack, righting a bench and sitting down opposite his brother, wiped blood from the corner of his mouth. Richard was pulling a rent flap of skin from the back of one of his knuckles. "Feel better?"

Jack spat the blood from his mouth to the floor. "Much. Not as satisfying as hitting you, but not bad."

✝

Jack had absented himself and Richard and Emilio had been seated alone for a while. Emilio scanned the smoky room before asking, "Where's Jack?"

"Gone back to the room I would imagine," Richard replied as he examined a bruise from a blow he did not remember receiving that was starting to mottle the back of his forearm.

Emilio finished his drink, slid the cup towards the middle of the table and made to rise.

Richard raised a hand to stop him. "Sit down, he'll be back soon enough."

Emilio, puzzled, dropped back onto the bench.

"Today has been near enough perfect for my brother. Food. A fight," Richard ticked these two off on his fingers, then a malicious smile drifted onto his face, "and fornication. A veritable trinity of delights for Jack."

"If that was meant to score a point or two, then you'll need to try a lot harder," Emilio observed coolly.

"Not at all. Merely an observation." Richard reached inside his doublet and retrieved a worn woodcut deck of cards that belonged to Jack.

"What shall the stakes be?" Emilio asked.

Richard pulled out his purse, let tumble from it the few coins he still had, and with them fell a neatly tied length of blue ribbon.

Emilio recognised the narrow strip of blue immediately. "Are you trafficking in trinkets now?"

Richard ignored him as he replaced the ribbon in his purse, leaving the few worn coins before him on the table. "Primero?"

"Primero," Emilio said in agreement, adding his own coins to the table and accepting the cards that were neatly dealt before him.

Richard won a steady stream of games, his attention was fixed on the game, and taking as many coins from the Italian in the short opportunity he had been afforded as he could. The games were quick, efficient, and mostly went against Emilio.

Notes from a flute peppered the air and Emilio turned on the bench.

Jack had made a reappearance and was sitting on the edge of one of the tables near the musician. A man with sandy shoulder-length hair, an accent that labelled him as Cornish, and a pleasant freckled face took up a song and the flute player backed him.

The song was halfway through when Emilio turned back to Richard. "Is he singing in English?"

"Only just," Richard said. He had gathered in the cards and was riffling them between his hands. "Another game?"

"In a moment, perhaps Jack will join us," Emilio said, turning again to see if Richard's brother was making his way across the inn towards them.

Jack, however, had settled himself on the table, legs swinging in mid-air, listening to the singer. He finished his song, and there was a murmur of appreciation from the men populating the tables in the Star.

"Why is he not joining us?" Emilio asked.

"There's an audience," Richard said wearily.

"I don't understand what you mean," Emilio replied.

"Oh, you will shortly," Richard replied, his eyes on the cards as he began to slowly place them on the table in a pile face up.

They had to wait for the man with the sandy hair and his strong accent to finish two more songs before Jack dropped from the table and spoke quickly to the flute player. The man nodded in agreement, tucked the flute into his belt for a few moments while he emptied his ale cup, and then retrieving it began to play the tune Jack had asked for.

"Here we go," Richard said, recognising the flourish of notes that heralded the start of 'There was a bonny lass.' Jack delivered the fast paced song, with a ribald chorus that would usually have the patrons joining in. If Lizbet had been there she would have been on the floor already, skirts hoisted and ready to dance, it was...one of her favourites. Richard's thoughts stopped abruptly, his hand holding a card he had been about to place on the table was motionless, and he looked across the room at Jack.

Why had he chosen this one?

Jack wasn't looking in his direction. Richard watched him carefully, the song ended to a loud chorus of cheers. Jack, as usual, had the audience's attention, and they were pressing him for more.

He followed up with another of Lizbet's favourite songs.

She wears red roses.

Richard's face was set in a stony mask. The message from across the inn was clear, Jack too was thinking of Lizbet.

Jack rejoined them after delivering a final song, the choice of which he left to his audience, and promising more later on he wended his way back between the tables towards Richard and Emilio. He took a seat, Richard rounded up the deck and handed it back to Jack. Their eyes met for a moment before Jack stowed the cards away inside his doublet.

"I'm tired," Jack declared shortly after to no one in particular, drained his cup and made to head back towards the room upstairs. Richard and Emilio joined him. The brothers let Emilio take the narrow stairs first, and Jack, his head close to Richard's ear said, "I'll have my share now."

Richard smiled, and opening his hand dropped from it into Jack's waiting palm half the money he had taken from Emilio. It was a relatively small amount, but when you had nothing, it was a lot. They could have asked Emilio for money, they could indeed have stolen it from him – winning it however saved them from an unpleasant combination of both humiliation and immorality.

CHAPTER FIVE

†

Morley doubted very much that it had been Robert who had fastened the bonds around the ageing body. He was not the type, he would have stood back, observed from a distance, while a lackey tied the knots.

But why?

The steward was dragged into the room formerly occupied by William Fitzwarren, by the soldiers Morley had returned with. Since Morley's last visit the evidence of abuse was missing. The furniture had been set back to rights, the bed made, hangings reattached, William's chair righted and his table set next to it, and the closet stool was missing. What did remain was the odour. Lurking beneath carpets, behind tapestries, trapped in the wood panelling, it permeated the whole room. A sensual declaration of what had occurred here even if the visual record had been erased.

Ronan, forced to stand in the fœtid room, was no longer the man who had forcibly ejected Morley from that house. In the presence of the soldiers and without the backing of Robert he was now clearly terrified. The thick dark hair that capped his head and covered his ears was serving only to accentuate how pale he had become, the wide black eyebrows often raised in support of a collection of angry features were lost now in a sea of white.

William's chair was vacant, Morley having chosen to perch on the end of the table in the room, giving him an advantage of height over Ronan. Morley tapped his thumb thoughtfully against his chin, and the steward, hands clasped before him, forced himself to stand still.

"I would like to know, where is Lord Fitzwarren?" Morley asked at last.

It was a simple question, and it seemed it was not one Ronan had been expecting. "He's... gone with Master Fitzwarren to Suffolk."

"And does he often go there?" Morley enquired, his voice still steady and reasonable.

Ronan shook his head. "Lord William has been in London for the last few years."

"Since he became ill, no doubt, and found it difficult to travel?" Morley said, head slightly cocked to one side, a look now of mild confusion on his face. "So why would he leave now, do you think?"

The steward swallowed hard before producing his answer. "I would not know, sir, it is not my place to ask."

"Not your place to ask...and quite rightly so," Morley said, pinching his lower lip between a thumb and forefinger, his voice still pleasant and agreeable. "And is it your place to tie your master to a chair and keep him there?"

Ronan didn't answer.

"Is it?" Morley asked, an edge with the coolness of sliced ice chilling his words.

"It wasn't me, sir," Ronan replied nervously, not meeting Morley's gaze.

Morley dropped from the table. "Let's abstain from these pointless denials, shall we? It was you, albeit at Robert Fitzwarren's direction, who put those ropes around him."

Ronan was silent, perspiration beginning to bead on his forehead and an erratic twitch at a corner of one eye betraying his nervousness.

"Answer me, man! Was it you?"

"I had no choice," Ronan admitted, the words leaving his mouth in one quick, confessional gasp.

"Who is your master?" Morley pressed.

"Lord Fitzwarren, sir, but Master Fitzwarren said it was for his father's own good, he'd lost his mind," Ronan stuttered.

Morley let the silence lengthen between them, the other man's agitation growing visibly. Ronan shifted his weight from one foot to the other looking very much like a man who was considering taking flight. Morley almost hoped he would try; outside the door were at least two of the soldiers he had arrived with, both of them more than capable of preventing his escape.

"I have spoken to Lord Fitzwarren recently, he did not strike me as having an addled mind. It was obvious from the state he was in that he had been there for some time. Naked, and stinking of shit – did you have no shame at all for your master?" Morley's voice crawled with disgust.

Ronan's eyes flicked from Morley's to the corner where William had been tied to the closet stool.

"How long was he there?" Morley's words brought Ronan's gaze back towards him.

"I'm not sure, sir," came the lame reply.

"Not sure!" Morley's voice boomed with a force his interrogee had not expected and Ronan jumped involuntarily.

"A week…" Ronan replied weakly.

"A week!" Morley's eyes went wide with shock.

Ronan, mistakenly believing his admission wasn't believable, added, "Maybe two."

Morley turned on the spot, flinging his arms wide. "My God man! How long was he tied on there – tell me!"

The hands that were clasped before the steward were knotted hard together, the knuckles white and they shook sporadically. "Since St Hilary's day. That's when they last argued."

Morley felt sick.

How could anyone restrain an old man like that? There were prisoners interred in The Tower to answer for crimes that might cost them their lives who were kept in better conditions than that!

Why?

"I believe there might be more to it than you are saying. Tell me, what do you know about Richard Fitzwarren, Robert's younger brother?" Morley asked, abruptly changing course.

Ronan seized on the new subject with the enthusiasm of a hound on the fox. "Very little, sir. I was appointed as the steward here after he had left the household. I know he is wanted for treason, and Master Fitzwarren is incredibly unhappy about that."

"How so?" Morley asked.

Ronan's brow furrowed. "I don't quite understand, sir."

Morley cast his eyes for a moment towards the ceiling beams. The man had not been appointed to his position on the merit of his wits, it seemed. "How do you know that Master Fitzwarren is unhappy about the charge of treason?"

"Anyone would be unhappy about having such a charge attached to their family name," Ronan said.

"Is that it?" Morley shot back. "You just think he's unhappy about it."

"I've heard him arguing about it with Lord Fitzwarren as well," Ronan replied defensively.

"Ah, a listener at doors! So what else have you heard that you were not supposed to?" Morley said, taking a few quick paces towards the retainer. When he did not get a reply Morley continued, his voice patient, as if outlining a wrongdoing to a child. "Shall I remind you that very recently you assaulted me, had me thrown from your door. Not the wisest of moves, and you have admitted that you have been complicit in restraining a Lord of the realm in his own home. Whether that was for his own good or not would be a matter for a court to determine. So I believe, Master Steward, that while I am affording you an opportunity to be useful, you take it. So what did they argue about?"

"Robert's brothers came to the house to see William and when he got to find out about it, he was furious," Ronan said.

"Brothers?" Morley's interest was immediately piqued.

"Yes. Richard and his bastard brother," Ronan explained.

"That's Jack, I believe?" Morley said. Ronan nodded. "Why was Robert angry?"

"He thinks they are after William's money, they've argued about it. I think William has wanted to make some grant or other to Jack and Master Robert is opposed to it," Ronan explained.

Morley smiled: here was the crux of the family feud, although the beneficiary was not the one he would have considered as likely. "To Jack? Are you sure?"

"Yes. I have only heard them argue about him," Ronan confirmed.

"And when did they visit their father?" Morley asked.

"It's a long time ago, must be getting on for over a year now," Ronan responded.

"And you saw them?" Morley pressed.

Ronan shook his head. "Charles, one of the other servants let them in. He has been with the family a long time and he recognised Richard, and with him was a blond who I am led to believe is his bastard brother."

Morley turned his back on Ronan and with his fingers laced together, hands pressed to his chin he stared across the room, seeing little. So the focus for Robert's fury appeared to be Jack and not Richard. If his father wished to share Robert's inheritance with a family bastard he could understand that, but his actions were beyond that, the conditions in which he had kept his father in were more than those merited by mere argument. And now he had removed himself, and William, from London, and for the moment from Morley's reach.

Morley subjected the steward to another long series of questions but it became apparent that he had little to add to the information he had already given. He was Robert's man, that was clear, but he was no more than a servant and had not been complicit in anything other than restraining Robert's ageing father. Eventually he dismissed Ronan, and stood alone again in the room regarding the wreckage. William Fitzwarren, old and infirm, had been a virtual prisoner in his home for a long time, that much he had gained from Ronan. Previously William had occupied rooms on the top floor but last year he had moved into these ground level rooms. The steward had confirmed it had been Fitzwarren's own decision to move and the servants had brought down his bed and other furniture, dismantling them and setting them up again in these rooms at the front of the house.

Families were often full of enmity, but the Fitzwarren one more so than was usual. Morley's eyes fastened upon a small green glass bottle with an enamel stopper.

Retrieving it from the floor he opened it, sniffed tentatively at the contents, wrinkled his nose and breathed out heavily to rid himself of the scent.

The questions he levelled at the other Fitzwarren servants did not provide any more answers either. It appeared the old Lord had been attended by Ronan recently, and before that by his personal servant, Edwin, who had now departed the house with them. The undercurrent in the household was one of fear, and while it was right that they should respect and honour their masters, some of their reactions were beyond that. Morley was sure that some of the servants were terrified of Robert, and trying to get any kind of sensible answers to his questions was proving difficult.

Morley, the small bottle from William's room in his pocket, decided to take his enquiries to the Fitzwarren physician. Ronan had supplied the name of Master Juris and within a few days he had an address, a note had been delivered requesting a meeting, and one had been confirmed for the coming Wednesday at Juris's offices, ones he shared with one of London's most expensive apothecaries on Mason Street.

Entering through the door Morley was met by the heady aroma of herbs. The air was thick with the perfume of medicine, the sweet cloying and over concentrated fragrance hiding other smells that were not as pleasant. Morley's senses informed him of acrid smells and of other pungent aromas buried beneath the surface of the rue and rosemary. He traced the malodorous stench to henbane, and also to some of the desiccated corpses of animals that hung from the roof. Rabbits, badgers, deer's feet, foxes and even fish hung in neatly-tied braces from the ceiling beams.

Before Morley's eyes had more of a chance to explore the apothecary's shop his attention was claimed by one of the efficient assistants who directed him towards Juris's door.

Master Juris, neatly attired in black robe and cap, greeted him warmly enough when he entered the room. It soon became apparent that Morley was going to learn little. Juris repeatedly made it abundantly clear that Lord Fitzwarren's ailments were not ones he was at liberty to discuss. Morley found that William had dispensed with Juris' services over a year ago, and had not attended him since. It was a short and disappointing visit.

†

It had been a longer journey than any of them had anticipated and all of them were thankful that it was finally over. Edwin, Jon and Walt, all charged with the task of looking after Lord Fitzwarren, had travelled with five of Robert's other men. They were told that they were going to the Lord's manor in Suffolk, however, after the first day Edwin had realised the route they were taking was wrong. His questions had not been answered and after two days he had stopped asking, realising that he would find out when they arrived.

William was installed in a covered cart, seated upon cushions that had been hastily placed in the back. Two of Robert's men rode ahead, securing accommodation en route, and Edwin and Jon were forced to carry him from the cart and into the inn each night.

Edwin dropped down the last two steps into the crowded room in the inn, looking around he found Jon waving at him from where he had secured them a table. Edwin wound his way through the throng and dropped down onto the bench next to Walt.

"Thanks, Jon. It's busy in here?" Edwin said, his eyes running around the crowded room.

"Market day is tomorrow so the place is full at the moment, apparently tomorrow it'll be empty, we were lucky to get rooms," Jon replied, then added, "There's ale and pies on the way."

Edwin smiled gratefully at Jon.

"How's his Lordship?" Jon asked, after a moment.

Edwin shook his head. "I think I preferred him when he was full of anger and fury, now I just don't know where to look."

"Oh, come on, remember what he was like? Christ – he made your life a bloody misery, and mine too. If he's lost his tongue and shrivelled up in shame then I don't care," Jon replied.

"It's still not right," Edwin continued. "I don't know who was looking after him, but he's covered in sores. If my arse looked like his I'd not be too happy about sitting in the back of a cart, I can tell you."

"You are never happy. No wonder your Alice says you are soft in the head," Jon tapped his temple with a finger as he spoke.

Edwin regarded him with a hard look. "All I said was it's not right, that doesn't mean I like the old shit does it? I hope my family looks after me a sight better than his are looking after him when I reach his age."

Jon leaned closer to Edwin, whispering confidentially. "He's brought it on himself. It's his fault Robert is like he is."

"True," Edwin conceded, then grinning he said, "still, its bought me a few days away from Alice, and for once we are being well looked after."

Jon nudged Edwin. "Shift over and let the lass put the jug on the table."

There was a general reshuffling around the table to make room for the ale jug, earthenware cups glazed on the inside, and a wooden trencher with a thick crusted sturdy pie.

Walt's one remaining eye was wide with disbelief as he viewed it. "Is that all for us?"

"I'm fairly sure it is, lad, so help yourself," Jon said kindly, and slid the pie closer to Walt.

Ronan, Robert's Steward, had deprived the lad of an eye when he delivered a beating the boy had not deserved, and both men felt sorry for the lad. Any prospects that might have once been open to him were now most assuredly lost. No one was going to want a retainer with an unsightly blind eye. Edwin was pretty sure this was why he had been sent with them, to remove him from the London house where he remained an unsettling reminder of Ronan's cruelty.

Their journey so far had about it the quality of an adventure. Robert's men were in charge of the route, the destination, and the purse. And Edwin, Jon and Walt were enjoying a quality of food and accommodation along the route that was beyond their meagre means. Both men, by the necessity of looking after Lord William, had to have a room near to his, and Walt, whose normal resting place was the stable, was delighted to have been afforded the luxury of a bed in an inn alongside the other men. Their food and ale in the evenings was also paid for, and none could grumble at what had been provided.

"That'll do us tonight and for tomorrow morning as well," Edwin said, gesturing towards the pie. Walt had cut the first wedge and Edwin slid his own knife through the firm brown pastry and picked up the slice in his hands. "Mutton, I think."

"It is," mumbled Walt, spraying Jon with a mouthful of pastry crumbs, and earning himself a playful cuff round the ear.

"Any more ideas on where we are going?" Jon said when he'd eaten his fill.

Edwin shook his head as he cut another thin sliver from the pie, skewered it with the knife and tucked it into his mouth.

"Well it's not Suffolk that's for sure, we are too far south for that now," Jon mused, his finger dabbing crumbs together on the table.

"Lord Fitzwarren has land all over the south. I've only ever been to the Suffolk estate, I can only assume they are taking him to one of his properties," Edwin replied.

Jon leaned across the table, the ale getting the better of his tongue, "Did it ever occur to you that Robert might be getting rid of him?"

The expression on Edwin's face was one of appalled shock. "Don't say that!" he hissed at Jon. "Don't even think of it. Is that something you want to be involved in?"

"It's something we've got to consider, and if they keep him bouncing around in the back of a cart for much longer then there's a good chance he'll die before we arrive anyway," Jon said.

Edwin could not deny that there might be a truth in that. William, quiet, withdrawn, and lighter than he had ever been, was no longer the tyrant who had bellowed at him. More and more he looked like a sick animal to Edwin, grey, pale, weak, and he too worried that he might find him dead in his bed one morning or dead on top of the cushions in the cart. Picking up his knife again Edwin set it to cut another thin wedge from the pie on the table.

"Steady on, there'll be none left for tomorrow," Jon warned, sliding the remains away from Edwin before he could help himself to another serving.

CHAPTER SIX

†

They saw the pall of smoke trapped beneath the huddled clouds before they saw the city. The chimneys from countless cooking fires, furnaces, forges and baking ovens delivered to the sky the grey marker beneath which was London. Another cold night had been little relieved by a weak sun and the grey clouds hung low over the city as if they too were seeking warmth from the fires below. A hard rain before dawn had added more unnecessary liquid to the slurry that ran between the houses on Watling Street, and their horses, plodding through the mud, were mired to the hocks.

Traffic was thick and slow, heavier entering the city than leaving, and they followed a wagon filled with firkins drawn by a heavy ponderous Clydesdale. Those travellers on foot were keeping to the edges where the road was firmer, and a long straggling line trod their way quickly into London, keeping pace with the horses. Acting as their noisy herald was a water carrier, stooped and with his pewter cups jangling noisily from their strung cords, he was at the head of the group on Richard's left.

On the right, hanging from nails along the front of a carpenter's shop were stools, small tables and benches all made of stripped, clean white wood. Shavings from the workshop were scattered thickly into the mire soaking up some of the water, and an apprentice appeared hurling another bucket of curled white shavings into the road. For a moment the smell of pine replaced the rotting smell of London.

Soon after they were passing Clerkenwell Street where one of London's more permanent markets took place. Richard remembered the last time he had been here, jammed under the eaves of the buildings along both sides of the streets were the leather sellers, the cobblers, the tin smiths and the fortune tellers. Pie sellers had jostled for position with those selling roasted chestnuts from smoking braziers while chickens, geese and pigeons freshly cooked and skewered could be bought hot and sizzling. Today were still sellers with their stalls in the street, but a lot fewer than there had been; it was no longer packed, and the milling noisy throng of Londoners pressing through the narrow gaps between the stalls was absent.

"Christ! Look at the place!" Jack sounded shocked. "This is not the London we left behind."

"Times have been hard for London as well," Richard said in agreement, pulling his horse to the left to avoid the spatter coming from one of the cart wheels in front of him. It had been his home for a long time. A vibrant, stinking, packed city, brimming with the life of its loud inhabitants. Some of the houses along the streets stood with their shutters closed, there was less traffic than he would have expected and fewer people were filling the streets.

London felt threadbare.

A few moments later all three men were forced to bring their horses to a standstill, the cart ahead of them having stopped to allow a flat bed wagon drawn by a small blinkered horse to rumble past in the opposite direction.

Emilio crossed himself and held his breath.

The back of the barrow was laden with five bodies. Two had been sewn into shrouds, the outline of the occupants showing through the coarse, tightly wrapped material, the other three had not suffered these final tender ministrations from friends or family, and their bodies lolled, pasty white, sunken-eyed and hollow-cheeked on the wagon bed.

Londoners leaving the city for the last time.

"Are you sure Carter will still be here? From what I've heard there are a lot of people who've left the city," Jack said, moving his horse closer to Richard's as the cart in front jerked forward once more.

"I don't know, but this is where we need to start," Richard replied.

Emilio had wanted to go straight to Thomas Tresham's. There, he could command a variety of resources, and offer them a degree of safety that they could not rely on receiving anywhere else in London. Richard had refused. They were heading straight for Christian Carter's house, they needed to know if Andrew had arrived before them, and if not, ensure that Christian and his family were safe.

†

Christian Carter's steward was more than a little alarmed when he was summoned by one of his master's servants to the kitchens to deal with a trio of unlikely visitors, and it showed clearly on his face. "Master Carter is out, I am afraid, and I would not expect him back until evening."

Richard stepped forward, he'd met the man before when, uninvited, he had let himself into Christian's kitchen the night they had made their escape from London. God, that seemed like a long time ago!

"I am a friend of your master's, and if you know where he is, please take me to him." The tone of Richard's voice gave the words the quality of an order and not a request.

"He's overseeing a delivery of Spanish wine at Rhys Clifford's. I could take you to him, if it's urgent?" The man's eyes flicked between Emilio and Jack, it was obvious that he would rather have all of them out of the house as soon as possible.

"It is." Richard's manner had the Steward fetching his cloak and leading them out into the street a moment later.

As they followed Carter's man Richard found himself grinning at Jack, who, from the expression on his face, was also sharing in his sense of relief. A sudden pressure had been released, and Richard felt as if his lungs could fill fully for the first time in months.

They were here first.

Andrew was behind them.

†

Carter's delivery was being unloaded and stored in Clifford's warehouse, half the wine already unpacked from the back of a flat bed wagon when they got there. Two of Carter's men were rolling the casks down ramped planks, guide ropes wrapped around them to slow their descent to the yard. Christian Carter, standing to one side, was overseeing the process, puzzlement showed on his face when he saw the figure of his steward appear in the yard.

His eyes on his newly arrived servant, Carter rounded the cart, he hadn't seen the other men behind him. "What's happened that can't wait?" he asked with a smile. "Has Tilly set the ovens on fire again?"

"These men have been looking for you, and I was assured their business was urgent, so I thought it best to bring them to you," the steward replied, turning and pointing to where Richard, Jack and Emilio were standing.

The expression on Carter's face changed immediately when he recognised that the man behind his retainer was Richard, his mouth forming an instant broad smile. He took a step forwards, realised that two men behind Richard were also with him, and the smile was replaced by a look of clear uncertainty.

Richard returned his smile and said reassuringly, "All is well."

Christian, waving his steward away, stepped towards him. "How long?" Was all he said.

Richard grinned. "I don't remember putting a time scale to it."

Christian, close to Richard, ran his eyes over the other man, his merchant's appraising gaze missing nothing. "I'd say it's been a sight longer for you than for me."

"Have I aged that badly!" Richard's words rang with mock indignation, "You always did know how to flatter a man."

"You look ..." Christian let his words trail away, "Damn it man, it's good to see you."

"Is there somewhere we can go? I have some matters of urgency we need to discuss," Richard's voice, crisp and direct, conferred the seriousness of what he wished to impart to Carter.

Carter's eyes flicked between Richard and the two men standing behind him. "Richard, for God's sake what is going on?"

"Perhaps your offices?" Richard suggested in reply. Christian was likely to have a fit of temper when he learned of what had happened, and he would rather that happened without witnesses.

Christian only hesitated for a moment. "Yes. Let me take my leave of Rhys. I can tell him there is some pressing business I need to attend to."

✝

They found Carter's workplace to be crowded and busy, his own office currently occupied by a clerk copying out bills of lading into ledgers in a tidy and steady hand. In the outer room two other neatly attired clerks were bent over a table, pens in hand, and looked up at Carter's arrival, their eyes widening when they took in the unlikely looking trio who attended him.

"Geoffrey. John. I have some private business." Carter put a coin on the table between them. "Take Charles with you and go to the Rabbit's Foot for an hour."

Geoffrey or John, a look of delight on his face, pocketed the coin, gave his master a warm word of thanks and, retrieving the elderly clerk from Carter's room, left. Carter waited until the door to the street closed before he stepped into his office. Emilio and Jack moved to follow, but without a word Christian abruptly closed the door on them, leaving them in the outer room with his steward, before he turned to Richard.

"I apologise for my sudden appearance, if I could have sent word, I would have," Richard said, his eyes meeting Carter's.

Carter dropped into the chair on his own side of the desk and gestured for Richard to take the other one. "Issuing an advance warning has never been one of your strong points. Anyway, it would just have made me worry. What happened?"

"I will tell you the details later. There is, I am afraid, a danger I need to guard against," Richard said, lowering himself into the chair.

"Oh, now there's a surprise!" Carter said, his words dripping sarcasm. "I told you dealing with that lot was going to end badly, didn't I?"

Richard raised his hand in acceptance of Carter's words. "You warned me. I know. I fell prey to avarice and greed and there is another man, a man called Andrew Kineer who also believes he knows what is in your warehouse and he is on his way to London."

"You said you'd not tell anyone?" Christian said accusingly, his eyes widening.

"I didn't," Richard replied, adding, "at least not willingly."

"This man, where is he? Is he alone? Who is he working for?" Christian placed the series of questions quickly as, hands on the chair arms, he pushed himself up from the seat.

"He has travelled from Malta to England, I don't know if we are ahead of him or behind him. All I do know is that he will try to take possession of the flintlocks, and to do that he needs you. Without you he will not be able to find them."

Carter dropped back heavily in his chair, the woodwork of the joints protesting with a series of crunched squeals. "And this man will come to London to look for me?"

Richard nodded. "Anne, where is she?"

"Thankfully I sent her, along with half of our household, to Norfolk to her parents. London is in the grip of another epidemic and it wasn't safe for her to stay," Carter said.

"Who remains at your house?" Richard asked quickly.

"My steward, and a handful of other servants," Carter's eye's widened. "And Harry!"

Richard rose. "Your steward is outside. Tell him to take one of the men I brought with me back to your house, then you've no need to worry on the boy's behalf."

"Who are they?" Carter replied.

"You can trust them," Richard said, then when Carter seemed to waver, he added. "I would trust either with my life."

Carter nodded. He had, Richard noted, paled a little, and had the tables been turned he had no doubt that he would be dealing with the situation little better.

Richard moved around the desk and opened the door to the outer office. "Jack, go back to Carter's house with his steward, make sure all is well."

"Coleman, take this man back with you, we will follow shortly," Carter said to his steward.

Jack nodded towards Richard, his face grimly set, and a moment later he had left the offices and headed into the street with Coleman.

"I need a short while," Richard said to Emilio who was sitting on the edge of desk the clerks had vacated, arms folded and a mildly bored expression on his face.

"Pray, do not rush on my behalf," Emilio snapped in Italian.

"He's French?" Carter stared at Emilio, but his words were for Richard.

"Not that now!" Richard quickly placed a hand around Carter's arm, steering him back into the office, ignoring the expression on Emilio's face.

"Who is he?" Carter said as soon as the door was closed, refusing to sit.

"A Knight of St John," Richard provided truthfully.

"In my office!" Christian blurted, his words loud.

"Yes, in your office. If you'll sit down I'll tell you why," Richard said, taking a seat himself, his voice calm in contrast to Carter's erratic one.

The account Richard gave was an honest and brief summary, he did not spare himself and soon Carter knew the seriousness of the situation. To his credit, once he understood what had transpired, Carter's thoughts immediately turned to the practicalities of how he could help.

"And the man outside my office? Is he here to conclude this deal for the Order?" Carter asked, pointing towards the outer office.

Richard nodded. "His name is Emilio, he is a captain in the Knights Hospitallers and he can help. Tresham is in London, the Knights can remove the flintlocks and protect you from Kineer."

"Well, I needed more space in my warehouse. I think I am right in assuming that this is a transaction that would be better concluded sooner rather than later, and that this man, Emilio, would like to view them? He'll need proof of their existence at the very least." Carter, a merchant to the core, had a very firm grasp on the process of the transaction that Richard needed to perform.

"I would be indebted to you," Richard said.

"You are already indebted to me on numerous accounts," Carter said dryly, pressing himself up from the chair, "Come on then, let's not keep the Order waiting."

†

Shortly afterwards, Carter, in the company of Richard and Emilio, arrived at his warehouse. The large double wooden doors, wide enough to admit a cart, stood closed, but after a firm knock the party were admitted through a side door. Carter led them between the stacks of boxes and bales to where the first of the cases containing the flintlocks still sat.

At Carter's direction Emilio and Richard lifted from the top of the first case two other boxes that were helping to ensure the anonymity of the case at the bottom. Carter left them for a moment and when he returned he held the tools needed to open the wooden box. Richard, taking them, began to lever open the top. Emilio stood and watched. When the wood was removed it revealed a number of long wrapped parcels, each one swathed in a closely woven waxed material. Richard lifted one out, produced a knife, and cut the material.

Before them, nestled within the slit packing, was a flintlock. Dull, coated in protective grease, and with fibres clinging to it from the wrappings.

Emilio stepped forward, lifted it and turned the gun over in his hands. Meeting Richard's eyes he nodded slowly. "Show me where the rest are."

†

Before the bells struck for another half-hour they were back at Christian's house. Carter was left there with Jack, while Richard and Emilio left to cross London to Tresham's. For the moment the security of Carter's warehouse was a matter of urgent importance to the Knights of St John. However much Carter protested that he did not like the idea, he had been forced to admit that if the Order were to take over the security arrangements for the warehouse, then it probably would be safer than it had ever been.

Jack found himself in Carter's house alone with the merchant.

"I suppose you'll need somewhere to stay?" Carter asked, his voice clipped and unfriendly.

"It would be appreciated," Jack replied He knew the other man had no liking for him, and he could understand why, and he made his tone as conciliatory as possible.

"My wife has taken most of the servants with her, but if I can find anyone I will get them to prepare a room for you," Carter grumbled, heading towards the door. At that moment there was a light knock, and when Carter opened it a mess of auburn curls adorning the head of a boy who measured up to the height of the door handle appeared. "Harry, I was wondering where you were," Carter said with evident pleasure, a hand ruffling the boy head.

"I've been in the kitchens, helping bring water in from the well," Harry announced proudly. "With all the men away Tilly needs me to help."

"Hmmm, I'm sure Tilly is capable of drawing water herself, but that was a kindness," Carter replied, then added, "I have a guest, can you tell Tilly to find us a tray of food and bring it back here please."

The boy disappeared into the corridor and Carter followed him. Jack breathed a sight more easily with Carter temporarily out of the room. This was not an office or a place of work but a home. Christian Carter had, until very recently, been a pile of packing cases in a warehouse. The end of a journey, the final part of a bargain. He had not been a man with a home and a wife. He was also not the man Jack had expected him to be. Instead of some rich merchant, fat and overfed, bristling with the efficiency of commerce he found Carter to be small and quiet, one who would be overlooked easily in a crowded room, and that Richard had declared him as a close friend was a surprise.

Carter returned a moment later.

"Coleman is having a room prepared for you," Carter said.

Jack took a breath and launched into a short, hastily prepared speech. "I appreciate Richard has left you in an uncomfortable position, and trust me sir, I am only here to ensure your safety until he returns. I thank you for your hospitality. It is, under the circumstances, a kindness not overly deserved."

Carter looked at Jack for a moment, and then exhaled loudly. "He doesn't get any better. He's been involving me in his escapades for the Lord knows how long, however this is getting a little extreme even by his standards. To date, my liberty and life have not been on the line. I don't suppose you would like to tell me more about what is going on?"

Jack adopted what he hoped was an apologetic expression. He was under strict instructions – "Leave Carter to me," Richard had said.

"I see," Carter said wearily. "Well, I shall have to deduce what I can from the facts I know, I suppose, until Richard, damn the man, steps back over my threshold."

"I hope, for both our sakes, that he will not be overly long in returning," Jack conceded honestly.

A knock at the door ended the stand off. Carter called over his shoulder, and a moment later the boy entered, a tray balanced on one arm.

"Put it on there, Harry," Carter pushed some papers to one side and cleared enough space on the desk.

"I am sorry, sir, this is the best Tilly says she can do with Mistress Turner having gone with your wife," the boy said as he set the tray on the table.

"If Tilly needs to apologise, in the future she can do it in person. Don't let her use you as a messenger," Carter admonished the boy, though it was a kind reprimand and the boy left the room smiling.

Jack's eyes ran over the fayre that had been placed on the table. It didn't look particularly poor. There were two pies, one with a latticed top decorated with leaves, both of them glazed and shiny. There was a plate with thick slices of cold pork, half a round yellow cheese, a small pot with apple sauce housing a wooden spoon, and a fresh cut loaf of bread leaking an aroma that was mounting a pleasant assault on Jack's nose. In the middle of the tray was an earthenware jug filled with ale, and set next to it, one inside the other, two cups.

Jack couldn't keep his eyes from the contents of the tray, and he was sure that Christian would be able to hear his innards complaining loudly that they had not been fed since dawn.

Carter waved his hand towards the food. "Eat. Help yourself. I'll not be seen as a bad host even when I do feel like I am suddenly a prisoner in my own home."

Jack did not hesitate, taking one of the sharp knives from the tray he cut into the glistening pastry. "English food is something I have missed."

"You've been out of the country with Richard then?" Carter asked.

Jack, his mouth full of a rich game pie, grunted in affirmation.

Christian Carter's brow creased. Picking up the flagon he filled both the cups and slid one of them towards Jack. "Were you on Malta as well then?"

Jack smiled apologetically, not about to be drawn by Carter's questions. Raising the knife he sliced another wedge. "I am sure Richard will tell you when he returns."

Carter grunted, raising his own cup and draining it of ale. Unlike Jack he didn't seem to have much of an appetite for the food that had been set before him. "I shall have to wait then until Richard returns after the agents of the Order of St John have finished securing my warehouse."

"There is a good man in charge of the force who will be there, and I can assure you that your warehouse and staff will both be safe," Jack replied honestly, cutting himself a good wedge of cheese.

"I wasn't so much thinking of their military efficiency, more of the association with the Order. They are not popular in every quarter you know," Carter said, a worried undertone to his voice.

"On that I can't comment," Jack said, then he diverted the conversation to another, more relevant course. "How many able men have you here?"

"Why?" Carter questioned anxiously.

"I'm to ensure your safety and I think it is wise to know what strengths you have," Jack replied, helping himself to more ale from the flagon.

"When Anne left I sent most of the household with her, I was more worried for her than myself. My steward, Coleman, remains, and there are two other capable servants in the house. I have more, but they are stationed in the warehouse at the moment," Carter summarised.

"Good, well have them secure every door and window and admit no-one, and we shall sit and await my brother's return," Jack said.

"Your brother?" Carter seized on the word immediately.

Jack looked at him over the rim of the cup, but didn't supply any further explanation.

"He told me about you. A half-brother. He found you in London when he was last here," Carter replied, looking very closely at Jack now.

A bitter smile crept onto Jack's face. "Aye, yes his half-brother."

"No one would ever take you for brothers, that's for sure. You are most unalike," Carter said still looking at him.

"So I've been told," Jack said dryly, putting the empty cup back on the table between them.

✝

Thomas Tresham was the representative of the Order of St John in London, and it was to his residence in The Strand that Richard took Emilio. The house was one he had ridden past years ago with Jack. Shortly after that journey he had had the beginnings of the idea that had led him full circle back to where he had started. With, he had to admit, little progress having been made in the interim.

That Emilio had been expected was immediately evident upon their arrival. Richard was left alone in an elegant room, warm and clad with both panelling and tapestries. Half a dozen chairs, high-backed and comfortable were arranged in a semi-circle around a stone flanked fireplace. Either side of the stone edifice was marked with the emblem of the order, picked out in black and white on shining polished marble. Like some alabaster tomb, the lintel wore a woven branch of leaves with cherubim, winged and holding trumpets in chubby hands facing each other in the centre.

Richard cast his eyes around the room, picked the chair in the middle and dropped into it then, scooping one of the fire dogs closer, he crossed his feet and rested them on top. If he felt out of place in this palace in his greyed, dusty, travel-stained clothes, it was not apparent from his manner. There was now nothing left to do but wait.

The door, thick and sturdy, made of solid shining oak and with a heavy warded lock clicked open with a solid sound. If Richard heard it he made no sign. Eyes closed, feet still resting on the polished brass, he sat, bathed in firelight, as if asleep.

"You sleep like the guiltless," said a familiar voice behind him.

Richard opened his eyes, observing the flames trapped in the grate, and said in reply, "Have I reason not to?"

"The worst of all deceptions is self-deception," Emilio replied acidly.

Richard turned his head to observe the Italian with a delighted expression on his face. "So Plato said. I see that now my brother is absent you are no longer keeping your thoughts to yourself."

"I hold you in no high regard, Fitzwarren, and I would have you know that," Emilio replied curtly.

Richard, smiling still, turned back to observe the crackling fire. "I am fully aware of the level of your disapproval."

Emilio dropped into the seat next to him. "The cargo will be removed in the morning. By the time dawn has broken it will be gone, and so shall I."

"Our bargain is then complete?" Richard stated.

"Once you present yourself in Malta, your sister and men will be released," Emilio replied.

Richard turned his grey eyes on Emilio. "That must rankle with you?"

"I doubt very much if your time on Malta will be an easy one," Emilio replied. "I have no worry that you will be afforded any favouritism."

Richard did not reply.

"Give this to Jack," Emilio held out the ring he had twice offered as a prize.

Richard's eyes rested on the gold Emilio held out. Then, without a word, he held his hand out, palm up, for Emilio to drop it into.

"Tresham has men here who will ensure you are escorted safely back across the city. After that your surety is your own issue, as is your return to Malta," Emilio replied coolly.

Richard rose. "I will make my own way back."

If Emilio heard, he made no sign, the door closing behind Richard.

CHAPTER SEVEN

✝

John Somer's house was further along The Strand near Whitefriars. Red bricked, walled and with a banked rear garden leading to a jetty giving access to the river. Scaling the outer wall was a simple task, and Richard dropped into the darkness of the kitchen garden, his boots crushing rosemary and thyme when he landed. The front of the house was in darkness. Making his way from the garden and through the orchard he rounded the back of the house. Richard scanned the windows, he knew from memory which of them was the study used by Somer, and he smiled when he saw a steady glow coming through the panes.

A vine, thick, twisted and with its roots wound deep in the soil held the back of the house in a wide caress. The wooded tendrils did not pass beneath Somer's lit window, but they did cling to the brickwork beneath another room further along on the same level. Quietly, hands gripping the hard, gnarled wood, Richard climbed to the second floor, only the slight rustle of the leaves recording his passage.

Moments later Richard was perched on the sandstone sill. The shutters were closed on the inside, there was no light leaking around them, and he knew the room on the other side would be in darkness. A thin scraping rasp betrayed the knife as it slid under the window leading, pressing against the catch and persuading it to open. Pulling the windows wide, the knife this time slid up between the middle of the closed shutters until it hit the resistance of the swivel lock on the other side. Lifting it slowly, the wood on the other side released from its rest swung free and a light touch moved the shutters back on their oiled hinges.

Quieter than a cat Richard dropped into the room, pulled the window and the shutter closed, and put the wooden catch silently back into place. As his eyes adjusted to the gloom it became evident that he was in a bedroom, one blessedly not in use, whether it was Somers' or not he did not know.

Equally dark was the corridor beyond the room. Two doors along from the bedroom was the room he wanted. He put his ear to the door and listened for a moment, then, satisfied that Somer was alone, he opened it and stepped quickly inside, closing the door soundlessly behind him.

Somer, bespectacled, and in the act of affixing a seal to a letter, looked up. Instant confusion furrowed his brow as his study door opened without the customary knock.

"The wax!" Richard exclaimed, stepping forward quickly.

"What?" Somer glanced down at his hand and swore. He had been about to pour liquid wax to seal the letter; his hand had tipped and he'd spilt a molten trail across the letter and onto the desk. "Damn it, man!"

Richard, quicker than Somer, snatched a knife from the desk and in one smooth movement scraped the drying wax from the parchment. "Not too much damage done," he said, grinning.

"Who let you in?" Somer demanded, a finger pushing his spectacles back up his nose.

"You need to reprimand your steward, and I recommend you buy a dog to guard your yard if you want to ensure your evenings are peaceful," Richard replied evenly.

"And that would keep you out, would it?" Somer demanded.

"No. But it would be a good deterrent for anyone else who wanted to enter your house," Richard replied, and leaning down he pulled from the side of his boot a sprig of rosemary, twirling it between his fingers.

"Sit down, man," Somer said, gesturing to a chair with his pen. "I need to finish this, one task at a time as they say. At my age if I don't complete it I am likely to forget, and this needs to be dispatched tonight."

"Its true success relies on sequential acts well done," Richard replied, shifting the heavy chair closer to Somer's desk.

"Aristotle?" Somer queried without looking up.

"No, my own advice, and one I singularly fail to adhere to." Richard sat in the chair and retrieved the green herb stem from Somer's desk where he had dropped it. He waited while Somer melted the wax, sealed the sheet, and applied a seal. Then, motioning Richard to be still, Somer pulled a chain attached to the wall near his desk, rising to meet the servant at the door who appeared after only a few moments, and handing him the letter. Richard did not hear the words they exchanged.

"Right, that's done. So now you can tell me why you've decided to ruin the peace of an old man's evening?" Somer said, rounding his desk again and dropping down heavily into the chair.

"I hardly think I've ruined it. I'm sure I've made you more than curious," Richard mused, pointing towards him with the herb.

Somers' mouth twisted into a sideways smile, pushing his glasses back up the bridge of his nose he regarded Richard critically. "Perhaps the evening is about to be a more entertaining one. There is indeed still a stain on the rug at your feet where you bled over it last time you were in this room. I hope you are not proposing to do that again?"

"Your kindness and your help were welcomed, and that is why I am here."

"So are you going to bleed over my furnishings again then?" Somer laughed, his eyebrows raised in amusement.

"Not unless I find myself under attack!" Richard smiled

"Verbally perhaps," Somer replied, taking his glasses from his nose he rubbed the lenses on his sleeve before replacing them. "I'm more than pleased that you are well. I had hoped to hear from you sooner."

"If I could have sent a message, I would have," Richard replied honestly.

"I could not fail to hear you connected to murders in London, and your name as well was on both Gardener's and Renard's lips. The words they used, I might add, were not favourable. Derby too it seems was another who strayed into your path, remind me why it is that I don't report you?" Somer's hands fetched together a number of pages he had obviously been reading, stacking them neatly and putting them to one side of the desk.

A mischievous smile spread across Richard's face. "Because you think I could be useful to you. That, and you enjoy the entertainment. I am sure you were highly amused when both Gardener and Renard found their schemes amounted to nothing."

"Wherever Renard is, trouble sprouts. He enjoys too much freedom, and he works openly for the Spanish cause. The councillors to a man know who his master is, and yet they still include him at the highest levels and fail to curb their tongues in his presence, and then act surprised when their opinions are thrown back at them," Somer finished, shaking his head, his hands open in a gesture of helplessness, before he let them fall back to the desk.

"And Gardener?" Richard queried.

"Remains an opinionated oaf," Somer replied quickly. "His policies are fracturing the council. Steering a clear path through the mire he leaves behind him is not easy."

"I am sure there are many who are thankful for your considered approach," Richard said.

Somer grunted. "Well, if there are they don't speak it."

"Women rule where rosemary grows, or so they say." The sprig of rosemary Richard sent spinning from his fingers to the desk.

Somer's eyes fell to the fragrant stems, and he grunted. "Women rule, or women are ruled."

As Richard watched he fished inside his doublet and extracted a thin chain with two keys attached to it. Pushing his spectacles up his nose he selected one of the keys and used it to open a drawer in the desk, from where he lifted out a wooden box. It was plain and unornamented, using the second key he unlocked it and lifted the lid; fishing inside he found the folded sheet he wanted and placed it on the desk between them.

Richard raised his eyes from the sheet to Somer. "You've still got it?"

"Of course, what did you think I would do with it?" Somer said levelly. "The havoc that would have wrought I could not have had on my conscience."

"I thought you used it to free Elizabeth?" Richard reached across the desk and picked up the sheet he had left with Somer years ago. He'd honestly believed it had been a card that had been played, so to find it stowed away in the shadows surprised him.

Somer smiled. "I did. You are not the only one adept at intrigue. That I knew of it was enough, and the lady was released."

"Why are you offering it back to me?" Richard asked carefully.

"I'm not." Somer reached across and snatched the sheet of paper from him.

"It is rumoured that the Queen is unwell," Richard said, changing the subject, his voice serious again.

"Rumour is right," Somer was nodding, pushing his glasses up he rubbed a hand over his tired eyes. "There is a lack of cohesion at the moment, the Queen has not settled the matter of the succession, and the real fear is that we will become a part of the Holy Roman Empire, a storeroom for Spain to raid and to use to support its war with France."

"I can see few being happy if the succession is vested in Philip," Richard said in agreement, a thoughtful expression on his face. "So what is the proposal? How to find an heir for England?"

Somer tapped the folded sheet on the side of the open box. "This will not help England. If the contents were made public all it would do is create instability. Which is why it has remained locked in here. Although privately I am wondering if it could be used to aid Cecil's quest to vest the succession in Elizabeth – he believes so."

"Cecil knows about this?" Richard replied.

"How else do you think I had the Lady Elizabeth released?" Somer replied. "I don't suppose you would like to tell me where you got it from? Last time you were here you collapsed before I could place the question, and left, if I remember, in the middle of the night without a farewell."

Richard grinned. "It was destined for Renard."

"My God! Renard! Does he know of its existence?" Somer's eyes widened.

"I don't think so. If he did then I am sure you would have heard about it by now," Richard replied thoughtfully.

"That's true enough," Somer said, dropping the folded discoloured sheet back into the box, and Richard watched as it disappeared and the lid closed over it. "I am grateful that it did not make it to its intended destination. Renard would have taken this to Philip, and the political carnage it would have caused can only be imagined."

"A moment ago you said you thought it might be used to vest the succession in Elizabeth? How so?" Richard asked carefully.

"It is a cruelty, but if Mary were aware of it then would not her pious nature make her realise that the rightful heir would be Elizabeth. That document undermines her mother's marriage, makes her illegitimate, and reinforces any claim that her sister has to the throne," Somer explained.

"That may be the case, but religious divide will not give Elizabeth the full backing of the council," Richard replied.

The corner of Somer's mouth was lit with a smile. "I know, however Cecil has a plan to deal with that and create accord amongst the privy councillors."

Richard leaned forward in his chair. "How?"

"A plan even you would admire. Both sides are to believe they are to succeed. You've told me who it was destined for, but as yet, not where it came from."

"I cannot help with that, it was amongst some papers the Archbishop of York had that were destined for Renard, that is all I know. That it had not been used until now did surprise me," Richard confessed, then added, "You keep that here? Is that wise?"

Somer smiled. "I have little choice. It is very safe, if the lid is lifted without the key then acid will spill in and burn the contents."

"Is that a warning or a threat?" Richard laughed.

"Both," Somer said placing the box back out of sight in the drawer again. "So what are you involved in now that brings you back to my door?"

"I have a task to complete, and once it's done I will be leaving England," Richard replied.

"Permanently?" Somer asked.

"Probably," Richard's voice bore a weight of resignation.

"Am I to assume that you have added more to your collection of crimes, that treason and murder were not sufficient?" Somer raised his eyebrows.

"I owe you much, so I will furnish you with an honest reply. I am being punished now for the sin of ambition, it seems," Richard said dryly.

"Who was brave enough to chastise you, then?" Somer asked, his voice sounding amused.

There was a moment's silence. Richard's eyes met Somer's before he delivered the answer. "The Knights of St John."

Somer sagged back in his chair, the wood back creaking in complaint, his face aghast. "You really know no bounds, do you?"

Richard's face darkened. "Do not worry, my wings have been well and truly clipped this time."

"So why are you telling me this?" Somer asked quietly.

"Because you at least deserve an honest answer, and I also have a small favour to ask," Richard replied.

The meeting lasted another hour, at the end of which Richard had what he wanted from Somer, and he left the same way he arrived, trampling on the herbs for a second time.

✝

It was late.

Jack gave silent thanks when he heard the noise of Carter's steward, Coleman, letting his brother in through the kitchen door. Carter had also raised himself from his chair and stood expectantly waiting for Richard to enter the room.

When he did, Jack watched Richard diffuse five hours of frustration and anger from Carter within moments. His greeting was warm, his manner apologetic, and his words sincere.

"It's done, and soon we will leave you and yours and it will be as if we had never been here," Richard concluded.

"Apart from a larger space in my warehouse, are you going to tell me now everything that is going on?" Carter's eyes flicked to Jack, obviously unsure whether Richard would continue in front of him or not.

Before either of them could say a word, Jack pressed his palms to the table and rose. "I'll leave you. I need to check if the steward has secured the house." He knew Carter was less than comfortable in his presence and would prefer to talk to Richard alone.

✝

Richard picked up Jack's empty cup and refilled it from the flagon. He waited a moment longer until Jack had closed the door before he spoke. "Christian, I am truly sorry."

"Come on then, what is it you haven't told me?" Christian said resignedly.

"I have secured a deal for all the cases of munitions in your warehouse, however life and liberty was the coin of the barter," Richard said, twisting the cup between his fingers.

Carter groaned and sat down, his arms wide. "What did I tell you would happen? You were never going to come off the better when you try to deal with the Order."

"It wasn't the Order that was the crux of my problems," Richard replied. "There was another man. He tried to trade in my identity and deal with the Order himself, and he nearly succeeded."

"Do I know him?" Carter asked, the thumb and forefinger on his right hand twisting a ring on his left.

Richard shook his head. "He is called Andrew Kineer, he used to be part of Seymour's household. I had thought I could trust him, and it seems I was wrong. He has, I am afraid, found out where the arms are and tried to deal with the Order directly, he is on the way to London, but we are ahead of him and I will deal with any threat he poses."

Carter's eyes widened. "Any threat? But the weapons are gone, or at least will be by tomorrow from what you have told me."

"He knows your name, and knows of a connection, I am afraid," Richard said, his voice serious.

"But if the weapons are gone, and if he knows that, then why would he continue to be a threat?" Carter repeated.

"That might be so. But when he finds out they are missing I fear he will do anything he can to strike at me, and I cannot risk you being caught up in the middle," Richard's grey eyes linked with Christian's.

Carter had paled. "So what are you going to do? Move into my house until he appears?"

Richard inclined his head. "I know a few people in London who he might contact when he arrives in the City, if he does they will let me know. Tomorrow I will send messages to them. I don't believe he will be far behind me, and I don't believe he will come here on his own either, there is too much at stake."

"He'd come here, with armed men?" Carter stammered.

Richard nodded. "Your warehouse is secured, the guns will be gone tomorrow, can you not leave the house as well for a while? Go and join Anne?"

"Leave? Are you mad? I've two shipments due in this week from Holland, they will be clearing customs in a day or so and if I'm not here the cargo will be snaffled by Forsyth or Caddock. No I can't leave," Carter said, and then added by way of explanation, "it's silk, you see."

Richard shook his head. "No, I don't."

"It's silk. I commissioned the voyage to bring it here, and if I am not around to take the cargo then I'll lose my investment, and that's something I cannot afford. So you, my friend, will have to work around that," Carter said firmly. "And that's going to prove none too easy is it? Not with the number of people you have looking for you. Damn it Richard, you've got the Privy Council after you, there's a warrant for your arrest for murder, and treason, and your father is after your hide as well."

"My father?" Richard repeated.

Carter was exasperated. "The Privy Council, treason and murder count for naught do they? But a mention of your father gets your attention? Dear God, Richard! Your father sent a message for me to attend him at his house in London. I couldn't exactly ignore a summons from Lord Fitzwarren could I?"

"I suppose not. What did he want?" Richard had folded his arms.

"You. He wanted to know if I knew where you were. There was little else to the meeting and once he was sure I didn't know I was dismissed quickly enough and made to promise that if I did hear word of you I would let him know," Carter supplied.

Richard looked thoughtful. "Perhaps you should."

"Richard! I think there are more pressing things to attend to at the moment than your family reunion," Carter said, though he was stopped from further complaint by a light tap at the door.

Richard rose and opened it.

Jack had returned.

"The house is as secure as it can be. There are a dozen ways to get in, the gates to the stables are poor and the wall round the back of the kitchen garden is so low it wouldn't keep a child out," Jack summarised quickly.

"Well, up until now I had no need to have security arrangements in place that would keep away marauding hordes, did I?" Carter's temper was rising at Jack's brief assessment of his home.

"It's a hard house to defend. There are a dozen entry points and if Kineer does try to get in, with just the few of us it's likely he'll be in here before we know it," Jack continued to give his report to his brother without paying attention to Carter.

"It has to be here, if we move Kineer will know we have arrived before him," Richard replied.

"Does that matter? If he knows we are here, and that the Order have taken the weapons, then there is no need to press Carter is there, surely he will be safe then?" Jack said.

"I like your thinking, that does make sense," Carter interjected, but neither of the men were listening to him.

"It might in your mind, but not in Kineer's. He'd do just about anything to strike at me, and if he finds the guns gone and that we arrived first he is still likely to press Christian for news of where we are, and where the flintlocks went. And he's not likely to politely ask and then turn on his heel and leave, is he?" Richard pointed out.

"Oh," Carter said, swallowing hard.

"Fair point, he's a malicious bastard, that's true," Jack replied.

"What have you done to me?" Carter dropped into a chair and covered his hands with his face.

Richard moved behind him and laid a hand on his shoulder. "Are all ventures of trade not fraught with a little risk?"

"A little risk? Are you mad?" Christian blurted, raising his head from his hands.

Richard smiled. "Christian, I am going to make this a very worthwhile venture for you."

"How? You've traded the bloody lot for your sorry lives and placed my own on the line as well! How is that worthwhile?"

Richard, smiling broadly and holding Christian's gaze, slid his hand into his doublet and retrieved a neatly-folded sheet of paper which he twisted between his fingers. "Does the name Marlow Crinson mean anything to you?"

A look of confusion settled on Christian's face for a moment. "He's one of the main purchasers for the Court."

Richard nodded and held out the white square for Christian to take.

"It's addressed to me?" Christian queried tremulously as he read the script on the front of the sealed sheet. Then, his eyes snapping up to meet Richard's, he asked, "What is it?"

"The answer to that question, I feel, will lie on the inside," Richard supplied, amused.

Christian, watched by both men, briskly broke the seal and read the short letter. His expression changed from concern to astonishment. "How did you get this?"

"You are pleased?" Richard asked.

"Pleased? This would be beyond any expectation I ever had. Richard, this would be incredible." Carter sat down heavily in his chair. "I can't wait to tell Anne... How did you arrange this?"

"Under the circumstances, it was the least I could do." Richard replied.

Jack looked between the two men. "Is someone going to tell me what's going on?"

Christian held up the letter. "It's a statement of preferential supply. I've been selected to supply Marlow Crinson with wine." His eyes dropped back to the letter again. "I honestly can't believe it, wait till Caddock finds out about this, he'll turn green with envy."

"And why is that good?" Jack continued, looking between Richard and Carter.

"I have a good business, my main trade is wine. But supply to the court and all the other institutions is practically impossible, it's hugely lucrative and merchants fiercely protect their rights. You cannot approach Marlow Crinson, you need to be invited. Once you supply the crown then there are a whole other number of buyers who will only buy from crown suppliers so the potential is...limitless," Christian explained, his eyes again dropping to devour the contents of the letter.

When Richard and Jack were alone an hour later, Jack said, accusingly, "So you spent the evening consorting with wine merchants? I'm glad it was something so important."

Jack was clearly annoyed.

"Amongst other things, yes," Richard replied.

"The man was after your blood. I honestly don't know how you do it, but he's eating out of your hand now and seeing the threat to his life some sort of minor inconvenience," Jack continued.

"They do say a merchant keeps his heart in his purse," Richard replied. "Anyway, it's taken his mind off the immediate situation, and Christian always did worry overly about things he could not control."

"I know how he feels," Jack said with a touch of bitterness. Then, changing the subject, "How are we going to find out if Andrew is in London?"

"There are a few people in London who Andrew knows, and I am hoping he will contact them when he gets here. He's not stupid, and I can't see him turning up alone at Christian's door, can you?"

"I just wish I knew where he was," Jack grumbled. "I want to know if we are days or weeks ahead of him."

"Anyway, it's not just Christian who is receiving favours tonight," Richard said. "Emilio has sent you a parting gift."

"He's gone? Without ..." Jack stopped himself.

Richard pulled from his purse the gold band of the ring and examined the front. That it had been made in Italy was apparent from its style, that it was valuable was also obvious from the jewels used in the decoration, and that it was going to look completely ridiculous on his brother's hand was also an undeniable fact.

The centre of the ring held a heraldic device; a sun picked out by a weighty diamond, the corners of a shield were pinned in place by rubies, and the shoulders joining it to the band were inlaid with green emeralds.

"Here, this is for you," Richard said, and held it out for Jack to take. "I believe it's the one he was betting with."

"Can we sell it?" Jack said as he examined the ring he held between his thumb and forefinger. "If these jewels are real it'll be worth a small fortune."

"They are real, have no doubt about that. Keep it though, I rather think Emilio feels it might be a lucky charm for you," Richard replied.

"A lucky charm," Jack repeated, trying to push the ring onto his middle finger and swearing when it got stuck just above the knuckle.

Richard retrieved it, seized Jack's hand and pushed it onto his ring finger. "There. I am sure Emilio will be very pleased."

Jack hauled his hand from Richard's grasp, delivering him a sour look.

CHAPTER EIGHT

✝

As Emilio had promised, the flintlocks were removed from Christian Carter's warehouse before the light had broken over the city the following day. The additional security that had been there to guard them was gone. Richard, careful to avoid places where he might be identified, contacted people he still knew in the city who might help him find Andrew, and also help ensure that Christian and his household remained safe. This had taken him to the notorious White Hart tavern in Cheap Street where Myles Devereux held court.

Devereux's mother, Frances, was the sister of William Courtenay, making Myles Devereux cousin to the exiled Edward Courtenay, Earl of Devon. This tenuous connection seemed to provide him with a protection from prosecution from his involvement in the darker side of commerce. If it was illicit, if you needed a debt recovering, if you needed protection, if there were some stolen goods you needed to sell, or some stolen goods you needed to buy, if you wanted to flee London for a crime, if you needed a witness for a court case, and *if* you had money, then Devereux would ensure the wheels of your transaction rolled smoothly.

Devereux held audience at the White Hart, an inn of questionable repute not far from the docks. His rank and wealth certainly meant he could have moved elsewhere in London, but Myles preferred to sit amidst the unsavoury and the debased, as if surrounding himself with a tangible layer of disreputable and contemptible human waste bolstered his own shameful reputation as the undisputed King of the corrupt. Richard was unsure whether or not he owned the tavern, but everyone knew that it was Devereux who was in charge.

Myles operated from the rooms above the White Hart. Richard entered the tavern and headed towards the stairs at the back of the room. Leaning against the wall at the foot of the steps, a stubby knife skilfully paring wood from a block in his right hand, was one of Devereux's guards. Myles surrounded himself with a small group of dedicated men whose sole purpose was to ensure the longevity of their master. They were known locally as Devereux's dozen; whether there were twelve or not was debatable since they were rarely ever seen together, and the occasional casualty was not unknown.

"Is he in?" Richard enquired, although the question was rhetorical, for had Devereux been absent the stairs would not have had a guard.

"He might be. And you are?" the man tucked the knife into his belt.

"Richard Garrett."

"I'll see," the man turned, efficiently took the stairs two at a time and disappeared through the door at the top.

Richard leaned his shoulder against the wall and waited. Devereux was never in a hurry to see anyone. How long he kept you waiting was a measure of your status. The longer the wait, the lower his regard for you. It was not a game Richard was prepared to play for very long today.

After five minutes, when Devereux's attendant failed to reappear, Richard broke all the rules of the White Hart by mounting the steps without an invitation. The main room of the tavern was lightly furnished with some early noon day trade. A serving woman, a pewter jug under one arm and woven basket with bread in her right hand, stopped dead in the middle of the room. Wide-eyed, she added her stare to those of the other patrons' as they watched someone make a fatal mistake.

No one entered Myles's rooms uninvited.

Never.

If Richard considered knocking on the door before he opened it, there was no pause of indecision, and he pulled it open immediately. There were three rooms used by Devereux, the outer one was where the monetary transactions were carried out and recorded. A ledger clerk and two of Devereux's guards, including the man who had been at the bottom of the stairs, were occupying it now. A merchant, seated opposite the clerk, was counting out coins under the watchful eyes of one of Devereux's men.

As Richard opened the door four pairs of eyes, two hostile, one shocked and the other incredulous turned upon him. He had an advantage of surprise: no-one, in the last three years, had been foolish enough to arrive unannounced. Richard made it half way across the room towards the door leading to Devereux before either of the men were upon him.

The clerk slammed the ledger shut, dragged it from the desk and clutched it protectively to his chest. The man who had been supervising the transaction scooped the money from the table, sluiced it into a wooden box, slammed the lid shut and placed himself between it and Richard. The one who had been the guard on the stairs threw himself at Richard and the pair, locked together, staggered back across the room cannoning into the recently closed door.

"I am trying to sleep!" A voice announced from the other room.

The sound of his master's voice was enough to stop Richard's assailant dead, though he didn't release his grip on Richard but maintained a tight hold, awaiting his next order.

"If it's not impudence personified!" the darkly dressed man slurred from where he was now stood, holding the door open. "Which rock did you recently crawl out from under, I wonder?"

Richard, still locked in the stationary fight, replied, "The same one as you."

The man near the door laughed. "Matthew, let him go." Then to Richard, "Come on in."

Richard sloughed off the hold, straightened up and followed Devereux into his room, closing the door behind him.

Any amused expression that had lightened Devereux's slack features immediately dropped, unwanted, from his face. "What do you want, Fitzwarren?"

"I can see we are on the same easy terms as always," Richard replied, his smile empty of anything pleasant.

There was a wide cushioned chair near the window. Devereux dropped into it and propped his elbows along the wooden back. "I've heard your name in all the wrong places. You still have a certain skill for upsetting people."

"And you don't?"

Myles shrugged. "I don't care."

"Meaning I do?" Richard retorted.

Myles laughed quietly. "I doubt very much that you've sold your soul. As delightful as it is to see you again, get to the point Fitzwarren, and then get out."

Richard perched himself on the end of the bed frame. A move that told Myles he had little intention of departing in a hurry, and a look of malicious annoyance settled on the seated man's face.

"Is that an invite?" Myles stated, his eyes resting on Richard's face.

Richard ignored him. "I need to hire four men."

Myles's eyebrows raised. "Four!"

"Four," Richard repeated.

"Can I spare four? Do I want to spare four?" Devereux enquired of the room.

"I said hire, not give," Richard corrected.

"True. Four men, anything else?" Myles said, brows raised.

Richard shook his head.

"What currency will you be paying in?"

Myles retained a bored expression for the next five minutes while he listened to what Richard had to say. When he had finished, he uncrossed his feet and rose from the chair, standing close to Richard.

"Alright. I will have the men you want sent over," Devereux said, then in a move that Richard had not anticipated a hand wrapped itself in the material of his doublet, twisted it and with a savage yank tore the material. Devereux instantly let go and turned, to send a pewter flagon that had been resting on the table to the floor. "Now get out."

Richard emerged from Myles's room, Devereux behind him resting against the door frame, a picture of calm indifference, watched him leave. "Matthew, take him out."

Matthew's eyes registered the ripped clothing on his master's visitor, and having heard the noise, he had a satisfied expression his face. "Come on. You heard Master Devereux. Out with you."

Matthew opened the door for him at the top of the stairs and Richard dropped down them back into the main room of the tavern. At the bottom of the stairs, and moving quickly out of his way, were gathered another glut of Devereux's stinking retainers. One of them, his filthy ragged plumage reeking of pitch and worse, saw an opportunity and clasped his hands together begging, until a solid thump in his back from one of the other men dissuaded him.

Richard swiftly exited the inn and as promised four men arrived at Carter's house an hour later. Richard introduced them to Jack, and left him in charge of the new resources to ensure the house and household were secure.

✝

After the race to arrive first, after the activity of the last few months, these first few days at Carter's house, trapped inside the walls, had hit Jack like a rock fall. Of the two of them Jack was the most easily identified and even Jack could see the sense of staying inside Carter's house. Richard knew he was suffering, it was a waiting game that neither of them was enjoying. There was little to do in the meantime apart from ensure that the new guard detail were doing as they had been instructed.

Carter had gone to bed leaving Jack and Richard alone in the kitchen. An orange fire, the flames fierce and intense, was busily charring the wood in the grate, and two efficient lamps hanging from the ceiling further pushed the dark into the corners of the room. The remains of the evening meal sat near Jack's elbow and he absently picked at some crumbling oatcakes that had been left.

Richard produced two evidently new dice, and Jack's eyes fastened on them, bemused and enquiring. Made from smooth, milky ivory, the cubes were held within a fine golden framework caging them along each edge.

"Those weren't cheap," Jack observed, watching as Richard cast them on the table between them. When they rolled to a halt they showed a pair of fives. "And weighted as well, I'd wager."

"Shall we find out? It might take your mind off your woes," Richard observed, taking the dice into his keeping again. "How about a game of King's Hazard?"

"You need four dice for that," Jack observed dryly.

Richard, smiling, produced two more.

Jack scooped them all from the table and rolled them over in his hand admiring them. "Where did you get them from?"

"One of Christian's trading partners brings these in from Italy." Richard took one from Jack's hand and twisted it between his fingers. "I rather think they have come from further afield than that though."

"These would grace a prince's table," Jack said, letting them roll from his hand back onto the table again.

King's Hazard was played with four dice. Once the first two were cast the player had the choice of either rolling the two remaining ones or one of them. The aim of the game was to get as close to a score of sixteen as possible without exceeding that number. If the player threw a double score with his first hand he was entitled to split them and play two hands as long as he doubled his stake.

Jack fished in his purse, pulling out a handful of coins, along with a button.

"What are you planning to spend that on?" Richard enquired, amused, watching as Jack picked it out of his hand and dropped it back into the purse. There was a pause while Jack seemingly gathered his thoughts. When he spoke, his voice was serious. "I keep seeing it, and I think to myself - I'll ask Lizbet to sew it back on for me."

"She won't be on Malta forever Jack, I promise," Richard's voice was reassuring, and his eyes, when Jack looked up, astonishingly dark.

"I let her down." Jack pressed the heels of his palms into his own eyes, his words edged with frustration.

"We both did," Richard pronounced with frank honesty, absently turning the dice over in his fingers. The only noise in the kitchen was the occasional muted thump as the logs settled in the flames.

Jack dropped his hands from his face, his naturally bright eyes found his brother watching him intently. "I actually miss the lass."

"I do as well." Richard's words, laden with regret, surprised his brother.

It was Jack who found himself trying to lighten the mood. "Let's never tell her that though?"

"Agreed." Richard raised his eyes from the table where they had rested on the still dice.

Jack broke off a lump of abandoned oatcakes and dropped it into his mouth. "When she comes back to England, you need to find her somewhere to go. A good house." Then, gesturing towards his brother with another piece of crisped cake in his hand, he added, "And get her a husband. She deserves it."

"Why is that my task?" Richard said, his eyes bemused and vivid.

"You're better at arranging things like that than I am," Jack stated simply.

"True," Richard sounded thoughtful, then suddenly, "she'd make you a good wife."

"Oh no," Jack shook his head.

"Why not?" Richard pressed, his expression innocent. "She can cook, sew, clean and put up with your snoring."

"Stop it," Jack's gaze, fiercely intense, met Richard's. "I've a debt I owe."

Richard sounded intrigued. "Go on."

Jack looked down at his hands clasped together on the table.

"You can tell me," Richard pressed.

"Another time," Jack spoke with finality, and reached for the dice.

"If I win, you tell me?" Richard wasn't letting his brother off the hook that easily.

"God, if you must know, the lass, Catherine. I owe her my life, she's lost everything and I cannot help but feel we played a part of it. I feel responsible," Jack said roughly.

"We are leaving a trail of wreckage in our wake," Richard sighed.

"I would like to help her. It would ease my conscience to know she was safe and happy," Jack continued.

"She's safe at the moment," Richard reassured.

"In London? How are you so sure she is safe?" Jack asked.

"As safe as she can be, and before we leave I will make sure she is, you have my word," Richard said solemnly. "Come on, King's Hazard," Richard continued, trying draw his brother's thoughts away from Catherine's current plight,

Jack cast the dice on the table, his first score a pair of fours.

"Weighted in your favour at least," Richard said.

They played a dozen rounds. Jack, not much engaged in the game, took the small cubes into his keeping and without enthusiasm released them onto the table.

"Eight," announced Richard.

Jack's eyes were drawn to the dice but hardly registered the five and a three he had rolled. "Eight," he confirmed. Jack rolled the two spare dice and Richard pronounced the score.

Richard took the dice into his hand and sent two of them rolling back across the table, the uppermost faces revealing a one and a four. "Thirteen."

Jack looked from the dice to Richard's face.

"Thirteen," Richard repeated.

Jack just stared at him.

"Jack, I have never seen you so distracted. I promise this will be over soon," Richard replied.

His brother's words revived Jack's attention and a moment later he realised what was happening, and he reached to stop Richard swiping the coins on the table towards himself. "You cheating cur."

†

Richard had spent another morning at Carter's offices where, for lack of anything else to do, he had begun to take on a role as his assistant. This had hugely annoyed one of the clerks. Geoffrey obviously had designs on his own personal advancement and this new man in the office, who obviously had a close tie with his master, was not welcome. Carter had introduced Richard as a man who was bound for work in the Venetian trading houses and was stopping with them until his passage could be arranged. The explanation, which did have a hint of truth, had done little to cheer Geoffrey.

Richard, carrying the ledger Christian had wanted, walked into his office and heeled the door closed behind him. The merchant, humming and happily tapping his fingers on the desk, looked up with a smile.

"You actually enjoy this?" Richard's voice was weary as he dropped the ledger on the desk. "Christian, I despair, I really do!"

"Here, enter those into that ledger," Christian ordered, ignoring his comment, and passed him a small pile of sheets. "They are already in date order. I need to get the bills over to the Parish Council today, they are paying me in advance of delivery."

Richard opened the wide leather bound volume and turned to the latest vacant sheet before pulling the documents towards him that Carter had passed. Flicking through them he paused, then looked up. "You are supplying the Parishes with Lime for the burial pits?"

Christian met his gaze and stopped humming. "You disapprove?"

"You always said I was the profiteering bastard with no morals!" Richard laughed.

"You must have taught me well. The key you see is speed. Anyone can buy it and bring it into to London, the commodity itself isn't scarce, but I have an arrangement to transport it in bulk quickly. And at times like this the Parishes certainly use a lot of it," Carter explained, then continued defensively, "Don't poke fun at me! London needs people like me, and so do you. Just think how bad London would smell without it?"

"I'm not. Christian, your business is a good one, and I envy your success," Richard replied, his tone sincere.

Richard's comment seemed to catch Carter off guard, and he put his pen down. "Do you?"

"My grand ambitions are not amounting to very much," Richard replied. "Perhaps I should have settled for something a little more mundane, but honest."

"What is success though?" Carter leaned forward a little across the desk. "Anne and I have no children. She wants them more than anything else, and that's something I cannot buy. Money, my success here," Carter waved his arms wide, "does not amount to anything when weighed against that score."

"You have Harry though, he's a bright lad. Does Anne know he's yours?" Richard asked.

Carter shook his head quickly. "No. And if she did, I have no doubt the lad and I would be finding somewhere else to live. I daren't even tell the lad in case he says too much."

"You should tell her. Anne likes him well enough, he's your son, and even if he's not hers she could treat him as such," Richard suggested.

"I do think about it, and I sometimes wonder if she suspects. His mother died of sweating sickness when he was three, and he's been in the house since. But if I judge it wrong she will make me pay for all eternity, you know what Anne can be like!" Carter concluded morosely.

"In my experience, keeping such family secrets as this, covered in layers of lies, does little good to anyone," Richard stated with an edge of regret.

"Ah, your brother. Why do you keep him with you?" Christian said, twisting the pen in his hand.

"It is not quite how it appears," Richard replied.

"I'm sure it's a good deal better for him than for you. The pair of you are worlds apart, it's a charitable thing you have done, but you cannot call him your brother," Carter said, pointing at Richard across the desk with the feathered end of the pen.

"Why not?" Richard asked bluntly.

Christian leant across the table a little further and pronounced, "Because he's your half-brother, a bastard. You just need to take one look at him to know where he was raised."

Richard rested back in the chair, folding his arms. "Since when did you become so jaded."

"It's just the way it is. Maybe, once, I was a little freer with my thinking, but as you get a little older you begin to see the constraints all around us, and you cannot break them. No one is going to accept Jack as your brother. You couldn't take him anywhere, just look at him!" Carter said, his right arm held out, palm up-over as if he were gesturing to Jack stood next to him.

"So for want of a good tailor he must remain in the shadows?" Richard queried.

"That's not what I meant and you know it," Christian's brows furrowed, a tone of rebuke in his voice. "It's good that you defend him, and natural as well, but he's only half your blood kin, remember that."

"I don't need to defend him, Christian, he's quite capable of doing that on his own," Richard replied, a slight smile on his face.

"Luckily there is no family resemblance between you. You should be thankful for that at least," Cater continued as if Richard had never spoken.

"He takes after his mother," Richard said simply.

Christian seemed quite shocked by the statement. "Did you know her?"

"Quite well, yes," Richard replied, sounding thoughtful, "Beautiful and hot tempered."

Carter opened his mouth to say something, then at the sight of Richard's raised hand, he closed it and remained silent.

"We have the same mother, Christian. He is my brother, he's not a bastard. I only tell you so you will hold him in better regard," Richard delivered the truth and watched shocked disbelief twist Carter's face.

"But he can't be. He doesn't look anything like you, are you sure?" Carter stammered in reply.

"Just accept it, for it is the truth," Richard replied.

The expression on Carter's face was a mix of disbelief and horror. "Richard, please don't tell me you have been taken in by some story, what sort of proof is there?"

"I told you only so you would have a better regard for him," Richard replied flatly.

"I hope for your sake you have not been duped. Believe me, he'll want something, they always do," Carter said with authority, tapping his finger on the desk.

"He does. And I am going to help him get it," Richard said, more to himself than to Carter.

†

Richard and Carter, along with two of Devereux's men, crossed London from Carter's offices to the Parish of St Bride's. The Parish practice was for debts to be settled at their offices, and so Carter needed to present himself to obtain his payment. The wet weather had continued, and as they passed East Smithfield the problem faced by London as it attempted to bury its breathless citizens became obvious. Work on two large pits had ceased and it seemed a heated argument was taking place between those paying for the burial works and those undertaking the labours. Both of the pits had filled with water, and rain still pouring from the sky was decorating them both with a myriad of concentric circles.

"We've dug the pit out where you wanted it, it's not my fault it's full of water is it? The base of it is clay, and it's as waterproof as a duck's arse," a man with a mottled face was pointing towards the flooded pit. Behind him, resting on their shovels, stood four nervous men. That they had been in the hole until recently was obvious, all of them were soaked and coated in ochre mud. The man with the red blotched face, better dressed and notably dry, appeared to be in charge of them.

"All I am trying to say is cut a channel from it in this corner here," a man wearing a knee length fur trimmed cloak and a wide, broad brimmed hat, pointed to one end of the pond, "to the road down there and the water will drain out."

Red Face was not accepting this simple solution. "That's a long trench, and a lot of work. Even if we dig that channel it is still going to fill back up again."

"I am paying you to dig this out for me. That was the agreement, and you agreed to that, and now look at it. We can't use this!" Fur Cloak pointed angrily to the water filled pond.

The labourer's spokesman shrugged. "You wanted a hole, we dug you one."

"But it's not one we can use!" The cloaked man's temper and frustration was rising, and he spoke the words through gritted teeth.

"Ah well, I'm a simple man, and we've done what you asked us to do. It's dug out where you wanted it, and to the depth you wanted it. It's a hole, it's in the right place, there's no arguing with that," Red Face said, pointing again to the pond.

The cloaked man raised his hands in a gesture of defeat. "Alright, Master Dent. Let me put it to you another way. I will pay you extra to dig that trench, whether it will or it will not work is my business."

The men with the shovels exchanged sudden bright looks, and two of them, heads together, conversed quietly. It was obvious that this was the crux of the argument. More work required more money.

"That's going to be one of the new burial pits, have you seen the size of it?" Christian observed, the leader of the work gang now involved in the detailed costings of his men's extra labours.

"They'd be better off taking them outside the city," Richard observed.

"I know," Carter leaned his head closer to Richard's for a moment, "the problem is, they've charged that scoundrel Devereux with disposing of the dead, and it'll cost too much to take them out of London and bury them. It's much easier if there is a central point like this to bring all the bodies to."

"Devereux?" Richard repeated the name.

"The man's a complete reprobate to profit from this," Carter said, disgust in his voice.

Richard couldn't help himself, and the loud laugh escaped before he could stop it.

"What?" Christian exclaimed, his eyes wide and questioning.

Richard wiped a tear away. "It's no different from your dealings in lime?"

"I'm an honest merchant. Devereux's a crook and a thief. He'll not do a decent job of this, he'll cut corners and line his purse. But who's going to stop him? There's no one else with the resources or the stomach to deal in the dead," Carter replied bitterly.

"If I didn't know better, I'd say you were jealous," Richard replied. "How did he get the job?"

"How does Devereux get any job? He knows everyone," Carter said gloomily.

"As now do you, don't forget Master Crinson," Richard reminded him.

†

It was an hour later that Carter finished his business in the Parish offices and returned to Richard, who was waiting in the outer office with Devereux's men. Carter did not say much until they were some way from the office, then leaning close to Richard he said, "It's a total mess."

"What is?" Richard replied.

"The burial pits are not finished and they are storing the bodies in a side chapel at St Bride's," Christian said under his breath. "They did have them in a building

194

at the rear, but it was a wooden one and the rats ..." Christian gave a shudder. "It's hopeless, I told you Devereux would cut corners, they can't bury the dead because the pits are flooded and they've nowhere else to put them."

"I hardly think you can blame Devereux for the rain, can you?" Richard pointed out.

"No, but still. If he'd done a better job then they wouldn't be stuck where they are at the moment," Carter continued.

Richard let Carter have the last word, and they made their way back through the drizzle to Carter's house.

CHAPTER NINE

†

While Richard was spending his days in Christian's company, Jack was finding his overly long. He had struck up a friendship with Coleman, and the steward was welcoming his offer of help with any tasks that needed completing around the house. He spent the morning, a coarse-pitch saw in his hand, cutting wood to repair the bottom of one of the back gates to the house. When the bells tolled out noon and his stomach told him it needed feeding he made his way to the kitchens, collected bread and cheese and took them back to the room he had been allocated on the third floor of Carter's house. Richard, he knew, had a room in the main part of the house near Carter's own. Jack didn't mind particularly. Christian had made it quite clear when he had first arrived that he did not hold Jack in any great esteem, though he seemed to have warmed to him lately, but Jack was still happy to remain apart.

His hand still on the newel post at the top of the stairs, Jack heard the noise from his room well before he got there. It was Harry's voice, and from the sound of it he was talking to himself. Jack stood on the other side of the partly closed door and listened for a moment, his hand on the latch, and a growing smile on his face.

"Take that, and that, die damn you!" Harry screamed theatrically.

Jack, rounding the door grinned broadly at the sight of Harry, Jack's sword in his hand, advancing upon his own shadow cast against the wall.

"Sword play in a small room, my lad, is never a good idea." Jack liked the boy well enough and he wasn't annoyed.

Harry, shocked by his arrival, let out a yelp of surprise, dropping the sword to the floor. The point spiked splinters from the boards, and the cross guard landed heavily on his foot producing a squeal of pain.

"See what I mean?" Jack said laughing.

"Sorry sir, I didn't mean any harm," Harry stammered nervously, hopping on one foot.

"None done I expect," Jack retrieved the blade from the floor, "I think your toes have saved it from any damage."

Jack held the weapon out, the sun flittering along the silvered length. "You need to have a care lad. Some men sharpen their steel fully when they feel they'll need to use them, but I've never been very good at predicting when that will be, so…" Jack leant forwards and in a quick movement plucked a hair from Harry's unkempt mop, the boys hand flew to his head. "I keep this one sharp."

Jack folded the hair across the leading edge and with very little pressure the brown strand parted.

"So keep your fingers away from it or you'll have a few less to count with," Jack said warningly.

Harry's eyes were wide. "I don't even think the master has one."

"Master Carter? Probably not," agreed Jack, hiding a sad smile thinking it was a shame Carter hid the fact that Harry was his son even from the child.

"I wish he would get one," Harry continued.

"But he has strong men to work for him so he's no real need to have one of his own," Jack said, trying to tread a careful path through the conversation.

"But if I was the master I would have one," Harry pronounced. Then he asked, "If you ever need it cleaning, sir, you let me know. I do all the tack for the horses, and Master Drake who runs the stables says I can get a shine on leather better than anyone else."

"Can you now?" Jack said, smiling at Harry's boast.

"I can sir," Harry affirmed.

"Right then, you can start with these and see how you do," a moment later Jack had divested himself of both of his boots and held them out towards the boy. Harry, not at all daunted by the challenge, took them.

"I'll need them back in an hour," Jack gave Harry a gentle shove and closed the door on him. Stretching out on the bed he ate the food he had brought, and a moment after he finished he was asleep. He woke an hour later to the sound of a light knock on the door. Opening it he was pleasantly surprised to find his boots waiting for him in a much improved condition.

They'd not looked that good since Lizbet... Jack's face clouded with guilt. Damn it!

†

Finally they had settled into a routine. Richard, along with two of Devereux's men, shadowed Carter when he left the house for his offices, Jack and the other men remaining at the house. Carter had already been to visit Crinson, and was so excited by the coming deals he would be able to broker, he had practically forgotten about the spectre of Kineer, and he was even tolerating Jack's presence in his house.

Jack and Richard were already in the kitchen, seated opposite each other, when Carter arrived for breakfast. With his wife, and most of the servants absent, he too chose to take his meals there.

Coleman had just taken delivery of the bread order and was setting the loaves on the table. "I'm sorry, sir, there's only half of our usual delivery here. The baker in Ouse Street died so ours now has twice the customers and he's putting his prices up."

"London is like an open graveyard at the moment," Christian grumbled as he seated himself opposite Richard at the kitchen table.

Richard cast his eyes over his friend. "Your standards are falling! Imagine what Anne would say if she knew you were in your kitchen in your nightgown?"

It was true, Christian was wearing a thick gown loosely tied at his waist, and beneath it his nightshirt. Christian laughed. "There might be one or two advantages of having the house empty of scolds. Right, what have we got?" Carter tipped one of the pots towards him to examine the contents, which turned out to be honey. The rest of the fayre, provided by Tilly, was basic but plentiful. Set out on the table were three types of cheese, bread, honey, ale, a high sided meat pie, and, from the griddle at the side of the kitchen oven, Harry was producing a neat pile of flat scones.

"Pass me some of those over here," Christian pointed towards the plate of scones. Richard, obliging, passed it along the table.

Christian selected four and dropped them onto his plate, drizzling honey from the pot on top of them.

Jack already had one in his hand, half eaten. "These are not too bad, lad." Jack smiled in Harry's direction and the lad grinned from ear to ear.

Carter cast a disparaging look in Jack's direction. "Harry is part of my household, and he's not your servant. I would appreciate it if you would remember that. He's told me you made him clean your boots."

Harry, his face bright red, turned his back on Carter and busied himself turning the cakes on the griddle.

Jack, his voice controlled, said, "I'm sorry if I have offended you, it'll not happen again."

"Just make sure it doesn't," Carter replied, his voice hard.

"Here, have some of these, while they are still warm," Richard said quickly, "you always were a grouch when you were hungry."

"Sometimes simple things make me a happy man," Christian said, folding one of the honey covered cakes in half and pushing it into his mouth.

"At least Anne need not worry that she'll return and find you nothing but a pile of skin and bone," Richard said dryly, slicing cheese from the block on the table.

Christian leant across the table and said, "I would be a more content man if she would leave my kitchens alone. There's a new fashion in London she's following and I'm forced to have fish and eels as the first meal of the day."

"Eels!" Richard exclaimed. "Not eels for breakfast. That'd even turn Jack's stomach, and he'll eat anything."

Richard received another plate of fresh hot scones from the fireside, and to Harry he said, "Jack'd eat his boots if the room was dark enough and he'd not notice."

Harry giggled with laughter.

"The damn things make me feel sick. But I can't tell her, can I?" Christian said morosely, then to Harry, "Do you think I could train that dog of yours to like eels, maybe I could slide them under the table to him?"

"I don't think so, sir, maybe the cat might though," Harry suggested helpfully.

"That's not a bad idea, you'll have to make sure the cat is under the table when I have my breakfast," Carter replied smiling at the boy.

Harry was eating the last of the scones, and Christian was idly scratching Harry's dog behind the ears. There was a strange calm to the morning, and none of them seemed keen to break it.

"This reminds me of when we used to go to Aunt Ado's in Cambridge. Do you remember?" Richard said, sitting back in the chair and making the wood creak.

Christian smiled. "Good Lord yes. We'd spend whole afternoons there, Adam kept on bringing us food and ale, and we just kept on eating. God knows where we put it all." He turned to Jack, "You'd have loved it. You paid her thruppence and you could stop all day, eat as much as you wanted, and you didn't have to leave until the bells struck for evensong."

"It was the company, not the food," Richard replied, "She was a wise old bird. Filled us up on bread and rye cakes and we'd have little room for ale or anything else."

"But she kept peat on the fire, and it was a damn sight warmer than it was in our rooms, remember?" Carter mused.

"Simpler times," Richard said, "Do you miss them?"

"Not often," replied Carter with honesty. "I can still acutely remember what it was like to not have enough coin in my purse to see the week out, and I like being my own master. Although you seemed to fare well enough? Always a scheme running if I remember rightly."

"I'm sure you don't," Richard replied smiling.

Carter's face split into a wide grin. "Do you remember that January when it was so cold in our rooms that even the piss froze in the buckets?"

Richard shook his head.

"Yes you do!" Christian turned to Jack and continued his tale. "It was bloody freezing. The snow was piled through the streets, and the winds whipping up a blizzard so they couldn't be cleared. We'd little money and nothing to spare for fuel for the fire. Christ, it was cold. Your brother disappears out of the window, he's gone for about half an hour, when he comes back he's carrying this great big bundle of long cut wooden slats. He disappears again and comes back with a second bundle. I didn't ask any questions. I didn't care as long as I was warm."

Jack, who knew his brother fairly well, had a good idea where this was heading. "Go on, where did he get them from?"

Carter threw Jack a sour look, it was clear he did not want him to be a party to the conversation, when he answered he directed his words toward Coleman and Richard. "The refectory roof! We went down the following morning and the place was filled with snow. The tables and benches had disappeared beneath it."

"Luckily we'd burned the evidence," said Richard grinning.

"Almost!" Carter began to laugh, "They found the foot prints leading across the roof to our window.

"So they caught him then?" Jack asked, turning to look at his brother.

"Did they hell as like!" Richard grinned, "I convinced the master that this was part of some plan to throw the blame upon us and the real culprits were elsewhere. Asking the master whether he really thought I would have been stupid enough to leave a trail of footprints in the snow leading to our room."

"And you got away with it? Even after that?" Jack asked, shaking his head.

"How was I to know it was going to stop snowing? I thought the tracks would be covered by the morning." Richard sounded hurt.

Soon after Christian, suitably attired and attended by his newest clerk, set off to the warehouse. Jack, relieved that Carter had left, remained at the house along with Coleman, Harry and two of Devereux's men.

✝

Jack heard the commotion and raised voices before he saw Harry, pursued by Coleman, running down the corridor towards him. The boy was carrying something in his arms and the Steward, hard on his heels, was trying to make a grab for the lad. Jack's first thought was that Harry had stolen something. Harry dived behind Jack, and the Steward was forced to abandon his pursuit.

"Give it here, Harry," the Steward said.

"No, I'll not," Harry shouted defiantly from behind Jack.

The Steward made to dive past Jack, but Jack, far quicker, flung his arms wide and blocked his path. "What's going on?"

"The dog's been run over, that's all. Harry'd rather see it suffer," Coleman growled.

"He's going to wring his neck, but he's mine!" Harry howled, and in his arms, wrapped in some Hessian sacking, the small white mongrel whimpered.

Jack, lifting back the sacking to better observe the creature within, asked, "What happened to him?"

"He ran under the blacksmith's cart, and it went over his leg," Harry couldn't quite contain a sob, "it's broken."

"*You* end the creatur's suffering, I tried. It's your problem now. But you can be sure I'll be telling Master Carter about this," Coleman grumbled at Harry, turning to stalk off down the corridor.

"Come on, bring him into the kitchen, I need a bit more light," Jack said, a gentle hand on the boy's shoulder.

At the end of the corridor they dropped down a few steps into the kitchen where Tilly was tying rue into even bunches at one end of the table.

"Right then, put him on the table," Jack said, pushing a bowl of eggs out of the way to make space.

"You're not putting a flea-ridden dog on my kitchen table!" Tilly said, rising and slapping down the rue on the table. "I'll tell Master Coleman. Get it off!"

"Hush your tongue, woman," Jack said, and under his unfriendly glare she sat down again in the chair, grumbling under her breath.

Lifting the sacking away it was fairly easy to see where the problem lay. One of the dog's front legs was clearly snapped, the bone had not come through the skin, but the splintered ends were making an ugly bulge in the flesh on the leg.

"What do you think?" Harry asked nervously, his arms reaching protectively to encircle the dog again.

"I think you are right. It's broken," Jack said, his big hand smoothing the fur down on the dog's head.

"Can you help him?" Harry asked.

Jack looked at the dog. Then back at the boy, and he changed his mind. "I can try."

Harry's eye's released a stream of relieved tears and he sat down heavily on the bench.

"I can see you're not going to be much help!" Jack said, grinning.

Harry wiped the back of his sleeve across his face twice to dry it. "Sorry sir."

Jack hid a smile and turned to Tilly at the end of the table. "I want some laudanum, have you any?"

"What! For a dog?" Tilly blurted.

"No, you simple witch, for me! Of course I want it for the dog! Have you got any?" Jack said.

"Mistress Anne would keep it locked in her cupboard, and she's not here now so I can't open it," Tilly said defensively.

"Is there an apothecary close to here?" Jack asked her.

Harry cut in, "Yes sir, in Silver Street, sometimes I go there on an errand for Master Carter."

"Good. Well go now and tell them I need laudanum, the smallest bottle they have will do," Jack instructed.

"You can't put that on Master Carter's account! I'm going to get the Steward," Tilly rose scattering rue heads to the floor.

"And you can pay for it with this," Jack continued producing a shilling as if the woman had not spoken. "Now go on, off with you."

Harry took the coin into his keeping and a moment later he had darted through the kitchen door.

"You'll not see that boy again now you've given him that much money, mark my words," Tilly said glaring at Jack.

"I believe I told you to hush your tongue, woman," Jack said warningly before returning his attention to the dog.

When Harry returned, his eyes were wide with fright when he saw the kitchen table was empty.

"He's over here," Jack spoke softly. He was sat in the chair he had ousted Tilly from, his legs stretched out before him and on his lap, curled up with one splinted leg jutting out was Harry's dog.

The dog was panting, tongue extended and eyes wide, its distress evident.

"Will he be alright?" Harry asked nervously as he approached.

"I don't know," Jack said, holding his hand out for the small brown pot Harry held. Taking it he shook some of the contents into his hand, scooped a little back into the pot and then before the dog could object opened its jaws wide and dropped the contents of his palm into the back of its mouth. Clamping the dog's jaws closed Jack rubbed its throat until he felt it swallow.

"He knows you and he needs to go somewhere quiet." Jack motioned for Harry to come closer. "Take him to my room; no one will look for you there. If anyone asks for you I'll tell them you are on an errand for me."

A grateful Harry lifted the shaking dog from Jack's lap and left the kitchen.

"It's not right what that lad gets away with," Tilly commented from the end of the table.

"Have you ever had a good word to say for anybody, woman?" Jack remarked, and before she could send a reply in his direction he announced that he was hungry, and if she knew what was good for her, she'd furnish Master Carter's guest with a plate of food.

✝

Tilly, half an hour later, a basket slung over her arm, was on her way back from the bakers armed with fresh loaves. She grumbled under her breath. Jack had eaten what bread there had been left, and she had been forced to go and get more. The miserable child was hiding in Jack's room with his damned dog, leaving her to do all the kitchen tasks on her own. There were extra mouths to feed now and Tilly was not getting any help – it was not fair. There was no point complaining to Coleman either; everyone knew Harry was the master's bastard, and the Steward had more sense than to take a rod to him.

She was about to round the corner into the street where Carter's house was when the basket was yanked from her arm. The harsh, sudden tug pulled her off balance, and Tilly fell to her knees, unable to save herself. The loaves tumbled out and were promptly stolen by two guttersnipes who disappeared instantly around the corner, the bread clasped close to their chests. Tilly was left in a heap, crying in the street. She sobbed loudly. No one stopped. Then a pair of boots presented themselves in front of her and a friendly voice said, "Mistress, are you hurt?"

Tilly looked up gratefully into a pair of warm grey eyes. A hand extended towards her and she took it.

†

It was some time before Morley could turn his attention again towards the Fitzwarrens. Cecil had occupied his time with more pressing matters; these had claimed both Morley's attention and his sleep for weeks. There was a division on the Privy Council, one he knew would never be reconciled, but one that his master, Cecil, had wanted an accounting of.

It had not been easy.

Privy Councillors were men of worth, possessing, on occasion, an arguably higher order of intelligence, and it had stretched Morley's skills of brokerage to obtain what he had needed. When his task was completed he knew, as did Cecil, who would support Elizabeth as Mary's heir, and under what circumstances that support would be freely given.

Morley had penned the report himself and presented it to his master. The document was short, and the few penned lines were a poor representation of the hours of work that had gone into its preparation. When Morley had handed it across the desk to Cecil he had watched carefully as his master had scanned the list of names, nodding. There had been a fleeting moment of annoyance as Cecil had announced that it was as he had supposed, and that Morley's report held no surprises. Morley though, didn't form a retort, he was well paid and if this was the report his master wished for then this was the one he would produce. Morley had suspected all along that what he had prepared was no more than a confirmation of what Cecil already knew. Morley was not a man to leave anything to chance, and this detailed preparation was a part of that process. Success rested in leaving nothing to chance and even less to speculation.

Morley had often mused that if Wyatt had counted Cecil amongst his supporters then the outcome of that event would have been a very different one. Wyatt's rebellion had failed primarily due to poor planning, and even poorer communication. Neither of these obstructions to success would have been an issue if Cecil had involved himself in the organisation.

†

Weeds skirted the wattle, stray grass seeds had taken up homes along cracks in the crooked timber frame and the door step was broken and sat askew. If he had not known any better Morley might have suspected that the building was derelict.

He already knew that Clement worked alone with his assistant Marcus Drover, and was not chambered with other lawyers. His previous enquiries at the courts, when he had been following the de Bernay case, had told him that Clement generally specialised in small legal matters such as property transfers and inheritances, but he was known mainly as a specialist in the recovery of debts. Morley knew that he had assisted Robert Fitzwarren twice: one instance had related to a serious assault he had been charged with and the second time with a debt he had owed to a silversmith.

Clement's reputation was not a shining one. His methods appeared to be legal but questionable, and he worked with some of the more notorious London debt collectors, including the worst of these, Myles Devereux. Producing writs, preparing cases, and keeping the Marshalsea debtors' gaol fully stocked seemed to be the lawyer's main source of income.

✝

Trouble was making its way through Clement's door far too often for the lawyer's liking, and now it arrived in the guise of a well-dressed Crown Servant by the name of Christopher Morley. Having delivered the news of the visitor to his master, Marcus made a neat and quick escape, a worried expression on his face.

Morley, smiling reassuringly, stepped further into the chaotic sea of files that undulated across the floor towards the desk. "You're certainly a busy man," remarked Morley, sidestepping a slightly higher pile and making his way along the narrow pathway towards the client's chair.

"Er... yes, please take a seat. How can I help?" Clement had risen from his chair and his voice, alive with nerves, was high-pitched and scratchy.

"I've a few questions to ask regarding one of your clients," Morley replied, lowering himself into the creaking chair he had been offered.

"Which client, sir?" Clement asked carefully. An unguarded look rippled across the little man's face, telling Morley that the lawyer knew exactly which client his query would be about.

"Fitzwarren," Morley supplied, his eyes locked onto Clement's face.

"Fitzwarren," Clement croaked. A variety of emotions settled momentarily on the lawyer's face before each one fled in the wake of its predecessor, growing apprehension, fear, and finally outright terror taking command of the small man's features.

"I understand your concerns, and I would ask you nothing relating to your professional dealings with Robert Fitzwarren," Morley said, raising a hand in a reassuring gesture.

"Of course, if I can be of any help?" Clement asked, still nervous, and his fingers, white-knuckled, fastened onto the edge of the desk.

Morley smiled. "There are some questions I have to place before Lord Fitzwarren and Robert Fitzwarren, unfortunately they are...unavailable at the moment. You have aided Robert, I believe, in furthering a charge he wishes to bring against his brother? Is that right?"

Clement swallowed. "Yes, there is a warrant for Richard Fitzwarren's arrest for treason, and Robert believes his brother, and half-brother, are complicit in his crimes."

Morley nodded. "It must be a distressing time for Lord Fitzwarren, to have his sons tether his family name to such a crime as treason."

Clement produced a small square of yellowed and frayed linen from a sleeve and applied it to his perspiring forehead. "I'm sure it must be."

"Indeed. His youngest son, Richard Fitzwarren, is becoming a byword for trouble," Morley, an adept reader of men, saw the fear in Clement's eyes and the breath catch in his throat. Like a hound with the scent of the hare, Morley, unsure where the trail was leading, pressed on, carefully selecting his next questions to see what else they may unlock. "Richard Fitzwarren seems to have begun to make a career out of opposing the Crown."

Clement remained stoically silent.

"Have you ever met the man?" Morley said suddenly.

Clement, unnerved by the question said, "Why would I have?"

"No reason, I didn't know how long you had worked for the family," Morley replied, "I thought perhaps you might have met him some time ago."

"From what I know, he is not in England, if he was I am sure he would have been brought to justice by now," Clement said, sounding suddenly hopeful.

Morley, detecting that Clement was very unhappy with the subject of Richard, sank his teeth in and pressed on, "That might very well be the case, we have heard a rumour that he might well be back in London so, as you say, it will only be..."

"In England..." Clement couldn't help himself.

Morley was forced to put his hand to his mouth, coughing quickly to disguise a laugh. "Apparently so, but from what I have heard from Robert the man is a fool. So I am sure his whereabouts will be soon discovered."

Clement visibly paled.

"Sir, are you quite alright?" Morley, feigning concern, partly rose from his seat. "Sit, you are looking quite unwell."

Clement did sit down - heavily. The hand that he placed on the chair arm to help guide himself into the seat shook visibly, and he had dropped the linen square to the floor.

"Can I call your servant? Perhaps a drink ..." Morley continued to fuss.

Clement waved his hand in the air, and a moment later, his thin voice said, "Robert Fitzwarren is a...difficult client, he would be most vexed if he found out his brother were in the country. Do you suspect both his brothers, Richard and Jack, are in London?"

Morley could not resist. "We do not know for sure, there have been some reports that Robert's half-brother has been seen, he seems to have quite a striking appearance. But as yet none of these have been confirmed. What we do know is that these men have always involved themselves in intrigue, so it would be wise to assume that they would be in London, or at least bound this way."

Clement gulped in air and his eyes cast nervously around the room as if seeking an avenue of escape.

"You seem nervous sir?" Morley said, and then went on to provide the excuse Clement needed. "I can understand that it must be a worry for you. Helping your client Robert to bring this charge of treason against Jack Fitzwarren has unfairly placed you in the middle."

"Quite so," Clement agreed, his hands fluttering in his lap.

"What I am trying to find out is if Robert has had any communication with Richard or Jack, and if he has any evidence to support the allegation against his bastard sibling."

"I cannot say for certain if he has met with him, it is not something he has mentioned, you would need to ask Master Fitzwarren I am afraid," Clement provided, his nervous fingers had captured the black serge of his lawyer's robe and were twisting it tightly.

"And the evidence, Sir. Why does Robert believe his half brother should also be charged with treason?" Morley asked, his brow furrowed his voice gentle and mildly confused.

"There is evidence that he has supported his brother, they are both wanted for murder, and both were together when Richard acted against the Crown. There is no reason to suppose that he was not complicit in his brother's crimes, and at the very least it would take a court of law to determine if he wasn't. It is a case that he should answer for, and if he has a defence, then he can provide it," Clement pronounced his lawyer's summary haltingly.

"It is a reasonable assumption, I suppose," Morley nodded in agreement. "If they are in London then it should not be too hard to find them. By all accounts Richard is not an easy man to miss in a crowd, marked out by his height and hair the colour of a canary apparently," Morley said, pressing his hands to the chair arms and looking very much like he was about to leave.

"It's the bastard who has that colouring, not Richard," Clement corrected.

"I thought you'd not met them?" Morley asked, his brows furrowed.

"I've not... Robert has told me," Clement replied, a little too quickly.

"Of course," Morley smiling rose from the chair. "I'll bid you good day, sir."

Morley began to thread his way between the walls of case files slowly back towards the door. "Did Robert ever find the de Bernay girl, or is he still continuing the fiasco without her?"

Clement gave a harsh laugh. "I've no idea where the girl is, and neither does he."

"Oh dear. I do hope you have not been a party to this impersonation of the plaintiff before the court?" Morley replied, his hand had been reaching for the door handle, but he stopped in the act.

Clement froze.

"I ... I'm not sure I know what you mean," Clement stuttered.

"Oh come now. I think you do. I was there when you presented Robert's case for the preliminary hearing, and the girl he brought was not Catherine de Bernay."

Clement threw his arms up in the air, wailed loudly and then clamped his hands over his face as if he were trying to block the world out. Morley made his way back silently across the room and retook his seat in the client chair.

"I think, Master Clement, that there are a few things you need to tell me. Don't you?" Morley said, his voice had lost its previous friendly tone.

"The Fitzwarrens are bastards to a man," wailed Clement, his face still covered with his hands.

"You might need to be a bit more choosy in who you add to your client roll in future," Morley pointed out unhelpfully. "Let's start with the de Bernay case, shall we? Why is Robert pressing a Chancery case for a writ of guardianship when he no longer has the girl?"

"I don't know, he's not told me," Clement let out a sob, "I had no choice, he threatened me, what could I do?

"Well that at least sounds like an honest reply. But surely you should not have involved yourself in this? At the very least you could be struck off the roll, and there is a more than a fair chance you could find yourself the subject of a prosecution. This is a crime, sir, and you know it," Morley sternly admonished.

When he dropped his hands away Morley could see that there were now genuine tears on Clement's face. His linen lost somewhere on the floor, he was forced instead to wipe his eyes, along with his wet nose, on the back of his sleeve. Morley waited patiently for Clement to collect his wits and settle his sobbing before he asked, "You have met Richard Fitzwarren, haven't you? Please think carefully before you furnish me with an answer."

Clement nodded his affirmation to the question.

"And Jack Fitzwarren? Have you met him?" Morley continued, and found himself delighted when Clement confirmed he had.

Clement continued to talk for nearly an hour, trying his utmost to extricate himself from the legal mire into which he had wandered. He told Morley that Jack had used a false name and had accumulated debts in London, he had tried to press William, his father to pay these, and then Robert. Neither of his family would honour his debts and Jack had ended up in Marshalsea. From there he had continued to try to pressure his family and Clement had been forced to intervene on Robert's behalf and assure Master Kettering, Marshalsea's Governor, that the debts would not be settled by the Fitzwarren family.

Somehow Jack had freed himself from Marshalsea and both Jack and Richard had held Robert's lawyer as responsible. When he had been in debtors' goal Master Kettering had directed some of his pleas for money to Robert Fitzwarren's lawyer, and that they had gone unheeded they blamed Clement for.

Clement had finished his tale, and if he was hopeful that this partial confession would be the end of his interrogation, he was about to be sadly disappointed.

"After Jack Fitzwarren escaped from Marshalsea, he came to see you, didn't he?" Morley asked.

"He threatened me. I told you, they blamed me for not getting Jack out of the gaol. They blamed me because his family did not pay," Clement said his head nodding quickly.

"So *they* threatened you? And what else?" Morley continued.

"What do you mean?" Clement looked genuinely confused.

"They came here, threatened you and then just left? Surely you don't expect me to believe that?" Morley crossed his legs and folded his hands in his lap, making it quite clear he had no intention of leaving in the near future.

"I was forced to pay them a large amount of money sir, that was the price of my safety," Clement replied. The lawyer licked his lips and his eyes involuntarily flicked to the drawer where he had kept the money he had paid Richard.

Morley nodded. "How much?"

"A hundred pounds!" Clement exclaimed. "I paid them a hundred pounds."

"And they left you alone. Then later Robert wishes to ensure a case is brought against his half brother for treason, and you readily agree because it will help to ensure your own safety," Morley summarised.

"Indeed, sir, that is the truth," Clement replied.

"Truth, sir, is something that we have had a lack of this afternoon, and I am not wholly convinced that I have a good measure of it now either," Morley replied coldly. "If there is more, you would be wise to tell me."

Clement repeated his story again, telling Morley there was no more.

Morley, knowing full well that Clement was still hiding something, left shortly afterwards fully aware that he would be returning to the lawyer's offices very soon.

✝

It had taken a week to arrive at their new destination. Edwin and Jon had supposed that they were travelling to Chichester when the road had turned south. Robert, as the Fitzwarren heir, had a sizeable manor there, and it made sense that this was their destination. Robert had another end point for their journey in mind. One that Edwin and Jon would never have guessed, and indeed William would never have even named it in his list of choices had he been asked.

When William had been granted the purchase of the monastic lands he had bought a huge swathe of farmland and forest that had formerly been part of the lands attached to Netley Abbey. The Abbey may have been dismantled but the remaining buildings had survived and were occupied by a tenant of William's who leased some of the land for his own benefit, while also supervising the tenants who rented the rest of it. Mark Todd and his family were living in what had formerly been the abbot's house, and that this was their final destination had come as a shock to Edwin and Jon.

Robert's men had ridden ahead, rooms had been prepared. A general excuse had been provided that the epidemic sweeping London and some of the northern counties made this a safe retreat for William. Robert believed the elderly Lord now required peace and somewhere like Netley could ensure that.

The man who had introduced himself when they arrived was Master Todd, and he took Edwin and Jon to see the rooms that were available for the Lord's use. William was left seated in the hall, a thick blanket around his shoulders, a small hunched form, abandoned near the remains of a cooking fire. The hall, rush-spread, filled with too many hounds and with every corner and wall supporting broken farm detritus, felt more like a barn.

The house was in a reasonable state of repair. It became immediately obvious when Edwin and Jon were shown the rooms that had been set aside for William that these had, until very recently, been occupied by someone else. In their haste to remove themselves not all their personal items had gone with them.

There were two adjoining rooms, in the corner of one a garderobe venting to the outside. One room was a bedchamber with a good-sized bed, two chairs against the wall under the wooden window shutters, a tall set of open shelves sat against an opposite wall. Two high-backed chairs, upholstered and wool filled, both more than a little threadbare, sat on either side of the fire. The fire itself was set into the wall, a sandstone hearth protruded into the room with an iron rail set around the edge.

There were three entrances to the room. To the left-hand side of the fire an oblong wooden door was set into the masonry, behind it was a steep, narrow spiral staircase. It gave private access to the main hall on the floor below, but it would be of little use to William. He could not make it up the stairs, and they were too narrow and treacherous for either Edwin or Jon to carry him up. The other entrance was through a larger door in the opposite corner that led out into a wide, short corridor.

The room itself was fairly comfortable. Set along the left-hand side were three tall windows and they gave a pleasant view of the land rolling away to the distant hills. The floor was covered with a dusty rug and in days long gone by it had probably served as a solar, a light airy room to sit and read in when the weather was poor. A further room to the right was also available for William; square, furnished with two low straw-mattressed beds and another, smaller, fireplace set into the wall. This would be Edwin and Jon's room. One wall, to the right of the fireplace was stained green, and glistened, the roof obviously leaked and the water had been running down the wall for some time. This whole section of soaked wall had been eroded of plaster, and the wet, dark algae-clad bricks winked at them in the gloom. The room smelt damp, and the air was laden with moisture.

At the end of the solar was a final door that lead to a wide stone staircase. It was still a spiral, but the steps were low and the spread wide enough for Jon and Edwin to carry William up.

"Christ! He's not going to like this," muttered Edwin to Jon as he returned to the main room with the large bed in it.

"It'll be a lot nicer when we get a fire going," Jon tried to sound cheery.

"I thought we'd be going somewhere a bit better than this," Edwin complained.

Jon had moved across the room and pulled open one of the wooden window shutters. When he went to open the second he found the bottom hinge had rotted through and the shutter, unsupported now by the sill, swung from the wall on its top hinge. It banged loudly on the wall, sending a flurry of loosened plaster to the floor. Jon, cursing, jumped backwards.

"God's bones! Will you look at that!" Edwin exclaimed. He had flipped back the covers on the bed. An aged and thread-pulled embroidered coverlet was camouflaging a stained straw-filled mattress, and his faced twisted in a grimace.

Jon moved to stand looking over his shoulder and elbowed him, laughing. "It'll look a damn sight worse than that when the old Lord has shat in it for a week!"

Edwin turned and gave Jon a withering look. "He shouldn't have to put up with this in the first place, no matter what it will look like after a week. Go and find out where Walt is and get him to bring up some firewood, I'll go and see if they've any linen."

"Linen!" Jon snorted through his nose, "you'll be bloody lucky."

Edwin's requests were, as Jon had predicted, defeated. One of Robert's men who had travelled with them informed him curtly that he could request anything he needed and it would be sent from William's London house, but until it arrived they would need to make do with what the manor had to offer.

Edwin had provided a verbal list to the man of some immediate essentials, but after a few moments he got the distinct impression that the man was taking little notice, and that his words were wasted. Still he reaffirmed his request for the Lord's linen, silver plate and his chair to be sent for as soon as was practicable.

If William had any opinions on his current situation he was keeping them to himself. Edwin had waited along the journey for a characteristic loss of temper, for abuse to be hurled at him either physical or verbal. When none came, when after a week he realised that he was now caring for no more than a weak, frail old man, he felt shame. He wasn't sure if it was for himself, having to serve such a pitiable master, or for William who was being treated so badly by Robert. Edwin had heard the arguments between them, the raised words, the shouts of anger and cries from his master when Robert had struck his father. What the exact reason was he did not know, although he could guess at it. Robert wanted to be Lord Fitzwarren, he wanted his inheritance and the wrinkled, decrepit shrunken form of his father stood in his way. Edwin could think of no other reason why William had been removed from London. He had been sent away to one of his rotting estates to die. What was worse, Edwin had finally realised, was that himself, Jon and Walt were also going to be stuck here until the old Lord was laid to rest and they could be released from their task. And that could be years!

†

Robert's men had left them the day after they had arrived, leaving them alone in the house with Master Todd and his family. They had obviously had to give over the two rooms on the top floor and his sour-faced wife, now relegated with her husband to a room on the floor below, was less than happy about the turn of affairs. The fact that Lord William owned the house and everything she could see and touch around her was a concept Mistress Todd did not seem able to grasp.

When Edwin had politely enquired about food for his master she had stared at him blankly. Then she'd produced a cooking pot and curtly informed him that he if wanted food then he'd have to cook it. It was then that Edwin had finally realised the situation he was in. They had filed William away on the top floor until he died.

"What are we going to do?" Edwin said to Jon after he had told him about Mistress Todd's response to his request for food.

"I'll find Master Todd, he can't just expect us to starve, can he?" Jon replied.

"This whole farm belongs to William, they can't just deny him – can they?" Edwin replied.

"Well, they just did. Edwin, think about it, if they are not prepared to even feed him do you think we'll be getting any pay? And who is going to feed us?" Jon said, his voice filled with concern.

Edwin paled. It hadn't even occurred to him that they, as servants, would be excluded as well. "But they have to. They brought us here. They can't just leave us without."

Jon raised his eyebrows. "Edwin, Robert's men have gone."

"I gave them a list of items to be sent from London, maybe when that arrives there'll be something for us?" Edwin sounded hopeful.

The pair sat in silence after that. Edwin was fairly sure William had already been forgotten about, as had they. He approached Master Todd who conceded to supply victuals to Edwin, although it was his responsibility to cook them, Master Todd pointing out that was why he and Jon had been brought from London. Looking after the elderly Lord was far too much of a burden for his already overworked wife.

†

Jon had a wife in London. After three weeks when he fully realised that they had been forgotten about, and that nothing was being sent from London, he left. Worse, he took Walt with him. The boy, an outsider marked out by his accent and the blind eye that Robert had given him, had suffered at the hands of the Todds. When Jon had found Master Todd's children standing around Walt beating him with sticks it had been too much and the following day they left. Jon had a little money of his own and if he was thrifty was sure it would be enough to get them back to London.

Edwin, crouched down, stirred a wooden spoon in the cooking pot set above the logs in the hearth.

"I heard you talking. I know Jon and the boy have gone." William had said little since they had arrived, and shocked Edwin jumped when he heard the frail voice.

"They've gone back to London, master," Edwin replied.

"And you stayed?" William asked.

Edwin was at once both confused and concerned. "Of course, My Lord."

William emitted a rough laugh. "If that was a title I once had, I think it would be fair to say I have been stripped of it now."

Edwin, biting his bottom lip, returned his attention to the cooking pot.

†

Master Kettering had his offices far too close to his work, at least that was

Morley's opinion. He'd been shown to Kettering's office efficiently, the man had offered him a seat, but all the time Morley was aware of the incredibly unpleasant aroma of the prison eking into the room. He had to suppose you got used to it over time. Perhaps Cecil's offices, which were not too far removed from The Tower prisons, had the same stench.

The questions he had asked Kettering so far had led to abrupt dead-ends. Kettering had never had any prisoners under his care by the name of Fitzwarren. He had heard of lawyer Clement, but that didn't prove to be of much use. In the current year alone the scrawny little lawyer's name had been associated with no less than ten debtors' cases under consideration.

"I wish I could be of more help," Kettering replied, his hands spread wide in an apologetic gesture.

"It appears I have been misinformed," Morley said, a tight smile on his face and his mind already on a conversation he would shortly be having with Clement.

"I never forget a name, or a debt, come to that," Kettering was saying. "Of course, it's all written down in the ledger, but I've got it all in here." Kettering tapped his cranium with a narrow finger.

Morley was about to rise from the chair, but Kettering's words stopped him. "Never forget a debt eh?"

Kettering smiled. "Never."

"This debtor would have been one owing a lot of money. Maybe the name was different," Morley prompted, hoping there might still be something to be gained from the meeting.

Kettering nodded. "It could be. Do you have a date for this debt?"

"Three years ago, in March. What debtors did you have owing large amounts then?" Morley asked.

"An interesting year! We had the Earl of Marlbrough's son, Henry, three times no less, but he's not your man," Kettering said laughing.

"Three times!" Morley raised a disapproving eyebrow.

"Gambling," Kettering muttered shrugging his shoulders.

"The sin of fools," Morley agreed. "Any others?"

"A few. Master Haden who sold his tannery business to two separate buyers, that was a debt of seventy-five pounds, then we had one other, Kilpatrick..." Kettering's brows knitted together, "There was something there, his wife provided some money for him and his brother redeemed the debt, but there was something odd about that case."

As Morley watched Kettering went to a side table and retrieved a leather ledger. "Here we go... March," his finger trailed down a list of entries until he found the one he wanted, thumping the page with his hand when he did. "This is it, Master John Kilpatrick. What was unusual was his wife asked for him under a different name. I'll be damned now if I can remember what that was, but we only found him by the description she gave."

"Go on," encouraged Morley.

"Blond as a Dane," Kettering replied.

"Would the lawyer attesting to the debt have been Clement by any chance?" Morley found himself holding his breath.

Kettering slid his finger sideways along the neatly penned line. "Yes, it was one of Clement's. And he collected the debt in person six weeks after it had been paid."

"Was it a hundred pounds by any chance?" Morley suddenly felt the small pieces of the puzzle begin to order themselves.

Kettering raised his eyes from the ledger. "Yes. Yes it was!"

"May I?" Morley rose from the chair and crossed the room to where the ledger sat on the table. The penmanship was neat, orderly and crisp. Morley squinted at it, but still he could hardly read it. Soon he'd be like Cecil with a pair of spectacles permanently gracing his nose. "Do you mind?" Morley asked,

"Not at all," Kettering turned the ledger towards Morley so he could see it more clearly.

"There we go," Morley leaned forward, smiling as his eyes focused on letters, and sure enough there was Clement's signature, next to the amount of one hundred pounds.

CHAPTER TEN

†

Christian's delight over Richard's introduction to the Court Head of Procurement continued, and, with Richard in tow in the guise of his clerk, he had attended some preliminary meetings, from which he had returned heady with excitement at the coming trade prospects.

His wife Anne remained at her mother's house, and despite several pleas, Christian had steadfastly refused to let her return. His reason had more to do with Richard's continued presence in his house rather than the epidemic that was still biting at the lives of Londoners. Richard was a man Anne disliked and disapproved of, and he would prefer that his wife did not know that he was in London again.

There was little to do, and it was a waiting game that preyed more on Jack's nerves than it seemed to on Richard's.

✝

The evening had darkened to night. Tilly had cleared the table of the remains of the meal and set between them a fresh jug of ale. Jack produced his worn deck of cards.

"Why not," Richard said as he watched Jack shuffle the deck.

"Are you two in?" Jack addressed Carter and Coleman who were also seated at the table. Carter nodded, and Coleman smiled broadly, obviously pleased to have been invited. Carter was still rebuffing Jack's overtures of friendship, making it quite clear that he had no great liking for him.

"My deck, so Primero," Jack announced and sent the cards across the table to land in front of the players.

Carter grinned at Richard, he'd deposited a coin in the centre of the table and was gathering his cards together. "I've not played Primero for years. Anne disapproves of card playing, there's not a deck in the house."

"Really?" Richard sounded quite shocked, while Jack sent each player a final card from the deck.

"Sadly yes. Anne believes gambling is a fool's game," Carter said, carefully rearranging the cards in his hand.

"She's right," Richard said.

"It's only a fool's game when you lose," Carter replied, his fingers tapping on the table, a thoughtful look on his face. Sending a second coin to the pot in the middle of the table he accepted another card from Jack, tucking it securely into his neatly fanned hand.

"Be warned, Jack. Christian might not have played for years, but he used to supplement his income with his card winnings," Richard said to Jack.

Carter laughed, "We both know that's not true."

Carter won the first hand, Jack the second and third. The deck had been played through now, and once the game was in progress it would no longer be shuffled. Jack dealt another hand, placed the deck down and turned over the top card. A three of clubs. Richard needed a four of diamonds, and that card should be three from the top of the face down deck. It would be Jack who would get the opportunity to take that card after Carter and Coleman had taken theirs.

Coleman discarded an eight of spades face up, and Jack's hand hovered, indecisive. Then, predictably, he went for the chance victory, and took the unknown card from the top of the deck. Richard, watching him carefully, recognised the disappointment on his brother's face. The new card was not going to offer him a quick win. Jack held the card and tapped it against the table, his eyes flicking between his hand, the new card and the eight of spades Coleman had discarded.

Reaching a sudden decision, Jack cast down the newly selected card on top of the eight of clubs.

Richard automatically began to reach for it and suddenly stopped.

The card Jack had laid on the table was a five of spades.

That was wrong! It should have been the four of diamonds, and after the four of diamonds the six of clubs. Richard reached for the deck and took the top card into his keeping.

Seven of diamonds.

Where in the sequence was the seven of diamonds? His mind ran through the cards, it should have been between the Queen of Diamonds and ... and he couldn't remember.

"Richard..."

"Richard, it's your turn," Jack's voice revived his attention. The card sitting face up on the top of the discarded pile was a two of spades.

Richard folded his hand and abandoned it on the table.

Coleman, delighted, won the game, sliding the coins towards him underneath his palm.

Jack gathered in the cards, reunited the pack, and began to deal the cards out.

Richard held his hand up.

Jack shrugged and sent his card instead to Carter who sat to his left.

By the end of four more games Richard could feel a dull ache settling uncomfortably at his temples. Jack was not shuffling the deck, and despite a second run through of all the cards he still could not place them. The argument between his belief in what the cards should be and where they actually were was one his mind was refusing to accept.

Rising from the table he left them to their game.

†

Allocated a room on the same level, but given discrete distance from Carter's own, Richard was glad on occasion for the solitude. Laid on his back, his eyes watched the fitful and fastidious spider above him as it worked on its geometrical perfection. It did not pause. Did not vary from its purpose. Moving outwards from the centre, slowly it created its wheel-like spiral web.

Then it would wait.

Its plan executed, its trap in place. But what if the window stayed closed and there were no insects? What if the errant fly failed to catch in the trap? Did the spider care? Did it worry? Or did it wait until it had starved to death? Did it pin its life on planning and execution and leave the final outcome to chance?

How many webs does a spider have to make before it catches a fly? How many webs were strung between branches in trees and dashed by the wind? How many clung to door frames to be destroyed in the morning when they were opened? How many spiders were scared from their constructions half way through by a hungry bird?

A lot.

But there were still spiders. They still survived, even though their food rested on the tiny chance of a small fly hooking itself in the sticky trap. Spiders were, on the whole, he concluded successful, even if chance was playing a large role in their survival.

An interesting thought.

His own rule was that nothing should be left to chance and maybe this was where he was going wrong. Maybe man could not, or should not, seek to control every outcome. Was that why success was constantly out of his reach? Had God shut the window and kept the flies out?

Was this why he could no longer predict the contents of a deck of cards? Was he being taught a lesson in control?

Richard rolled over, picked up the cup. Realising it was empty he fished for, and found, the bottle of aqua vitae on the floor. Pushing himself up on the bed he was about to refill the cup. His shoulders slumped and instead he sent it flying across the room, watching it bounce from the wall and roll to a stop at the foot of the door. It would be quicker if he bypassed the cup.

Inclining the bottle he tipped a third of the contents into his throat, feeling the raw spirit send something akin to warmth down his throat. He knew he'd stop only when he lost consciousness, when the bottle slithered from his hand, and his mind slipped into the blessed empty darkness.

✝

Jack, with nothing to do, was becoming a liability in the small house, and Christian, despite Jack's best efforts, had yet to express any liking for him and regularly cast disparaging glances in his direction. Harry, however, was of an age when he was readily and easily impressed by this new addition to the household. Jack, armed with much more than the pens that were the tools of Carter's trade, and exuding a hard professional soldier's competence was an attraction that Harry could not resist. His master might have told him on several occasions to avoid Jack's company, but the draw was too much.

Harry walked past Jack, flipping a coin into the air, and whistling brightly. He'd not seen Jack, who neatly snatched the coin from the air.

"Hey, that's mine," Harry complained.

"Here, you go," Jack flipped it from his thumb and Harry captured it between both hands. "What are you doing with a sixpence, lad?"

"Master Fitzwarren said I could have it," Harry said, sliding the coin away defensively.

"Did he now?" Jack hadn't seen Richard all morning and he'd assumed he was with Carter. "Why did he do that?"

"He asked me to go buy him some bottles from The Ship at the end of the

Street, and said I could keep what money was left," Harry replied truthfully.

Jack groaned. "How many?"

Harry looked confused.

"Don't worry lad, you're not in trouble. How many bottles?"

"Two," Harry replied, "I took them to him in his room this morning."

Jack ruffled the boy's hair, and then found another coin of his own which he flipped towards Harry. "That's yours, and let's keep this little story between ourselves. There's no need to tell Coleman or Master Carter?"

Harry nodded, his eyes on the second sixpence he now owned.

✝

Jack stood in the corridor and looked at the door to Richard's room, debating whether or not to open it. His brother only drank like this when something was wrong. Once, he'd told Jack he did it because it was the only way to stop his thoughts, and that some of them burned in his head like fire. He'd not been overly lucid when he'd made that confession, as

Jack recalled. Should he leave him be? Let him find some peace inside a bottle?

He was about to turn away when Lizbet's voice rattled around the inside of his head noisily.

Jack, you can't leave him, he could be blind drunk, drowning in his own vomit!

How many times had he let Lizbet deal with him? A few. He didn't hit her, he didn't abuse her. But he supposed she was used to dealing with drunk men. Squaring his shoulders he tapped on the door.

Nothing.

"Richard," Jack added the word to the next, louder rap on the door.

Silence.

"Oh, for God's sake!" Jack grasped the handle and pushed the door open, it sent a cup drumming across the floor boards to bounce off the wall under the window. His brother was on his knees, head on the window sill, one hand on the opener, asleep.

"What are you doing. For God's sake it's not even noon?" Jack closed the door behind him, his voice exasperated.

The man propped against the wall didn't move. "Richard, come on you can't stop there."

Jack shook his brother's shoulder, and for a moment Richard's eyes flicked partially open. "What are you doing? If

Carter hears about this he'll not be happy."

Richard's gaze, blearily drunk, followed his hand up to where the fingers still rested around the window opener. "Letting the flies in." His hand pushed the window open, then his head dropped with a hard crack onto the stone of the sill, and his eyes closed again.

"Oh, for God's sake!" Jack repeated, exasperated, and realised that Richard was suffering just as badly from this forced waiting as he was. A hand under each of his inert brother's arms, he picked him up and dropped him on the bed. On the floor were the two bottles Harry had brought from The Ship. One was empty and Jack discarded it back on the floor, the other, when he shook it, proved to still be a third full, and Jack poured that out of the open window before closing the door and leaving his brother to a dreamless sleep.

When he got back to the bottom of the stairs near the kitchen he found Harry waiting for him.

"Do you think he might need me to go and get him another bottle from The Ship?" Harry asked, obviously hopeful of making himself a little more profit.

"No, Harry, I think he has enough. And remember – this is our secret," Jack said tapping his nose conspiratorially.

Harry nodded enthusiastically and tried to match Jack's stride as he headed towards the kitchens. Jack hid a grin and shortened his paces. "Come on, I'm starving, let's find out if there is anything to eat."

There were oatcakes, and Harry lifted down the honey pot from a shelf and put it between them on the table.

"Tell me the story about the Turks again, go on please," the boy pleaded, elbows on the table and his knees on the bench.

"Again?" Jack said, exasperated. "It doesn't change you know."

"Go on, tell me about the battle with the Turks. That's the one I like the best!" The boy leaned across the table and tugged Jack's sleeve.

"I can't keep on telling you the same story. Soon I am going to make a mistake and get my facts wrong," Jack complained, adding honey to the top of an oatcake.

"No you won't, please," Harry pleaded.

"Haven't you got work to do?" Jack said, changing the subject abruptly.

Harry looked suddenly crestfallen. "I suppose I do."

Jack relented at the sight of Harry's expression. "One last time."

The boy smiled in delight.

"Grab some of those oatcakes and we'll go and sit in the sun," Jack said, rising.

Harry, a handful of crumbling cakes, followed Jack out into the kitchen garden. Jack settled himself with his back against the wall, stretched his legs out in front of him, crossing his feet. He suppressed a smile when Harry, settling next to him, adopted the same position.

Jack leaned over and helped himself to one of the biscuits from Harry's grubby hands. "We were on a ridge high up above the sea looking down into the bay..."

"That's not the start, you started down near the sea, with the Turks coming towards you from the ships," Harry interrupted, his words negotiating their way around a mouthful of crumbling pastry.

"Whose story is this?" Jack rebuked, giving the boy a friendly shove, "This time I'm starting way back at the beginning, before the Turks landed."

✝

Richard was in his room, having returned with Carter from his offices, and Jack was determined to talk to him. Richard only ever drank to those excesses when something had happened, when there was something he didn't wish to face. And Jack wanted to know what shit was heading their way this time. He'd brooded over it all day, there was something his brother was keeping from him, and Jack badly wanted to know what it was.

Jack's knock on the door was a formality only, and he immediately opened it, finding his brother seated on the edge of the bed in the process of pulling his boots from his feet.

Richard cast an annoyed glance in Jack's direction. "Well?"

There was a small table set against the wall, and Jack leant against it folding his arms. "I want to know why you got drunk?"

Richard pulled the boot from his foot and discarded it with a bang on the floor. "Does it matter?"

"Yes, it does," Jack said forcefully.

"And do I interrogate you every time I find you insensible?" Richard shot back.

"We both know what you are like. You drink like a man who wants to die, and you only do that when something has happened, usually bad, so tell me, what's happened?" Jack said, shocking himself by his own directness.

"Nothing has happened," Richard said, then relenting added, "You have no need to worry."

"Don't I?" Jack said sceptically, then when he didn't get a reply he tried a different track, "Try honesty. Why did you drink two bottles of the worst aqua vitae in an hour?"

Richard pulled the second boot from his foot and with his head lowered he regarded the floor between his feet. "Sometimes, Jack, I can't think. My mind doesn't work, I can't plot a course, I can't plan, all I can see is the immediacy of the situation before me."

Jack, sounding confused, said, "I don't know what you mean?"

Richard let out his breath suddenly, and loudly. "Like when we were playing cards. I should know what's in your hand, what's in Carters, where the aces are in the unplayed deck. And I don't, not any more, I can't order my thoughts."

"Is that all?" Jack was hugely relieved.

Richard looked up, anguish on his face. "What do you mean is that all?"

"I thought something had happened, that you'd had news of Andrew, or worse, from Malta, or of Lizbet. I was worried you were keeping something from me," Jack spoke with evident relief.

"I was," Richard said wearily.

Jack laughed then. "So, you can't card count any more! Welcome to the world I live in! I've never been able to do it. I thought the other night when I won a few games you were just being overly generous."

"It's not just cards, Jack," Richard said.

Jack managed to stop himself from making a quick and thoughtless reply. After a minute he said. "Times have not been easy, especially not for you. What happened to you wasn't your fault. Lizbet thought she was helping, just give yourself more time."

"Maybe," Richard accepted.

"And another thing?" Jack added.

"Go on," Richard replied his voice wary.

"Eat some more, will you. If I shook you I'd be left with a pile of bones," Jack said, smiling.

†

It was Sunday, Christian was working in his office in the house, and Jack, after helping Coleman finish the gate repairs, was sitting again in the lee of the wall in the kitchen garden. His knees drawn up, a pie balanced on one of them and a cup of ale in his hand on the other, engaged again in retelling a story to his small, but eager audience.

"...and what did you do next?" Harry asked Jack.

There was the sudden sound of boots crunching on the gravel of the path from the kitchen door. Jack, a hand shading his eyes from the sun, saw his brother approaching.

"Have I interrupted Jack's story on how he saved all of Malta from the Turkish invasion?" Richard said, dropping to sit next to Jack.

"No, sir," Harry replied.

"And you," Jack said pointedly to Richard, "weren't there."

"True." Richard leaned around Jack and said to Harry, "Master Coleman is looking for you, and I told him I'd seen you in the stables, you might want to make your way there."

Harry was on his feet in a moment. "Thank you, Sir."

They both watched the boy dart across the kitchen garden and disappear through a gap in the wall into the stable yard on the other side.

Jack turned an inquisitive and somewhat disapproving gaze on his brother.

Richard returned the appraising look with one of his own, grey and curiously limpid. "What?"

"Andrew might never arrive, he could be dead. Malta is a long way from London, perhaps something happened?" Jack vocalised the thought that was haunting both of them. "How long do we wait?"

"We wait until we know what happened to him. I'll not leave Christian, I would never forgive myself," Richard replied.

On the other side of wall they could hear the sound of Harry's high-pitched laughter.

"He reminds me of me," Jack said laughing.

Richard picked up a pebble from the ground and sent it skittering across the gravel path. "The lad's bright enough, his only flaw is that he thinks the sun shines out of your ..."

The scream was panicked and penetrating. Both men were on their feet in a moment.

Richard, a hand against the wall, pushed himself forward into a run, a stride ahead of Jack he reached the break in the wall where Harry had disappeared through earlier.

The scene in the yard was one of utter chaos. A horse, still attached to a cart, was rearing. The wagon bed had smashed back into the well in the centre of the yard, shearing off the whole wooden structure.

The scream had become a terrified choking wail.

"When the cart hit the well it knocked him in," Coleman bellowed, trying, and failing, to fasten a hold on the rearing horse's bridle.

"Where's the rope?" Richard peered over the side of the well and could see the boy below, arms above his head, sobbing and trying to grasp hold of the side of the well shaft.

"The rope's gone down with the bucket," Coleman called, having finally got a hand wound round the horse's halter. The animal had stopped rearing, and the cart was no longer careening dangerously across the yard.

Jack was already halfway over the stone ledge of the well shaft.

"Go. I'll find a rope," Richard darted across the yard towards the tack room leaving Jack to climb down the shaft.

"Keep hold of the side, lad," Jack called down to him.

It was narrow enough for him to have a foothold on either side of the shaft, the top ten feet were easily navigable, but then the moss and stunted ferns took over and the stones became furred and lethally slippery.

Harry let out another gurgling scream.

Jack doubled his pace. The brickwork of the shaft was roughly finished and between the stones there were ample ledges and holds. Finding another gap for his right foot he stepped down quickly, his hand seeking out another hold in the darkness of the well shaft. His boot, the sole smooth leather, slipped on the edge of the stone. Nails raked down the stonework, fingers fastened on a stone ledge, halting his fall momentarily until the friable edge of the rock broke away. Skin peeled from the palm of one hand as it dragged past the coarse rock, his descent halted suddenly when his boot jammed against a course of masonry jutting from the cylindrical shaft, ten feet above Harry's head.

The boy beneath him was crying, one hand grasping the wall, the other reaching futilely up towards him.

The well shaft from this point down was cut into the rock, there were no ledges or gaps where the mortar had fallen away, the sides of the shaft smooth sandstone, coated in an algae as slippery as eel skin.

Harry lost his hold on the rock. His cry was cut off as his head slid beneath the water.

Jack had no choice. Lowering himself as far down from the last brick course as he could, he hung by his hands for a second before he dropped into the cold well water at the bottom of the shaft. The icy water clamped a tight hold on his chest, and the air in his lungs gasped from his body. If he'd hoped his feet would find the bottom he was disappointed, the shaft was deep and tapped into a subterranean spring. His head breached the surface, air refilled his lungs, and he frantically felt beneath the water for the boy.

Please God, don't let him drown.

Above him he could hear his brother's voice, but around him nothing. Nothing! Just the noise he was making in the water.

Harry!

The back of his hand banged into the soft form of Harry and a moment later he had hold of his body and the boy's head was dripping next to his own.

"Harry, Harry!" Jack shook him, but the body remained limp in his arms.

No, no, no!

Jack shook him again. Nothing.

"What do I do?" The shout was directed up over at his brother.

Before Richard could answer Harry's eyes opened, unfocused and glazed, and he retched, spewing well water down Jack's back.

"God lad! Christ you scared me half to death! Just keep your arms around my neck. Richard'll have a rope down to us soon enough." Jack, his own body shaking, had one arm clamped tightly around the boy and another holding on to the wall.

Looking up he saw the light dim as his brother leaned over the wall and prepared to let down a rope. The first rope was too short and they were forced to wait, immersed in the cold water while Richard spliced two ropes securely together and lowered the longer length down to Jack.

"Put it under his arms and I'll pull him up," Richard called down from above.

The rope had been tied in a loop already and Jack slipped it over the boy's head and under his arms. "Put your arms up, and hold the rope, and as Richard pulls you keep your feet on the wall." Harry nodded, and Jack watched from below as the boy was hoisted from the well.

He was more than a little thankful when the rope dropped back down the shaft a second time. With Richard's help from above, and Coleman also hauling on the rope, he soon had his hands on the wall that circled the well entrance. Then a none too gentle hand grabbed onto him and pulled him over the edge.

"Is he alright?" Jack looked to where Harry was sitting in a spreading pond of water shaking, tears pouring down his face.

Richard scooped the boy up. "Let's go and see if that kitchen fire is on and have a proper look at you, shall we?"

Coleman followed them in, bellowing orders for hot water and warm clothes. The noise soon reached Carter where he had been working in his office.

"What happened?" Carter burst through the kitchen door. "Coleman said Harry fell down the well?"

"The lad did, but it wasn't his fault. One of the horses reared and he got knocked in," Richard returned his attention to one of Harry's hands that he was examining, "Hold still lad, and let me see, it's a bad cut but I think it will be alright. You've properly covered yourself in lumps and bumps falling in there haven't you."

Carter looked then at Jack who was sat dripping still, arms wrapped around himself shivering. "Good Lord – did you end up in the well too?"

"Well, I couldn't send Richard down there, he can't swim!" Jack said grinning at the boy, who smiled back.

"What are you trying to say?" Richard adopted a hurt expression, "Next time I'll leave you at the bottom and you can climb out on your own."

Richard, satisfied that the boy's injuries were minor, sat back and regarded his brother across the table. "Any scraped knees you want me to look at?"

Jack threw his brother a sour look, then sniffed loudly and followed this with a monumental sneeze. "No, but you could find something to warm my insides."

"Yes, I'll get something for both of you." It was Carter who answered and then scurried from the room, returning a moment later with a bottle from his study.

"You get some of that inside you, lad, and it'll soon take your mind off your cold feet," Jack reverentially poured a measure into a cup and handed it over to a wide-eyed Harry.

Harry put the cup to his mouth, took a large gulp, and gasped as the liquor burned his throat and then set a course down through his innards.

"Told you!" Jack laughed.

"Drink it slowly, lad," Carter said, then he turned on Tilly who sat wide-eyed and gawping at the end of the kitchen. "Can't you see these two are half frozen, couldn't you at least get a fire on rather than standing there staring at them, woman!"

Carter poured a second cupful, handing it to a shaking Jack. "I think I owe you an apology, sir."

Jack met Carter's eyes, his blue eyes filled with relief. "You owe me none. I was glad to be able to help."

☨

Richard judged that if he did not remove Jack from the house in the near future there was going to be a calamity. Either he was going to incite Harry to some reckless act that Christian would disapprove of, goad his steward into violence, or start an unnecessary argument with their host or himself that would lead to nothing but acrimonious regret. Jack, bored, was almost as unpredictable as Jack, hungry.

Carter had been as scandalised by the suggestion as Jack was delighted. The prospect of spending the evening in the Angel variously enjoying female company and cards put Jack in an irrepressibly good mood for the whole day. Christian, on the other hand, was dealing with the event in a wholly different manner. Outwardly shocked by Richard's suggestion, but nervously delirious about the prospect which amused Richard.

There was still a degree of danger to their passage across London which leant an even greater thrill to the event. Should they be apprehended there would be little doubt that capture would lead to their demise. They took a circuitous route through the city, cloaked and silent, and made their way quickly to the street where the Angel nestled anonymously between two respectable black framed buildings adorned with diamond panes and lime-washed wattle.

"You're sure Robert is not going to be here?" Jack had asked as they made their way across the city.

"He's away from the city, at Cousin Harry's father's, by all accounts," Richard reassured, and then he added, "I don't think he'd ever dare to show his face again in the Angel after what we did to him last time he was there."

Carter, nervous, hung back behind Jack while Richard advanced and knocked firmly on the door. A well used wooden panel slid sideways, and before it had been replaced the noise of the metal latches on the other side of the door being withdrawn could be heard.

They made a quick entrance and the door was closed, latched, and secured before the huge form of the doorkeeper turned, grinning. "Master Fitzwarren, it's good to see you sir, and your brother," Nathan whistled through his broken teeth, folding his bare arms over a muscled chest. The knuckles, several askew, whitened with scars, bore testament to his efficiency as the door keeper at the Angel.

"If I remember, last time, we never did get to have that game of cards. Perhaps this time?" Richard said.

"If you've time," accepted Nathan.

A perfume, as heady and light as it was memorable, entered the room like an aura around their plump and radiant hostess.

"And you I certainly remember." Arms outstretched, Nonny made a direct route for Jack. "You brought him back!"

"How could I deny you?" Richard replied graciously.

Releasing Jack she clapped her hands, and two women who had been seated in an anteroom rose and attached themselves to a grinning Jack and a red faced Christian. Nonny, her arm linked through Richard's, steered him down the corridor. "Spare me a little of your time before you enjoy the hospitality of the house."

Opening the door to her rooms she stepped inside, Richard following, enveloped completely in the folds of her perfume.

"I have to thank you." Nonny was selecting glasses from an elegant tray on a side table.

"Thank me?" echoed Richard.

"You successfully reduced my clientele by two," Nonny replied, passing him one of the filled glasses.

"Robert?" Richard asked, taking the glass and settling into the rich red fabric of the silky cushions, embroidered and springing up around him.

Nonny discarded two of the cushions to the floor and deposited herself gracefully in the cleared space. "Thank you. He was a more than a nuisance. Some men enjoy violence in the bedroom a little too much."

Her free hand strayed to a brooch at the top of her dress, where it pinned a long plume of translucent silk that wrapped around her shoulders and descended towards the floor.

Richard smiling, asked, "Are you angling for more gifts, ma chéri?"

Nonny adopted a mock hurt expression. "You are being unfair, your company is pleasure enough."

Richard sipped the wine. Warm, spiced and overly sweet it reminded him of … what did it remind him of?

"I don't have your attention, what is it that you are thinking?" Nonny reached a hand up and ran it down the side of his face.

Richard, meeting her eyes, said, "You miss nothing, do you?"

"You have let the cares of the world rest on your face," her words were spoken thoughtfully.

"Are we in the confessional?"

Nonny took her hand from his face and laughed. "Of course we are. Why else do men come here? To escape their cares, their worries and their wives. So unless you are wed, which I much doubt, then you must be here for the first two."

"I might have a wife," Richard replied reprovingly.

"No, I don't think so," Nonny said smiling.

"I could be here to escape her scolding tongue,"

Nonny shook her head. "Certainly not."

"Can you really be so sure?"

"How long have I known you?" She countered.

"A while," he admitted.

"A while," she agreed. "And you, my pretty, are out of favour at the moment, so where would you get a wife from? If ever anyone was born to wed for an advantage it was you my sweet, and that's not a possibility at the moment is it?"

Richard laughed out loud. "So you think I'll settle for nothing less than an Earl's daughter?"

Nonny tapped her chin with a ringed forefinger. "De Vere has two daughters and then, of course, there is the Earl of Lincoln's sister." Nonny went on to provide a surprisingly comprehensive list of eligible daughters, sisters and widows that would provide an advantageous match.

"But, not, as you say, at the moment," Richard concluded.

"Are you in London long?" she asked, changing the subject.

"My presence here has a certain elastic quality at the moment. I am not sure," He replied thoughtfully.

"If you could maybe return before you leave, I have a gentleman who I believe would like to meet you," Nonny said.

"A client of yours?"

"Sometimes. Before you go I will arrange a meeting, now shall we go and find out if your companions are enjoying themselves?" Nonny asked, beginning to rise.

"Not yet. I might not have a wife, but I do have cares and worries I would rather forget for a while."

"Well then, let me help you forget your cares for a little while, mon cheri."

A short while later, his mouth pressed against that of one of Nonny's willing girls, he tasted again the thick sweet wine that had been on his own lips. Slipping a hand around the back of the girl's neck he pulled her closer...then froze for a moment. The memory, the aroma of cheap warmed wine flooded into his mind. It had been in another country, with another woman: he'd drunk the spiced wine from the earthenware jug before he'd lifted Lizbet's wet and dripping body from the water where she'd fallen asleep.

A worried expression crossed over the girl's face. Smiling, he moved to allay it, holding her face between his palms and kissing her deeply, the hint of the spices lingering still in his mouth.

†

He found Jack and Christian at the card tables later. Jack's shirt hung open and a girl was attached to his side, her arm wrapped around him beneath the linen. Christian, who certainly did have cares, worries and a wife, had abandoned them all and was playing cards with Jack and two other men at the table, a small red-headed girl balanced on one knee helping him with his game.

Richard dropped into an empty seat. A servant appeared, wordlessly providing wine, and a side table was set next to him with sweetmeats.

"Do you want to play?" Jack asked.

Richard, stretching his feet before him, shook his head. His mind was, for once, comfortably empty, and he'd no desire to clutter it with the mechanics of a card game. Instead he drank and watched his brother and his friend. That a brothel should offer a feeling of home was outwardly wrong, but it was a feeling he was enjoying too much to analyse..

"I can see you've been treating yourself, Fitzwarren! Who's the blond?" A voice as indolent as it was insolent asked from behind him.

Richard's expression didn't change. "Devereux. Did anything ever come out of your mouth that was not born from foul thoughts?"

A satisfied smile spread Myles's mouth wide across his face. "I try my best." There was an empty chair next to Richard and he flopped down into it uninvited, one leg hanging over the arm and the other booted foot rested on the chair, his knee drawn up to his chest. Devereux was swathed in black saturnine velvet slashed to expose the dark silk of his shirt, his wrists emerging from delicate fringed lace that lay just a little too far down the pale hands. Two of his men were standing a few paces away, confident and at ease. His appearance at the table had drawn the stares of Jack and Christian, but Myles was oblivious to everyone else in the room.

"Perhaps I shall join your game," Devereux suddenly declared, raising a hand in the air. One of his men handed him a red velvet purse and the other moved the table closer to their master, marooning Christian's and Jack's cards.

Richard, sighing, collected in the cards, pulling the deck back together.

"Oh, you disapprove," Myles said, his brows knitted and disappointment clinging to his words.

Richard silently cut the cards and was about to deal a round when Myles reached across and took the deck from him.

"In the name of fair play, I cannot allow you to deal," Myles said smiling, then turning he held the cards towards Jack. "You deal, blondie."

Jack, his eyes darting between Richard and Devereux, confusion on his face, was forced to rise and pull his chair closer to the table. Taking the offered pack he shuffled the suits and then dealt a neat hand amongst those seated around the table.

Richard won the first game and Myles the second. The conversation had stopped and the only noise was the clatter of coins on the wood.

Myles won the next game.

He left his winnings in the middle of the table, so after Jack had collected the cards, he slid the coins towards the victor.

Devereux's eyes, dark as coal, flicked towards the coins and a moment later, quicker than a ferret, his hand trapped Jack's wrist in tight hold. Twisting it for a moment, he angled the fingers towards him before Jack wrenched his hand from the unwanted touch.

"Well, my treasure, where did you get that trinket from, I wonder?"

Jack ignored him and sent another set of cards across the table to each of the players.

Richard won the next two games.

Myles cast his cards on the table in disgust and in a quick move, unfolded himself from the chair and stood looking down at Richard. "Come on then, if you want to know what I have for you."

A moment later, Jack and Carter were alone at the table exchanging concerned looks.

"That was Myles Devereux wasn't it?" Christian Carter asked at the first possible opportunity when they had left The Angel.

"I am afraid it was," Richard confirmed.

"It doesn't surprise me that you know him, he's a bloody maggot. My idiot cousin Harry used to borrow money from him and then spend weeks avoiding his men when they'd call for payment – never a good idea," Jack said, shaking his head.

"Are you well? Are you actually feeling sorry for Harry?" Richard asked, sounding shocked.

"Not at all. Harry didn't pay and once Devereux's men came 'round to his London house and when they didn't find him there they took their temper out on the servants instead – Christ, what had they to do with it?" Jack said angrily. "And you must have heard of what he did to the Hansons? Devereux's men tied him and his whole family to a wagon bed and let the tide come in. There were people there, and they stood and watched them drown, they were so scared of what Devereux would do to them if they went to help."

"Jack's right, Richard, Devereux is a dangerous man," Christian chimed in.

"What, I wonder, did he want to talk to you about?" Jack asked, even though he knew he would not be getting an answer.

CHAPTER 11

†

Jack's nose detected the smoke before he saw it; the scent caustic, sharp and pungent. It was not the pleasant smell from a cooking fire, and it was too early in the evening yet for the flames in the hearths to have been rekindled to warm the house. This biting aroma was the stench of something much worse. A whetstone and the knife he had been sharpening fell forgotten from his hands, a moment later he was on his feet, heading through the house towards the source of the fire.

The tension dropped from him when he heard Coleman berating Tilly. The volume of the tirade notched up as the pair emerged from the kitchens into the corridor, both of them surrounded by a plume of soot laden smog. Coleman's tirade of maledictions was punctuated with violent coughing, and Tilly, her eyes streaming, was trying to stay out of the range of his fists.

"The chimney's blocked and the idiot woman didn't put the fire out. Now the whole ground floor is filled with smoke. Get out with you!" Coleman planted his boot on Tilly's backside and propelled her down the corridor.

Jack, fastening a malevolent stare on her, stepped sideways to allow the wailing Tilly to pass, tears cutting clean lines down her blackened face.

Richard, with Carter on his heels, joined them a moment later. Carter's eyes were wide and concerned, and there was a questioning look on his brother's face.

"It's safe sir. The chimney's blocked..." Coleman was forced to pause as his lungs emitted another barking hack, and he leaned a hand on the wall for support. "...Tilly didn't think to douse the fires."

"At least the house is not ablaze. We need to get some air through the place or everything is going to stink of smoke for weeks. If we open the kitchen doors to the yard and the ones at the front the air will drive the smoke from the house. Richard, can you close all the doors upstairs to keep the smell out?" Carter was already hurrying towards the back of the house grumbling. "If Anne comes home and her linen smells like this I'll never hear the last of it!"

Jack headed to the front of the house, pushing open the door, and cool clean air sluiced around the jamb. The grey mist of the smoke from the kitchen swirled behind him and he stepped outside into the busy street. Kicking a rock to the foot of the door, he wedged it open. Inside he could hear Carter now shouting at Tilly, and he hid a laugh. Useless bitch!

Leaving the door open, he crossed to the other side of the street, away from the haze that was wafting gently from the doorway. Jack's gaze drifted towards the roof.

His heart hammered in his chest – Jesus Christ!

The chimney, which he had no doubt led to the kitchen was blocked, but it wasn't an accumulation of soot that had caused the chaos. The top of the chimney was closed off with straw, pale yellow sprigs emerged from the aperture making it resemble a badly packed scarecrow.

Heedless of the traffic, Jack darted across the road, diving back into the cloudy interior.

"Carter! Carter!" Jack ran headlong into Coleman in the corridor. "Where is he?"

"I've just seen him sir, he's in his office just past ..."

Jack didn't wait for him to finish. Carter's office was on the other side of the kitchens, reaching it he ripped the door open.

Empty.

Cursing, he ran back to the kitchens, then out through the still open door into the yard at the back. He was in time to see Carter being pushed through the gate by a man in a brown cloak before it snapped shut. The other side of the gate led directly onto the busy road of Bank Street. Jack was across the yard in a dozen steps and in another he was in the open street.

There was no sign of Carter.

Sense told him they would have headed away from the busy centre of the City. He ran right, down the slight hill, away from London. Very soon he realised he was wrong. Jack alone could move much faster than a man pressing a captive before him could, and when he didn't catch him quickly he knew he had taken the wrong route. Doubling back he met Richard, and behind him Devereux's men, spilling though the gate at the back of Carter's house. After a quick exchange the pair ran, side by side, up the hill, eyes desperately scanning the road ahead for any sign.

Jack finally caught sight of Carter. Wearing only a linen shirt when he'd emerged from his office to find his house flooded with smoke, the white was marking him out amongst the mottled grey and brown of London.

As they closed upon Carter it was evident that the hooded man pulling him through the crowded streets was applying a knife to his ribs, one hidden beneath the folds of a fouled and much begrimed cloak. The pair were side by side, but the rhythm between them was jostling and inharmonious. He was also no match for his pursuers. A fateful backwards glance told him he was being followed, and also about to be caught. The ragged beggar abandoned his captive, shoving Carter as hard as could towards them, then ran with a lolloping gait, hoping to evade capture.

It was Richard who cannoned into the bundle of filthy, malodorous tatters, sending the man to fall against the corner of a cobbler's stall. The prop, knocked out from under a wooden table, sent a display of ladies' pattens to slide from the drooping shelf into the road. The stall owner, last in hand, moved forward, but he stayed his advance when he saw the knife blade glitter between the group. At the sight of two of Devereux's men on the edge of the fight he lowered the iron in his hand.

Richard had a tight hold on the wrist holding the shabby blade, and a knee rammed painfully into his chest held the man down. A kick to the head from Jack's boot, and the knife fell from an open hand and the struggling man collapsed in a limp heap beneath Richard.

"It's not Andrew!" Richard exclaimed, pushing himself back up and ripping the hood away from the man's straggling mop of matted hair.

The pile of rags on the floor was reanimating itself and had becoming alarmingly aware of the perilous situation it was in. Quicker than an eel, with the fleetness of the threatened and the liveliness of the terrified, on his hands and knees he scuttled for freedom. Richard was left holding the filthy soiled cloak that had been shrugged from his body, Jack lunged for the lithe little man, catching him by the arm and staying his escape.

The man, wild with fear, kicked, wrenched and twisted against the hold, frantically trying to pull free. A filthy, black-nailed hand left a double line of leaking red tracks down the side of Jack's cheek, a moment later, adjusting his grip he had the man locked in a hold, arms trapped at his sides. His legs though were still free and he kicked back hard into Jack's knees.

"See if you can do that when you can't breathe, you bastard," Jack shifted his grip and brought a forearm hard across the man's throat. He struggled desperately, but Jack increased the pressure at his throat and spittle ran from a contorted mouth along with a gasping rattle. Angling his head sideways he made one last effort to sink his teeth into Jack's arm.

"Be still, damn you!" Jack's hold was restrictive, his arm safe from the discoloured blackened stumps that littered the man's gums.

"Where is your master?" Richard demanded, a hand in the greasy hair he pushed the man's head back and glared into the feral eyes.

"Let him breathe Jack. Just one last time, remind him of what he is about to miss. Permanently," Richard instructed, never letting his gaze leave the man's face. Jack loosened his hold long enough for the man to let out a choking, slavering gasp and replace it with another, before he clamped his forearm hard again across the hairy throat.

"I'll ask again. Where is your master?" Richard's voice was brittle with anger.

The man's lips moved, but the only sound that emerged was an animal-like guttural grunt. Jack slackened his hold again. The man opened his mouth wide and stared at Richard. The stump of a tongue, hacked away for an age old misdemeanour, stared at him from the rotting cave of the man's mouth.

Richard cursed. Fixing a hand under the hairy jaw, the nails biting deep into the skin he said. "Right you scruffy little shit.

You might not be able to tell me, but you bloody well can show me. Is it far?"

The scraggy head shook.

Richard scooped the tattered cloak from the floor. "Keep hold of him, Jack." Then to Devereux's men. "Go back to the house, and take Master Carter with you."

"No, no," Christian stammered.

Richard placed a firm hand on his arm. "Please, this is no place for you."

Carter relented and a moment later he was heading back to his home.

Re-clothed in his reeking filthy layers, with a knife pressed persuasively to his ribs, Carter's aggressor led them down Bank Street, at the junction with Penny Lane he took them right towards St Bride's. Then, he dug his heels in to the road and stopped, a scabbed finger stabbing the air in the direction of the church.

"In there?" Richard pointed towards St Bride's.

Tendrils of matted hair swung around his ears as his head bobbed in affirmation. Jack propelled him towards the church, and his feet slid on the road, clearly not wanting to cross towards it.

"Let him go, it seems he's more terrified of his master than of us," Richard advised, his eyes on the stone edifice facing them.

"It could be a trap." Jack eyes ran over the building while still retaining a tight hold on his captive.

"It probably is," Richard replied, "and one we are not going to spring. Not while we don't know what his strengths are."

"I agree," Jack released his captive, sending him stumbling foreword with a fist in the small of his back.

They made their way quickly back to Carter's house. Jack was feeling strangely elated, as if a weight had suddenly been removed from his chest and he could breathe freely. It had felt good to squeeze the life from the beggar, it wasn't Andrew, but that time, that confrontation was getting closer, and Jack was ready for it. The brief taste of violence had given him an appetite for more.

"What do we do? Go back, get some more men and return to St Brides?" Jack enquired as they strode rapidly back.

"Maybe."

"What do you mean – maybe? We're not leaving that shit to slip away again. Not this bloody time." There was real anger in Jack's voice.

"It seems ..." Jack didn't hear what else Richard said, they were already back at the gate and he was already on the other side. He had another knife in his room, and he was going to get it.

Striding quickly through the kitchen and into the wide corridor that led to the stairs to his room, he found Harry's white mongrel hopping on its one good front leg towards him.

"I told Harry, you're not to be running around for another week," Jack admonished the dog, scooping it up as he passed. The dog had a bed in Jack's room and Harry too had been sleeping in there.

"Harry," Jack called, as he took the stairs two at a time, carrying the dog.

The door to the room stood open.

Jack lowered the dog to the ground.

The mongrel growled.

Jack knew why the dog had been downstairs even before he saw the disarray in the room. It had obediently followed its master when he was dragged from the house. A chair was knocked over, an earthenware jug smashed on the floor, its contents still pooling on the wood. On the floor – the knife.

Christ, no!

Blood covered the length of the blade and a thin trail of droplets was spattered on the floor. It took a second, the blade he wiped clean on cloth he'd used earlier, then he dragged it across the floor. Carter needed to see none of this.

Jack's feet touched the stairs just three times before he practically fell into the corridor, pointlessly shouting Harry's name. The kitchen door opened, and Jack found his eyes lock with Richard's for an instant as he realised exactly what had happened. They'd been drawn away and Andrew had taken Harry.

Jack felt sick. The corridor was suddenly airless and his senses reeled.

Richard had both his hands pressed to his forehead and his eyes, wide and unseeing, stared along the corridor.

"What's wrong?" It was Carter, then when they didn't answer, growing concern in his voice, "Richard?"

"Andrew's taken Harry," Richard managed, his voice hoarse.

CHAPTER THIRTEEN

†

Carter's face had taken on an ashen, bloodless quality. A shaking hand reached out for the support of the wall.

Jack, swearing, sent a fist, fuelled by frustration and anger, into the wood work, splintering the thin oak.

Richard was the only one to speak. A speculative gaze switching from Jack to Carter. "How did he know Harry was Carter's son?"

Jack, his fist still among the splinters and spikes, glared at him. "Does it matter?"

"Yes. Yes it does. Someone told Kineer. Someone from this house had to have told him. Otherwise Harry was just a stable hand, a servant and totally worthless to Andrew," Richard summarised urgently.

Jack was nodding as understanding began to dawn.

"Who knew?" Richard turned the question on Carter, as both of the brothers looked at him.

"No one knew!" Carter's eyes flicking between them, then, his voice anguished. "Christ! We just need to find him."

Coleman was standing at Carter's shoulder, weight shifting between his feet, clearly unsure how to cope with the situation. Richard switched his attention to the steward. "Who knew Harry was the master's son?"

Coleman flushed, his eyes on Carter. "No one, sir."

"Don't lie to save your master's face. Tell me! Who knew?" Richard demanded.

"For God's sake! Just answer him," Carter said roughly.

Coleman dropped his eyes to the floor. "Everyone knows."

"What!" blurted Carter.

"Everyone, saving Mistress Anne," Coleman amended hastily.

Richard held up a hand to still Carter's words. "Someone in here has been talking to someone outside, we just need to find out who."

"It wasn't me, I'd never discuss the master's business," Coleman said defensively.

"There are two lads in the stables, Tilly, and yourself. That's a pretty short list of people," Richard stated bluntly.

"That woman hates Harry," Jack observed instantly.

"Agreed," Richard turned on his heel, and pulling open the kitchen door found Tilly on the other side, her face puffy from crying and mottled with the soot. "Who did you talk to about Harry?"

Tilly moved quickly to put the safety of the table between herself and Richard. Jack dropped down the steps and stood, arms folded, behind his brother. "Come on Tilly, tell us, who've you been talking to?"

"I've done nowt wrong," Tilly protested. "Nowt, do you hear me?"

"I do, and I haven't time for this. Now, tell me who you've spoken to!"

Tilly's eyes flicked towards the door to the kitchen garden.

"Do you really think you can make it to that door before me? Are you that stupid, woman?" Jack strode across the room blocking her exit.

Tilly looked between them, seemingly trying to gauge which of them was the greater threat. She edged further from Jack, but the action brought herself dangerously close to Richard. A hand caught her wrist in a vicious grip. Tilly wailed, her free hand trying to pry his fingers from where they pressured the joint.

"Let go!" Tilly shrieked, twisting against the hold.

"I'll let go when you tell me who you've spoken to." Richard increased the pressure, Tilly's shriek increased in pitch and Jack's face twisted at the sound.

"There were robbers in the street, they stole the bread from me and he helped me," Tilly sobbed.

"When was this?"

"A week ago, last Saturday. The little bastards knocked me to the ground and stole the bread. Please let go, you're hurting me..." Tilly pleaded. Tears cut tracks down her sooty cheeks.

"Not until you are finished," Richard said through gritted teeth.

"He told me he was in the wine business, and I said Master Carter was as well, that's all," Tilly's shrill voice finished.

"There was more, come on. He wanted to know who was in the house, didn't he?"

"I told him you were here, and Coleman, and the master's bastard, Harry," Tilly cried.

"And you've not seen him since?"

Tilly shook her head.

Richard discarded her arm and she dropped, crying, onto a bench.

"Go on, out with you," Jack took a false step towards Tilly and she belted from the kitchen, skirts held high as Carter pushed past her to join them.

"He's been watching the house for a week. He'll know we are here, and now he's got himself some security as well. I'm missing something," Richard muttered, his expression hard and intense, and he addressed his words to no-one in particular.

"Will he have taken the boy to St Bride's?" Jack asked helpfully.

Richard turned his back on his brother, palms pressed to his face. "Quiet! Let me think."

"We need to do something, my boy ..." Carter's words tailed off.

"If that damned woman, Tilly, hadn't gossiped to Kineer in the first place," Jack began.

"Stop it!" Richard commanded. He left the crowded kitchen, still faintly reeking of smoke, and went into the garden. There was something, today there had been a connection. Richard closed his eyes – what had it been? Somewhere in his mind was the answer. Slowly, painfully, he replayed the events. Running again up Bank Street. The flood of relief when he'd seen Carter through the crowd. The lunge for the filthy man who'd held a knife to his friend's ribs. Fighting to find the man's arms through the filthy wrapping of rags. Gasping against the stench of urine and tar... Pitch!

Richard spun on his heel and was back in the house in a moment. "Jack, arm yourself. We are going to St Bride's."

†

The church of St Bride's was built over the original Roman building that had first occupied the site. The crypt, well below the street level, was a testament to the antiquated architecture of its foundations. A wide, squat building, having a long nave and two proportional wings that reached out to form the shape of a cross. Traffic in the streets was thinning, the evening was drawing to a close, London was readying itself for the end of another day.

Richard was in no hurry. Jack, on his right, was trying to force the pace to become a faster one, but Richard slowed him. "The evening service won't be over yet."

Jack cursed.

Richard needed to order his thoughts and at the moment St Bride's would be filled for Vespers. They paused for a moment on the opposite side of the street, staring at the rising buttressed walls. Nothing seemed out of place.

Together they entered the dim interior.

It was lit near the altar with oil lamps and candles burning in high, bright-polished holders held upright upon bases of clawed feet. Richard slid onto the end of a vacant pew towards the back of the church and Jack settled heavily and noisily next to him. Richard resisted a comment.

A crepuscular interior was lightly littered with worshippers; the first five pews were seated to capacity, and from there on back the faithful were more erratically spaced. The air, heavy with incense, curled between them, a lit brazier to the left of the altar sending spirals of grey, heavenly smoke snaking towards the rafters.

Jack sneezed. "How long do we wait?" he muttered under his breath.

"Until it empties. Have no fear, he'll find us," Richard assured him and rested back against the pew. Closing his eyes he focused his mind on his surroundings.

The chanted liturgy coming from in front of him.

Dues, in adiutorium meum-intende. Domine, ad adiuvandum me festina...

Jack shuffled on his right, sniffing loudly.

Richard elbowed him. "Be quiet."

Behind him came the light patter of leather soles on the ochre floor tiles. From the right, the scuff of shuffling feet. Above him, trapped somewhere in eaves, a wood pigeon cooed.

The liturgy continued.

To his left, a stifled cough stabbed the air, and then, slightly further away, a dissenting murmur of disapproval. Somewhere to his right, the repetitive neat click of a rosary. A draught, from the east facing open door behind him, licked at the back of his neck. Jack shifted his position on the narrow seat, a steel buckle prong dragged against the woodwork. A sudden increase in the breeze, followed by a click and solid boom from the distant left, told him the Devil's door in the north transept must have been opened, drawing the air through the building.

The service finished.

There was a recurrent low thunder of noise. A pew, pushed back on his left, scraped the tiled floor. In front of him a book of psalms, or hours, fell from a lap uttering a staccato slap as it landed. There was the collective sound of feet, slowly filing past the narrow pews to the nave, shoes grazing the terra-cotta squares, accompanied by an occasional hushed voice. The door behind was open, fresh air, clear of the church aroma flooded in, the door in the northern wall must have also been open.

Richard opened his eyes.

St Bride's was emptying, or at least it was emptying of worshippers.

Richard rose to his feet, squeezed Jack's shoulder fleetingly, and made his way along the line of the pews to the aisle. At the end he began to move along the south wall towards the transept. The solid strike of boot heels on the marble tomb markers in the floor told him his brother was at his back.

A high window, black now, the intricate glass pattern denied life by lack of light, hung above them like a dark vertical pond. At the end of the transept was another, smaller altar, raised on a round dais with marble steps leading up to it. Hanging above the altar was an effigy of St Brigid, and in the floor before it was a brass inlaid sheet with a depiction of the saint and worn Latin script.

A tomb to the right, marble topped, supported a forever sleeping effigy of the interred. He was flanked by metal baskets holding tall oak shafts topped with worn heraldic pennants. Dust, age and the sunlight from the south transept window had long since robbed them of any splendor.

Standing in front of the altar, a look of suppressed expectation on his face, was Andrew Kineer. If their journey had been a difficult one it was obvious that Kineer's had been as well. His face was gaunt and thinner beneath his beard, and hair that had once been scattered with the odd grey strand had now been stripped of half its colour.

"Fitzwarren!" The voice was pitched to carry no more than the distance between them.

"A long overdue reunion," Richard delivered the words irreverently.

Kineer ignored him. "So, what are you going to offer me?"

"How do I know you still have something left to bargain with? You carelessly left a trail of blood. How do I know he is not dead?" Richard asked flatly.

Andrew laughed bitterly. Raising his left arm, they could see at the wrist, bound tight, a linen wrap. "Not the little shit's blood, I am afraid."

There was a relieved exhalation from Jack behind him.

"I don't believe you," Richard replied, dubiety playing in his eyes. "Show him to me. Then I will tell you what I have to offer."

Kineer seemed to weigh the words for a moment, before producing the briefest of nods. Walking to the end of the transept and rounding the corner, he exchanged a quiet word with a man who was standing there, hidden, before returning to stand near the altar. All three of them waited.

Richard's face was blank.

Jack's a troubled playground of hatred and rage.

Kineer's wore a malevolent sneer.

Richard's peripheral vision became alerted to the movement of men behind pillars, taking up positions behind him. There would, he had no doubt, be more than he was aware of.

They heard Harry before they saw him, the noise of a protesting child's voice clashing with the guttural sound of his captor's orders. If there was any relief it did not show on Richard's face. The noise ended behind Richard with a scuffling of boots on the stone floor and gasps of complaint from the restrained child.

"Harry, it'll be alright." It was Jack behind him who spoke the quick words of reassurance.

"Oh, but will it?" Kineer interjected cheerfully. He raised a hand in the direction of his man and Harry was dragged back out of the transept. "What do you have to offer for him Fitzwarren. It is, after all, your fault he's here."

"It depends upon what you want?" Richard was rewarded by a darkening in Kineer's face when he detected the undercurrent of insolence in his voice.

"Don't play games with me! You've completed the deal with the Order. Where's the money?" Kineer's eyes were narrow.

Richard smiled. "You can have me, and you can have my brother. But that is all we have to give."

Kineer pushed himself away from the altar he had been leaning irreverently against, advancing a few steps towards Richard. "I have the child. My men surround you. What will you offer me?"

Richard put a hand to his face, his fingers slowly drawing across his cheek, a thoughtful look on his face. When it dropped away it rested on the hilt of the sword fastened to his belt, his demeanour was that of a man possessing both authority and control. When he spoke his tone was scornfully derisive. "Perhaps I should put the question. What are you going to pay me?"

Confusion flitted onto Kineer's face, his eyes darted, with an increasing uncertainty, between Richard and Jack.

"Your men surround me? Do they? Look again. How many men did you have? Half a dozen perhaps? How many stand in the shadows now? Ten? Twenty? You've not been outnumbered Kineer, there's been a coup, and they are now working for me," Richard explained patiently.

Kineer laughed, the harsh barking noise rang around the transept. "You expect me to believe that? You are the one who is trapped Fitzwarren."

"I expect you to believe the evidence," Richard replied.

"What!" Kineer gasped the word.

"You hired men from Devereux didn't you?" Richard folded his arms, a pained look of exasperation on his face.

Kineer was now looking beyond Richard and Jack to the men in the shadows. To those behind the pillars, propped against walls in the gloom or standing in the aisle.

"Myles Devereux owes me his life. He has sent more of his men here and now word has passed between them and they are, sadly, no longer working for you," Richard explained.

"The child! Bring the child here! Now!" Kineer's voice was loud, bruising the beams in the vaulted roof.

Harry, small, quiet and pale appeared again from around the stone corner. This time though, without a restraining hand.

"Oh dear," Richard said simply, a dangerous and threatening smile settling on his face.

Before Andrew could move, Jack had a hold on Harry's arm, pulling the boy behind him and wedging him into the safety between himself and the stone wall of the church.

Andrew, by his own device, was trapped in the oblong of the south transept. Four of Devereux's men had appeared across the exit to the aisle, blocking his escape.

Among them was one of the men who had been stationed at Carter's house.

"Take the boy back," Richard instructed, his eyes never leaving Kineer.

CHAPTER FOURTEEN

†

It was a foreordination.

Kineer drew his sword.

Before Richard could step forward, Jack took a tight hold of his arm, stopping him. "Are you sure? He's good." Jack's quiet warning was spoken softly, near his ear, the offer apparent.

Richard arched his brows, his grey eyes impenetrable, his stare adamantine.

"Wait! Before you go." Jack's quick hands took charge, reaching forward he pulled the sword belt a notch tighter, saying hastily as he did, "He has a vicious right swing. Watch for it. He'll feint to his left, give you an easy defence and then come in three times as hard from the right. Don't let him break your guard. We both know you are not as good as you could be. Give me your arm." Jack transferred the wrist guard he habitually wore that held a knife, "And take this as well." Jack gave him his poniard.

Richard tucked it into the back of his sword belt, clapped Jack on the arm, and made to move past him. In one smooth, flowing movement bare tempered steel glinted, unwavering, in his hand.

"I'll not let him live, you know that." Jack assured.

Richard paused. "I'm inspired by your confidence!"

Before Jack could say more Richard had moved towards the platform holding both saint and sinner. Walking slowly down the right hand side of the transept he passed the ornate, flagged, crusader tomb, pausing at the edge of the steps to the platform. Andrew stood beneath the slicked black window, illuminated by the moving candlelight flickering on both sides of the altar and by oil lamps set into sconces in the east and west side of the walls.

"You are a fool to have come. Your brother might have stood a chance, but not you." Andrew's word dripped contempt; turning his head sideways he observed Richard closely.

"It was inevitable," was all Richard said.

"Predictability, isn't that what you despise in others? I then, at least, should please you," Andrew replied, suddenly laughing.

"My judgement erred. It happens," Richard replied.

"So has your father's bastard assured you of his fealty then? Is he all you have left to side with you?" Andrew scoffed, the words spoken loudly enough for Jack to hear. "Does he know, I wonder? Or were you keeping his heritage secret for your own ends?"

"He knows," Richard countered.

The look on Andrew's face was momentarily unsettled. His next words were for Jack. "Has he told you that you are William's heir? I doubt it. He's using you, Jack, like he used me."

"Don't bother, Kineer. I know perfectly well who I am, and what you are," Jack's pronouncement rang around the transept.

Richard had circled around so that he stood at the bottom of the three low steps that led up to the platform where Andrew stood.

"You can stand there all day. I'll not come down. If you want to meet me then bring your steel up here," Andrew said, a chilling smile biting at his lips.

In the shadows of the church Devereux's men had begun to move forward, drawn to the spectacle, but unwilling to be a part of it. The columns on the nearest side of the nave had a line of men strung between them.

Slowly Richard set his feet on the low steps and made his way on to the platform where St Brigid was interred. Andrew

302

stood in the middle, his back to the altar, away from the steps, Richard was all too well aware of the danger he faced fighting near them.

It was Richard who took his blade to Andrew's first. Andrew, grinning, pressed the younger man back the way he had come in three fast decisive strokes.

Richard sent Kineer's blade back towards him, the steel squealing in complaint. The smile dropped from Andrew's face. He redoubled his efforts, his attack as vicious as it was efficient, Richard using all his skill and strength to keep the sharpened steel from his body. Andrew's attack pushed Richard back again, so that he was only paces from the treacherous polished marble trap.

"The steps!" Jack called out the warning from behind him.

If Andrew knew it as well, he kept his face schooled and his eyes from the steps. He closed the gap giving Richard no choice but to move a foot back in retreat.

His balance was hopelessly lost.

In the second that he fought to regain it, and shift his weight, Andrew's blade sliced horizontally, hooking the sword from his hand. The steel rattled across the floor fetching up with a clamorous clatter when it reached the base of the crusader's tomb.

The sword lost to him, Richard now had a poniard in each hand.

Andrew was laughing. "Lad! What are you going to do? Scratch me to death with them?"

Kineer had, though, backed a pace away. Throwing verbal taunt rather than pressing an advantage. Richard soon found out why.

"I'll let him go, Jack. He's a worthless shit. You are far better than him, and that's the way it should be. Let me help you, Jack," Kineer was offering Richard's life for his own.

Richard could see Jack out of the corner of his eye, and Kineer received his answer quickly enough. To his brother's right was the iron basket with the ancient poles, topped with the flag of England. Jack didn't hesitate. His whole body against the wooden axe shafts he pushed, they moved a little, and he let them rock back to the vertical before he heaved them forward again. The second time they rocked further, and the third heave gave them enough momentum to topple over. The poles and flags were set on a path to land on Andrew.

Jack hadn't waited to see if they hit their mark; the hilt of Richard's sword lay near him and dropping to his knees he took it in both hands and sent it spinning back across the smooth tiles. Richard had already dropped to the floor, his hand outstretched, ready to receive it. Rearmed with the sword he was back on his feet, and was now well on his way back up the platform. Kineer was near the altar after having leapt back to avoid the falling shafts.

"You never could fight fair, could you, Fitzwarren?" Andrew angrily kicked away one of the poles that lay across the brass tomb marker. The wooden shaft rolled from the platform and bounced noisily down the steps, the sound resonating up into the high galleried roof.

Richard gave him no more time, the other two fallen poles had rolled behind Andrew, and he had every intention of forcing him on to them.

"Do you think me a fool like your brother?" Andrew scoffed, stepping sideways and, by degrees, making Richard swap places with him. "I'll tell you something else as well, that sister of yours was a tasty delight."

"Ignore him!" the warning came from Jack behind him.

Kineer forcing Richard's blade down grinned maliciously. "Didn't you know the slut had been sharing my bed?"

The steel seared together again, the biting sharpened edges had still to cause injury.

"She wasn't too happy about it, but we reached an understanding," Kineer continued, licking his lips, his face twisted in a lascivious leer.

Richard kept his thoughts to himself – not fool enough to be drawn by Andrew's verbal goading. So far his temper was still in check. He knew the fight on his side was reactive and unplanned, Jack had been right – it was a confrontation he was not prepared for. His skill was blunted by his lack of anticipation, he was fighting in the moment, and that was a dangerous place to be. The traded blows were robbing both men of their strength, and Richard was fighting a man whose stamina now was greater than his own and whose skill was now at least on a par.

The only opening would be when one of them made a mistake, weakened, or found themselves wrong-footed. The longer this went on, the more likely the finish would be owed to a fool's mistake.

It was Andrew who drew the first blood, his eyes flashing with delight as he saw the red gash his sword tip had made down the younger man's arm. The blow had been forceful enough to cut through leather and linen to the skin beneath; although the doublet had lessened the blow, the blade had still sliced into his left forearm.

He heard Jack swear loudly behind him.

Richard knew his arm holding the poniard should have been higher. Then the short blade would have blocked the sword, or at least lessened its impact. A memory of another fight at Burton came back to him, a fight where he had been worn down, his skill stripped slowly from him, until he could barely stand.

That wasn't going to happen today.

Tightening his grip on his own sword, his knuckles white, Richard focused on the execution of every move. Andrew's delight was short lived. The cut on Richard's arm was not a bad one, and the sting of the cold steel was a reminder that if he was going to pick his moment, he had better do it soon. Blood was dripping from his hand, if he had a moment to look down, he might have found it amusing that it had obliterated the Latin word 'misericordiae' on St Brigid's epitaph.

He picked his moment well.

The throw was unexpected. Andrew twisted away from the poniard as it cut through the air. It didn't meet its mark, but it forced Kineer to turn and Richard's blade seared towards him and cut a debilitating blow into the older man's wrist. The injury was disastrous, stilling his opponent for a moment and allowing

Richard to force his blade hard into Andrew's stomach.

Drawn close by necessity their eyes locked. The sword loosed from Andrew's grasp and bounced on the stone flags, the noise echoing through the church.

There was the sound of hurried running feet, and Richard knew his brother was close behind him. Jack's arm circled him, adding his own tight grip to the hilt, crushing Richard's hand onto the sword he still held. The twist of the blade was vicious and sudden, the scream from the man impaled on the steel inhuman. It stopped when Jack let the blade lower and Kineer slid from it, choking now on his own blood which ran from between his twisted lips.

For a moment Richard leant back heavily against Jack, his hand still covered by his brother's on the sword hilt.

"I think there are at least two of my fingers you've not broken," Richard's voice was a hoarse whisper.

Jack loosened his grip, the sword slid from Richard's hand to join Andrew's abandoned blade on the top of the tomb. Richard swayed, and Jack's arm's wrapped around him holding him upright. Tipping his head back he rested it against Jack, his senses swimming.

"I warned you to watch for that cut from the right, didn't I?" Jack's words were quiet, spoken close to his ear, and were filled with relief and concern.

Richard, recovering, pushed away from Jack and stood looking down at Andrew. He wasn't dead. Not yet. But there was not a physician in the world who could save him, blood coursed from between the hands that the dying man had pressed against the wound, and his breath came in ragged, whooping gasps that shuddered through his body.

Jack had dropped to his knees next to Andrew's bleeding body and began systematically working his way through the man's clothing. Andrew, still breathing shallowly, was beyond resisting. Finding a purse Jack slung it on the floor, underneath his shirt he found a gold chain holding a crucifix, and a quick efficient twist broke the links, then as Richard watched, Jack set to pulling the two rings from the dying man. The hand was slick with blood and Jack's fingers slipped, unable to gain a purchase on the silver.

"For Christ's sake! You're still a pain in the arse when you're dying." Jack wiped his hands on Andrew's hose, removing the worst of the blood, the offending ringed hand he had dropped palm-up on the floor. Planting a boot across the wrist Jack pressed Dan's knife between the knuckles and the fingers, severing them. Holding them up in front of Andrew's still focused eyes he shook them, releasing the rings from the bloody stumps before tossing them towards the wall of the transept.

"And those, you shit, are for Lizbet." Jack said, wiping the rings on Andrew's clothing.

Jack had settled back on his haunches, his eyes fastened on the white bloodless face. Andrew was looking back at him, the mouth leaking blood and saliva, the lips moving wordlessly. The only noise was now a guttural rattle coming from inside his torn body.

"I could sit and watch this all day," Jack spoke quietly, evident pleasure in his voice, "but I am afraid I probably need to get rid of your body, so as annoying as that is, I'm going to have to help you along."

As Richard watched, Jack's hand fastened over Kineer's face, denying him another breath.

CHAPTER FIFTEEN

†

They weren't alone. The shadows were filled with men watching the scene unfold silently, waiting to see what the players would do next.

Both of them stared at the body.

Jack was still kneeling. Richard, behind him, rested a hand on Jack's shoulder.

Despite the nausea that was attacking his stomach, there was something else spreading through him, it took Richard a moment to recognise it – relief. Involuntarily, something halfway between a nervous laugh and a gasp escaped from his throat before he could stop it.

"Christ, I feel better," Richard confessed.

When Jack straightened up, Richard found the expression on his brother's face was also one that was also curiously bright.

"I didn't realise just how good killing that bastard was going to feel." Jack's words were heavy with relief as well. "Bloody shame I can't do it again."

"In one way it's over, and in another it's not," Richard replied, his voice resigned.

"I know. It felt like an end, but until we see the Order adhere to their deal we can't be sure of the outcome," Jack said, then grinning he elbowed Richard, "it still felt good to feel a sword in that bastard's guts."

"As good as it felt, we can't leave him here," Richard said, his voice still a little breathless.

As Richard watched Jack leaned down and quickly untied the linen from around the cut Harry had inflicted on Andrew.

"Give me your arm, let's not leave anyone a trail someone can follow." Jack rising, fastened the material over the wound. "I did tell you to watch for that trick of his, didn't I?"

Richard grimaced as Jack pulled the linen tight. "I know you did."

"You did well. I am sure Emilio would have found some faults," Jack said, tying the linen ends in a knot, "but I..."

Richard interrupted. "Jack, can we leave the post mortem of my faults and failures until later – we need to get rid of him."

"We're already wanted for murder. Will another one make that much difference?" Jack cast his eyes back down towards the still leaking corpse. "Even if we get rid of him, he's bled all over the floor – if I'm honest, that's not going to pass off as a bit of spilt communion wine you know."

Richard found himself suppressing the urge to laugh. Jack was right, Andrew was laid in a red pond that had covered most of the brass of the Saint's memorial.

"We could just leave it. Do you think it'll be seen as a saintly miracle from Brigid?" Jack continued.

Richard raised his eyebrows. "Probably not."

"What do we do with him?" Jack asked, his eyes casting around for some available place to dump the corpse.

Richard, looking beyond Jack into the gloom that soaked the rest of the church, became aware of the moving shadows in St Bride's, a reminder that they were not alone. Devereux's men were still waiting.

"Devereux's men are still here, they might be able to help." Richard's eyes roamed the shadows in the church where the men stood in dark anonymity.

Richard stepped back up onto the platform and retrieved his blade from the floor and, a little way further on, the poniard he had thrown. Irregular and angled now, the point of the knife had been sheared away by whatever had stopped its flight. The only weapon that remained now was Andrew's fallen blade, the end reddened with his own blood. Richard lifted it from the floor. He recognised it, once it had been the sword of an ally, a friend; or so he had thought. In a sudden angry movement he threw it behind the Knight's tomb. It fell, clanking, between the back of the stone coffin and the wall – out of sight – lost, like so much else in his life.

Jack had rounded up the fallen poles, righted the iron basket, and replaced them. If the faithful looked up tomorrow they might notice that the poles no longer held flags, and if they hunted for them, the would find them behind the tomb, balled and stained with drying blood.

Retrieving the weapons, his back to Devereux's men, had given Richard the moments he needed. When he turned towards them he moved with confident strides, his demeanour again one of control. Dropping from the saint's resting place he stepped towards the row of men, from the centre a man stepped forward, a man he knew. Matthew.

"I need somewhere to get rid of him. Is your master still keeping bodies in the crypt?" Richard asked, his voice calm, his words confident.

Matthew inclined his head, his fingers tucked into his belt. That he didn't like Richard was evident on his face, but he was under orders. "He does."

"Well then, lead the way. I'm sure one more corpse will make little difference," Richard said, extending an arm in the direction of the stairs to the crypt.

Matthew summoned over another man, they exchanged quick words, then to Richard he said, "Bring him, we'll show you where you can put him."

Richard turned, but Jack had already heard Matthew's words. He'd raised Kineer's knees, jammed a foot against his boots, and grasping the dead man's left arm hauled him onto his shoulder.

Jack closed the gap between them, hefting the burden on his shoulders until he got the weight where he wanted it. Richard moved to help, but Jack shook his head. "There's at least twenty of Devereux's men, you make sure they stay on our side. I'll manage his stinking corpse."

Richard nodded. It made sense.

Richard followed Matthew and another man carrying a lit oil lamp, and behind them Jack followed, his steps heavy on the polished floor.

The steps to the Roman crypt were steep and narrow, made of a friable sandstone with a heavily worn central tread. Before they were halfway down air carrying a hint of the scent of death met them. It would be a lot worse inside the crypt. Richard knew Jack had been locked in a store room at Marshalsea with the rotting corpses of the dead debtors, and the stench, that cloying, sticky, all pervading aroma of death, was one he would recognise only too well.

The man Matthew had spoken to was ahead of them unlocking the door that was set into the wall at the bottom of the steps. A moment later it swung open. The crypt was below ground, dry, walled, and cool enough to slow the putrefaction of the corpses. Despite that, the smell was foul. The evil air released from inside wrapped around them both and Jack, behind Richard, gagged.

"Do you want me to take him," Richard, turning, asked quickly.

Jack tightened his hold on the body and shook his head.

Dim light from a lamp Devereux's man held illuminated the interior and Richard could see the lined rows of dead, some in shrouds, one or two in coffins, but most were naked, or near enough so. Laid out on the floor of the crypt at St Bride's the corpses waited for burial. The unfortunate victims of the latest sickness to strike London were now doubly unfortunate, the weather and circumstance even denying them, for the moment, a final resting place.

Jack dumped Andrew on the floor just inside the door, the body landing heavily, the skull producing a dull thud against the dusty flagged floor. Richard, taking hold of Andrew's boots, one under each arm, dragged the body to the furthest end of the crypt, away from the light. The arms trailed behind the body, and it left a smeared line of blood on the dusty floor.

At the far end in the near pitch darkness, Richard took the time to arrange Kineer's body to become part of the neat line of dead awaiting burial. There was little he could do about the blood stains, but by morning they will have dried to a deep brown and have lost their lustre.

"Get that door locked, and let's get out of here," Richard instructed, returning.

Matthew's man didn't delay, slamming the door shut on the stench of decay. He fumbled for a moment to find the key, the oil lamp locked precariously in the crook of his arm while he searched for the one he wanted on an iron ring.

Jack, who had been holding his breath, released it in a loud gasp, taking the steps two a time he headed back to the ground level, and fresher air. Jack stopped halfway up the flight, breathing raggedly, bent over, hands on his knees, and white as a shroud.

"Are you alright," Richard asked quickly.

"The smell, it's so bad," Jack said as he straightened up.

"Let's get back to ..." Richard stopped abruptly. He was interrupted by the sudden noise of the main door banging open and the sound of feet running into the church.

"Shit!" Jack said under his breath.

"It's the bloody watch. Hurry up!" It was Matthew at the head of the stairs. By the time Richard and Jack arrived at the top of the stone steps Matthew had gone, and Devereux's men appeared to have disappeared as well.

The sound of boots on the stone flags increased. The noise was coming directly towards them. Outside the clouds had cleared and a full moon was sending a fragile silver light through the high windows on the south side, enough to dimly illuminate the interior. Enough to see the dark shapes heading towards them. Richard and Jack were both standing near the top of the steps to the crypt; to retreat was to be trapped. The main exit was directly in front of them, but to traverse straight towards it was too dangerous.

"There's a Devil's door in the north transept, you go for that, I'll go 'round the opposite way," Richard instructed, giving

Jack a quick shove before he ran into the gloom in the opposite direction.

There was, just beyond the south transept, three highly polished candle holders, taller than a man, they were set against the wall at the end of the pews, and beyond them the door to the bell tower. That was where Richard was headed. Keeping to the walls, moving in the shadows, and hoping Jack could make it to the north door in time. Devereux's men, had absented themselves from the church it seemed. The sounds now were urgent voices, footsteps that were loud and did not care if they were heard.

Coming towards him along the south aisle was the noise of those hunting for him. A canopied tomb set against the wall provided a black niche of darkness for him to press himself into as they ran by. Why were they here? Who had reported the fight? He could only hope that Devereux's men had made it safely back to Carter with Harry.

His path clear, Richard squeezed out from the narrow hiding place and made his way towards the bell tower door. His right hand quickly pulled over each of the three brass candle holders before he dived through the door into the bell tower. One of the candle holders fell on to the end of a pew splintering the wood, the other two impacted on the floor, sending solid echoing bangs cannoning around the church interior.

The door to the bell tower had a latch only, and there was no way to lock it from the inside. Worse, with the door closed the tower, a hollow oblong, was in virtual darkness, some grey light pierced the top where the bells sat, but the walls from there on down were solid and windowless. Access to the top of the tower was via a wooden staircase set against the wall.

Richard, in the middle of room, in the consuming darkness, raised his arms above his head, traversing the room three times until his right hand found what he wanted. A bell rope. Looped up, off the floor, to prevent them from being chewed by the rats. Without hesitating Richard hauled on it, released it, and ran for the wooden stairs leading to the top of the tower.

†

Richard was gone before Jack could utter a word of objection. Jack dived away from the exposed position at the top of the steps, flattening himself behind a pillar. The running had stopped, there were shouts between the men as they began to search the church. Jack was still near the south transept, he needed to cross the aisle and then the nave to make it to the north wing and the side door to the church.

On either side of the altar the choir stalls stood. Polished seats fitted into a high-backed carved wooden screen, separating the altar from the aisle. A hand on the hilt of his sword to prevent a rattle, he skirted around the Norman pillars towards the back of the church, away from the entrance but also away from those searching for him.

The route Jack had taken soon had him cursing silently as he found himself trapped between the back of the wooden screen and the stone of the church wall. He needed to get through it; on the other side was the nave, and beyond that the northern transept. As quietly as caution would allow he made his way backwards towards the west end of the church, hands pressed to the wood panelling hoping for a break that would allow him through.

A door!

Low, closed and narrow, it was set into the wood. It gave access for the choir to the stalls rather than them having to enter and leave via the nave. An iron-ringed handle invited him to open it. Jack took hold of it, twisting the metal slowly. Would the ferrous bar on the other side give his position away as the latch jolted open? God, he hoped not!

There was a metallic clank. It sounded deafening and Jack swore. A moment later, on the opposite side of the church, there was a crashing cacophony of noise that reverberated around the nave and drowned out any noise that he had made. Whatever Richard had knocked over was large, and three separate crashes echoed around the building.

It was Jack's signal to move. Pushing the door open he squeezed through the narrow gap, emerging amongst the wooden choir stalls. Above him, set high into the end wall of the church, was a huge paned window, moonlight scattered down lighting the chequered tiles that led to the altar. There was no one amongst the stalls, and he could hear feet running towards the noise on the other side of the church. There wasn't time to worry about his brother, he needed to make it around the other side of the church, towards the Devil's door. Pressed between the dark carved wood of the stalls framed between two angels, he could see several men advancing towards the altar. At the moment they couldn't see him, but when they drew level they would.

Without warning the bells rang out from the tower, one round sound followed by three lesser clattering ones, lacking conviction. The men walking down the nave stopped, turned on their heel and took flight, heading towards the noise. Jack grinned–his brother had found the bell ropes.

Directly opposite him was another door, like the one he had just come through, one that would take him to the north aisle. Quickly he crossed the diamond tiles, his boots making more noise than he would have liked.

Jack reached for the latch on the second door when he heard the sound of footsteps that slithered to a halt on the smooth floor behind him. Dropping a hand away from reaching for the iron ring, he instead pulled Dan's knife from his belt, and turned.

Halfway down the aisle was a man. Broad shouldered, barrel chested, with hairy corded arms and a long knife secured in his broad belt. As Jack face him, silvery light flashing along the length of the steel in his hand, his pursuer raised his hands, palms spread wide and took two precautionary steps backward.

Then he stopped.

Meaty shovels of hands, forgotten, dropped to his sides, and recognition rolled out across his fat round face, followed by an expression of delightful expectation.

"You bathtard!" His pursuer announced with a distinct lisp.

Shit!

It was Bartholomew. Jack had relieved him of several of his front teeth years ago when the man had hunted him down for a fictitious debt and thrown him into Marshalsea.

"Ladth! He'th over here!" Bartholomew shouted over his shoulder.

The lisp might have been funny when Jack had given it to him – but not today.

Any moment now the passage down the aisle was going to be blocked. Already there was the sound of heavy boots on the marble heading towards Bartholomew. The large man, sensibly awaiting reinforcements, was standing now, a few paces back, now with knife in hand.

Jack, with no choice, dived for the iron ring of the handle. As he turned his back Bartholomew set his feet towards him. Blessedly the door opened. Jack fell through it, shouldering it closed in Bartholomew's face.

The big man, fuelled by revenge, already had the door open. Jack heard the delicate wood of the small door splinter as it was slammed hard against the screen.

He didn't look back.

The sound of Bartholomew's boots was lost now amongst those of his companions. If Richard had been trying to draw them from him, Bartholomew's shout had pulled them back. There were men blocking the route to the north transept, there was nowhere left to hide, the only escape was through the main door opposite the altar, and to reach it Jack needed to run the full length of the aisle. On the right side, between the church wall and the end of the rows of oak pews he headed for the door at a dead run. Half way along he was forced to a skidding halt, as another man was running towards him up the narrow gap.

Quicker than a fleeing fox, Jack jumped up onto the polished oak of the nearest pew. His right boot on the back of the long wooden seat, he felt it begin to tip with his weight. Jumping to the next he ran along the backs of the pews, tipping them over. Behind him he could hear the bangs as the pews fell, landing on one another, mixed with the curses of his pursuers whose path was now blocked by the upended woodwork.

Dropping from the last pew back to the floor, Jack could see the door. There was a high-pitched screech, the sound of brass on the ochre tiles as a candlestick, taller than a man, was slung across the floor. It rolled over into the aisle, snared Jack's ankle and sent him twisting to the floor, landing heavily on his side.

One elbow already pushing him back from the floor, he tried to rise. But before he could Bartholomew's bulk landed on him, flattening him against the floor. The man had his knees in Jack's back and a clawed hand was holding his head against the cold floor.

"You fucking bathtard!" Bartholomew growled in his ear.

The lisp still wasn't funny.

Jack closed his eyes.

Ten minutes later he was wishing they'd hit him harder. The blows to his stomach had emptied it, those to his ribs had cracked or broken a few, and the ones to his head had closed one eye and he was fairly sure his nose was broken. His every sense was filled with blood: his own. He could smell it, taste it and feel it. When he was no longer capable of any resistance, two of the men had dragged him by the feet towards the crypt. His head had bounced down the steps, the skin tearing from his right cheek, but even that had not delivered his mind to darkness.

When he was halfway down the crypt stairs, when he heard his tormentors laughing, then he realised with sickening horror what they were going to do with him. They dropped his feet, and he heard the sound of the door being opened, one of them kicked one of his legs out of the way so the door could swing fully open.

"Jesus, Bart, it bloody stinks," one of them said.

"Well hurry up and get him in there," Bartholomew replied impatiently.

Jack was hauled from the floor and onto his knees and bodily shoved into the crypt. As soon as he was on the threshold they began to close the door and used it to send him sprawling into the room on the other side. With a bang that echoed around the church and sliced into Jack's nerves the door closed.

Jack lay still on the floor, his cheek pressed to the cold gritty sandstone of the floor. His eyes were closed, and he kept them that way. Opening them would confirm what he didn't want to know – that it would be just as black, just as dark. His broken nose was a blessing, he couldn't breathe through it, and the smell, the vile, putrid rotten smell of London's recent sufferers, did not impact as badly on his senses as it otherwise might have.

Jack listened.

How had it gone so wrong? Andrew's body was not far from where he lay now, still warm, the blood not yet congealed. The sense of near elation he'd felt when he'd grasped his brother's hand and forced the blade to twist seemed to have happened so long ago. And now he was laid in the same burial chamber, beaten, bleeding and with no hope of escape.

Jack was laid on one of his arms, and it had become uncomfortably numb. The pain in his chest was telling him that several of his ribs might have cracked during Bartholomew's assault. Moving his free hand he pushed himself up to release the trapped arm. Gasping in pain he dropped back onto the floor, pinpricks of light playing behind his closed eyelids.

Not cracked – definitely broken!

He lay still, letting his breathing recover and the pain subside before he tried again. This time slower, and by degrees he pulled his arm free.

Was there any sound beyond the door? Had his brother escaped?

Please – don't leave me here!

Apart from pulling his arm free Jack had not moved– he couldn't. He focused his mind entirely on the sound of his own breathing, of the feel of his breath. The air drawn into his mouth, bypassing his useless nose, drying his gums, turning the blood into a sticky glue that made his tongue adhere to the roof of his mouth when he swallowed.

Then the long shaking breath left his body, warm and dry. The breeze of it touching his lips. There existed a moment of stillness. A moment before he took in the next long breath, a moment when he was not breathing. Was this death? If only his body would stop, cease to take in another gasp of air. Then it would be over. Simply and quickly over.

Jack swallowed, his tongue automatically trying to moisten his dried lips. The simple movement gave him again the taste of blood in his mouth. He sniffed, which did nothing but release a clot of blood into his throat, and he gagged. All the time keeping his eyes closed – *keep them closed. Tightly closed.*

Jack realised he had lost his focus and frantically tried to haul his wandering mind back from the dark corners of the room that it was straying towards. Back to his breath, back to the simple quiet sound. The air was cold, he could feel it on his front teeth as it snaked passed them to his lungs. Cold and damp and...and something else.

Don't think about it.

Don't think about what's in the dark.

Panic gripped his body and a shudder ran through him. Broken ribs grated together. Jack cried out in pain, screwing his eyes shut even more.

"Jesus wept!"

For a moment he hadn't realised he'd spoken the words aloud. The agony from his right side was too much and he couldn't lie on the broken bones any more. Drawing in an arm he tried to press himself up on an elbow. The pain was like a knife blade in his side. There was a vague memory of a harsh stamp from Bartholomew's boot that had been the cause of the breaks, but it hadn't hurt half as much then as it was beginning to now.

Pressing some weight on to his arm Jack tried to lever himself up. Even if he could just make it onto his back, anything would be better than having his whole weight on top of his cracked ribs.

Jack cried out again, but forced himself to move, finally rolling onto his back, a last harsh sob escaping from his lips, his breathing ragged.

Then he heard it. A small noise. Getting closer. Panic started to fasten a harsh claw inside his chest, squeezing his heart, stopping the breath from leaving his throat.

Then there was a sound he had not expected. The noise of the door opening. The sound of voices.

"There he is!" Whoever it was had a lamp in his hand and was holding it out, the light somehow making it through Jack's closed lids.

"Is he dead?" said a second speaker.

"I dunno," the first voice said.

A kick was abruptly delivered to Jack's injured side that made him cry out in pain, his body twisting around the injury.

Both men laughed.

"The other body is over there, can you see?" The first man said, and there was the accompanying sound of boots scuffing the sandstone floor.

Jack listened in silence as the men retreated, the door was left open, and he could hear their muted voices along with others. Then what sounded like a dozen feet scurried down the crypt steps, and before he had a chance to prepare himself his limbs were grabbed and he was half carried, half dragged back up the steps. It was then that he did open his eyes, but all he could see were the wooden roof beams in the church, the back of the man who had an uncomfortable hold around his right leg, and the arm of the man walking to his left and carrying the lamp.

He was dropped on the stone floor on the church for a while, and was aware of a muted conversation taking place above him, after which he was carried out and hoisted onto the back of a wagon, and then something wet and cold was dumped next to him. If he had retained possession of his senses, if he had turned his head to the right, he might have found some irony in the fact that he was once again in the company of Andrew Kineer.

CHAPTER SIXTEEN

†

Narrow coarse timber steps zigzagged up the inside of the west wall of the bell tower. Before Richard had reached the top he heard the door pulled open and men pounding up the wooden stairs; he felt the vibration as more than one set of feet ran up them behind him. Emerging from the last tread he found himself on a broad wooden platform. Two bells were mounted on a broad oak stock, both ends of the mechanism flanked with huge iron spoked wheels around which thick bell ropes ran. Wooden slatted shutters allowed some light into the tower and kept out the worst of the weather. Squeezing between the wheel and the shutter on the west side of the tower, Richard shouldered the woodwork.

He hoped he had guessed right. On the other side was either a sheer drop to the ground, or access to St Bride's roof.

Rotten, brittle wood gave way too easily on the second impact, Richard's hand caught on the wooden frame saving him from falling through the opening after the tumbling slats. Twenty feet below him was the steeply angled church roof.

Reverberations from the pounding of booted feet told him his pursuers were at least half way up the tower. Dropping to his knees, he swung his feet over the edge and lowered himself towards the roof, hanging by his fingers

It was a lot further below him than he'd hoped.

The pounding on the wood increased.

"I can see him!" A voice called from the bell platform. Richard dropped from the tower onto the slate tiles. All his weight landed on his left foot, the ankle twisting savagely beneath him producing an exclamation of pain. A moment later the rest of his body hit the roof.

Above him he heard the angry shouts of his pursuers as they watched him slide down the roof.

Supporting the church wall were two buttresses, stone structures that ran from the top of the walls at an angle to the ground. Richard guessed that the first was about ten feet along the roof.

He rolled over twice, then ripped the broken knife from his belt, jabbing it hard against the stone in an effort to slow his descent. There was no way to stop his fall, the roof was flush and the angle steep. He was either going to exit the roof and land on the buttress, or he would be jettisoned into the air before plummeting to the cemetery yard below. Richard realised that if he got this completely wrong he'd land in one of Devereux's flooded pits - then at least they wouldn't need to bury him!

The edge of the grey roof was coming towards him at an alarming rate. With every ounce of strength he forced the knife hard against the stone. For a moment the broken point wedged between two tiles.

It slowed him.

His weight yanked against the blade, riving the tip from the narrow gap. Both hands now around the hilt, the jagged point continued to scream as it scored two parallel, pale lines down the roof.

To his right a tile, missing a nail, hung loose, exposing a hole in the roof. Loosing one hand from the hilt he managed to fasten his fingers around the top of the exposed edge, the thin slate cutting into his fingers. Feeling his hand beginning to lose its grip on the tile he abandoned the knife and lunged with his left hand as well for the opening. Below him he heard the knife sliding down the roof, there followed a moment's silence before he heard it land, rattling, on stone.

The falling blade had missed the buttress.

For a moment his descent had stopped. He'd lost his knife, and when he let go of the edge of the tile he was going to fall, and there was nothing left to slow his descent. If the buttress was not directly below him then he was about to fall to his death.

Completing the accurate assessment of the situation, forehead pressed to the cold slate, Richard took a deep breath - and let go. His final thought a silent plea for forgiveness directed towards both Jack and Lizbet.

It was only ten feet to the edge of the roof, and he was now sliding slower. His right boot left the roof first and met with nothing but air, and the left soon followed it.

Attached to the outer church wall, the top of the buttress was flat before it began to descend towards the ground, sitting three feet below the edge of the roof.

He landed on it heavily, and too far to the right.

For a moment it felt as if he would roll from the top, then both hands, scrabbling desperately for purchase, found ragged holds in the mortar between the sandstone blocks.

His momentum was checked and he lay, trembling, on the top of one of the southern buttresses.

Centring himself on the masonry, Richard began to climb down the stone support. Ten feet above the ground he could hear no sound. His pursuers had not been stupid enough to follow him onto the roof, and as yet they had not made it around to this side of the church. He practically dropped down the wall, landing in the grass of St Bride's Cemetery, startling one of the goats kept by the Parish to trim the grass. The animal, wide-eyed, bleated in terror when it was kicked in the head by the descending man.

"Over there!" Richard heard the shout from his right.

Cursing the goat, he set off in a limping run in the opposite direction.

Rounding the outside of the southern transept he ran headlong into a group of men coming towards him.

✝

Two blows to the head had rendered him unconscious. When he recovered he was in the back of a wagon, gagged, blindfolded and with his arms tightly bound. They had done an efficient job with the knots and there was little he could do to free himself. Jack's knife was still in the wrist guard, but the lashings around his hands were too tight for him to reach it.

Church bells sounded out and he knew he'd been laid in the cart for over an hour. Then the wagon creaked and tipped as a driver mounted, and after a short jostling journey he had been dragged from it and guided up a flight of stairs and through several doors. Richard was pressed into a room by a firm hand. For a moment only, he had no idea where he was.

Although he couldn't see the room he was aware of it. There was heat from a fire that was gently crackling in front of him. A slightly disappointed sigh came from his right followed by a tiny click that might well be a glass being set down on a table. To his right the man who still had one hand on his shoulder, and another capable paw wrapped around his right wrist just above the bonds, sniffed twice. If all that was insufficient evidence to explain his surroundings, then the scent confirmed it.

"Untie him, Matthew." The unmistakable voice of Myles Devereux commanded from the direction of the fire.

The blindfold was removed, the bonds at his wrists cut, and Richard himself pulled the gag from his mouth.

Myles, comfortable, relaxed and looking quietly pleased with himself, lolled in a chair in front of the fire. His feet were crossed and supported on the edge of a second vacant chair. He waved a hand absently towards Matthew; the man silently retreated, closing the door soundlessly behind him.

Myles smiled.

"The man I was with, where is he?" Richard demanded the moment the door closed.

"Would that be the dead one, or the live one?" Myles replied unhelpfully, his brows raised in enquiry.

Richard's eyes narrowed.

"Blondie? He will have been arrested by now, I should think," Myles replied, retrieving his glass from the table and holding it delicately in both hands.

"What for?" Richard moved forward, leaning down he roughly shoved Myles's feet from the chair they were resting upon, and dropping onto the edge of it he glared at Devereux.

"Fitzwarren, have the words 'thank you,' ever crossed your lips?" Myles straightened in the chair, his ebony eyes furious.

"Has the word 'sorry' ever passed yours?" Richard shot back.

Myles gurgled with laughter. "You really must be more careful with your trinkets."

A second later two fists were wound into the soft velvet of Devereux's doublet and he was hauled from the chair and dragged upright by Richard. The glass fell from his hand, bounced from the chair arm sprinkling ruby droplets cross the floor, before ending its descent in a dozen angular pieces.

"Where. Is. He?" Richard pronounced the words with menacing singularity.

Myles didn't pull from the hold, instead he rested himself against Richard, draped an arm over his shoulder, and matching Richard's tone replied, "In. The. Tower."

Richard growled, released Myles and sent him backwards into the embrace of the chair then, turning, he ran his hands through his hair. "What happened?"

"Excuse me?" Myles sounded genuinely surprised, pulling himself to the edge of the chair he sat with his hands on his knees. "You were the one with the dead body, correct? My men extricated you from the church after the Watch arrived. You could be a little grateful," Devereux said, sounding mildly hurt.

"So why was he arrested?" Richard turned back to face Myles.

"Are you going to make me repeat myself? The dead man? Mutilated as well, by all accounts – not your usual style, Fitzwarren," Myles said, feigned distaste evident in his tone.

"Why was he arrested? What went wrong?" Richard said bluntly.

Myles's face twisted in a grimace. "The fault of that seems to be down to Bartholomew's missing front teeth. Your fight was reported, the Watch were on the way, my men would have brought you both here, however Bartholomew had plans of his own for Blondie. Seems he owes his crooked nose to him - and his lack of teeth. So he threw him in the crypt with the body you attempted to hide."

Richard dropped back into the chair and lowered his head into his hands.

"Which brings me to the body. You can't just dump them anywhere, you know. I have to dispose of those, you shouldn't just add to the pile whenever you feel like it. You could have at least asked?" Myles said, leaning forwards in the chair.

"Myles, shut up. I need to think," Richard snarled at the younger man.

Myles hooked a leg over the chair arm and watched him speculatively.

"Are you certain he is in The Tower?" Richard asked, forcing the anger from his voice.

"He's probably there by now. Bart told Matthew they were on the way for him," Myles supplied.

"Can your men find out if he has been taken to The Tower, and how long ago?" Richard asked after a moment.

Myles shrugged. "I suppose so."

"Well, will you?" Richard replied.

Myles looked skyward, a bored expression settling on his face. Then, lowering his leg from the chair arm, he banged his boot heel hard on the floor three times. A second later the door opened and Matthew's face appeared. Myles, his neck twisted round to observe him said, "The man who was with him," he waved a hand toward Richard, "can you find out where he is now? It is a matter of some urgency." Matthew nodded, closed the door, and left. "There – better now?"

Richard didn't reply.

"Helping people is supposed to be good for the soul. I've done so much of it today – why is it then that I'm not brimming over with feelings of joy?" Myles mused, a ringed hand tapping the arm of his chair absently.

"You can't sell joy, so you wouldn't even know how to recognise it," Richard replied bitterly.

Myles, smirking, selected a new glass from the side table and filled it, continuing to watch Richard over the edge of the expensively engraved rim.

A light tap half an hour later brought the confirmation that Richard had not wanted. Jack was indeed in The Tower.

Richard turned a clinical gaze upon Myles when Matthew had retreated. "How do I get him out?"

Myles's eyes widened, setting the glass down he leant forward in his chair. "Out! You don't get anyone out of The Tower, unless of course you are referring to the pieces they get rid of every now and then."

"Come on Myles, you must have some contacts in there." Richard dropped into the chair opposite him.

Myles tipped his head back and regarded Richard along the length of his nose for a moment. "I do."

"So, can you get him out?" Richard placed the question again, desperately clinging to his temper.

Myles was shaking his head slowly. "No. As much as I would like to help, once you are inside The Tower there is no chance of escape."

"I imagine there would be if I was paying enough?" Richard replied.

Myles raised his hand. "Don't try to blackmail me with money you don't have, Fitzwarren. I can't get him out."

"Alright then. Can you get me in?" Richard asked.

Myles's eyes were suddenly wide and bright, the orange from the firelight playing in their bottomless depths. "Get you in?"

"That's what I said," Richard repeated.

Myles steepled his fingers together and rested his chin thoughtfully on the apex. "That would indeed require a lot of trust on your part. You are wanted for treason, Fitzwarren, I could make myself a tidy profit and be rid of you all in one go."

A smile twitched at the corner of Richard's mouth. "But you wouldn't."

"Why are you so sure?" Myles said quietly, the flippant tone replaced now by a hard, serious edge.

"The blond," Richard stated bluntly, "is my brother."

"Is that the truth, Fitzwarren?" Myles said, his voice suddenly cold.

"It is," Richard's eyes locked with the darker ones. "I know you can find out easily enough."

Myles dropped hands in to his lap. "I can get you in. How you get out though is your own business."

"Thank you," Richard replied.

"We pick up the bodies from The Tower prison. Hunt normally sends a message when he needs a collection, no one would suspect anything if they went without a summons, a simple mistake. The guards let them through readily enough. That would get you in," Myles was tapping his fingers on the arm of the chair.

"That sounds easy enough. When can we go?" Richard asked.

"In the morning. Not however, looking like that!" Myles waved a hand in Richard's direction.

†

"Stop right there!" Myles, seated behind a desk, was out of his chair, a hand raised to stop Richard's advance any further into the room.

Richard, swaddled now in a sloppy arrangement of rags, his head crowned with a greasy cap, his face and hands blemished with dirt, looked, and indeed, smelt the part.

"What are you looking at me like that for?" Myles complained. He was partly dressed, a clean linen shirt hung from his shoulders, still unfastened, the cuffs and neck leaking ties.

"I'm amazed to find you awake." There was genuine surprise in Richard's voice.

"Keep that observation to yourself. It is a commonly held belief that I've never seen noon sober and standing. It provides me with a certain amount of freedom early in the day. If it got about that I was available sooner there'd be a line of petitioners outside my door at daybreak."

Richard raised his eyebrows. "Petitioners?"

"What else shall I call them? Customers?"

"Fools," Richard replied.

"And a fool and his gold are soon, sadly, parted," Myles intoned happily.

"Will you hold these for me?" Richard's hand held out a purse.

"What's in it?" Myles asked, making no move to take it.

"I didn't really want to wear my riches beneath the rags, bit of a giveaway," Richard supplied.

Myles's eyes dropped to the desk. Richard threw the purse and it landed with a light thud.

"Not many riches then," Myles observed dryly. "Remember what I just said about fools and gold? You are not going to find him, and you'll certainly not get him out of there."

"What would you have done for John?" Richard asked, his voice serious.

"I would have dragged the Devil out of Hell," Myles replied, his voice suddenly brittle. "He liked you. God knows why."

"He was a good man. I wish I had been here," Richard replied.

Myles shook his head. "You couldn't have helped. I tried everything. I paid men off, blackmailed as many as I could, but I couldn't get him out of The Tower."

"He didn't deserve it," Richard said solemnly.

"No. No he didn't," Myles said quietly. The flames burnt in the hearth, wrapping themselves around the logs. Myles, suddenly pale, dropped into his chair, his head covered with his hands. "I watched. I stayed until the end. He begged me to leave. Before the fire took hold he held my gaze for as long as he could. Then I realised what I had done," Myles sniffed loudly. "Because I was there, he bore the agony of it in silence. He never cried out, and that was my fault, mine!" Myles's fist banged down heavily on the table twice, the first impact making an ink well jitter, the second sending it onto its side, the black liquid leaking across the desk.

Richard's filthy hand righted the glass pot. "I wish I had been here, for you."

When Myles looked up there were tears coursing down his cheeks. "Get your brother out before they burn him. Or worse."

CHAPTER SEVENTEEN

✝

Jack was jarred painfully back into the land of the living when the cart he had been loaded onto was unhitched from the horse. The cart bed tipped and he slithered to the ground, while the corpse next to him benefited from a securing rope under the arms and remained where it was.

"Up you get!" A voice said from above him, a moment before a boot was kicked into his back.

Jack, groaning, one arm held around his battered ribs, pressed the palm of the other to the ground and slowly forced himself to his knees.

"Come on. I've not got all night," grumbled the impatient voice of his captor, then to someone else it said, "Where shall we put him?"

"No idea, we'll have to ask Jeriah," came the reply.

Jack realised that moving on his own was probably going to be a lot less painful, and haltingly he made it slowly to his feet, his right hand found the side of the cart and he leant against it heavily for support.

"Come on," a hard push was delivered to Jack's back, and grunting against the pain he followed in the direction they wanted him to go.

Where was he?

A dark yard lead to an even darker corridor. Part way along light spilled from an open door.

"Go on. In there," the man behind him gave another unnecessary push and Jack staggered into the room.

Two men were playing cards at a rough wooden table, seated opposite each other on upended barrels. The man on the right was bearded, with a right eye drooping permanently downwards, the corner pulled by the white scar running across his cheek. He looked up, annoyance clear on his face.

"He's just come in," the man behind Jack said by way of explanation.

"Can't you see to him? It's not my turn." The bearded man returned his attention to the cards held in a tight fan in his hand; he hesitated, and then twitched one from the left side fitting it snugly into the centre of the cards.

"Jeriah, get off your arse and see to him. I don't care whose turn it is or isn't, it's certainly not mine," the man behind Jack evidently held a higher office than Jeriah did. "And hurry up, I'm not waiting here for you all night."

Jack's eyes took in as much as he could, his battered brain desperately trying to work out where he was. He had been arrested, of that he was sure - but where was he? A voice in his head was repeating one short warning to him over and over.

Be careful Jack!

Jeriah ignored the instructions, instead waiting for his fellow player to take his turn, ending it when he discarded a three of clubs on the grubby table. Jeriah grinned, revealing the splintered blackened stumps of what had once been teeth, snatched the three of clubs and laid it down next to the rest of his hand before swiping the coins from the table. His fellow player slapped his useless hand face down on top of Jeriah's winning cards.

Jeriah twisted around on top of the barrel, dirty hands on his knees and glowered at Jack. "So you're the piece of shit that has turned up to ruin my evening then?"

Jack, uncertain whether to reply, remained silent.

Jeriah shook his head, the man who had been playing cards with him laughed.

"Are you deaf?" Jeriah asked after a moment.

Jack could suddenly sense a game, a vicious one, of which he was about to be the quarry.

Careful Jack.

"No, master," Jack supplied, his voice level and calm.

Jeriah moistened his lips with the tip of his tongue, anticipation bright in his eyes. "I'm not sure I believe you. I'm not sure you were listening to me." In his right hand a knife appeared. "They didn't listen to me either." Jeriah nodded to a short plank behind him. Holes at either end were threaded with cord, and the cord hung from a nail hammered into the mortar between two stone blocks. Along the plank, variously crisped and desiccated were nailed a series of ears, the exception being the last one that had yet to shrivel. The knife used on the newest one had not performed a clean removal, and a long length of blooded skin hung from just beneath the lobe.

Jack felt sick.

It this wasn't Hell, it wasn't far from it.

Jeriah grinned. "I'll not ask you again. What's your name?"

Be very careful.

"John Warren," Jack replied, meeting Jeriah's eyes. A partial truth was always easier to maintain, his spinning mind reasoned.

"Well then, Master Warren," Jeriah said, "let's get you to your room for the night, shall we? I'll need payment first, rooms at The Tower are not cheap, are they lads?"

Jack's throat tightened so much he thought the air was not going to pass. He was in that one place where Hell had leaked through from the hereafter into the present world.

Jeriah might have been vicious, sadistic and even slow witted, but he wasn't stupid, and he didn't miss the look of terror that had momentarily blighted Jack's face. "Did you not know where you were? That's a shame."

A moment later the knife was impaled, blade down, the point piercing the wood of the table top next to the three of clubs.

Jeriah tapped his finger on the top of the wood. "On here now, anything you have. Money, and those rings an' all."

Jack hesitated for a moment too long and received a hard punch in the back, the force of it jarred his broken ribs and he staggered a pace closer to Jeriah.

"Put your hand on here," Jeriah stared at him, a string of saliva hung between his snarling lips, and his hungry eyes bored into Jack with heartless ferocity.

Jack swallowed.

Jeriah twisted the knife from the wood, the force pulling up an ugly line of splinters from the grain, tapping the point on the wood he said again, "Put your hand on here, now."

"He's not listening to you, Jeriah," his card playing companion said laughing in breathless expectation.

The man behind Jack pushed him forward another pace, and added, "It'll be a sight quicker if you do what he says."

Jeriah laughed at that. "On the table, now."

A quick and unwanted vision flicked into Jack's mind of what he had done to Kineer, and his arm involuntarily pulled back to his side.

A sudden scuffle of movement, and a forceful shove had him lurching forwards. Jeriah rose and rammed his left shoulder into Jack's damaged chest leaving him limp and gasping, and with his hands tight around Jack's wrist he smacked his hand down hard on the barrel top.

Jack yelped at the pain of sliced skin, and a gurgle of joyful laughter erupted from the seated man. The one behind him effectively and quickly searched his clothing and removed his purse.

Jeriah released his hand and Jack, already pulling against the hold, staggered backward. Blood ran down the back of his hand from where one of the splinters had pierced his third finger. It was bereft only of rings.

"Get rid of him, Jeriah," the man who had led him to the room sounded bored now that the entertainment was over.

"Where to?" Jeriah complained.

"I don't know! Find somewhere to put him until Master Hunt arrives in the morning. And give me that lot here."

Jeriah reluctantly handed over the rings he had prized from Jack's hand before hefting a lamp from the corner of the room. "Come on, Simon, you as well, I can't get the bloody doors and hold the lamp on me own, can I?" Then to Jack, "It's a shame I didn't get to add an eighth ear to my board."

Jack didn't reply.

His ear would have made a total of nine and not eight, however pointing out the inaccuracy in Jeriah's mathematics seemed neither wise nor important.

✝

It wasn't a dark cell he was led to, but instead an open chamber. Leaking in from two high, grilled windows came grey moonlight and the noise of the river could be heard beyond the walls. Jack rightly guessed they were in that part of The Tower that flanked the Thames, and from the damp in the room either level with the water or even below it.

In the middle of the room a wooden framework sat, the wood dark and stained, the straw littered on the floor rank and putrid, much of it damp and rotting. A fire burned in an iron brazier against one wall, adding its dim light to the lamp Jeriah had brought. Next to the brazier hung irons, branding irons, tongs and pincers, all of which would be at home hung near a blacksmith's forge, but here they were heated with different purposes in mind.

A manacle was clamped around Jack's right wrist, then after the ring was closed and the chain rattled through the iron retaining loop, Simon pressed one of the links over an iron spike higher up the wall and then stepped back, chortling under his breath. Jack soon realised why: the linked chain would allow his wrist to go no further than his shoulder. He would be either forced to stand or hang from the manacle.

Jeriah kicked at a crumpled heap on the floor before he left. The soiled mound of rags emitted a low moan at the impact and Jeriah, turning to Simon, said, "He's never going to go is he? He fucking stinks. How can a man live without his guts for three days?"

Jeriah gave the bundle three more savage kicks before Simon intervened. If Jack thought that Simon was trying to save the injured man he was soon corrected.

"Bloody well stop it, Jeriah. That's not fair. You bet he'd live three days, I'm down for four and Stan said five. He was a right fucking stubborn shit, we all said he'd not give in easily, just 'cos you've lost don't spoilt it for the rest of us."

"I've not lost yet, the bastard might still be dead before dawn," Jeriah said, getting in a final kick before he mounted the steps.

Jack listened to the two gaolers bickering as they retreated up the stairs, taking with them the lamp. Soon the room was lit only by the squalid grey light from the moon. The noise around him was equally as fearful. Rats were moving in the straw, braver as soon as the men had left. A sudden stinging pain as a set of yellow incisors belonging to the first rat to scale his boot sank into his flesh just below the knee, causing him to jump in surprise.

Jesus Christ!

Another sound filled his ears, it was his own uncontrolled harsh breathing and the rattle of the iron links as his shaking body pulled against the chain. With only one hand chained to the wall he was able to repel the assault that was intent upon attacking him from the floor. Jack soon proved too hard a meal and the attacks lessened. Sick to the pit of his stomach, he soon realised why. From the ragged bundle near the steps the sound of intermittent mumbled prayer mixed with weeping drifted to his ears.

The rats were settling for an easier meal.

The dying man was repeating over and over Job's plea to the Lord to save him.

"Oh, that You would hide me in the grave."

Each line was painfully pronounced between weak sobs.

"That You would conceal me."

Another harsh gasp of pain.

"Until Your wrath is past. That You would appoint me a set time, and remember me!"

The prayers finally stopped and gave way to feeble cries for help. Jack wanted to cover his ears, he wanted to shout to block the pitiable sound, anything so that he didn't have to listen. With the manacled hand against one ear and his head pressed against the wet stone of The Tower he managed to keep the terrible sound from his ears and his eyes fastened on the grey squares high in the wall, two patches of night sky, two sections of the world outside this Hell.

When the grey lightened a degree he could hear other noises. The sound of a boat passing The Tower, men's voices distant and indistinct. That seemed to make the rats slightly less bold and he was no longer aware of the noise of them scurrying through the straw, or the sound of them tearing at the flesh of the dying man in the corner.

CHAPTER EIGHTEEN

†

Myles had despatched him to the taproom of the inn where he was to wait for the group who had the task of removing the less animated of The Tower's occupants. The room was empty, moonlight leaked through the shutters, but the floor was a trap of stools and benches hidden in the dark. Richard had paced the room, accidentally kicking a stool that had sent the inn's mouser fleeing, a furry ball of loud and vociferous feline displeasure. A yell of complaint from the adjacent room made by a disturbed sleeper persuaded him to sit on one of the benches and wait.

The cut on his arm throbbed, he'd not even looked at it since Jack had tied the linen tightly over it, closing the wound.

Jack!

Richard rubbed his hands roughly over his face.

He had to find him.

How, didn't matter, just so long as he did.

Fortune's dice had landed, bounced, and presented to him yet again a different face. In a simple and brief hour everything was painfully different, as Heraclatus had annoyingly, yet accurately, pointed out, "nothing is permanent except change."

The cards had been neatly laid out, but now the process and the order was wrecked. Return to Venice, free Lizbet and the men, and set Jack on a course to redeem Catherine and claim his birthright. For a brief moment, when he had gazed into Andrew's fading eyes, he'd thought it was possible. They were at that moment free to leave England, free to return to Venice. For a brief and idiotic moment there had even been a dizzying sense of elation.

Jesus! How fleeting had that been?

The taste now was bitter.

The cards, useless, tumbled from his mind, forgotten and unwanted.

This was a new game, played with a new deck.

What the next card would be he had no idea, and Fate's liking for vicissitude was not one he was currently sharing. All Richard did know was that he would not leave Jack to suffer alone. If the roles were reversed, if Jack were outside The Tower, he knew full well his brother would throw his life away in a moment to save his. Jack was incarcerated within the worst prison in England, the fault of this was his and he was not about to leave him to suffer alone.

His impatience was about to demand he wait no longer when his eager ears heard the sound of muted voices and a cart drawing up outside the inn.

Angry, his blood fuelled with fury, Richard Fitzwarren set himself on a journey that was as unplanned as it was reckless.

✝

As the bells tolled for Lauds, an early light saw Richard leading a plodding, squat, milky-eyed horse towards the river. Grey, damp fog lay across London in a thick insubstantial layer that stole their feet and hid the holes in the road. The piebald gelding drew a short, two-wheeled, flatbed wagon towards the entrance to the Tower. The iron rimmed wheels rattled discordantly on the road, and the loose wagon axle shook the aged cart making the decrepit timbers groan and creak against their nails. The Tower rose from within the centre of a still grey lake of fog, the briar, the detritus and the clogged moat all concealed by the river's smothering film.

Even for London it was early. The business of moving the city's dead was one that took place outside of the normal hours of commerce. They had another hour yet before for city woke and began a new day.

The outer defence to the pale stone fortification was the moat, breached by a narrow stone bridge, flanked on either end by towers. The road leading down to these was rocky and narrow, a further bottleneck, slowing traffic and preventing a broad attack. It was wide enough, just, for two carts to pass with care, but there was little extra room, halfway down was a cutting into the right side which acted as a passing place.

The man to the right of the horse, holding the short whip, was Isaac. A short, balding man in his thirties, he wore a long leather jacket that ran to his knees and was pocketed like a smith's. On the front and from the bulging apertures emerged a host of things Isaac felt of importance—cord, wooden pegs and iron pins, and from his belt swung a hammer. He was in charge of this weekly delegation that approached The Tower; Devereux's men collected any deceased and added them to the Parish's bodies he was tasked with disposing. At the rear of the cart walked two other men, the shabbily dressed remainder of Isaac's team.

Isaac had been less than pleased to find out that he needed to go a day earlier than was normal, and that a new man had been drafted onto his team amused him even less. He was not in charge of much, but he had made it very clear to Richard, as he applied the whip unnecessarily to the old horse, that he was in control of this endeavour.

Despite the night time hour, there was a queue of early traffic already on the narrow road down to The Tower. Supplies came in daily, and the delivery drivers were waiting their turn to trundle carts through the gates.

Isaac couldn't help but grumble, his voice obviously meant for Richard's ears. "It's this bad because it's Wednesday, we always come on a Thursday. There's no waiting on a Thursday, straight in and straight out we are."

Ignore the bloody idiot!

He threw an accusing look at Richard. That he blamed him for this reschedule was clear. They were now within earshot of The Tower's outer defence; the last thing he needed was a fight with one of Devereux's idiots here. Tightening his fists and forcing the burning anger from his mind, Richard regarded his feet, his shoulders hunched beneath the brown ragged layers.

Isaac, tired of complaining about the new collection arrangements turned his attention to the newest member of his crew instead. "How long have you been working for Master Devereux then?"

Richard, silently cursing, shrugged in answer.

Ignore him!

"How long I said?" Isaac repeated, louder this time, so the rest of his men could hear his interrogation.

"Dunno, since just after last Easter," Richard replied in a voice that he hoped sounded quiet, uncertain and nervous. They were nearly at The Tower. A few more minutes and he would be inside. He needed them to leave him alone!

"God! You're a bright one. How come I've got stuck with you?" Isaac's right hand clipped the back of Richard's head making the cap fall over his eyes. The action was greeted with a chorus of loud, jeering laughter from the two other men walking at the back of the cart.

Richard, the cap clasped in his fingers, the leather squeezed between hands that were shaking with rage, forced the anger from his voice. "I'm sorry, Master. I'm just a simple man."

Don't lose your temper!

"You're simple alright." Isaac aimed a blow at Richard's right ear which was neatly avoided.

"Get him Isaac!" one of the men at the back of the cart yelled in encouragement.

"Come here, you little shit," Isaac lunged forward, fastening a fist into the filthy material wrapping Richard's body.

Richard allowed himself to be pulled forward and a blow to the right cheek left his ear ringing.

"Pass him here, Isaac," another man called, and a moment later Richard was sent staggering backward into the violent embrace of another of Isaac's men.

"'Ere you lot. Pack it in. We're moving," Isaac announced suddenly.

Isaac's shout came a second before Richard lost his temper. He had pulled Jack's knife from the wrist guard and a moment later it would have been buried in Isaac's back.

Richard was saved from further torment as the blockade on the traffic was removed and the cart in front began to move slowly forward toward the narrow bridge.

Isaac was known by the men at the gates. There was a brief exchange of ribald comments and coarse remarks and then the cart was making its way across the bridge. The prison section was on the right, occupying that part of the fortification that flanked the river, two levels were cut into the ground beneath them, the lowest one having access to the water.

"You lot, behave," Isaac commanded as the horse drew to a halt. Straightening his jacket with an air of self-importance.

The location lent a seriousness now to the proceedings and the other two men, now ignoring him, stood in quiet conversation at the back of the cart. Workmen had not arrived, but the tools of their trade and the materials stood around in piles. Sliced timber, pale, aromatic and seasoned, stood piled on trestles to keep it from the ground and sheeted with oiled cloth to keep it dry. A shave horse stood ready, surrounded by a sea of curled wood cuttings, and next to it was a heavy workbench, its surface a littered topography of cuts, nicks and dents.

With mounting impatience Richard watched Isaac ready himself for his meeting. Isaac took his time, squaring his shoulders and making his stomach and packed pockets jut out absurdly.

Get on with it!

Finally Isaac set his foot on the step before the low arched door and disappeared inside.

Centrally located, the White Tower presided over the enclosed community. It was the final bastion, and with no entrance at ground level the only way in was via a wooden staircase to the first floor. Surrounding it were the outer defences, with one side flanking the Thames and containing Traitor's Gate. Included within these walls were royal residences, armouries, workshops, chapels, bakeries, barracks and a prison. If he was going to find Jack then this was where he needed to look.

Richard forced himself to wait, otherwise he'd be on Isaac's heels. Pressing a hand over his eyes he forced himself to remain by the aged horse's head for a moment longer.

Finally, like a hound released, blood kindled for flight, he flew up the steps into the dark. He ran, a voice in his head chiding him. This was a direction few men, if any, had ever run.

Out, yes!

But not in!

✝

A narrow corridor ran left and right, in front was a set of steps going down and another leading up. A hand on the wall, he forced himself to stop.

Think! Listen!

Isaac's voice came from his right, joined in jocular conversation with another whose rounded accent and peculiar pronunciation placed his origins far to the west of the city. Another snippet of crude conversation told him Isaac was not in a hurry.

Where was Jack?

Up or down?

A hand on the stone newel post, he took the worn steps leading downwards, his feet light and silent on the stone.

Abruptly, the staircase spilled into another corridor, where the only illumination came from the ashen light that crept down the stairs behind him. Giving his eyes a few moments to adjust to the gloom, a palm pressed against the wet wall to guide him, he turned right and headed along the corridor. A series of rooms were revealed on the left, his hand finding the recesses housing the doors, the outline of a grill showing as a dark square near the top of each.

Solid. Iron studded, And locked.

The passage snaked down further into the bowels of The Tower, the smell feral and acrid and the sudden sporadic clank of looped chains dragging through iron rings told him he had found the cells.

From his right came an abrupt ferine moan, the sickening sound twisting his stomach.

Myles might have been right.

Groping blindly along the passage he found door after door in the dark, though there was nothing to distinguish them. Something unseen in the blackness trapped his right foot. Richard stumbled into the next doorway, his shoulder banging heavily against the oak door.

From behind the wood came the quick mechanical rattle of a chain pouring through a loop. A hand, pallid in the blackness, shot through the grill next to his head, the fingers blindly seeking anything. It caught and fastened itself into his hair, dragging his head against the iron bars. Richard pulled against the hold, but the fist had closed tightly pulling his face against the grill. Both of his hands tried to prize away the rigid, gnarled fingers, when a second hand reached between the bars and sought to place a second hold on him.

"Let go—damn you!" he said, voice pitched low through gritted teeth.

His words were greeted by an angry growl, and the nails of the man's hand bit painfully into his head.

To his right another chain snaked through a securing ring, ending with a sudden reverberating clank as it reached its limit, and then behind him the same noise followed by a wordless shout.

Richard tried one more time to free himself, forcing his thumbs under the hand, trying to break the hold. The man's second hand found his wrist, and an iron grip pulled him hard against the door.

A whooping shout from the cell to his left echoed along the corridor.

Richard let go with his right hand, rived the knife from the wrist guard and dragged it hard against the hand trapping his head.

A scream of animal surprise was followed by a slackening in the hold and he ripped himself free.

Crossing the passage he leant for a moment, his back to the safety of the wall, breathing heavily. Shakily, Richard pressed the wet knife back into the guard. All around him were the disturbed noises from those in the cells mixed with the metallic jolting clanks from the iron loops.

One more mistake like that and it would be his last. Any help he had intended to offer Jack would be ignominiously lost.

If he called out Jack's name he would have every poor unfortunate trapped in the dark answering him. There were grills on the doors, but without a lamp there was no way to see who was on the other side. Richard pressed on to the end of the

369

passage way; it ended with a dark black well where a stone spiral drilled further down to a deeper layer in the building. Retracing his steps to the stairs he had descended, moving along the corridor to the left, he found the layout was the same, and it was equally dark. Reaching the end, he turned back and found the grey oblong outlining where the stairs led back to the upper level. Back at the top he listened before rounding the post. Isaac's loud voice still rang out from where he was talking with the gaolers.

He needed light.

But where to get one?

Richard returned to ground level, and from there took the stairs that headed up. He passed no one. The steps emptied out onto a corridor running left and right, closed doors faced him on both sides a short distance along. A hand to the first confirmed what he had thought—locked.

Richard kept going up.

When the stairs cut across the next passage the door to his right stood invitingly ajar. Pushing it open he found himself in the middle of a workshop. Wood was propped against one wall. The floor joists were bare and long lengths of wood had been laid across them to provide a walkway. There was nothing of any use. Crossing the plank bridge he entered another unlocked room with a recently laid bare floor, pale and smelling of fresh cut timber. In the middle of the room was a makeshift table constructed from the old flooring, the surface littered with crisp dry crumbs and several wooden cups.

Richard stopped himself abruptly.

What am I doing?

Richard hit the heels of his hands off his forehead hard, twice.

Think, damn you!

If he couldn't string a coherent series of thoughts together quickly he was going to be caught, and Myles's prophecy would end up being highly accurate. He needed a bloody lamp—that was all!

Just a lamp!

Laid over a bench was a long leather apron next to a mason's tool roll. Richard shrugged off the filthy rags, dumping them in the corner, and pulled it on. It belonged to a stone mason, the front had two deep tool pockets, and the leather was ingrained with pale stone dust. Dressed as a workman he was assured a certain amount of freedom of movement around the areas where repair work was being carried out. Hands on either side of the window surround he looked out across Tower Green. Staring back at him with the five high arched windows was the Chapel Royal of St Peter ad Vincula; stacked neatly beneath the second window on wooden rests were sections of cut creamy yellow sandstone. Some worked, some awaiting the touch of the mason's chisel.

Striding with purpose, Richard dropped quickly back down the stairs and set his feet in the direction of the Chapel Royal. As he approached he could see that scaffolding encased the end of the church and the main door stood open. Along both the north and south walls were set oil lamps in the sconces, providing constant illumination inside the chapel. Richard retrieved one from the nearest alcove and left the chapel, heading back around the edge of the green towards the cells.

Isaac's wagon was still standing near the doorway, the horse, its head drooping to the floor, stood miserably in front of it. Devereux's men were propped against the back of the wagon, involved in an animated debate. They saw him approach but didn't halt their conversation and paid him no regard. Without his outer plumage of rags and the greasy felt cap they didn't recognise him.

The lamp, warm in his hands, gave off a yellow glow, enough to see his way by, but not enough to light up the whole passage. Back in the passage with the first line of grilled doors, he cautiously held it up and looked inside. The poor light did not penetrate far enough into the cell, all he could see was a dark shadow in one corner which he assumed to be the occupant. All he could hope was that his brother, if he was in here, would be more alert.

With the light he saw on the floor a coil of rope that he had tripped over before and avoided it along with the door which he had fallen against.

If he had thought his passage along the corridor had gone unnoticed he was wrong. It seemed these prisoners knew the habits of their gaolers so well they were aware that his presence was unusual.

When he held the light to the next grill his own found a pair of eyes staring back at him, the lamp light reflecting eerily from the pupils.

It wasn't Jack.

A hand shot out towards him, palm up and a voice, cracked and hoarse, broke the silence of the night. "Have pity on me, Master."

The words seemed to send a message along the corridor that travelled faster than fire. Chains ran through loops, hands clenched at the bars, faces turned towards the dim light, arms outstretched, all open palmed, and half a dozen voices began a soulful plea.

"Have pity on me, Master...have pity on me."

Richard found himself surrounded by a line of beggared prisoners, their hands held out towards him.

For Gods sake! Not again!

Then he risked it, adding to their noise his own plea in the dark. "Jack. Jack, can you hear me?"

He was answered tenfold.

"Here."

"Have pity, Master."

"Jack's here."

"Help me, please."

The voices all rolling into one long repetitive report.

His hands shook. The top and bottom of the lamp rattled together in his uncertain hold, and the corridor was once again in darkness. He'd drowned the wick.

The lamp was out.

Richard abandoned the dead lamp. Cursing silently he rubbed his hands over his face, the smell of the oil pungent in his nostrils. If he kept this up he was going to end up in one of these cells himself very soon.

This was becoming a fool's mission.

Leaving the corridor, and the prisoners he had awakened, Richard found another set of steps, again leading down. From somewhere beneath him air was rising, the breath of a slight breeze touching his skin. The stones of the wall beneath his hand were wet, furred with a moss he could not see, and his descent was now in complete darkness.

Beneath him was a sudden scrabbling scuffle, punctuated with an angry squeal.

Rats!

They would have scurried clear if anyone had passed this way recently. Confident his way ahead was clear Richard quickened his pace, aware that at the bottom was a grey square of light, wherever he was heading towards was lit.

Rounding the stone frame he found himself on the edge at the opening to a large chamber.

Centrally placed, unoccupied and waiting, the rack sat in the middle of the room, ropes leading to pulleys disappearing upwards in the dark to their fixing blocks. By the wall on the other side of the wall, illuminated by the dim glow from a brazier was the room's prisoner. Manacled at one wrist, propped awkwardly against the wall, an eye swollen shut, caked in black dried blood, a cut on his head darkening his hair, clothes ripped, torn and dishevelled.

Jack!

About to take a step toward him. Richard stopped.

From behind him came the sound of voices. Noisy steps told him there were a number of men descending the stairwell.

Shit!

Before they arrived the light from the lamp they carried banished the dark. Five steps above him, a black opening he had not seen when he descended beckoned. Richard dived for it, disappearing into the darkness of a narrow corridor a moment before the men rounded the steps and saw him.

From where he stood he could see five of them step down into the chamber.

All he could do in the face of that number was surrender.

Edging along the corridor as far as he dared, Richard tried to listen to the voices. They were too far below him, the damp stone was soaking up the sound, denying him a sense of the words. A few moments later the voices were coming towards him—they were leaving the chamber.

"I'll talk to Morley," one of the men said in answer to a question that Richard had missed, then the same voice asked. "Are you sure Jeriah didn't help himself to anything?"

"A few coins maybe, but he gave me everything else." It was the heavily accented voice Richard had heard earlier talking to Isaac.

"He's a thieving bastard," the other man returned, his words met with laughter from the others.

Richard pressed himself back further along the corridor into the dark, he was fairly sure they were going back up the stairs the way they had come, and he was right. Edging quietly forward he watched the lamp light disappear marking their exit.

He had a chance.

He just needed to find something to break the iron chain.

Emerging from his hiding place he set a foot onto the steps down to the room below before he realised that all five men had not exited together.

"What the Hell..." said a man glaring up at him from the room.

CHAPTER NINETEEN

✝

Barrel chested, flat nosed, with thinning hair grazing his shoulders, and now with a questioning scowl imprinted on his face. It took only a moment before the man realised Richard was not supposed to be there, and he lunged up the steps towards him.

His companions would be only half a flight above him. If he made a noise or shouted for help, then Richard's bid to free Jack was over.

Richard raised his hands, taking two quick steps back up the stairs.

"Sorry, Master, I got lost," Richard replied, his voice nervous, his tone apologetic.

"No one gets lost down here. Come for a bit of a look, did you?" The man's beady eyes ran over Richard's mason's garb before returning to his face.

"It was a bet with the lads," Richard offered meekly, then added, "I lost."

"Too right you did!" The gaoler grunted a laugh.

"Give me a groat and I'll show you what's down 'ere," Flat Nose said, folding his arms.

"A groat!" Richard's eyes widened in dismay.

The gaoler's eyes narrowed. "A groat, that's the price of getting out of here without getting your hide tanned."

Richard let a look of resignation settle on his face, followed by an audible sigh of defeat.

The gaoler licked his lips and grinned. "I'll show you some things that'll make your blood run cold, and I'll find you something to take back up to show your mates you've been down 'ere as well."

Richard nodded in acceptance and slid his hand beneath the mason's apron, when he pulled it back he held it cupped, as if it contained coins, the fingers of his left hand sorting the invisible money. "All I've got is…"

"Let me see," the gaoler growled and mounted the three steps between them, intent only on seeing how much Richard held in his hand.

Richard allowed him to close the gap.

A puzzled frown settled between bushy brows as the gaoler's eyes lifted from the empty hand to Richard's face. Before understanding could find a clear path through his confused brain, Richard had wrapped his fists in the man's jacket, hauling him forwards. Twisting past him, Richard landed on top of him. The man, winded by the fall, wheezed loudly.

"The keys?" hissed Richard in his ear, a blade pressed to the man's throat.

Below him Flat Nose tried to propel himself backward away from the blade, elbows and hands frantically trying to give himself some distance from the sharp steel.

"The keys. Now!" Richard repeated, pushing himself forwards, keeping the knife edge against the other's skin.

Richard's face was inches from the gaoler's, the eyes below his wide and fearful.

"The keys!" Richard growled again. "Give me the keys and I'll let you go."

"I've not got them... Jeriah... he's in charge," the man beneath him stammered.

Footsteps sounded on the main stairs above them.

Richard cursed under his breath.

"Get up!" Richard commanded, the knife still held threateningly close.

The short man scrambled to his feet, taking a step back away from the menacing blade.

"Where does this lead to?" Richard pointed behind the man, along the narrow dark passage he had sought sanctuary in earlier.

"To the river," came the quick reply.

"Go on," Richard stabbed the air with the knife in the direction he wanted the man to go. "Make a noise and it will be your last."

Further along the floor began to descend slightly, the unseen walls on either side closing in. Around them the air became markedly colder, and Richard could hear his feet splashing in shallow puddles.

What was he doing?

Now he had a bloody captive, and a useless one without any keys.

Think!

The man before him stopped suddenly.

"Keep going." Richard put the flat of his hand on the man's back and shoved him forward.

"We're at the gate," was the nervous explanation he received.

"Is it locked?" Richard placed the point of the blade against the man's back.

"Barred on the inside," came the reply.

"Open it," Richard hissed in the dark.

From in front of him he heard the sound of an iron bar being withdrawn. It was pitch black, the man must have known where it was and was working by touch alone. He grunted with the strain of moving the metal, and Richard took a precautionary step back.

A second later a vertical line of light broke between the door that had just opened and the stone frame, growing wider as the wooden door was drawn back. Beyond it were three low steps, the bottom one covered by the lapping water of the river. An iron grille sat across the opening, the hinge had rotted through on the right hand side and the metalwork now hung at an angle, only partly blocking the entrance. The bank side vegetation that grew halfway up the height of the grille obscured the gate from the view of river traffic; it also told him it had been a very long time since it had been used.

Opposite the hinge sat an iron panel, a black keyhole evident in the rusted plate. Where the hinge had rotted through, the grille had dropped and there was space at the bottom for a man to squeeze between the iron and the stonework: it would be tight but Richard judged that even Jack could get through the space.

Richard had a way in, and more importantly, a way out.

He tightened his hold on the knife. He'd have to hope the body was not found quickly, and that the man was not missed. Even with the grey light flooding past the door it was still dark and the first blow was a poor one. The gaoler wore a thick over jacket, fastened with buckles and the force of the knife was deadened when the point hit the metal of a fastening.

Realising the danger, the man lunged past Richard, diving back in the direction that they had travelled, a cry for help bursting from his lips. A second was cut off as Richard caught him up. An arm tight around his neck and a kick to the back of the knees brought him swiftly to the ground. Richard heard him spluttering, water splashing up around the guard's head. The man's face was in one of the puddles. Shifting all his weight on to the gaoler's shoulder's Richard held him down. Beneath him the fight became a frantic struggle to pull his mouth from the water. To breathe. Both of Richard's hands were fastened onto the back of his neck and a boot trapped one arm, holding him down. The struggles lessened as the body weakened. The arm beneath his boot went limp. Finally, when the body had stopped moving, and the last gurgling gasp bubbled the puddle as the choking breath was released, did he let go.

Two hands around the gaoler's boots, he dragged him back towards the open river gate. The man's hands trailed behind him, dipping in and out of the puddles as they went. Richard pulled the door fully open at the end and dragged the man out of The Tower and onto the river steps. His body could not be seen from above as the doorway was recessed into the wall, and it was safely hidden from passing river traffic by the lush green reed mace that twisted up through the iron grille. Coffined in the small gap between the grill and the steps, the gaoler sank into the silty embrace of the bank.

Through the grille Richard could see the river, where already some early traffic was passing. Directly opposite the gate was the spire of St Catherine's, and standing on the dead man's back, his hands against the grille he turned his eyes to left. He judged that the main river entrance to The Tower was not far from where he was, but there was little clue as to whether Traitor's Gate was to his left or right.

Richard retreated, closing the wooden door, but rather than pushing the securing bar home he left it unbarred, leaving the entrance accessible from both the inside and the outside. There was no noise from along the passage. The man's final cries for help, in a building used to such frequent pleas, had not been heeded.

Now he just needed to get Jack.

When he got back towards the end of the narrow passageway he realised he was too late.

"Where's that useless bastard, Simon, got to?" A voice, annoyed, rose from the chamber below him.

"I dunno, you know what he's like. He'll have sloped off somewhere for a sleep.

Remember last week, we found him snoring in one of the empty cells," a voice said in reply.

"If I find him in one this time, I'll lock the bloody door and he can stay in there," growled a voice heavy with a Cornish lilt.

Richard pressed himself into the sanctuary of the darkness. A quick glance around the edge of the stone entrance told him there were two of them. His hand tightened on the knife.

Richard listened to the voices below him.

"That bastard's still alive an' all," one of the two said.

Richard edged towards the end of the narrow corridor, sliding silently a step further towards them, still trapped within the concealing shadow.

"Are you sure? He smells dead," the Cornishman replied.

Both men were leaning over a mound of rags heaped to the left of the stairs.

"He's smelt like that for days. Look," there was the sound of a kick followed by a low and feeble moan.

Richard, the knife held ready, stepped from the protective dark embrace; both men still had their backs to him. Slowly he moved down the steps towards them.

"When he's dead Simon can clean him up. I'm not touching him," the Cornish voice said, grunting.

Five more steps.

"How can a man live when his guts have spilled out like that? How many days did you bet?" The man who had delivered the kick asked.

"I've lost, and so has Jeriah, it's between you and Simon now," Cornish said, he straightened — his back was still towards Richard.

Three steps to go.

The other man clapped his hands together, saying gleefully, "It's about time I had a bit of luck."

Higher than the two men, Richard's eyes flicked for a moment to Jack, and found his brother watching his descent with his one good eye, his expression blank.

"Did you bet more or less days than Simon?" The Cornishman asked.

Two steps to go

"Less," the man replied.

One step to go.

"If that shit, Simon, doesn't show his face shortly then finish him off. I'll say nothing," the Cornish accent suggested.

The sound of a sudden rush of footsteps clattered down the stairwell from above him.

Richard froze.

The men began to turn.

Richard backed up two steps.

"Are you bastards ignoring me?" Jack rived the chain through the securing loop, the links clanked loudly.

Both men turned towards Jack.

Richard taking the steps two at a time retreated back into the passageway. From below him he heard the sound of a blow and his brother gasping in pain followed by the little man's shrill and unsettling laughter.

Three more guards dropped down the steps, missing Richard and joining those in the chamber below. Another high-pitched howl of delight met his ears attended by the sounding of his brother falling against the support of the chain.

Richard set back off up the steps.

Keys...or something to break the chain with.

The agony of realisation sliced through his head. There had been mason's tools in the rooms above where he had stolen the apron from. Taking the steps two at a time Richard headed back to the level where the floor was being put down, the workers had not arrived as yet. A soft leather tool roll sat on a bench near the table. Shaking it open Richard took what he wanted. A dusty masonry chisel and a hammer, both chalked with soft fine limestone powder.

Cautiously, he descended again.

He could hear them coming up the steps from the lower levels, an undercurrent of meaningless conversation and rising above it the high-pitched laughter of the man who had taken his fists to his brother.

The group split, half heading back towards the room Isaac had gone to, the rest sauntering along the corridor in the opposite direction. One of them holding aloft a small bleeding trophy.

"I told him to listen to Jeriah, didn't I," the sing-song brittle voice said before breaking into another bout of shrill laughter.

Richard waited for them to pass, before setting his feet again onto the steps leading below. This time when he neared the chamber it was occupied only by the prisoners. Sparing a quick glance at the immobile ragged, rotting heap of humanity near the steps, he could thankfully see where the ear had come from. Across the other side of the room his brother hung from the manacled wrist.

Richard was across the room in a moment.

"Jack. Jack can you hear me?" Richard's voice was urgent in his brother's ear. Jack's free arm he wrapped around his shoulder and heaved him upright. "Jack, come on Jack. Help me."

Blood was running from Jack's mouth, from which a sound emerged, though if it was a word Richard couldn't decipher it.

Jack coughed and groaned, and managed to say, "They'll be back soon."

"Hold the chain tight," Richard pulled the manacled wrist down, tensioning the chain, and produced the hammer and chisel.

A brief and lopsided grin settled on Jack's broken mouth.

The tip of the chisel pinched the link against the wall, holding it still; Richard hit it as hard as could.

Sparks danced in the dim light.

Richard's right hand holding the chisel collapsed against the wall as the tool snapped. Half of the metal shaft breaking away and dropping to the floor.

What was left was blunt.

Cursing, Richard dropped to his knees, his hands searching frantically for the broken point.

"Get out, I can hear them," Jack's voice above him croaked.

He found the end of the chisel which still carried a point.

He fitted it inside one of the links, praying he could use the taper to split the chain.

"Richard, get out!"

A hard blow ricocheted from the uneven end of the chisel, the hammer head sliding from it; the chisel shard rattled the chain and fell again to the floor.

"Richard!"

This time he found it straight away and applied it again to the link.

"Please!"

Richard, ignoring the plea, fitted the sharp end back to the link and struck it again. Widening the link, the chisel sank in, fitting tightly between the rusted iron.

Richard heard Jack's quick intake of breath next to his ear, and the reverberating sound of boots on the steps from above him.

Striking the iron tool again Richard watched in dismay as it split lengthways and dropped again to the floor—useless.

"For God's sake. Go! You are little use to me dead!" Jack now had his one free hand against Richard's chest and pushed him backward, the action leaving him gasping with pain.

Richard made it back to the sanctuary of the narrow passage a moment before the guards reappeared. Hidden in the shadows he could hear the men moving in the chamber below. Other noises met his ears, the sound of distant hammering drifted down from above him, the muffled calls of the trapped men from within the cells— The Tower was waking up. Soon the building would be alive with all those who frequented her rooms during the day, the workmen, the courtiers, the court officials... The court officials.

Like John Somer.

Richard realised with sudden clarity that he was going to have to abandon his plan. All it would lead to now was his capture. But he had a way in and a way out if he needed it, and his daytime hours he could put to different uses.

Could he leave Jack in here for a day?
Would tonight be too late?

†

Soon after, Richard was dressed again in the stinking rags, crowned with the close fitting felt hat, and hovering near the horse's head waiting for the return of Isaac. Richard looked at the animal. His brother would have had something to say, he had no doubt. The harness was tight, ill-fitted and it had rubbed the flesh to an ugly band of sweating sores around the side of the horse's neck. One eye, milky blind and the other weeping, would see little good in the world.

Richard rested his head against the horse's neck and ran a hand down the matted coat toward its withers.

Neither of us are faring any better.

The horse, unused to this gentle treatment, snickered, pressing a prickly hairy nose into his ear.

"Nowt to pick up, lads," Isaac returned eventually, thumbs tucked into his belt, an accusing look cast in Richard's direction.

His disappearance, noted by Isaac's men, was swiftly reported upon their leader's arrival. Discipline within these intimidating confines was beyond Isaac's bravery and Richard received only a series of hard kicks and verbal abuse growled in his ear, warning him of the violence to come once they were outside.

With a cart loaded with two dead prisoners they turned the horse around and headed back the way they had come. Passing the guards at Bayward Tower the horse trudged, its head low, across the thick wooden boards that led to the moat. They crossed the festering swamp via the narrow bridge strung between the two towers. Although The Tower sat on the edge of the Thames, attempts to feed the moat from the river had twice failed, so the water in the defensive ditch was a stagnant, weed ridden, silty mire that filled the broad ditch around the three sides of the walls, the fourth wall having been built along the edge of the Thames. Reed mace and saltgrass clung to the bank between outer tower wall and the brackish water and a heron fished, fearless, on the pale stone defences.

Richard, a hand in the poor beast's halter, steered him through the final gate, the wheels catching in the worn stone ruts. The horse abruptly stopped, his head raised, pulling from Richard's hold as Isaac, on the opposite side, forced the horse to halt.

"And you!" Isaac rounded the front of the animal, his face bright with rage, eyes deep and glinting from within the fleshy folds of his face, and his fist clenched around a hammer shaft.

If there was anger painted on Isaac's face, it was nothing compared with the burning frustration Richard was suffering. Isaac's boiling rage was flushed from his features and replaced by an expression of surprise when he found himself suddenly upended, flat on his back on the cobbles. Surprise fled in the wake of nervous fear as the blade from Richard's wrist guard nicked into his hairy neck, the cold steel stinging.

The other two men witnessed their leader's humiliation but did not hear the words Richard growled in his ear. Isaac, clambering from the road, returned to the safety of the other side of the side of the horse, away from the lunatic with the knife.

†

Myles Devereux was out, but Matthew was in. His brown eyes ran over Richard's returning form with evident distaste. Wordlessly he beckoned for him to follow, and soon Richard had his clothes and the purse he had left in Myles's care returned. His enquiry as to Devereux's whereabouts went unanswered, and once he was dressed again in his own clothes he was unceremoniously shown the door.

The journey across the city was one he didn't remember. A sense of his surroundings returned only when he was crossing the street towards the front door of Christian's house. Coleman opened the door; Carter, having heard the sound was already hard on his servant's heels.

"Christ! Where've you been? I've been worried to death," Christian blurted, then a second later, his eyes glancing beyond Richard, he asked, "Where's Jack?"

Richard's eyes flicked towards Coleman, and Carter quickly said, "Come on, let's get inside.

The two men dropped down the steps to kitchen. Harry was on his knees feeding wood to the fire, a lump of cheese in one hand. At the sight of Richard he discarded it immediately on the table, a wide grin breaking out across his face.

"Harry, lad, go and find that dog of yours. I've some business to discuss. I'll send for you when I'm finished," Carter instructed, and looked pointedly in Tilly's direction as he waved towards the door. Harry and Tilly left, and as soon as the door closed Carted asked, "What's happened?"

"Kineer is dead. The Watch were called, Devereux's men got me out of the church, but not Jack," Richard said as he sank onto one of the benches.

"Is he alright? Where is he?" Carter stood at the end of the table, his hands resting wide on the surface.

"In The Tower," Richard replied quietly.

"Christ Almighty! How did that happen?"

"Quite easily," Richard replied wearily.

"Don't stop there! I've heard from Harry what happened until Devereux's men brought him back here. What happened after that?" Carter said sliding onto the bench opposite Richard. "Tell me, man!"

Richard provided Carter with an edited summary of events, finishing with, "I'd no idea what I was going to do when I got inside. Or how I'd find him. It was a stupid waste of time borne out of the need to do something rather than nothing. It's the sort of ill thought out action I'd expect from Jack."

"Must run in the family then," Carter pointed out bluntly. "So now you've had time to think about it, what are we going to do?"

"We?" Richard said.

"He saved my son. I'd like to help," Carter said gravely. "How long have I known you? I can tell from your face you've thought of a way of get Jack out of The Tower."

"We've brought enough trouble to your door already," Richard turned his serious grey eyes towards Christian's face.

"That didn't answer my question though, did it?" Carter said pointedly.

"You never were easily diverted," Richard replied, his voice tired.

"And I'll not be now either. So how are you proposing to get him out?" Carter asked directly.

"Somer. John Somer," Richard replied.

Carter's eyebrows headed in the direction of his hairline. "Somer! I didn't know you knew him."

"He and I are friends, of a sort," Richard replied, "Though after this we may not be."

†

Morley heard the knock on his door and called out an invitation to enter without bothering to rise from his desk. Master Hunt, the controller of The Tower prison, appeared inside the room a moment later.

Morley smiled a greeting, and then his face crumpled as a sneeze took control.

"Bless you, Master Morley," Hunt said.

"It's this confounded weather. I've not been warm since last Easter," Morley said before he was forced to inhale suddenly as another ferocious sneeze set upon him.

"Bless you," Hunt politely provided for a second time.

"How can I help you?" Morley asked, applying a linen square to his dripping nose.

"We had a prisoner come in last night, and he had these on him. I thought it best to bring them straight to you this morning." Hunt wasted no time and dropped the purse that had been taken from Jack onto Morley's desk.

Morley folded the linen and pushed it up his sleeve out of the way before pulling the purse strings loose and upending the leather, letting the contents rattle to the desk.

Sitting on the oak desk staring at him were four rings. One exquisite, enameled and jeweled was of a value he could only guess at, the second a gold signet ring bearing a crest, and the other two of poorer quality, the silver smeared with blood. Sitting next to them a crucifix on a broken chain, and a single gold angel.

Morley looked up at Hunt quickly. "No other money?"

Hunt's face twisted behind his beard. "The lads took him in during the night, it's tradition, they get any coins they find. Not gold mind you, the lads know they are not to pilfer them."

"Well then, that's all right, as long as they don't take the gold!" Morley said with a level of sarcasm that was lost on Hunt. He had the brightly decorated ring between his fingers, the device on the front was one he worryingly recognised. Scooping the jewellery together he rose from the desk.

"Where is he?" Morley asked.

"I'll take you down myself, I'm going that way," Hunt said and Morley, lifting his cloak from the back of his chair set to follow him.

Within minutes Morley again had the linen extracted from his sleeve; this time though, he was not trying to suppress a sneeze, instead he was using it to blanket his nose to keep the smell of the dungeons from it.

Morley made a conscious effort to keep away from the walls, and anything else in the place. Not only did the smell of the place linger, but it was filthy. Following Hunt he emerged into a room where the main central position was occupied by the wooden mechanics of the rack. Two of Hunt's men were busily trying to bundle together the remains of a corpse that was discharging an oozing, noxious aroma into the air. Morley made the mistake of casting his eyes sideways, meeting the dead man's stare, realising that the eye sockets had been completely hollowed out by the rats and his lips gnawed back to reveal a set of sneering, blackened gums.

Morley cursed Hunt silently under his breath. In the future he would insist on the prisoners being brought up, rather than having to travel down into this subterranean mess.

"There he is," Hunt announced, extending an arm towards where a man was chained against the opposite wall.

Morley took in the man before him in a moment. He wasn't as well dressed as the ring they had taken from him might have indicated, yet he was not a peasant. He wore good clothes that looked like they had suffered recently. His stance was unnatural: one wrist in chains was level with his head, and the other was braced against the wall in an effort to take some of the weight from his feet. Despite that he was regarding Morley with an intense stare across the gloomy room.

Morley rounded the wooden apparatus until he stood a safe distance from the prisoner. Hunt at his side had an iron rod in his hand, and Morley knew from experience he'd not shy from using it.

"Your name?" Morley asked, his eyes locked with the blue ones.

The stare never varied and the words, though hoarse, were level and insistent. "Get me out of here."

"I can, perhaps, but I need your name," Morley replied.

There was an almost imperceptible shake of his head and a repetition of the request.

"Tell Master Morley your bloody name," Hunt stabbed the man with the end of the iron rod. Morley could only assume it had connected with some existing injury as the man cried out in pain, his legs collapsing beneath him until he swung suspended, gasping, from one wrist.

"For God's sake, Hunt!" Morley exclaimed, "Get him down from there, I'll be back shortly."

†

Morley carried the purse into Cecil's office. That his master was not expecting him was obvious from the expression on his face.

"What is it, Morley?" Cecil asked, irritation apparent in his voice.

"There is a prisoner in The Tower, I think might be of interest," Morley replied.

Cecil's shoulders dropped. "I'm busy, Morley. Is this really something you need to bring to me? There are dozens of prisoners in The Tower, and all of them believe they are of interest to someone."

"Yes, but..." Morley tried again.

"Deal with it, Morley. I doubt very much that this needs my personal attention." Cecil had already turned his attention back to the papers before him, muttering under his breath.

Morley gave up on words, fished in the purse and cast the ring on the desk. It rolled to a glittering halt near the nib of Cecil's pen.

"Oh!" was the only word Cecil uttered. The pen was cast aside, the glasses pressed a notch further up his narrow nose and Cecil picked up the jeweled ring from the desk. "It's not De Cominero again, is it?"

Morley shook his head. "That was my first thought, but I've seen him, and it's not him."

One of Philip's courtiers, Ferdinand De Cominero, had ended up in The Tower twice. Once for shooting arrows at the ducks on the roof of St Bartholomew's, caring little for the fact that the stray ones were embedding themselves in passersby, and a second time for entering into a duel with a man and killing him in front of a dozen witnesses.

"Who is it then?" Cecil asked, still twisting the ring before his eyes, as if the answer would be written upon it somewhere.

Morley shook his head. "The man has not come back to his senses, he's had some rough handling I would say. There seems to have been a fight reported at St Bride's, the Watch recovered a body and this man."

Cecil groaned. "Where is he now?"

"Master Hunt has him in one of the lower Tower dungeons. When they were going through his belongings Hunt found that and had the sense to seek me out," Morley pointed to the ring on the desk.

"For God's sake get him out of there, put him somewhere more appropriate until we find out who he is. Did he have anything else that might help to identify him?" Cecil probed, raising his eyes to Morley's face.

"Everything is in here." Morley passed the purse Hunt had given him to Cecil.

"Go on, get him moved, and I'll try and find out who he is." Cecil opened the purse and waved a dismissive hand at Morley.

The bells had struck for noon before Morley returned. When he did, he found his master in a less than happy mood. The purse sat to one side of the desk and the elaborate ring he had brought to Cecil's attention sat next to it along with another three others which Morley knew had been in the purse. It was the policy to remove anything of value from prisoners when they entered The Tower.

Morley's eyes roved over the small collection of jewelry, then leaning forward he picked up a signet ring with a deeply engraved crest.

"Recognise it?" Cecil questioned.

Morley, whose eyesight could benefit from glasses but who was refusing to acknowledge the fact, took the ring and held it a little distance away, allowing his eyes to focus on the heraldic device on the ring. Looking up from the ring his eyes met Cecil's.

Cecil nodded. "I doubt very much if it's Lord Fitzwarren we have interred in The Tower. So who is it? Or do we have a thief?"

Morley looked again at the ring and the Fitzwarren crest that stared back at him, then he said thoughtfully, "I wonder if we have ourselves Jack Fitzwarren."

Cecil's brows knitted themselves questioningly. "Jack? Why so?"

"I know little of him, apart from the fact that he resembles his mother, and the man who we have has hair as fair as a Dane," Morley replied thoughtfully before he set the ring back with the rest. There were two more, base in comparison, and, when he inspected them more closely, blood stained. Hunt had provided him with the details of the other body that had arrived with the prisoner and he could guess where these two gruesome trophies had come from.

"Has he come to his senses yet?" Cecil asked.

Morley shook his head.

"When he does, fetch me," Cecil ordered.

†

Pain seared through the tortured muscle and tendon of his shoulder like a burn. His back against the wall, and a shaking hand pressed to the soaked wall behind him Jack managed to return his feet. He'd feared that he'd pulled his shoulder joint apart when he'd fallen and swung from his manacled wrist, but as he regained his footing, and took the weight from his wrist the pain began to subside.

The well dressed man, out of place in the filth of the pit he had been consigned to was gone, as was the remains of the weeping penitent from the corner of the room. The rats, fed and fat, were gone, and for the moment he was alone.

There was a scream, sudden, high pitched and desperate.

Jack felt his stomach muscles tighten.

"No...no...please..."

The words ended with another scream, one of a different type. The first had been filled with a terrible foreboding, but the second was the animal noise that told of pain beyond endurance.

Jack closed his eyes, his body rigid, casting around his mind he found the string of words the dying man had repeated over and over. His voice was cracked and dry, but he was still able to give sound to the words. Anything to set against the pitiful screams.

"Oh, that You would hide me in the grave."

Then what?

"That You would conceal me,"

Jack searched his mind for the missing words.

"until Your wrath is past."

The last line, what was the last line?

"That You would appoint me a set time, and remember me!"

Christ, was anyone going to remember him?

Jack repeated the words again and again, staring across the chamber, his gaze fastened on the blue sky beyond the windows, his eyes avoiding all the torturous devices littering the walls.

As abruptly as the screaming had begun it ended. Jack finished the last line of Job's plea and rested his head back against the wall. Was the man dead? Had he given them what they wanted? If he was still alive had he been reduced to a dying mess like the man in the corner? Jack didn't want to think about it, but it was a route of thought his mind was refusing to turn away from.

Footsteps pattered on the stone of the steps leading to the chamber, and a moment later Jeriah's leering face greeted him. The corners of his mouth were marked with spittle, a thin line of red splatter marked his unscarred cheek and his right hand was mottled with blood. Jeriah was breathing heavily, whatever he had been doing had been heavy work.

"You got me into trouble, you piece of shit," Jeriah announced, "Master Hunt was asking where the rest of your money went."

Jack watched the goaler carefully.

Jeriah, on the opposite side of the rack to Jack, unhooked a long black iron from the wall, the end hammered flat with a rounded point.

"Doesn't look much, this one," Jeriah said as he turned round holding the metal bar up in his hand. "I need to hurt you where no one's going to look."

Jeriah shoved the iron rod into the brazier, the black crust broke away and after a few more stabs the glowing coals lapped by the fresh air began to glow orange. With care Jeriah lay the end of the rod amongst them. "They say that's how old King Richard went, killed by a poker up the arse."

Jack's whole body tightened, the linked iron chain pulled through the loop above him with two sudden clanks. He was only chained by one wrist so he might stand a chance of defending himself.

As if Jeriah had just read Jack's mind he said, "I'm going to strap you face down over the edge of that," Jeriah nodded towards the rack, "Simon and the other lads are coming to help."

Now Jack knew he was going to fight. He would fight them, and he would die fighting, better that than ...

Jeriah spat on the iron rod, the spittle dried quickly. "Got to wait until it spits back, then it's hot enough. Don't worry I'm not going to kill you. I'm just going to make your shit boil inside you."

They would have to unlock the manacle if they were going to drag him to the rack, at that moment he would be free.

Jeriah, arms folded and leaning against the wall near the brazier, suddenly straightened, a smile on his face, "Here come the lads."

Jack felt sick as he too heard the sound of footsteps on the stone stairs. Was The Tower going to reverberate to the sound of another scream very soon, another plea for help, another pitiless wail.

Three other men appeared, one Jack recognised from the night before.

"Get him on here," Jeriah commanded, sending another globule of spit towards the iron rod. It sizzled and Jeriah cast a malicious look in Jack's direction. What Jack hadn't bargained for was how skilled these men were in restraint. A bar, forked, and wrapped in leather, wide enough to fit over his neck was rammed into place before he had even realised what they were going to do. With his free hand Jack fought to press it away, but there was little he could do against the weight of two men holding it in place. With no air his struggles were rendered ineffectual, they reduced the pressure long enough for him to take in a gasp of air before reapplying the throttling hold.

Jack felt the manacle being released from his wrist. He tried to use the freed hand to press away the fork, but there was little he could do, and he could feel his vision beginning to fold in around the edges.

"That'll do lads, shift him," Jeriah had judged the moment right. When they dropped the restraint away Jack fell with it, his knees buckling, while he was still gasping for air they'd dragged him the short distance to the edge of the wooden rack. Between three of them they had his unresponsive arms and legs pinioned to the wood, his chest flat against the slatted top, his legs, fastened above the knees to the frame.

Jeriah, the flat of his hand on Jack's back, leant down, bringing his face close to Jack's. He didn't utter any words, his eyes were fastened on Jack's face, watching him as another of the men ripped down his hose, exposing his pale skin to the cold air.

"Shall I let the lads have you first?" Jeriah finally said, a crooked leer bringing the drooping eye even closer to his foul mouth.

✝

"What the Hell!" Master Hunt shouted from the doorway.

Jeriah, the poker in his right hand, spun round at the sound Hunt's voice, the heated end laying a burning trail across the upper arm of the man to his right who yelped in pain.

"Jeriah! What have you done?" demanded Hunt.

"Nothing, Master Hunt," Jeriah stammered, "We was just bringing him."

"Really!" Hunt looked around the room and took in the scene in a second. "He'd better be alright, Jeriah, or you're dead." Hunt advanced into the room, buried a hand into Jack's hair and hauled his head back. "Can you hear me?"

"Yes, I can hear you," Jack replied through gritted teeth.

"Thank God for that! Get him off here, get some bloody clothes on him and take him to Bart's room, and find Harper to clean him up. He's too precious for horseplay, do you hear?" Master Hunt commanded, then to Jack, "I've no idea who you are, but you are one lucky bastard."

The leather straps were released, and Jack was lifted between two men and guided back towards the stairs. The process took place under the watchful gaze of Master Hunt, who followed them once they left the chamber, Jack supported between two men who half carried, half dragged him up three flights of stone stairs. When he was delivered to the new cell and deposited on the bed he lost all sense of where he was. He had an impression of someone asking him questions, but his mind seemed to drift away before he could make a reply.

The next time he woke he was aware of hammering. The noise, woodpecker-like in its intensity, seemed to be prying his skull apart. Jack groaned and raised his hands to his head.

"You're back with us, are you?" said a happy voice to his right. "You'll soon regret it. I've had to listen to that bastard with a hammer all bloody afternoon, my head feels worse than yours looks."

Jack turned on the bed to look in the direction of the speaker. The pain in his side stopped him. A harsh gasp breaking from between his cracked lips.

"A drink, I'm guessing," the speaker said, and a moment later a small fat man, carrying a jug and pewter cup came into view. "My name is Master Harper, I've been charged with seeing to you. Now don't go getting any ideas. Master Hunt has men outside and one yell from me and you'll not be getting up off that bed for a week. Do you understand me?"

Jack attempted a nod.

Harper poured ale and helped Jack to drink. He was still on his back but managed to raise his head towards the cup. Some of it made it into his mouth, for which he was grateful, and some of it flooded into his broken nose for which he was not. Spluttering, he fell back on the bed, eyes shut, a hand to the pain in his side.

"You've some bonny colours under your shirt lad. I'd not be surprised if a few of those ribs aren't broken," Harper observed.

"You think so?" Jack managed after a moment when the pain lessened.

"I do. Your ribs are the colour of a thunderstorm in June," Harper continued, having missed the edge of sarcasm in Jack's words.

Jack reached towards the cup again, and obligingly Harper helped him to raise his head to it. The ale poured into his mouth and Jack choked.

"Steady lad, just a little at a time," Harper advised, pulling the cup from his lips.

Jack still coughing painfully, ale running from his mouth, dropped back onto the bed.

"I'll leave that here for you. Harper has to go and see Master Hunt now, but I'll not be long," the little man announced, and a moment later Jack heard the door close.

Jack wasn't sure if perhaps he had slept. But from somewhere a noise seemed to revive him and he became painfully aware of the hammering again that pervaded the room.

The hammering stopped.

Jack opened his eyes. Seated in the window embrasure was a neatly- and darkly-attired man, his arms folded, observing him with an interested expression. "I'm pleased to find you awake ..."

The hammering started.

"What are they doing?" the dark-dressed man, exasperated, his voice loud, asked Harper, who was hovering near the end of the bed Jack was laid on.

"It's a new floor, Master Morley. The old one was rotten and they are laying new planking sir," Harper provided.

"Good Lord, is there nowhere quieter?" Morley continued.

"I don't know, sir, it's Master Hunt who decides which rooms are used," the little man provided apologetically. Then added, "We have lost a whole floor with the repair work going on, so we're having to make do with what we have."

Morley rolled his eyes.

The hammering stopped.

Morley turned his eyes back towards Jack. "My name is Christ …"

The hammering started.

Morley's face darkened.

The hammering stopped.

Morley spoke a little quicker. "My name is Christopher Morley and it would help, sir, if we knew …"

Bang… Bang… Bang… Bang… Bang.

"God's Bones!" Morley slithered from his perch near the window and dropped to the floor. "Wait here, Harper."

The door closed with an even louder bang, Jack winced, and Harper shook his head. "I doubt he's going to find anywhere quieter, not unless we go back down a few floors."

Morley, accompanied by two other men, arrived back in a very short period of time.

Bang… Bang… Bang… Bang…

"Get him up between you, come on Harper, there is a free apartment across Tower Green, we can use that," Morley announced from the doorway.

Jack was hoisted to a sitting position on the edge of the bed by hands that were clumsy, but genuinely helpful.

Master Harper advanced, one of Jack's boots in each hand. "Give me a moment, lads, to get these back on him, and then we can go."

Jack wasn't much help when he tried to push his feet into the right boot, the pain in his side had him reaching out for support and cursing in pain.

"I'll get them on, lad," Master Harper reassured, pulling the right boot up, the backs of his white puffy hands looking more like two unbaked small loaves than appendages.

With his boots on, Jack found himself efficiently grasped under each arm, and raised to his feet. They gave him a moment as they felt him sway, but even Jack was surprised by how well his legs were behaving. The damage, it seemed, was confined to his upper body.

"Right then," Morley announced with satisfaction, "let's go somewhere quieter."

As they left, the cacophony increased in ferocity from the ceiling above them.

There were three floors of stone, spiral steps. Keeping as far to the right as they could, they were thankfully wide enough for Jack and his two supporting helpers to descend together. Each jarring impact sent another spasm of pain shooting through his body. The men on either side of him, well accustomed, he would imagine, to carrying the less than able, were doing a good job of taking his weight. But Jack was forced to move at their pace, and it was a faster one than he was ready for.

The last step was hollowed, angled and horribly worn. Jack's right foot slipped from it and his knee buckled beneath him.

"I've got you lad," the man on his right uttered close to his ear as he changed his stance and shouldered Jack's weight. The other man matched his hold, now they carried him with their shoulders pressed under his arms. The man on the left was taller, and Jack found his feet trailing on the ground.

"Come on, it's the one over there," Morley announced, striding from the stone doorway at the foot of the stairs and out into the light.

Jack squinted as the sunlight lanced into his eyes. The two men on either side of him increased their speed to follow Morley, and Jack found his feet trailing beneath him as he was carried to his new accommodation. The three of them side by side filled the path, and a woman, basket over her arm, was forced to take a side step onto the grass. Jack was only aware of her trying to look elsewhere as he was carried past her. He wasn't surprised she averted her gaze - if he felt this bad, then Christ knows what he looked like!

Morley arrived first, holding open the arched wooden door for Harper. It was not wide enough to admit Jack and his helpers and they awkwardly shifted their positions and passed him through the door.

Inside it was cold, and smelt of damp, the contents showing that it was currently being used as a storeroom. There was no bed, and on the right side of the room a pile of chairs were stacked on top of each other.

"Get some of those down," Morley pointed towards them.

Harper moved to oblige and a moment later a chair was set behind Jack and his grateful helpers lowered him into it.

"God, they don't get any lighter," complained the man on his right straightening his back. Then to Morley, "Will that be all, sir?"

"Wait outside until Master Hunt arranges a suitable guard for the door," Morley said as he lowered himself into another chair provided by Harper.

In the distance, work was continuing on the new floor and the banging, now only faintly audible, continued.

Morley and Jack were alone.

"Sir, your name, please?" Morley asked, the words painfully polite. "I suspect the one you gave might not be wholly correct."

Jack tried to sniff through his blocked nose, the act making him choke for a moment. Feigning a pain worse that he was experiencing, an arm wrapped around his injured side, Jack tried to force his battered brain to think.

He was in The Tower, no longer incarcerated in the dungeons? Why? Who did they think he was? What did they think he knew? And where the hell was his brother!

Morley waited patiently.

"Sir, your name?" Morley prompted again.

What name should he give? A false one? The truth?

There was an audible sigh from the man opposite him, seated cross-legged in the chair. "Sir. You were found with a dead man. Some fight appears to have occurred. At the moment we don't know the identity of him, or yourself. We have some indication that one of you might be a man of means, however, which one we don't know."

Jack regarded the man with his one good eye. Silence was not a course he could resort to for much longer.

"The gates of Castille?" Morley placed the words carefully between them.

It was a description of the device on the centre of ring Emilio had left for him, and Jack rewarded Morley with a glance in the

418

direction of his hand where the ring should have been.

Morley smiled. "Good. Now we just need to establish who you are, sir, and why you had that ring. Was it given to you or did you perhaps..."

Jack watched him though his one good eye, his interrogator had been careful not to use the words "stolen." An absurd and involuntary urge to laugh pressed up from within his chest, it emerged as a choking cough that painted alarm over Morley's face. "It was given to me by Emilio de Nevarra," Jack delivered the words as clearly as he could, and they were met with utter silence. Jack for a moment wondered if he had been heard, but then realised that it was shock that was written on Morley's face.

"Thank you sir. And your name?" Morley said after a moment.

"Jack Fitzwarren."

"And the dead man?" Morley asked.

"A robber," Jack provided.

Morley nodded, his hands pushing off the chair arms he rose from the seat. "If you will excuse me for a short while, I will have Master Harper see to you needs."

✝

Morley was back in Cecil's office shortly after leaving Jack.

"Who is he then?" Cecil demanded as soon as he saw Morley entering through the door.

"Jack Fitzwarren," Morley confirmed.

"And this?" Cecil picked up the ring that still rested on his desk.

"He recognises it, and indicates that it was given to him by Emilio de Nevarra," Morley replied.

"Emilio de Nevarra," Cecil repeated, and put the ring back down with a sudden thump on the desk. Grumbling under his breath, Cecil pushed himself from the chair. "The dead man, could that be de Nevarra? Could he have stolen this from him?

"It's possible. Hunt has the body in the yard near his office," Morley conceded.

"Morley, do you know who Emilio de Nevarra is?" Cecil asked, rounding the desk.

Morley was forced to shake his head.

"Ferdinand of Castille's son, he joined the Knights of St John years ago," Cecil replied.

"I'm sorry sir, I'm not certain..." Morley began.

"For God's sake, Morley. Emilio de Nevarra's father is Philip's brother," Cecil clarified.

Morley's eye's widened at that. "He's the King's nephew!"

"Exactly! Get me my cloak," Cecil announced to the room in general.

†

Catherine was stunned. Unable to move, she stood and stared after the man who was being half carried, half dragged between two men following Morley down one of the paths along the side of Tower Green. They arrived at an iron studded, low arched doorway. Morley disappeared inside and the other two men manhandled Jack through the doorway.

Catherine suddenly realised she was standing, stock still, in full view of everyone. Gathering the basket she was carrying closer to her she set off to walk slowly along the same path by which they had just taken Jack. She passed the now closed door, reaching a wood store at the end of the path. Setting the basket on the floor she began to slowly fill it with kindling.

The two men who had carried Jack between them emerged, followed shortly after by a short balding man who headed back towards the prison section of The Tower. Catherine leaned forward, selected more wood and continued to add to that already in the basket. When the door opened again she had the sense to stay bent over her task, and Morley didn't see her, his steps quickly taking him from the door.

What should she do?

Was it really Jack?

Had she made a mistake?

There was only one way to find out. Before she had a chance to change her mind Catherine had filled the basket, hoisted it to her hip and was briskly making her way towards the door.

"I've been told to come and set a fire," she announced, trying to sound as confident as possible.

The two men exchanged a quick glance. The one on the right shrugged and without a word pushed the door open for her to enter.

Catherine stepped into the interior. It was a small set of rooms, much like the ones Elizabeth had been allocated. A narrow passage ran from the door, leading to rooms on the left and right. The door on the right stood open, revealing a room half filled with chairs stacked upon each other.

She was about to turn towards the other room when the sight of a booted foot caught her eye. Stepping into the room and rounding the corner she found him.

Seated in the chair where Morley had left him, staring into the middle distance was Jack Fitzwarren.

If he had heard her enter he gave no sign.

Jesus, he looked a mess!

One eye was fully closed, and a cut on his forehead had leaked blood down one side of his face and into his hair, darkening it and sticking it together in a matted mess. He looked odd, he must have been laid down when the blood had poured from the wound and dripped to the floor and it had made half a dozen lines across his face and neck. The lines were horizontal now as he sat in the chair. His clothes were filthy and torn, and the backs of both his hands showed knuckles ripped of skin. Jack must have sensed her approach, heard her skirts on the floor or the scuff of shoes on the bare boards or the creak from the basket she still held, and his head turned towards the sound. The closed right eye didn't see her, and Catherine had to take two more steps into the room before she found herself returning an unforgettable blue gaze.

Catherine clutched the basket closer and took a step back, her face flushing pink.

Jack's lips opened, and his one good eye was fixed on her face.

"Jack, what happened?" Catherine managed to whisper, the words quiet, the breath choking in her throat.

"Christ, lass! You are the last person I ever thought I'd see," his voice shook, it lacked the timbre she remembered, but it was still Jack.

Words from outside, a conversation exchanged between the guards at the door and another man made Catherine jump. She turned abruptly, dropped to her knees and set her shaking hands to building a fire in the grate.

"I've brought you something to drink, and Master Hunt is sending someone over to see to that cut on your head," a man said, and then he spoke to her, "Woman, set a table next to him so I've somewhere to put this lot down."

Catherine turned from the fire. Holding a wooden tray laden with cups and a jug was a short bald man she had seen leave earlier before Morley. Among the jumbled furniture pressed against one wall of the room was a three-legged stool. Catherine twisted it free from the wooden wreckage and placed it near Jack's right knee. As the man set the tray down and turned his attention back to Jack she grabbed the empty basket and darted through the door.

"You've not lit it!" She heard him call after her.

Then Jack's voice. "I told her to leave it, I'm too warm."

Catherine retreated as quickly as she could to the rooms where Elizabeth was housed. Every step outside was one when she could have bumped into Morley, and she couldn't chance that, she knew her feelings would be written plainly on her face – and Morley missed nothing.

Closing the door to her own room, her legs finally gave out and she sagged on to the edge of the bed.

What had happened? Had he finally come for her?

As much as Catherine wanted to believe in that she knew she couldn't. There had been too much open shock on his face, and his words had been an admission that he had not expected to find her there. So why then was he here? And what had Morley got to do with it?

There was only one way to find out. She was going to have to ask Morley.

CHAPTER TWENTY

✝

Morley knew where the body was and led the way, Cecil trailing impatiently behind him. Ducking through a low Norman arch they passed along a short dark corridor before exiting and emerging into the light. They were in a small enclosed yard, their entry greeted by the angry caws of two crows, startled into flight. A two-wheeled cart, unhooked from a horse, the bed at a perilous angle, stood against the wall. Weighing it down was the body that had accompanied The Tower's latest prisoner.

Laid on its back, the crimson of his blood now an ugly black-red against pallid skin, the spoiled corpse gazed at the sky with sockets picked clean by the carrion. Morley's eyes took in the stomach wound that had boiled with blood, soaking the corpse to its knees, and the right hand missing two middle fingers, both of them cut neatly, just above the knuckles. The clothes were disorderly. The doublet had been torn open, the buttons not undone but ripped from the fabric—someone had hastily searched it for whatever they could find.

Morley stepped back so Cecil could take a closer look.

Cecil pressing his glasses up his nose, circled the cart, examining the corpse from every angle. Morley was sure he'd miss nothing.

"He's wearing a sword belt. Did a blade come in with him?" Cecil asked, pointing towards the empty scabbard.

Morley shook his head. "I asked about that, but there was nothing, it might be the one found at St Bride's. I will check."

"Make sure you do, it might help to identify him," Cecil's eyes were fixed on the severed fingers. "I'd like to know why that happened."

"Robbery?" offered Morley.

"Christ, Morley! The man was dead by the looks of it, they'd no need to do that to him," Cecil replied.

"Perhaps they were stuck," Morley regretted his words as soon as he had spoken them.

"Have you seen the rings that were on those fingers? Silver, and poor silver as well by the looks of them, and that crucifix on the broken chain was pressed pewter.

They were worth very little. They weren't taken from his body because of their value, Morley, they were taken for another reason entirely," Cecil said stepping back, a finger tapping his chin thoughtfully. "His boots are worth more than those trinkets, and they are still on his feet. This was not robbery."

"I am sure you are right," accepted Morley.

"Where is he?" Cecil announced, looking at Morley.

"In one of the apartments near the Byward Tower," Morley replied.

"Byward Tower?" Cecil questioned.

"The noise was too much. Have you heard the hammering? The floor is being replaced, and I couldn't hear myself think, let alone listen to his answers. So I had Hunt find somewhere quieter," Morley explained, applying a fresh square of linen to what was becoming a very sore nose.

"I'm halfway across the Green and even I can still hear it," grumbled Cecil as he headed back towards the corridor and the apartments where their prisoner was held.

When they arrived, Hunt's men were still dutifully positioned on the door, and inside they found Master Harper and their prisoner, though unfortunately only one of them was animated. The little man, delighted to be hosting such important visitors, was on his feet, wide-eyed and beaming helpfully.

"I've seen to him, like you said to, Master Morley," Harper replied happily. "He's had some ale but wasn't too interested in the food what I brought."

Morley looked between Harper and Jack Fitzwarren. "How long has he been like this?"

"He fell asleep about an hour or so ago. The lad has had a right good beating, so I thought I'd just leave him be," Harper replied, standing back so Morley could approach.

"Christ! He's not asleep. He's a fever on him by the look of it," Morley replied.

"Do you think so, sir?" Harper took a step towards Jack, his eyes screwed up to better observe his charge. "I thought he was just asleep."

Jack still sat in the chair, but if the support of the sides had been removed, he would have slithered to the floor in a heap. His head lolled to his shoulder, eyes closed, sweat had caught in his hair and it was stuck erratically to his forehead. A visible shiver ran through his body as they watched.

"I see what you mean," Harper acknowledged, then added by way of explanation, "nothing that I knows about, I can only think that it was because of where they found him."

"Where did they find him?" Morley asked, placing the words carefully.

"Locked in the crypts, with all the corpses at St Bride's," Master Harper provided helpfully.

Morley and Cecil vacated the presence of the prisoner very quickly.

"Come back to my office Morley, we need to tread a careful path through this mire," Cecil commanded, and the pair headed back around the green to Cecil's busy office.

Cecil divested himself of his cloak, one of his attendants taking it from him, before stepping into his private office. Morley, a pace behind him, followed him in and closed the door.

"I'll not loose him, Morley," Cecil replied, and he found a folded sheet on his desk and waved Clement's letter in the air. "If that's Jack Fitzwarren, and it looks like it probably is, then he's likely to become Lord Fitzwarren in the very near future. He's too valuable to release back through those gates. His father might not be on the Privy Council any more, but if this man Jack takes his place, as Lord Fitzwarren, he might find himself placed there, and we know very little about him."

"We know his background," Morley supplied, "he hardly sounds like a man who has been raised to take on such a role."

Cecil glared at Morley. "It's a matter of control, Morley. Let this man go from here, a man who is heir to half of the counties west of London, and what do you think will happen? Eh? Someone will realise his worth." Cecil waved the gold ring in the air, "It seems he's already connected with Emilio de Nevarra."

"We don't know why though, or how?" Morley tried to say reasonably.

"Power. Emilio is a member of the Order, can you imagine the coup on his part if he managed to bring this man into their fold? His inheritance, his estates, everything Lord Fitzwarren owns now would fall under the control of the Order of St John, and that, Morley, is not going to happen. And even if he doesn't join the Order with their backing and support, it's not unlikely, is it, that he'll appear on the Privy Council or in some other office at court in years to come, and that still gives the Order a powerful position if they have influence over him."

Morley did see the dilemma, and he also recognised the more immediate one. If Jack Fitzwarren was carrying the sickness, he should be removed as quickly as possible from the confines of The Tower. The fact that Morley had been in such close proximity himself was starting to worry him, and as a fresh sneeze began to form, he wondered if this one might have a more sinister origin.

"What would you like me to do?" Morley asked cautiously.

Cecil dropped into his chair, discarded the sheet of paper onto the desk and began drumming the fingers of his right hand on the wood. "We can't lose control of him."

"But we can't keep him here?" Morley blurted. "You know the procedures, anyone suspected of carrying the sickness should be removed immediately."

"We don't know if it is or not. He looks like he's been beaten within in an inch of his life," Cecil replied, a deep frown creasing his brow. "Keep him where he is, make sure no one else goes in or out, and contact Tresham. Tell him we have a man claiming association with de Nevarra who needs a physician, tell them he's too ill to move, they can look after him here. After all that's their bloody calling isn't it?"

Morley nodded. It wasn't a bad course of action.

"This way it will look like we've acted on this," Cecil picked up the ring Emilio had given Jack, "but we have retained a controlling hold on him at the same time. And Morley?"

"Yes, Master."

"Keep me informed. If he recovers I want to know about it, immediately." Cecil cast the ring towards Morley, "If you are going to see Tresham you'll need this."

Morley collected the ring from the table and left Cecil's office. His first destination was the apartment near Byward Tower where he informed the guards on the door that no one at all was to be admitted, and that Harper, who was caring for the prisoner, was not to be let out either. Any food was to be handed over at the doorway, and no servants were to enter. If the guards thought the orders strange, both of them were sensible enough not to say so.

†

Sleep, if it had been sleep, slipped from him by degrees. Jack opened his one good eye and closed it again instantly. A tide of nausea rolled unchecked through his body. His right hand lay on the on the wood of the chair arm, and his fingers fastened tightly around it, the flesh stretched thin and white across his knuckles. The left hand flung sideways found one of the uprights under the chair arm and clutched it so hard the wood creaked in complaint. Jack held himself rigid, braced against the pain and dizzying sickness, breathing in tight, controlled breaths, until he felt the attack begin to lessen.

Slackening his hold on the wood, Jack let his body relax and slump in the chair. Without warning a second wave hit him, he couldn't find the wood of the chair, and instead he sat gasping through clenched teeth, his right fist clenched, and the nails of his left hand biting hard into his leg. When he thought it had receded a third shock rolled through him, this one convulsed his muscles viciously, forcing the scant contents of his stomach from him.

Pain seemed done with him after that. It had left him shaking and limp in the chair. His legs, had he tried to use them, he knew, would have provided useless support.

Jack chanced a second glance from his good eye. The closed right one tried to open in unison, but the congealed crusted blood had sealed it shut, he could feel the skin pulling against the muscles. The tangle of wooden wreckage filling the wall opposite him gave him no clue as to where he was. There was a memory of the sound of hammering, and of being carried between two men, and he'd needed to be carried after what Bartholomew...

...Bartholomew.

The night at St Bride's sliced through his mind.

Every detail suddenly remembered. His brother telling him to go towards the Devil's door — where was Richard now? Jack's body straightened in the chair involuntarily, the muscles tightened and the pain from his ribs had him gasping for breath again.

Imprisoned within the blackness of the crypt, they had left him laid on the floor. The side of his chest where Bartholomew had stamped on him throbbed with pain, every careful breath pressuring his broken ribs with agony. He'd been dragged from the crypt, hauled back up the steps, he remembered staring up at the dark wood-beamed ceiling of St Bride's.

Then...Jesus Christ! The Tower!

Had it been real?

Jack's good eye dropped to his right wrist, and what he saw told him that it has been real enough. The manacle had carved a deep livid cut in his wrist, and the skin was blackened, bruised from the iron. There was the man dying in the corner. He even had a sense of his brother being in the room. If he had spoken though, Jack had no memory of the words.

And Jeriah! He remembered being saved from that fate just in time.

He wasn't there now.

Jack's next memory was waking on the bed. Master Harper helping to hold a cup to his cut mouth, then questions...then a calm and reasoned voice asking him his name, and about... Jack's thumb on his right hand moved automatically to the base of the finger where the ring had sat.

Gone.

Missing.

The "Gates of Castille," the voice had said. Someone must know Emilio? Was Emilio here? Had he heard his voice? Jack wasn't sure.

His face felt suddenly hot. Jack's good eyed dropped to the fire place, it was unlit and did not account for the feeling.

As the minutes dragged on he recognised it more and more as it took hold of his body. A pressure in his ears, the throbbing in his dried lips, a burning feeling flickering across his skin, his heart beating rapidly inside his battered ribs.

It was fever.

†

When Jack awoke next he was in a bed. Before he had thought of the request, a cup was placed at his lips. Cool water sluiced into his mouth, breaking through the gritted tight feeling, allowing his tongue to move, the second mouthful seeming to make it further into him rather than just being absorbed by the desiccated flesh.

A hand, cupped behind his head, helped him to drink, and when it was gently removed he became aware of the soft pillow his head lay on.

"Can he hear us?" A voice asked.

Jack wanted to say he could, and he very much wanted to ask where his brother was. There were more words exchanged, he heard them and he wanted to say something, he wanted to reply, but he couldn't.

It must have been night when he woke again, his good eye opening and focusing, with difficulty, on the room. He was laid on his back in a bed in a small room. Against the wall a table stood, upon which was a pewter flagon and cups, next to it a small brazier burnt and a thin stream of undisturbed smoke, like a thread, ran towards the ceiling. Candles burnt in wooden holders near the fire. Twin wicked, they emitted a steady bright light, and the fire added a warm orange glow to their illumination.

A scrape and a bump to his right made him turn his head. A small, brown-robed monk, a rosary tucked into his knotted belt, had risen from a stool next to the bed. Wrinkles around a pair of bright inquisitive eyes and a mouth that formed a genuine warm smile produced a feeling of relief in Jack. Wherever he was, he was in no immediate danger.

"So you are awake are you, lad?" The monk asked as he moved to pour water from the pewter jug. "Toby and I were wondering if you'd open your eyes this morning."

The monk returned, cup in hand. "I'm brother Angus, and that fat lump laid on your legs is Toby. Come on, you'll have to move now."

Jack realised brother Angus was addressing a fat striped cat that was indeed laid across his legs.

Brother Angus set down the cup and scooped a hand under the complaining cat, lifting it further down the bed. The brown striped feline stretched, exposing its white claws, meowed loudly, then settled back down to sleep.

"Worst mouser I've ever known," Brother Angus announced, shaking his head, then returning his attention to Jack. "Can you sit up?"

Jack, hands at his sides, pushed himself up in the bed, the effort of moving leaving him shaking and breathless.

"Sit back," Brother Angus had dropped a pillow behind him and he was efficiently propped up in bed. The cat raised its head to observe the disturbance to his slumber before settling back on the bed and stretching to take up the space formerly occupied by Jack's feet.

†

Catherine had never sought out Morley, but then she had never wanted to. He found her when he needed her, when he had a task he needed performing or a question he needed to ask. So now that she wanted to find him, Catherine found that she had very little idea where to look. The fact that her own freedom was fairly limited as well did not help. She was allowed free movement within the rooms appointed to Elizabeth and to the gardens adjoining them and she could accompany her mistress to meals. The only other time she would find herself alone was when she made the short journey to bring in kindling for the fire. It did not afford her much opportunity to find him.

Instead she was left with the frustrating task of looking out for him, seeing if he would reappear near the room where she now knew Jack was being held.

What had happened to him?

When Catherine finally saw him, urgency overruled caution and Catherine ran from the apartments along the path and fetched up a few paces before Christopher Morley. His brow furrowed for a moment, and then a genuine smile settled on his face.

"I wanted to speak with you, sir," Catherine said.

"Of course," Morley hooked his arm through hers, "however, perhaps not when we are standing in the middle of Tower Green assailed by stares from all sides."

Guided by the darkly clad Morley she allowed him to lead her across along the path skirting the green towards the room where Jack was. There were, she still noted, guards on the door. They passed the door and Morley released her arm, pushed open the next one along for her and held it while she stepped over the threshold. It was identical in layout to the one next door and her feet took her automatically into the room on the right of the corridor.

"I did wonder," Morley said, folding his arms and leaning against the door frame, "Master Harper told me a servant had been in to set a fire. So as we thought, we do have Jack Fitzwarren next door."

Catherine whirled around to face him. "What's happened to him?"

"That is something only he can tell us, and at the moment he's lost his senses," Morley replied.

"What have you done to him?" Catherine said accusingly.

"Nothing, believe me, he's running a fever and for the moment no one is allowed in or out. So for your own safety, my dear, don't try and get into his rooms again, please. Did he tell you anything when you saw him?"

Catherine shook her head.

"Are you sure? Surely you asked him what had happened?" Morley questioned.

"I did, but a man came into the room before he could reply," Catherine said.

"That's a shame," Morley replied, his voice sounding filled with genuine regret.

Catherine found the arm of the chair, leant heavily upon it and then, heedless of Morley in the room, lowered herself into it. A hand pressed to her face, the tears ran from her eyes and her shoulders shook.

"Oh, my dear, I'm so sorry," Morley said, laying a hand on her shoulder. "He is to be cared for here. If he recovers I will let you know.

"Get off me!" Catherine pulled from his touch, her voice angry and loud.

✝

441

John Somer rarely attended Court. Pleading his age, he preferred to work from his home which was only a short river journey away. Such was his efficiency and competence that his absence was rarely, if ever, questioned. Today, however, he had been forced to his office in The Tower by the climax of his wife's plans for an extravagant entertainment and a lavish meal which seemed to require the upheaval of every room in the house. The addition to his household of his wife's mother, a wizened shrew who revelled in the art of complaint, had persuaded him to leave his house early, when the fog still lay on the river.

Concentration though, was proving to be an elusive commodity. Every time he tried to put together a string of coherent thoughts, or turn his mind to reading, it would be punctuated at irregular and inappropriate points by the continuous and noisy repair work taking place across the other side of Tower Green.

"For the Lord's sake!" Somer exclaimed to the empty room, casting down the sheet he had been trying to read. Discarding his spectacles on the desk, he closed his eyes and massaged the bridge of his nose with a thumb and forefinger.

The noise had finally abated.

Sighing loudly Somer settled the spectacles back on his nose, adjusted the angle, and slid the sheet back in front of him. It was a letter that required a reply and, dipping a pen into the ink, he was about to begin when he was disturbed again.

The next tapping noise though was of a different order, it was a steady knock on his closed office door.

"I concede defeat!" Somer growled under his breath. Opening a drawer he dropped the sheet he had been reading inside before calling out an invitation to enter.

The man who stood on the threshold was about as welcome as the noise.

Cecil.

Somer forced a welcoming smile onto his face. "Come in, come in. I was just looking for an excuse to stop work."

"What coaxed you to join us?" Cecil, smiling equally as falsely, entered Somer's office.

"It was a bad decision, and one based on misinformation!" Somer said, rising from behind his desk and gesturing towards a chair. "My wife has some great entertainment planned, and she has her mother visiting as well, so I had thought to find myself somewhere quieter to work, but just listen to it..."

"I know. It's been like this all week. Three full floors are being replaced, I've been told it will be another week at least before they are finished." Cecil ignored the chair Somer had offered, instead crossing the room he stared from the window towards the source of the clattering. "I feel like I have my head in a barrel full of woodpeckers."

Somer laughed as he lowered himself back into his chair. "I agree. I would rather put up with my wife's mother than this. I've no intention of coming back to this tomorrow."

"I just wish they had given some notice. I could have relocated myself for a few weeks," Cecil replied gloomily, leaning on the stone window sill.

"It's got something to do with the weather," Somer replied.

"The weather?" Cecil turned towards Somer, confusion in his voice.

"The timber is seasoned," Somer said by way of explanation. When Cecil's expression remained blank he continued, "They can't keep it all dry in this weather, the damp is getting to it. If they don't use it soon it will warp, that's why they have every free carpenter in London in there at the moment."

"Ah, I see, well at least it will be over soon, which will be a blessing." Cecil, his hands clasped behind his back, moved towards the chair.

Somer, considering that sufficient pleasantries had now been exchanged, asked, "I'm sure you didn't come to discuss The Tower repairs?"

Cecil, also acknowledging that courtesy had been served, said, "I've come to return this to you."

Cecil produced a marked and aged square of parchment from inside his doublet.

It was one that Somer immediately recognised. Without a word he rose from his chair, rounded the desk, crossed to the door, and twisted the key that rested in the lock.

Rather than offer the sheet to Somer, Cecil had lowered himself into the chair, tapping the square absently on his knee. "You seem surprised?"

"I did wonder if I would ever see if it again, yes. Can I assume then that the Devise has been settled?" Somer asked, raising his gaze from the paper in Cecil's hand to the other man's eyes. Cecil had been working for months now to settle the succession, and Somer suspected that it was now concluded.

Cecil nodded. "The Queen has signed it."

"Does Philip know?"

"She signed yesterday, at the moment few know. Many might suspect, but only those who directly witnessed her signature know, and they are sworn to keep silent on the matter," Cecil said. Somer noted that the younger man had let a slight hint of triumph edge his words. Had he possessed any liking for Cecil, he would have advised him that it was a fault he should address. The Court much preferred a condition of competent indifference from its administrators; success was something to be reserved for those of higher rank.

"Will she write to advise him? Do any of his courtiers know?" Somer placed the questions quickly.

"I don't think she dares to tell him, and it matters little," Cecil replied, pulling the corner of his robe over his knee. "We have ensured that the Devise has popular support, and soon it will be ratified by the Privy Council."

"And what about the keystone upon which this agreement was secured? Two sides, both in agreement, but for different reasons?" Somer's right hand had found a pen and he was rolling it between his fingers, his expression thoughtful, his eyes watching Cecil carefully. As yet he did not know why the man was sitting in his office.

"Courtenay remains an issue, that's true. One we could do without, he's still in Italy at the moment, and under Mary's orders banished from England, so he can't return here," Cecil said in agreement. The noise had begun again outside. Annoyingly, Cecil's tapping of the paper on his knee was out of synchronism with the hammering.

"Not yet. But that's only a matter of time," Somer, discarding the pen, flung his hands wide.

"It is a problem that requires a solution," Cecil replied. "Those who supported this, wishing to see Courtenay wedded to Elizabeth, are pressing for a proxy marriage. Courtenay has approached the Pope and he might well get dispensation."

"Has he had a reply?" Somer leant forward slightly in the chair, was this to be the crux of Cecil's visit?

Cecil shook his head. "He has not received an answer. There will be a price attached to this and my sources tell me Courtenay is short of funds, his supporters will by trying to find the gold he needs to sway Rome."

"That's all we need," Somer said wearily. "And from here we can hardly stop him, can we?"

"Yes, it is somewhat of an issue," Cecil replied pointedly.

Somer's eyes narrowed—here it comes. "You have a solution?"

"Perhaps," Cecil replied, then he added, "You are against this match?"

"You know the answer to that," Somer replied.

"Then I know I can count on you to help me with the problem," Cecil said smiling, twisting the parchment between his fingers for a moment before he slid it back inside his doublet. "There were some men who were very curious as to where that came from. You can, of course, rely on my discretion."

Any warmth dropped from Somer's face, his grey eyes taking on a winter quality. "Are you saying that to prevent this I need to act?"

"No, just that I am hoping I can count on your help," Cecil said smoothly.

"Get to the point, Cecil," Somer's voice was harsh and abrupt.

"John, please, I mean nothing personal, both of us work for the good of the Crown, we are on the same side." Cecil's words dripped affability.

"Get on with it," Somer said, ignoring his amicable protestations.

Cecil shrugged, but appeared little perturbed by Somer's cool words. "What do you know about the Fitzwarren family?"

The question caught Somer off guard, as it was meant to. Despite his best efforts

Somer was sure Cecil, a skilled dissembler, had seen a look of uncertainty flit across his face, though there was no reciprocal expression to confirm this on Cecil's calm features. Somer knew his reply also came a moment too late.

"Lord Fitzwarren has been away from court for years, and his son, Robert, is a wastrel of the highest order," Somer, back in firm control, placed the words carefully.

"Didn't one of his other son's work for you for a while?" Cecil asked, then he added unnecessarily, "the one who is wanted for treason?"

Every nerve ending was alive in Somer's brain: where was this going?

"Richard, yes, years ago, after Seymour was executed, not for long though," Somer accepted, it was after all a truth that there was little point in denying.

"It seems there might be another brother, Jack, with a connection to the Order of St John, and I was wondering what you might know about that?" Cecil asked pointedly.

"A third brother? That's not a name I've heard before," Somer said with genuine honesty.

A third brother? And the connection with the Order he did know about—this was getting far too close for comfort.

"There was a fracas at St Bride's, and a man who we believe is Jack Fitzwarren ended up in The Tower," Cecil was still watching Somer carefully.

"Is he a member of the Order? If my memory is correct there was another member of the family who joined," Somer tapped his fingers on the desk, he knew exactly who it was; the ruse of forgetfulness, though, was buying him a few moments to get his mind ahead of Cecil's. "A cousin I think, but the name eludes me."

"I'm sure it does," Cecil replied, sounding not at all convinced. "I believe you are thinking of Edward Fitzwarren?"

"Yes, that's the man. Joined years ago, much against his father's wishes if I recall," Somer said in agreement.

"Richard Fitzwarren, would you know where *he* is?" Cecil shifted slightly forward in the chair.

Somer shook his head. "As far as I know, Richard is out of the country, wanted for treason, and not likely to return until the reason for that is gone."

"I was wondering if he might be a little closer, especially given that his half-brother is in London. He's a man wanted for treason, but that is a transient charge that is likely to vaporise, especially in the face of the Devise. The reason for the charge was his loyalty to Elizabeth, would such a man not be ideal to assist with the issue of preventing this proxy wedding?"

"He might be. However, I've no idea where he is," Somer's reply was blunt.

Cecil drummed his fingers on his knee for a moment, then seemed to reach a decision. "One of my men has been making enquiries, and it seems that Lord William might have fallen prey to Robert. He seems to have taken control of his land and property and has locked his father away somewhere, in rather poor conditions from the sound of it."

Somer's eyebrows raised a degree. "If that is so it is a sad state of affairs. No man in his dotage deserves to be dealt with by the heavy hand of his sons. I am not sure why you are telling me."

"I thought there might be a chance that your path might cross with Richard Fitzwarren, he might not be so pleased at the treatment of his father," Cecil said. Somer knew that Cecil was giving him leverage, something he hoped he would use to manipulate Richard.

"And this other man, Jack, you are sure he is son of William? Why not impart this to him? Would he not be equally as interested?" Somer countered, moving the conversation away from Richard.

"He has, temporarily one hopes, lost his senses to fever. He was found badly beaten and is being cared for here at The Tower. We could not overlook his connection with the Order, and Thomas Tresham has provided one of their members, versed in medicine, to care for him. So the questions I have for him will have to wait." Cecil suddenly slapped his palms down on his legs in a gesture of finality, and a moment later rose from the chair. "Well, I am sure we both have much to do."

Somer didn't rise, but watched in silence as Cecil walked to the door, turned the key and without a backward glance let himself out of Somer's office.

Damn the man!

Somer leant back in his chair. There was much to consider.

This Devise was going to be hugely unpopular with Philip. If Mary died then he would move to make himself her successor, and Mary, his loving wife, had been persuaded to block him in favour of her half-sister, a woman she had many reasons to dislike. Somer knew Cecil had used the paper that hinted at Mary's illegitimacy to secure her signature. An ill and ageing lady, manipulated by a clever and deceitful advisor. Somer managed to keep the distaste from his face. He also recognised that even if he had not been party to that conversation, his provision of the evidence made him just as complicit as Cecil. His motives, he assured himself, were borne from a desire to serve England, and to save her from Spain. Cecil wanted to be the power behind the throne, and his tireless work to help place Elizabeth there would, he hoped, not only retain him his current position, but earn him even more recognition.

Cecil had made the threat quite clear. He wanted rid of Courtenay, and he was pressuring Somer to aid him in that by retaining the parchment. He was probably right; Fitzwarren was an ideal candidate for the job—but where was he? He doubted very much that the information that his father was suffering would be a lever he could use, there was little love between the pair, that much he did know. However, this new member of the family, one that he had not heard of, Jack, might be the key to obtaining Richard's assistance.

Somer's head throbbed.

If Richard's half-brother, who had some connection with the Order, was in Cecil's custody then Richard would not be far away.

Somer just needed to find him.

CHAPTER TWENTY-ONE

✝

Carter's insistence that he sleep had made unwanted sense.

He had blundered around all night without a plan, and Richard knew if he continued on this journey, his senses, now deadened by exhaustion, were not going allow him to provide much help to Jack.

By the time Isaac's group had returned, he had been reunited with his clothes and found his way across London, it was past noon. After an hour's discussion with Carter it was even later and Richard had been reluctant to sleep, he wanted to talk to Somer. Carter though, had been insistent, and had promised to wake him after an hour. Richard, trusting his friend, slept well; his sleep was not one troubled by the worry of not waking.

"Come on, up with you," Carter's voice had him instantly awake, he'd slept dressed, and just needed to pull on his boots.

"I've one condition," Carter continued, folding his arms and leaning with his back against the wall.

"What's that?" Richard asked, reaching for the second boot.

"Have something to eat, there's food in the kitchen," Carter said, holding the door open for Richard to pass. "I don't expect you to sit and eat it, but take some with you."

Richard, grateful for his friend's understanding, smiled. "I will."

Within a few minutes, his hands full of bread and cheese, he was once again in the street outside Carter's house. This time he had the outline of a plan. Persuade Somer to help, whatever the cost, and if that failed, then he had hopefully left himself a watery entryway back into the Tower. He would have to just hope that the dead gaoler, floating face down amongst the reeds, had not been found. The bells were striking for two by the time he set his feet back across London and it was nearly four by the time he was in The Strand, this time presenting himself at Somer's front door.

Somer was out.

To the left of the door was a comfortable reception room, he was shown in there while the servant went to enquire if there was news of Somer's return.

Richard paced across the room. This had not been part of his plan. Somer rarely left his house, he hated Court, and part of his condition of working for it was that he could do so from the comfort of his home. Other officials would have a room at court, they would stop there rather than return home—would Somer?

A sound from behind him made him turn abruptly.

"Richard Fitzwarren," said a voice he remembered. Standing in the doorway, small, neat, and expensively jewelled was Somer's wife, Lucy. One hand on the door handle and the other against the frame she blocked the exit, regarding him with a cool quizzical gaze. "The last time your name came up in conversation, there were several other words included in the same sentence that I'd rather not have my husband associated with."

Richard preformed a quick bow, and his tone, when he spoke was sincere. "I beg just a few moments of your husband's time, nothing more."

Lucy laughed, a bright blue enameled necklace dancing with the rhythm. "Do you think I don't remember you? There's always something more, you are a byword for trouble."

"I will promise not to return to your door again, if you would grant me one final meeting with your husband," Richard asked, his voice serious and his grey eyes fastened upon hers.

"Don't take me for a fool. He is due back in an hour, we have guests arriving soon. You may talk to John, but be quick, and by God leave him in a good humour or you'll be answering to me," Lucy's mouth twisted at one corner into the tiniest of smiles.

Richard returned the smile a hundredfold and said with relief, "May God grant you peace and hear your prayers."

"Humph, He very well might, but I doubt there will be any eternal peace while you are around. Can I send in some food and wine while you wait? I could take you to join my other guests, though while that would be both delightful and highly entertaining, I am not entirely sure it would be wise." The smile widening, she added, "Lady Burghley is here."

Lady Burghley was William Cecil's second wife.

"Then I agree, that your arrangements are entirely prudent and wise," Richard replied. "There is no need to send servants this way on my account."

Lucy nodded. "I will send John here as soon as he arrives. And remember, be quick!"

She released the door, and Richard found himself once more on his own.

It was a long hour before the door opened again, and this time John Somer walked into the room, pulling it quickly closed behind him.

There was no shock or surprise on the elderly man's face.

"You expected me?" Richard stated.

"Sit down, my legs are tired and I'll not have you hover over me like an expectant child." Somer rarely sounded agitated, and Richard thought he could also detect an undercurrent of anger in his voice.

Richard pulled the other chair across the carpet, seating himself close to Somer. He did not wish for his words to carry.

Somer removed his spectacles and rubbed his eyes. There was a smear of ink across one cheek. Once it would have made Richard smile, but not today.

"Confounded things. It has got so that I can't see with them and I can't see without them!" Somer cast his spectacles into his lap. "It's a curse of old age, one you should be thankful is not upon you yet."

There was a light knock at the door and a servant entered carrying a silver tray with wine and glasses.

"Set it down, there," Somer pointed to a small side table, and the servant, his work done, left, closing the door noiselessly behind him.

Somer pinched the bridge of his nose between his fingers. "Let me pour myself a glass. I think I am going to need it when you tell me of the mire you have found yourself wading through."

Somer picked up the decanter and, pulling the glasses towards him, filled them. One he slid towards himself, the second, his hand on the base, he pushed across the small table towards Richard. The glass, although smooth, resisted against the gilding on the wood and wobbled precariously. Wine pitched itself towards the rim, and a moment later Richard's hand closed around the glass, steadying it.

"You must be a drain on your household, if it's not glasses, its oil lamps. If it's not those, it's ink pots," Richard said, shaking his head. His voice though was weary, and there was little humour in his words.

"I might break or lose the odd item, however that's nothing in comparison to what you have recently mislaid, is it?" Somer's voice reprimanded.

Somer now had Richard's complete attention, he sat the glass back on the table soundlessly. "What have I mislaid?"

"More of a who than a what by the sounds of it. Do you wish to tell me about this troublesome knave?" Somer replied, both hands around his glass, a thumb running around the twisted stem.

"Jack Fitzwarren is my brother, how do you know about him?" Richard asked.

"Cecil has him in the Tower," Somer replied.

Richard nodded, his expression grave. "How is he?"

"He's in The Tower gaol, that's all I know," Somer supplied. "Dare I ask how he got there in the first place?"

"Carelessness," Richard replied. "There was a fight."

"So I gather. Knowing you, that would not have been a random act of violence. You are here to ask for my help, so I think it would be prudent to tell me what happened. Don't you?"

"I don't know if prudent would be an ideal word to describe it. I'll concede you an explanation, and I do need your help," Richard replied.

"This at least should be entertaining," Somer said refilling his glass.

"That observation depends very much from where you are viewing the situation, I am doubting my brother would describe it as such at the moment," Richard replied coldly.

"Well then, get on with it, man," Somer said.

Richard summarised their situation in very few minutes. He had expected more questions, but Somer listened to the narrative attentively, and when Richard finished he sat in thoughtful silence for a few moments before he responded. "Cecil has your brother at the moment, as far as I am aware there are no additional charges made against him."

"What would I need to do to get him released?" Richard asked plainly.

Somer twisted the stem of his own glass in his hand for a moment. "Edward Courtenay."

"The Earl of Devon, yes, I know him," Richard replied evenly.

"How he survived Wyatt's plotting was a mystery even to me. However thin it might be, his veins run with royal blood and he is at the heart of every conspiracy and plot to take the throne. The man's mind is addled by his ambition," Somer finished.

"He had an unfortunate life," Richard said carefully.

"Don't give the man excuses," Somer reprimanded.

"Is charity an excuse?" Richard replied calmly.

"In Courtenay's case it is. In the last year he might as well have set up a market stall in the centre of London selling his pedigree. There is not a faction he has not approached in the hope of advancement. Mary likes him well enough, and forgives him his duplicity, but this time he has gone too far."

"Go on," Richard put his glass, the wine it held barely touched, back on the desk.

"If he marries Elizabeth he believes his position will be unassailable, two tenuous claims will make one solid one," Somer said.

"Elizabeth's claim is hardly tenuous," Richard pointed out.

"I will say this only between these four walls, if Courtenay marries Elizabeth then her claim will be extremely tenuous and very short lived. Without prior consent from Mary the marriage would be tantamount to treason and that would spell the end for both of them," Somer replied.

"As you say, between these walls, I cannot see Elizabeth agreeing to this," Richard replied.

"I doubt she would, she's already turned him down once, however he's headed to Italy where he either intends to press the Pope for the possibility of a proxy wedding and failing that there is a plot afoot to remove Elizabeth from England and force her into the marriage," Somer replied. "This is, however, not the crux of the problem. Cecil has been using the possibility of the wedding, to secure the Privy Council's support for Elizabeth as heir. There are those who have backed her if she marries Courtenay, and those who support her if she does not marry him."

"And why are you telling me this?" Richard asked carefully.

"Cecil has secured the support of both sides, and now the Devise is completed and approved, Cecil needs to ensure the wedding, proxy or otherwise, will not take place," Somer said.

"I am not sure how you feel I am involved in this," Richard said.

"Because I think you will be leaving England very soon, and I want Courtenay stopped, that is to be the condition," Somer said with finality.

"Stopped," repeated Richard.

"Yes."

"There is only one way to stop that fool from being a threat to the succession," Richard observed dryly.

"Exactly, he needs to be removed from it," Somer said. "I will not allow a fool and his ambition to sink England, and there are many others on the Privy Council in agreement."

"Supporters of Elizabeth?" Richard queried quietly.

Somer nodded. "In return I will ensure your brother's safety."

Richard cocked his head. "I would have one condition."

Somer raised his eyebrows. "A condition? Are you in such a position to ask for one?"

"I would speak to Lady Elizabeth, I'll only act if it is in accordance with her wishes," Richard replied.

Somer tapped his fingers on the desk. "I can arrange that, and I think you can be sure it will not be a wedding that she'll favour. Stay here tonight, and I will arrange for you to meet with Elizabeth in the morning."

Richard nodded in acceptance of Somer's words.

Somer's mood changed abruptly, he said cheerfully, "It does seem that I might be able to do you a favour, if you wish it, before you leave England."

"Is this another poisoned chalice?" Richard's voice was weary now.

"It might be, or it might not be, that depends I suppose. It concerns your father," Somer replied.

"Is he dead?" Richard said bluntly.

"Maybe. We don't know. Your brother, Robert, has spirited him away from London, allegedly to Suffolk, and he's not been seen since," Somer said. "Morley was sent to question Robert who flatly turned him away, but before he left the house he found your father tied naked to a chair. By the time he returned with Cecil's men Robert and your father had gone."

"My father and I are not on the best of terms," Richard supplied.

"Perhaps you should be," Somer replied, his eyebrows raised.

"Why?" Richard read the look on Somer's face and placed the word slowly.

"It appears he has disinherited his son,"

"He does that a lot, which one this time?" Richard's tone was acid.

"You know damn well who I mean. He has disinherited Robert in favour of Jack. You seem surprised?"

"I am," Richard said.

"All I can say is that if your father dies, and that fact becomes known, then the inheritance will fall to your brother. He's tainted with treason and murder and it will be more than I can do to remove him from custody when the Fitzwarren estates are forfeit, that will be a prize Mary will not let slip through her hands." Somer said.

"What do you suggest?"

"I suggest that you leave England, and quickly, and if you want to take the opportunity to find out where your father is on the way, then I have given you the opportunity," Somer replied.

Somer rose from his chair, Wait in here, I will have a servant prepare a room for you and collect you when it is ready. My wife has quite a number of guests tonight, I would advise you to remain inside until the morning."

†

Somer did not immediately join his wife, instead he made his way upstairs to his office. He lit a lamp and settled down to pen a letter that would ensure that Richard Fitzwarren had no difficulty whatsoever gaining entry to the Tower the following day.

CHAPTER TWENTY-TWO

†

Shortly after Somer had left, Richard was escorted by his Steward to a small room on the same floor as Somer's office. A tray of food had been provided along with wine.

He couldn't stay in the room. Confined. Within him there was too much turmoil, too much desire to do something, even if he had no idea what that something was. To spend the night, inactive, alone, was beyond him. Escaping from the room was fairly easy and he could return in the morning before Somer realised he was missing.

Richard's original intention had been to leave Somer's house and return quietly to Carter's home. Christian's quiet, competent companionship was preferable to spending a night alone in Somer's house.

As time went on, his plans were becoming more and more intangible, with no more durability than a spider's web and with less purpose. His feet took him across London, but not to Carter's house, instead he found himself shrouded by the drab shadow cast by the church spire opposite his father's house.

Lost in thought, he watched the house prepare for the end of the day. Like an old dog with bleary eyes the shutters were closed on the lights on the ground floor as the house went to sleep. The upper floors had been in darkness since he had arrived, and the only light showing now at the front of the house was that seeping around the jamb of the front door. There would be a lamp burning there until the morning. It was a sign that the house was occupied, that this was a Lord's house.

His mind filled with what Somer had offered.

His brother for Courtenay.

It was not a deal he had to think about for overly long. It had been a better outcome than he had thought it would be; he had only hoped that Somer might hold some sway to help release Jack, he had not been ready for a deal to be offered to him.

It had been too quickly offered.

It was too neat.

Somer and Cecil knew who Jack was, Richard had been expected.

What was he missing?

Was his brother dead already?

Was Cecil using him?

Was Somer using him?

And why tell him about his father?

He had little reason to doubt Somer's words. He could well believe that Robert had dealt cruelly with their father, and he didn't overly care.

Richard rested against the wood of the opposite building, lost in thought for an hour before he finally headed toward the house. He abandoned any thought of approaching unseen from the rear and instead marched directly across the street, hammered on the front door, and waited.

From behind the door he could hear the slow uneven tread of footsteps. As he waited he saw the vertical slice of light brighten as the lamp on the other side was turned up.

Richard rapped on the door again. "Charles, its Richard."

He'd recognised the uneven limp of his father's oldest retainer, he'd last seen him four years ago, and it surprised him that the man was still alive. He'd been with the family since Richard had been a child.

"Master Fitzwarren!" The shaky, aged voice addressed him from the other side of the door uncertainly. "It's late, master and I've been told to open the door to no one."

"Not even to me?" Richard replied.

"How do I know it's you?" the shaky voice replied.

"You recognised my voice, didn't you?" Richard said reasonably.

"My old ears could be playing tricks on me, I'm not sure I should open the door," Charles replied nervously.

"Charles, it's freezing out here, open the door!" Richard felt his patience beginning to fray, after everything that had happened to be denied by an old man in the night was too much.

Something in his tone must have told the old man of his rising annoyance and the old voice snapped back, "Come back in the morning."

"Charles, wait, please. I am sorry, I have had unpleasant day. I am the same Richard Fitzwarren who stole your boots after I lost my own in a card game. It's cold, Charles, please open the door," Richard said, his voice losing its impatience, now just tinged with weariness.

After a second's silence there was the rough rasp of an iron bolt being drawn back through securing loops, the noise was repeated a second time and a moment later the door was swung open before him. Charles, bent-backed, his head tilted, defying the stoop of age squinted at the face before him, his right hand holding up the lamp.

"Charles, you fool, unless your eyesight has improved I know you can't see me, but you can hear my voice," Richard replied.

A face cracked with age grinned, exposing a row of pink bereft gums. Charles stepped back, his arm swinging the lamp out of the way to allow Richard to enter. The old man fumbled with the handle on the lamp, and it was Richard who closed the door and set the latches back in place.

"Robert, I assume, is elsewhere?" Richard asked quickly.

Charles nodded. "He's been gone for months, we thought he was with Lord Fitzwarren."

There was the harsh tread of boots further along the corridor.

Charles paled. "Ronan." Twisted bony fingers pulled the blanket he had shawled over his shoulders closer.

Richard stepped in front of the aged retainer a moment before a door opened at the end of the corridor and William's Steward, and Robert's man, filled the frame. He paused for a second only, fury lighting his face, before he began to stride towards Richard. "I'm in charge here, and you've no place in this house. Out, do you hear me?"

"Still your tongue and your feet, Steward." Richard's voice was cold and lethally edged.

Ronan ignored the warning. A big man with a vicious streak, it was obvious he had every intention of enforcing his threat personally, and he continued to close the distance between them.

Charles let out a nervous whimper and pressed himself against the side of the corridor. "You'd best do as he says, lad."

Ronan had closed the gap and a readily prepared fist swung through the air, its destination Richard's head.

The blow did not connect.

Richard stepped quickly towards Ronan and brought the heel of his hand up hard under the man's jaw. There was a sickening crack and blood poured from the right hand side of Ronan's mouth painting a livid trail down his chin. The swiping fist recoiled and turned into a hand flattened against his bleeding mouth. Richard's fist connected next with his cheek, the two rings he wore cleaving two bleeding tracks across his face. If Ronan had any thought about a retaliatory assault his mind was abruptly changed when Richard levelled a knife blade at his chest.

"Lord Fitzwarren is absent, and so is my brother, which places me in direct control I would think. Now, what to do with you?" Richard said, obvious pleasure on his face as he registered the dismay in Ronan's eyes. "Charles, has the tack room still got a good lock on it?"

Charles hesitated for a moment only, until he realised what Richard meant to do. "It has, Sir."

Richard's smiled widened. "Excellent, go on Ronan, lead the way."

Five minutes later Ronan was secured in the locked and windowless room attached to the end of the stable block where the tack and saddles were kept, and Richard, placing a guiding hand on Charles' arm, took him back into the direction of the house.

"Do you know where Robert has taken my father?" Richard asked.

"I don't, it's Jon you need to talk to," Charles said.

"Jon?" Richard queried.

"Jon Ushart, he was one of Lord Fitzwarren's servants. Months ago he went with the Lord and Edwin, he came back a few weeks ago thinking he could rejoin the household here and Ronan threw him from the house," Charles finished.

"Where do I find Jon?" Richard asked.

"His wife Anne, she worked here as well, one of the laundry women, and when Jon came back he turned her off as well. I've no idea where they went," Charles said sadly.

"Would Ronan know?" Richard asked.

"I doubt it. Milly Wade, one of the cooks, was friendly with Anne and she's still here, she might be able to tell you where they live," Charles said.

Richard clapped Charles on the arm, "Let's go and find Milly then, shall we?"

"She's likely as anything to be in the room she shares, I can go and get her," Charles said, sounding delighted now by this turn of events.

Milly Ward, nervous and unsure of why she was being asked questions about Anne Ushart, arrived in the kitchen accompanied by Charles a few minutes later. She looked utterly horrified to find a man seated on the edge of her kitchen table helping himself to plums from a bowl in the middle.

"It's young master Fitzwarren," Charles said, by way of explanation.

Milly Ward looked utterly confused, and quite sceptical, but put in a quick curtsey anyway.

"He's quite right, Milly. I am Richard Fitzwarren, and I am trying to find my father. Last seen, it appears, in the company of Jon Ushart, would you know where I might find him?" Richard said, his voice level and serious. He dropped from the edge of the table and now stood.

Milly's eyes flicked between Richard and Charles. "He's not in trouble, is he?"

"Of course not. I just want to find out where my father has gone, and I believe the only person here who might know is Jon. If you know where I might find him I would much appreciate it," Richard said.

"I don't know if I can help," Milly said, her voice nervous.

"I can understand your loyalty might lie with…"

"No, I mean, I think they've left London," Milly said quickly. "They rented a room over The Fox in River Street, but Jon couldn't find work and he was going to go back to his parent's house near Norfolk, I think they might have left by now," Milly explained.

"When was the last time you saw them?" Richard replied.

"A week ago, Anne came to say goodbye," Milly said.

"Do you have any idea where in Norfolk?" Richard said.

"All I know is that his father had a farm and his brother had taken it over. He was going back there hoping he could find work and somewhere to live with his family," Milly provided.

"Where in Norfolk? Do you have a village name?" Richard asked.

Milly shook her head, her brow creased, then suddenly she said, "Yes, I think Anne said Dareham, but I can't be sure."

"I'd like to talk to the rest of the servants, assemble them for me," Richard said.

"But it's the middle..." The look on Richard's face stopped her words.

"The quicker we do this, then the quicker you can all get back to your beds," Richard advised.

Lord Fitzwarren's household was assembled shortly after. All of them summoned to the room at the front of the house normally used exclusively by Robert, on the opposite side of the corridor from where William had been trussed and tied. There were eight other kitchen and house staff, including Milly Ward, eight men with various posts around the house and in the stables. Robert's room, carpeted, plush and expensively decorated was not a place the servants felt at home, and it showed on their faces. They had all hastily dressed, and two of the women wore long thick shawls over their linen shifts.

Charles had summoned them, and they had hesitantly entered the room, the door left ajar. Richard was seated on the edge of the table, his arms folded as they filed in room, asking each of them their name. Charles arrived last following in a tall man whose stained clothes told of an outdoor occupation.

"Is that everyone?" Richard asked.

Charles cast his watery eyes over the collected servants, and apart from Ronan, everyone was accounted for. "Yes, Master Fitzwarren."

Richard let his eyes run over the assembled crowd. "My father is absent, and my brother, so you will be taking your orders from me."

Richard paused and there were a few quick nervous glances exchanged.

He turned his attention to one of the taller of the men. "The Steward is in the tack room, can you bring him in here please."

There was uncertainty on the man's face.

Richard added, "Use any force that is necessary."

That produced a broad grin from the man. "Aye, sir, I'll have him for you in a moment."

Silence settled once more on the assembled group. All of them became aware of a heated exchange taking place outside the room as Ronan was being escorted down the corridor.

The door opened, Ronan was pulled in, the man having a tight hold on the steward's arm.

Ronan twisted free from the man's hold and turned to face Richard, a sneer on his face.

"Is he a good steward?" Richard asked Milly Ward suddenly. She flushed and looked at the floor. "Charles, is he a man who has my father's interests at heart."

Charles shook his head firmly.

Richard regarded the furious man calmly. "Not a good recommendation for a master. Is it?"

Ronan looked between them all, his face hardening. The faces of the other servants had changed after Richard's words, now they were sending him derisory looks.

"Should I keep Master Ronan as steward, Charles?" Richard asked, folding his arms.

"No sir," Charles's reedy thin voice was heard by all of the occupants of the room.

Richard nodded. "It seems you have been fairly well condemned, Master Steward."

"You can't do this!" Ronan managed, anger finally breaking through. "None of you can do this. You wait until Master Fitzwarren gets back and you'll all be out of the house. Do you hear me? Do you?"

"I think they do, however, until that unhappy state comes to pass it is you who is going to be turned out of this house," Richard pronounced.

The nervous expressions on those in the room had now changed, some of them wearing a sneaking smile.

"It's Geoffrey, isn't it," Richard said to the man who had escorted Ronan into the room.

"Aye, Sir," Geoffrey said in acknowledgement.

"Show Ronan out of the house, please," Richard said.

"You can't do this! I live here, my belongings are here," Ronan protested as Geoffrey clamped a large hand around the steward's upper arm.

"Geoffrey, let Master Steward take what he can carry from his room and then eject him from my father's house," Richard replied.

Richard spent an hour in which time he spoke to each of the staff in turn. Some were still too nervous to reply and shook their heads when he asked questions about his father, fearing implication in what had taken place. The rest of the staff knew little and had witnessed even less. Edwin and Jon had cared for the master, and fear had kept their tongues tightly tied. Arguments had been heard, but what else had gone on behind the doors to William's room could only be guessed at by the rest of the house staff.

When Richard had finished with the last of them, he crossed the corridor and opened the door to William's room. Now it was neat, tidy and clean. There remained nothing to show what might have happened to William. Eleanor stared down at him from her portrait and Richard found himself returning her cool, appraising gaze.

It was after midnight when he left. He would spend the last few hours of the night with Christian before he returned to Somer's house.

When Richard returned to the house it was Carter himself who opened the front door, his expression worried.

"Good God, man, you've been hours!" Carter exclaimed.

Richard looked at him, he wasn't even aware of what the time was. It had been an evening where one hour had rolled into another. He supposed he must have been a long time, first Somer's house, then his father's.

Carter propelled him down the hall towards the kitchen. "Come on man, there's ale and Tilly has left some food out."

Richard dropped onto one of the wooden benches at the kitchen table and let his eyes stare across the room while Carter busied himself setting a cup and food before him. Attached to the side of one of the ceiling beams was a cobweb. Richard stared at it. Tonight, when he left, his mind had woven a plan to place before Somer, a plea and a request to help his brother. Now it seemed he had trapped himself in a web of his own making as well.

"What's the matter?" Carter said dropping heavily onto the bench opposite and planting his elbows on the table, making the ale in the cup swill.

Richard looked up and met Carter's eyes. "I don't know. Something is wrong."

"We know that, Jack's in The Tower. Did you find out anything about him?" Carter asked.

"He's still there. I've been set a task for his release..." Richard's voice shook.

Carter's eyes widened, "What?" Then when he didn't get a reply, Carter leaned across the table and shook his friend's shoulder, adding, "Richard, tell me, what's happened?"

Richard dropped his head into his hands.

"What do they want you to do?" Carter said, his words pitched now at the level of a demand.

"I can't say," Richard spoke through his hands.

"Oh God! What have you done?" Carter said.

"It doesn't matter. I had no choice," Richard replied his voice tired and strained.

After that they sat in silence until Richard wordlessly took himself off to bed.

When Carter rose in the morning, Richard had already left.

CHAPTER TWENTY-THREE

✝

Richard left Somer's house early in the company of the elderly minister. Necessity had forced him to sleep and his body was alive with a nervous energy as they took the boat down the Thames towards the Tower. Every sense told him that he needed to play whatever cards were dealt to him today with smooth and efficient competency.

Somer, clad in a thick fur coat and moaning about the lateness of the previous night, and the effect his wife's choice of menu had upon him, refused to be drawn into further conversation. All he would say on the subject was that he had arranged the meeting with Elizabeth that had been Richard's condition.

As the boat, rocking on the slight current, moved in towards the jetty, Richard could see down the side of the Tower that flanked the river. Recessed into the middle of the wall like a dark mouth, open and swallowing the water, stood Traitor's Gate. On one side of it was the recessed doorway where he had dumped the gaoler's body —that seemed like an age ago.

How long had it been?

Christ!

Yesterday morning!

How long had it been since Kineer had died?

A day earlier. Only two days ago!

For a moment he felt again the crushing hold on his hand, as his brother had wrapped his own around the hilt, twisting the blade. He had been tired, shaken by the force of the fight, Jack's steadying grip had been welcomed, allowing him to guide the sword in that final violent twist.

Together.

A moment they had shared, and one they had deserved to.

Jack had got him through so much, his handling was often brusque and brutal, but he was always there. Jack had tried his best, presented Richard with his life more than once, and he did not deserve what had befallen him. His brother wanted him to be the man he had once been. Jack turned his eyes from his weaknesses, supported him, held him up, backed him up. Richard knew he needed to be that man again, face himself, accept what he was, and use it to his advantage. If he had ever lacked purpose, that was no longer the case.

Richard closed his eyes for a moment. Taking in a deep breath he exhaled slowly, letting it take with it all the unwanted thoughts and fears, clearing his mind. He could feel his thoughts settling, like a silent cold blanket of snow. Releasing another breath, a clarity, crystalline, sharp, and one that he had not experienced for so very long began to return.

The boatman had jumped onto the jetty, a rope in his hand, and he looped it with practised ease around one of the securing bollards.

When Richard's boot left the uncertainty of the rocking boat and pressed onto the firm wood of the jetty he was filled with something else—recognising it, he smiled. Whatever was coming he welcomed it with an eager anticipation.

He might be out-manoeuvred, he might have little to gain, but he cared little so long as his ends were served. Richard recognised he was no longer a creature of ambition, he had become something more, something reactive, adaptive, something far more dangerous. Someone who no longer cared about his own future.

He was on the bank before Somer, and watched the elderly man stand uncertainly in the rocking boat, steadied by the boatman's arm and helped ashore by a liveried servant. Richard, who might under other circumstances have offered help, watched, a look of mild impatience on his face, and his expression was not missed by Somer.

"Do you wish to tell me something before we enter?" Richard enquired, his voice irenic and calm.

Somer ran his eyes over the younger man's face, but declined to reply. Hefting his long-furred cloak to keep the hem from the filth he set off towards the first guard tower. Ahead of them strode the liveried servant. Somer, a man well known, would not be held up by the formalities. Richard, for the second time in as many days, passed over the clogged Tower moat and into the city's royal fortress.

At the second gated entranceway a servant was waiting for Somer. Brief and quiet words were exchanged and a look of annoyance descended onto Somer's features. Whatever was about to play out was not going according to Somer's plan, Richard noted with speculative thoughtfulness.

The liveried servant led them towards a door that Richard had recently been through. On the other side of that single stone step was the prison, and at the bottom of a flight of steps was his brother. For a moment he thought that they were going to use the crudity of Jack's captivity to secure his compliance. The servant though, turned left, heading in the direction Isaac, Devereux's man had gone only a day before. As they passed the room, an argument drifted through the door into the corridor.

"I reckon Jeriah has scared him off," a voice said.

"Nah...more likely he owed him money and he's scarpered," came the reply.

Richard hid a smile.

They continued on towards a low arch that opened into a small courtyard.

Waiting for them, neatly dressed, his cold eyes narrowing at the sight of Richard, was Cecil.

The entrance was narrow, allowing only one man through at a time. Somer stepped through first, Richard following. There was, among the three of them, a moment of infinite silence.

It was Cecil who broke it, turning to Somer he said, "If you would excuse us, John."

"We had an agreement, and I'll be damned if I will let you leave here with both sides of the deal," Somer spoke directly to Cecil, his gaze intense and his voice hard.

Cecil gave a slight shrug of acceptance, producing immediately a folded sheet from inside his doublet, and held it out towards Somer.

Somer took a step forward and retrieved the sheet. Flipping it open briefly he scanned the contents before stowing it away beneath the folds of his own clothing.

As Somer turned to retrace his steps his eyes, for a moment, met Richard's., If he had hoped for shock, then he was to be disappointed. Richard matched his cool gaze and took a measured step sideways allowing Somer access to the exit. Somer no longer had a part to play.

"You know who that is, don't you?" Cecil asked when they were alone, pointing unnecessarily towards the body strapped to the wagon bed.

"Is that the only mystery you wish me to solve for you?" Richard asked, his voice cold.

"You killed him. Who is he?" Cecil demanded.

"His name is Andrew Kineer, he was a member of Seymour's household and after that he worked as a mercenary, and now..." Richard took a couple of steps towards the body, "...you really need to find a pit to throw him in. I know a good man for the task, if you like I could..."

"Enough! Why did you kill him?" Cecil's voice rose in pitch.

"He blamed me for a number of deficiencies in his life," Richard replied, his nose wrinkling with distaste he took a step away from the body. "He's not keeping well, is he?"

"Let us go somewhere more private. I have some more questions I wish to put to you," Cecil replied, his tone icily crisp.

"I think he can keep your secrets," Richard said, leaning towards Cecil and nodding in Kineer's direction.

"Somer might find you amusing. I don't," Cecil replied bluntly.

"Regrettably, Somer's uses for me extended beyond simple amusement, it seems," Richard replied, his eyes bright and his mouth twisting in a sardonic smile.

Cecil let his eyes lock for a moment with the grey ones before he turned and stepped from the courtyard. Richard followed him, and behind them two more liveried and armed men, who had been waiting in the corridor, followed them. Within a few minutes they had travelled around the edge of Tower Green and were alone in Cecil's office.

Cecil rounded the desk and lowered himself into his chair, observing Richard over steepled fingers.

Richard sighed loudly, and without invitation pulled a chair noisily away from the wall and across the floor until it was on the opposite side of the desk from Cecil. Dropping into it, he folded his arms, and observed Cecil coolly. "You had questions?"

"We have a man in our keeping that you wish to be released?" Cecil said, getting to the point.

"You do," Richard accepted, adding, "Somer had presented me with a solution."

"I know. I am not as trusting as he might be," Cecil replied. "You had a condition, apparently?"

"Two." Richard stated.

"Two?" Cecil repeated, his tone mocking.

"I am sure you know what they are?" Richard repeated.

"And if the Lady were to suggest otherwise, then you would not carry out this task? You would leave your brother confined here if she was against this course of action? If that is the case, then I fear holding your brother is not sufficient leverage either if you would be willing to sacrifice him for a woman's words," Cecil said drily.

"Maybe you can persuade me otherwise?" Richard replied. "Those are my conditions."

"For a man with a charge of treason hanging over his head you have a lot of demands," Cecil said, sitting back heavily in the chair.

"Two is not so many," Richard replied, his eyes never leaving Cecil's face.

†

If he had hoped to speak to Elizabeth alone he was to be disappointed. The meeting was to be a brief one.

The woman who stepped through the door was not one he remembered. Four years had narrowed her face, her mouth was pressed into a thin line and her eyes took in everything in the room in a moment. Elizabeth exuded a fragile and dangerous energy. Her face, schooled and calm, held no smile of welcome; her eyes locked with Richard's for a moment only before moving on and engaging with Cecil.

"Madam," Cecil bowed with exquisite precision, "A question has arisen, and we would know your mind. Edward Courtenay has approached the Pope regarding a proxy wedding with yourself, does he do this with your consent?"

"You know the answer to that question," Elizabeth replied, directing her words towards Richard.

"We wish to hear your mind on the subject," Cecil said firmly.

Elizabeth's mouth hardened even further, it was clear she did not want to answer the question. "It is not a marriage I favour. Was that the only question you had?"

A moment later she was gone. All that remained was the scent of roses.

"And my second condition?" Richard said.

Cecil shook his head. "We need to have a little mutual trust. Your brother will remain here, as surety."

"I want to see him. Now." Richard held Cecil's eyes as he delivered the words.

Cecil seemed to consider the request for a few moments before his face creased in an expression of assent. "Very well."

†

Before Richard was escorted from The Tower he was taken, under guard and in Cecil's company, to a room on an adjacent side of the Green to the prison entrance.

The door, guarded on the outside, was opened to admit them. Once inside he was taken to the doorway of second, which, when it opened, revealed his brother.

Jack, propped up on pillows, his chest bound in linen, pushed himself up the bed at the sight of his brother. His mouth opened, but a shake of Richard's head silenced him. The door was closed a moment later on Cecil's instruction.

If there was any relief that Jack was no longer chained to a wall it did not show on Richard's face, and shortly after he was again being escorted through the gate at Byward Tower.

CHAPTER TWENTY-FOUR

†

Although the weather was not warm, the gaoler's corpse had ballooned in the water. The gas, collected and festering within his guts, had turned the corpse over and arms and legs hung down in the water, attached to a bloated stomach that broke the surface like some small domed island. One of his arms had become fastened under the metal grille, and with the buoyancy from his distended abdomen, it had become tightly wedged there.

If Richard had thought his re-entry to The Tower would be a quiet and silent affair, he was wrong. Removing the blockage of the rotting guard was an act that sent a heron from its perch and a flock of roosting moorhens paddling furiously across the river. Finally, cursing under his breath, he freed the arm from the iron hold, and leaning through the grille, he pushed the floating body away. A coil of rope hooked around his body he shrugged off and passed through the bars first, then he squeezed between the disintegrating iron and the wall. His entry required a degree of submersion, and the gap was a narrow one—there remained a nagging doubt that a larger man might not be able to press through. That, however, was an issue that was so far along a list of other possibilities that it was currently not a consideration.

Rising up the submerged steps, and over the decaying gaoler that was trapped between the door and the iron grille, Richard pressured the door gently.

It gave beneath his touch.

The bar on the inside was still withdrawn. Pushing it open, he was inside a moment later and encased within the ink-black of the passageway. Dumping a dark shirt and sodden hose on the floor, he pulled dry clothes from a waterproof skin fashioned from a cow's stomach. He had little intention of leaving a trail of sodden footprints to mark his passage through The Tower.

His left hand on the wall to guide him and a knife in his right, he made his way along the passageway quickly. Eyes, becoming accustomed to the dark, picked out the grey outline marking the end of the passage. Beyond this, and down to the right, was the chamber containing the rack, and to his left the steps that would take him to the prison entrance and to Tower Green.

Listening at the end of the passage he heard nothing that told him of the presence of guards. The only noise was a sudden metallic clanking. Somewhere, a chain was being hauled against a retaining ring.

His boots soundless on the worn steps Richard headed upward, away from the river.

Above him was the main guard room. Pressing against the wall at the top of the stairwell, he could see the yellow glow of lamplight spilling into the corridor from the opened door and the muted sound of conversation accompanied by an occasional sporadic laugh he recognised. It sounded like they were playing cards.

A moment later Richard was across the corridor and outside the prison. He stood against the wall, in the shadow where Isaac's cart had waited. There were guards stationed at the two towers on either end of the bridge over the moat and also patrolling around the inside of The Tower.

Turning around the stone newel post, he headed up towards the recently laid wooden floors and the table where one of the workman had recently lost a number of his tools.

The rooms were empty, redolent only with the heavy scent of fresh cut timber. Richard seated himself on a bench near the table, moonlight from the diamond panes casting enough grey light into the room to work by. With the back of his hand Richard swept the table clear of sawdust and set on the surface the other items he had brought with him. Using a knife he split the stretched skin of a sheep's stomach. Inside, dry and wrapped in crisped hessian, heated almost to the point of ignition over a fire, was black powder. The small bag was still bone dry. Piercing the packet with a knife point, Richard tapped out a line of powder that was about twice as long as his forearm.

It was a bloody short fuse.

He lacked enough powder for a longer one. Short notice had meant this was as much as Myles had been able to acquire, and Richard knew that for a reasonable explosion he needed as much as possible for the sparking fuse line to ignite.

The second split parcel revealed a tinder box and the third an earthenware jar that had lost its lid. Pouring a small circle of powder onto the table, Richard inserted the rest into the jar, turned it over and stood it at the end of the powder trail. An arched nick in the rim showed where it had recently been attacked with a knife to allow the powder's angry flame inside the jar. He'd learnt enough from Scranton to know that if the explosive wasn't contained, its effect would be much diminished. It needed to be pressured as much as possible.

Emptying out the small tinder box at the other end of the powder trail, he picked up the flint and sent it across the striker. A shower of bright orange pin pricks sparked, bounced, and died—none of them catching on the dried tinder.

Below the window he heard voices.

An exchange between two guards.

Steady hands set to their task again. A second shower of sparks, bright in the dim room sprinkled across the charcloth. One of them caught for a moment, the tiny orange core glowing. Before he could move to bring the spark to life it winked out.

The flint scraped across the steel again.

Another shower of feeble sparks jumped on the charcloth.

Two glowed. Two together.

Discarding the steel and flint he quickly added a twist of soft dried cotton taken from summer flax, folded the charcloth around it, and added his breath to the bundle. A gentle warm draft to coax the flame to life.

Another light steady blow on the cloth.

Nothing.

Richard inhaled and blew one more time. The spark, igniting, took hold within the charcloth. A tiny white wisp of smoke that he smelt, rather than saw, sneaked from beneath the folded cloth.

Another breeze of air and the ember had lit the flax seeds. A second later a silent flame fed hungrily on the cloth.

Richard dropped it onto the end of the powder trail and ran.

Sparks entered the jar as Richard reached the open doorway. The earthenware erupted. The bottom, the thickest part of the fired clay pot, remained intact. Spinning from the room, it first grazed the sandstone of the window frame before slicing through the diamond set panes, taking glass and lead moulding into the air on the other side with it. Then, like a billowing sheet shaken from the window, came a pall of white smoke.

The walls of the jar, thinner, jig-sawed into a hundred fragments. All of them angular and jagged—one, spinning, violently carved a neat cut along the back of Richard's exiting shoulder as he dived for the safety of the corridor beyond. Running further along he made it into the room where the floors were still being laid before the sounds of the first footsteps and shouts of alarm reached him.

The smoke had worked better than he could have imagined. White and thick it clogged the stairwell, flooding from the room where the powder had exploded.

Within the grey acrid mist friend could not be separated from foe. His face hidden behind a rag he passed two men on the smoke-filled stairs, clapping one of them on the back as he passed and pointing to the origin of the detonation.

Tower Green was a scene of chaos.

Emerging from the bottom stairs he remained within the protective bloom of smoke that was rolling out to silently fill the open courtyard. Men were running, some armed, some holding lamps, some just running. All of them, though, were heading towards the scene of the explosion.

Men behind him were shouting.

"There's a fire!"

Twisting his head behind him and looking up for a moment he saw that there was indeed a fire. The explosion had lit the planks that had been set to make the new floor. Dried and aged, they'd made ideal fuel.

Richard added his own cries to the general alarm.

"Fire! Fire!"

"On the second Floor!"

"Look! Fire!"

Skirting the edge of the Green, remaining in the shadows, he ran against the current of men heading towards the prison. The path took him first toward Byward Tower where guards, alarmed, stood nervously, alarmed but not daring to leave their posts. Richard ran past them, he looked very much like any of the other Tower inhabitants who were careening around Tower Green senselessly.

Richard, though, had a destination in mind. Running along the path towards the church he veered left. With a quick backward glance, Richard set his foot to the side of the woodshed and in a few steps he was pulling himself up onto the roof.

Pitched smooth slates made for a difficult climb. He was reminded of another roof and another climb, but pressed the memory from his mind and concentrated on reaching the apex of the current roof as quickly as possible. The building to the right had a higher pitched roof and using the masonry wall and a knife in the lead flashing he pulled himself towards the ridge tiles.

Once he reached the top of the roof he flipped himself over. From here no one could see him. Before, anyone looking from any number of windows in The Tower could have witnessed his climb, but no longer. Letting out a breath of relief he slid the coil of rope from his shoulder. The hemp, already knotted along its length, had a loop already spliced in one end and Richard dropped it over the top of the chimney stack. A firm tug told him it was secure and, holding the rope, his boot toes curled under him to slow his slide, he made it down the steep roof, his feet soon finding the horizontal support of the guttering that ran along the bottom edge.

Lying full length on the tiles, his feet hooked into the guttering and his left arm clamped around it, Richard chanced a look below him. If there was light burning within the rooms the shutters must be closed against it as there was no sign of illumination along the back of the wall from a window. A moment later he was hanging from the guttering, and after that he dropped silently into the overgrown garden at the back of the rooms. He was sure his brother was in the quarters he was now behind. The back of the building showed two windows and a central door.

Locked.

This wasn't a prison and the windows were shuttered on the insides. Leaded panes, framed and latched, provided little resistance. Pulling open the right hand of a window that had not been opened in a long time the hinge, sticking, complained. He released the window open as it issued a high-pitch squeal.

There was no noise of investigation from inside. Hopefully all their attention was fastened on the chaos on Tower Green as the guards sought to identify the cause of the sudden explosion.

Pulling the opposing pane, the two windows, partly open, provided sufficient gap to enter the room.

The room beyond was in darkness.

Feet over the sill, Richard lowered himself into the room, dropping noiselessly to the floor.

There was a sudden yelp followed by a double thud from the room beyond the one he believed Jack was resident in.

Richard flattened himself against the wall next to the door a second before it was drawn open filling the room with a flood of weak candlelight. On the threshold stood his brother, breathing heavily.

"You heard my message then?" Richard said, grinning.

"What the hell did you blow up?" Jack gasped.

"Nothing much. We need to leave over the back roof, have you anything else to wear?" Richard asked, looking at the crisp white linen shirt Jack was wearing. They might as well deploy a flag to mark their position as they made their escape.

Jack ducked back inside the room and Richard, following, found he had to step over the unconscious form of a small man, a bump already stretching the skin of his forehead. Jack had one arm already in a doublet and was fishing painfully for the second sleeve, his broken ribs making it a difficult task.

"Here," Richard held it while Jack wriggled his arm into the fabric. "Can you manage your boots?"

"It would be quicker if you helped," admitted Jack.

Richard held them still while Jack, grimacing against the pain, pressed his feet into them and Richard pulled them up. If they were to leave by the route he had planned that meant retracing his steps and clambering over the roof. He doubted very much that Jack was fit for such a task.

"How many guards are on the door?" Richard asked.

"Two usually, and they have the key, so we are locked in," Jack provided.

"What about him?" Richard nodded towards the unconscious man.

"Harper doesn't have the key," Jack said.

"We need to climb the wall at the back, can you manage?"

"If it means getting out of this shit hole, just watch me." Jack was already on his feet, and Richard set off towards the back room and the open shutter. Sitting on the edge, raising his legs up and over the stone ledge he dropped quickly into the garden beyond, waiting for his brother to do the same. Luckily there were no observers. Jack, using the support of the window frame, hauled himself slowly onto the window edge. He twisted, grimacing, and his shoulder hit the wooden shutter sending it swinging backward to bang loudly on the wall.

Richard contained a curse. Wondering how on earth his brother was going to pull himself up ten feet of wall if he couldn't manage to climb out of a window.

Richard put a hand up to stop his brother lowering himself from the ledge.

"You'll not make the climb," Richard said urgently, pointing at the wall behind him they needed to scale. "How many ribs have you broken?"

"One, maybe two." Jack tried to push himself out of the window to join Richard, pain suddenly twisted his face, Jack, gasping for air was immobile on the ledge.

"Are you sure?"

"Maybe a few more," Jack managed through gritted teeth.

Behind them, inside the room there was a sudden moan as the gaoler, Master Harper, began to awake from his unscheduled sleep on the floor.

"It sounds like he is about to make a recovery, let's persuade him to invite the others in and get that door opened," Richard suggested quickly.

A moment later Richard was back on the ledge, sliding through the window. Dropping into the room once more, he handed his brother a knife and darted through the door into the room where Harper, lying in an untidy heap, was beginning to reassert control over his fallen limbs.

"Not a sound," advised Richard from behind Harper, a knife blade fastened just below the man's Adam's apple.

There was an audible double thud which Richard took to be his brother's feet landing back on the floor again. Stealth was not going to be among his brother's attributes tonight.

"The men on guard outside," Richard said, "tell them there is a noise at the back in the yard. Tell them you want them to come and look."

The knife close to the flabby throat was acting as a deterrence to a visual confirmation.

"Did you hear me?"

"Yes, yes!" a small voice, mouse-like and immensely at odds with the gaoler's stocky body, confirmed.

"Come on then, up with you," Richard commanded, then to Jack, "will that back door open?"

"It's barred on our side, yes. Do you want it open?" Jack responded quickly from the dark.

"Yes, just partly open. Jack, come in here out of the way," Richard commanded. Then to the man before him, the knife now prodding in his back, he said, "Let's get this right. Tell them there's a noise in the garden, when they open the door you run towards the open door and on through it. Understand?"

The round head bobbed in quick affirmation.

"And I'll be standing right here to make sure you get it right," Richard said, sliding against the wall to the left of the door hinges. He would be hidden when the door opened.

Master Harper played his part better than Richard could have expected. He hammered on the door with a fleshy fist, his calls were met with quick responses from the other side and a moment later a key rattled in the lock.

The door was flung open.

Master Harper took a quick step back, his eyes connecting for a moment with the silver blade in Richard's hand. "Outside, in the garden, there's men trying to break in," he wailed, and ran towards the garden.

Both of the guards overtook Harper. Already on the alert after having being forced to stand and watch men run to and fro after the explosion they were more than ready for action. Richard was behind Harper and as he neared the door he gave the short man a vicious shove that sent him flying into the man in front of him, causing both of them to fall sprawling through the door.

Richard, a foot on the middle of the back of the fat gaoler, was over them and upon the second guard who was already tearing a short blade from his belt.

It had to be quick. And it was.

Richard's assault didn't pause, with the advantage of momentum the blade went neatly through two of the man's ribs. Before the look of sudden shock had even settled on the man's face a second stroke cut through his throat from left to right.

Behind him was the noise of a choking plea. As he turned, the guard was trying to push out from under the weight of Master Harper who was still trapping him on the floor. Without hesitation the dripping knife in Richard's hand cut into a second neck, the man fell from his hands and knees to the floor. A boot rammed across the back of his neck held him momentarily immobile until the knife had cut through his windpipe.

Master Harper was on his knees, pallid hands held up, terror on his face.

"No!" It was Jack who had spoken. "Leave him be."

Richard looked between the pair of them for a moment. Then, reversing the knife, the hilt in his fist, he brought it hard against the gaolers temple knocking him unconscious for a second time.

The two dead men wore red jackets emblazoned with the Tudor rose on their chests. Richard forced one of the bodies onto its back and quick fingers began flipping open the toggle and loop fastenings. Once undone he peeled it from the man's body, it came away accompanied by the noise of the tearing of strained stitches.

Richard, shrugging the jacket on and beginning to refasten the toggles, grinned at his brother. "We'll use the front door then?"

Jack, confusion on his face, looked at the other dead gaoler, a scrawny man, smaller than his brother. "That's never going to fit me!"

Richard, on his feet, found the man's cap, complete with black plume, and rammed it on his head. The broad sword belt across the jacket completed the uniform. "I know, but looking like this I should be able to escort you to the prison. Come on."

Using a knife he sliced the bottom two feet from the rope that hung from the roof.

"In front or behind?" Richard asked, the rope held out, stretched between his two hands.

Jack, realising what he meant to do, raised his wrists. "In front."

A moment later there was a visible but ineffectual binding around both of Jack's wrists and between them a knife was concealed.

Richard, standing behind him, one hand on the front door, about to open it, said. "Once outside we go right, along the path towards The Tower entrance, then left towards The Tower prison entrance."

"The prison!" Jack exclaimed.

"Trust me." Richard gave his brother no more time to complain and pulled open the door.

Jack's prison cell was now unbarred and unguarded.

"Come on," Richard deftly snuffed the candles sending the room to darkness as he dived for the door, Jack limping, in front of him.

Outside every armed man The Tower possessed was being marshalled. The smoke pall had cleared from most of the yard and was no longer offering any useful cover. They needed to make their way along one side of Tower Green, and from there to the prison entrance.

The courtyard and the green were now full of soldiers, every able-bodied man in The Tower having been summoned to arms. The portcullis was down barring the wooden gates near Byward Tower and behind it a contingent of twenty men stood on guard. Richard was fairly sure it shouldn't be too hard to escort a prisoner across Tower Green to the dungeons.

Jack, prodded on by Richard, walked, head down, along the path.

A man, a yellow sash across his red jacket declaring his rank, stepped forward from the men, a frown on his face and a question on his lips. "Where are you going? Didn't you hear the orders? No one is allowed out."

"Sorry sir, Master Hunt's orders. He needed this man moved back into the prison," Richard said, a firm hold on Jack's arm.

"And you are on your own? Is Hunt mad?" The officer said, his eyes switching between Richard and the much bigger man before him. Calling over his shoulder he said, "Lucas, go with these two over to Master Hunt's office."

A moment later a man, wearing a sergeants sash, detached himself from the orderly rank and stepped forward, his eyes alight with obvious interest.

"Thank you sir," Richard said, immediately making a move to push his prisoner in the direction he wanted to go. The unwanted Lucas fell into step next to him.

"I've not seen you before," Lucas said.

"Not surprised," Richard replied, giving Jack an extra push in the back, "I've been ordered to work for Master Morley."

"Morley, eh? One of Cecil's men," Lucas replied, then quizzed, "What's he doing with a prisoner in the middle of the night then?"

"I don't know. He'd been questioning him in the rooms over there," Richard gestured behind him, "I was just told to take him back to Master Hunt."

Lucas looked across the green. "Tim Harper was on guard on the door over there? I ran past him just after all the windows in The Tower over there blew out. Where's he gone then?"

Richard shrugged. "Do they know what caused the explosion?"

"No," Lucas shook his head, his eyes making a careful inspection of Richard, and the expression on his face told he did not like the results. "Came from the floors where all the work is being carried out, but there's nothing up there."

"I thought we were being attacked," Richard said, a conspiratorial grin on his face, "I could use a bit of action, nothing ever happens in here."

"If you've so much time on your hands, man, you should spend some of it on your uniform. Have you seen the state of it?" Lucas prodded at a stain on the doublet, showing as dark patch in the moonlight, his fingers coming away wet from the cloth, a look of revulsion settling on his face.

"Sorry, sir," Richard replied, "I was in such a hurry to dress I knocked an oil lamp on to it. I will clean it as soon as I am able."

"Make sure you do," Lucas replied briskly.

They had arrived at the entrance way to the prison.

"Thank you sir, I'll find Master Hunt," Richard said, and was relieved when Lucas, his nose wrinkling already by the smell emanating from the prison below, remained on the threshold. Light from a lamp hung on a bracket near the doorway illuminated the entrance.

Richard pressed Jack to the right, his eyes still on Lucas.

The guard, about to turn and leave, dropped his eyes from Richard's to his hand, sticky with oil from Richard's jacket. In the dim lamp light Lucas saw his hand was not covered in oil. His eye's flicked to the stain on Richard's doublet.

Blood!

Lucas's eyes shot wide open, his right hand reached for his blade in the same moment his voice raised the alarm.

"To arms!" Lucas's shout rang out.

Jack dropped the loose bonds from his wrists, exposing the knife in his right hand.

Richard moved in, so close that Lucas's reflex action to draw his blade was a waste. Richard had a hand at his throat and a second sent a knife into the man's side beneath his rib cage. Richard let the wounded man drop to the floor, he could already hear men running to obey the call.

"Shit! Run! This way!" Richard, a hold on Jack's sleeve, pulled him towards the descending stairs.

Jack resisted only for a moment before he followed Richard down the dark stairwell. Behind them was sound of running feet, the repeated shouts of alarm and Lucas' continued shouts—"They've gone down to into the prison."

"Christ, Jack! Run."

Richard wanted to take the steps two, even three at a time, but his brother, a hand against the wall for support, was dropping down them at an uneven stagger. He was going as quickly as he could but that was nowhere near fast enough. The dark passageway was still a floor below them.

"There's a passage on the right before the last chamber. It opens to the river. Go, go..." Richard turned on the stairs, a knife in each hand.

"No!" Jack fetched up against the wall, gasping for breath. "Terrible apart..." he managed between uneven breaths.

"And even more stupid together..." Richard finished for him through gritted teeth. "Go, they won't kill me! I'm working for Cecil."

Jack's face clouded for a moment, Richard reaching forward gave him another shove down the stairs.

"On the right, there's a passage...don't miss it."

The first man down the stairs towards them, a drawn blade in his right hand, had the advantage of height, but not of surprise. Richard, tight against the central newel post of the spiral stairs delivered a knife to the back of his calf muscle. With a cry of dismay the man's leg buckled beneath him, and he pitched forward down the spiral, face hitting the gritty steps. The sword fell, bouncing once on the pommel, before it flipped end over end and slid down the stairs. Its descent was arrested by Richard's boot, and a moment later the weapon was in his hand.

The fallen man had bought him seconds. They were scrambling over him but Richard, descending the steps at a lethal pace, quickly caught up with Jack. A hand in the middle of his back, he pushed him hard into the narrow passage and at the same moment he sent the stolen sword skittering down the rest of the steps towards the chamber with the rack.

The guards followed the noise.

A hand on Jack's back he pushed him along the corridor.

Behind him the shouts told him they had found the chamber below empty.

"Keep going!"

When they reached the end there was the sound of boots hammering down the passage behind them.

It's narrow so they would be in single file.

Richard dived beyond Jack and pushed open the wooden door, flooding the passage with moonlight.

"Go..."

Behind him he heard the sound of splashing water.

In front, filling the passageway, was Jeriah. Eyes blazing, a knife ready in his right hand and a cudgel in his left, he headed the advancing line of pursuers.

Richard threw the knife in his right hand towards the man's head. It didn't stop him, but for a moment it paused his advance, his arm flying to his head to protect himself. Without turning, Richard stepped backward quickly through the open doorway. Jack was ready with the door and as soon as he was clear had his shoulder against it, slamming it shut.

"We can't hold them for long," Jack said, his whole weight pressed to the closed door. A second later the door was pushed hard from the inside and it took both of them to keep it closed.

"Ideas?" Jack asked. He'd switched his position, his feet were now against the rusted grating and his back was against the door.

"One." Richard, ankle deep in the water on the steps, his hands in the soaked material covering the dead man's back, hauled him up the steps. The gap between the door and the grille was just enough for the door to open.

There was a second attempt to push the door open from the inside. Jack, his face contorted in pain, his hands on the stone door frame, locked his body against the door. It pushed open a few inches only and slammed back shut again.

"Hurry up!"

Richard had one of the dead man's legs threaded through the grille and was pushing the second through when the door was forced again from the inside.

"I can't hold it!" Jack spoke through gritted teeth.

"Let it go," Richard had the second leg between the iron bars.

Jack remained braced against the door.

"Let it go! Jack! It can't open far enough," Richard, a hand on Jack's arm, pulled him from the door.

He was right, the door could open no more than a third of the way before it came against the body. After that it couldn't open any further as the body was trapped between the door and the grille.

Pushing the reeds away from the side where the hinge was broken, he showed Jack the gap. Lowering himself down the steps and into the water, he submerged his head for a moment and was through the gap and into the river beyond.

The guards had not given up and the door was banging repeatedly against the skull of the dead gaoler, angry voices making their way threateningly through the narrow opening.

Gasping, Jack lowered himself into the water feet first, as his brother had done, Richard, holding the bars, watched as Jack began to force himself down the steps between the grille and the wall. They didn't have long. He had no doubt men had already left the prison and were heading around the side The Tower.

Come on Jack!

Richard had his hands on Jack, pulling him down and under the iron bars. He felt him turn sideways to slide his body between the gap. His legs were through, then his chest.

Jack stopped.

His head was almost submerged on the other side of the grille. Richard could feel him struggling against the hold of the iron.

"Take the doublet off!" Richard changed his grip, instead of pulling he was pushing, sending his brother back. It was the thickness of the jacket that was trapping him as he tried to force his way between the narrow gap.

They had brought up something heavy to batter the door with. The impacts from the other side had taken on a solid, wood splintering quality.

Jack, gasping on the steps, desperately tore the doublet from his shoulders.

"Come on! Try again!" Richard said urgently.

An upright in the door began to give way, the planking breaking and blistering under the battering from the inside, white spikes of wood cracking away from the grain.

Slopping the soaked material down Jack slid again down the steps, twisting sideways, his head this time submerged. Richard's hands under the water found his brother's arm and pulled—hard.

Jack's breath broke the surface of the water in a series of bubbles. But Jack remained stuck, wedged between the wall the grille. Richard realising what he had done, but having little choice, braced his feet against the grille and with all his strength hauled on Jack's arm. There was a moment of brutal impasse, and then Richard fell back into the water as the hold the wall and iron had on Jack was released and he emerged spluttering for air on the Thames side of the barrier.

A boat, its pilot watching closely for two sodden swimmers had already begun to move silently towards them. By the time Jack wrapped an arm around the rusted iron grille for support it was alongside them. The craft was one of the wide cargo carriers that moved constantly up and down the river, and she carried three men whose willing hands soon had both Jack and Richard aboard.

Jack was white. Blood was pouring down his side where the skin had been torn away by the brickwork and his breathing was coming in painful and erratic breaths.

"Just a couple of ribs? You're a lying bastard!" Richard said settling next to his brother.

Jack tried to speak, thought better of it, and screwing his eyes shut concentrated instead on breathing.

"Have you had enough of England?" Richard asked a few moments later.

Jack nodding. "I'll go anywhere you like."

Richard grinned. "Italy it is then."

EPILOGUE

†

A dozen men, under orders they would not veer from arrived at the manor. Capable men, riding good horses. Their leader dropped from his saddle, passed the reins to another of the mounted men, and waited.

He had seen three servants scurry from the yard as they had ridden in, and he was in no doubt his presence would be quickly reported. Trained eyes told him he was standing in little more than a farm, and one that was under a degree of financial pressure as well. Broken walls, a hanging shutter, and a yard that was pockmarked with unfilled holes told him as much. The fields he had ridden through as they had approached held poor animals kept inside walls that spoke of neglect and poor crops that failed to fill the fields. This was not an affluent place.

A man, a cudgel in his hand, backed by another man similarly equipped appeared in the main doorway to the building. "What'll you be wanting?" He called from the top of the steps.

"Lord Fitzwarren. We are here to escort him back to his home in London, under orders from his son," Myles Devereux replied, pulling one glove carefully from his hand, a finger at a time.

"But I never heard anything about that, he never sent word?" The man replied, sounding confused.

"You have word now," Myles Devereux replied, tucking his gloves into his belt.

Suspicion ran across the man's face. "How do I know you're from his son?"

Devereux let out a long sigh, fished inside his doublet and produced a folded sheet of parchment. He didn't offer it but simply held it out. "I doubt you can read, this is for Lord Fitzwilliam from his son, and I am to deliver it. If you would take me to him I would appreciate it."

"Give it here, I'll see it gets to him." The man extended a hand.

Devereux shook his head. "No. Take me to him. Now."

The man took one step back up into the house, it was clear that he intended to slam the door shut against them.

Myles turned his eyes skyward. Then gesturing towards the armed and mounted men, he said, "Take some sage advice and bring me to Lord Fitzwarren, now."

"I'll have him brung down to you," the man conceded and slammed the door.

What the Steward didn't realise was that Myles Devereux didn't wait for anyone.

Turning towards the mounted men behind him he nodded towards the door and stood back, arms folded as he watched a capable and armed troop of men force the door and enter the manor. He heard shouts of protest and a woman's high-pitched shriek. Impassive, he waited. After a few moments one of his men appeared back in the doorway.

"Lord Fitzwarren is being brought down now," Matthew reported from the doorway. "Would you prefer it if we brought him outside, it's not fit for beasts in here."

Myles smiled with satisfaction. "Don't worry Matthew, even if I sup with beasts it doesn't mean I shall become one. I would speak to him alone, ensure that is the case."

Matthew, nodding, ducked back through the door, reappearing five minutes later when the necessary arrangements had been made.

Myles entered the hall. His men were spread throughout the occupants. Solid, armed and menacing. He let Matthew lead him towards a door at the end of the mired hall, opening it for his master to step through.

It was the first time that day that Myles's expression had been unsettled. What he found on the other side of the door was not at all what he had expected. He had expected Lord Fitzwarren— powerful landowner, Richard's formidable father, privy councillor, friend of Henry VIII, a man of military prowess and undeniable animal cunning. What he was met with instead was a decayed old man, in rancid clothing, with hollowed cheeks who stunk like a midden pit.

Myles, turning on his heels, strode back into the main hall. "Is this a joke?"

It was Matthew who stepped forward. "I'm afraid not. That's his servant there," Matthew pointed in the direction of a man standing nervously near the doorway.

Myles fastened his eyes on the servant and took a quick step towards him. "Are you seriously telling me the man in that room is Lord Fitzwarren?"

The servant nodded his head, then said, loudly enough for the whole hall to hear, "He has been badly treated since he arrived."

"Badly treated!" Myles repeated, his voice incredulous. And then to the servant, "Can he speak?"

"Yes, yes he can, Sir," the servant replied.

Myles turned back on his heel and returned once again to the small room and the wizened man. Closing the door behind him, he observed Richard Fitzwarren's father, who was returning his stare with an equally cool gaze. "Your son sent me."

"Which one?" William Fitzwarren replied. The voice hinted at a strength long since gone.

Myles folded his arms. "The one who cares, it would seem."

William's mouth hardened into a bloodless line, and he watched as Myles produced again the sealed letter he had earlier waved in the yard. As William watched, Myles broke the seal with his thumb, scattering wax shards among the foul reeds covering the floor. He held the sheet in front of William's face.

"They've taken my glasses," William stated.

"Shall I?" Myles asked, his eyebrows raised.

He received a nod of affirmation from the aged head.

Myles reversed the sheet. "Let me see. 'Should it please you to do so, I have provided the means for you to be removed back to your house in London, which is again your own. Ronan has been removed, and men are in place to ensure Robert cannot return. The price of your salvation is a matter of negotiation between yourself and Myles Devereux. Signed Richard Fitzwarren.'"

"And your name would be Devereux?" William asked, his voice dry and rasping.

Myles folded the sheet and replaced it inside his doublet and nodded, then said with a degree of sarcasm. "I can see age had not deprived you of your wits."

William's eyes narrowed at the slight.

"Careful, old man, you might not like what you see, but I am the light and I am your divine bloody salvation, so shall we get to the issue that I wish to discuss and you wish to avoid?" Myles replied.

"What's that then?"

"How much are you willing to pay for me to get you out of this shit hole?" Myles replied.

Printed in Great Britain
by Amazon

45388858R00300